"Please..."

Her voice, in that broken plea, jerked him back to the moment at hand. "Please what?"

"Don't take me to the hospital."

So she wasn't catatonic after all. Or in total shock. Both good signs that filled him with relief. At least it didn't appear she was going to collapse on him, a fear he hadn't heretofore wanted to address.

"That's where you belong," he stressed, disturbed anew that she would even hesitate.

"If you try to make me go, I'll get out of the car."

"And do what?" He knew his sarcasm was lost on her, but he couldn't stop the words.

"Keep walking."

"And die?"

"That wouldn't be a bad thing," she said, her voice breaking.

MARY LYNN BAXTER

BAXTER

Like Silk

ISBN 1-55166-902-1

LIKE SILK

Copyright © 2002 by Mary Lynn Baxter.

Visit us at www.mirabooks.com

Printed in U.S.A.

Like Silk

One

Were there any skeletons in his closet?

Collier Smith would rather not dwell on that subject, but he had no choice—not since he'd just found out he was being seriously considered for the federal judgeship in the central district of his home state.

"Yes, yes," he muttered out loud, thinking how incredibly lucky he was to even be in the running for such a prestigious position at the young age of thirty-eight. What was even more incredible was that he had no political experience.

A federal judge. Awesome. His dream come true—if it happened, he reminded himself, jerking the reality chain. But if the cards fell right and he ended up as the president's chosen one, he would not only make himself proud, but his stepdad, Mason, as well. Collier knew Mason wanted this position for him with every fiber of his being, and Collier feared the consequences if it didn't come to fruition.

He squirmed against the pinch of guilt that tightened his gut. It should be his stepbrother, Jackson, who was vying for the job, not him. If only Jackson hadn't been in that accident and lost the use of his legs. If only... There were so many of those in his life that Collier couldn't begin to sort through them all.

His mind reverted back to his buried skeletons, but he

quickly dismissed them again. He refused to dwell on the negative. For the moment he wanted the luxury of indulging himself and basking in his good fortune.

Unable to contain the excitement building inside him, he slapped the steering wheel with one hand, then felt the vehicle swerve.

Sudden fear tightened Collier's fingers back on the wheel and forced him to pay closer attention to what he was doing. A man couldn't drive unfocused through these rolling hills, especially with a slow drizzle hitting the windshield and numerous multicolored leaves falling from the trees that surrounded him.

Though it was nearing darkness, he could still see and appreciate the beauty of early fall in Tennessee. Rarely did he get the chance to sneak away from the booming law office where he was a partner and treat himself to a weekend alone in the family's rustic cabin nestled away from the hectic wear and tear of everyday life.

However, he wasn't on a pleasure jaunt, he reminded himself, facing reality once again. The high-profile case he'd taken had turned out to be more complicated and demanding than he'd expected. He needed some quiet time to study and prepare.

Too, he needed some space from the woman he'd been seeing for some time now. Lana had been pressuring him to set a wedding date, which would mean an engagement ring, announcement party, the whole nine yards. None of those held any appeal. He wasn't even sure he loved her. Even if he did, the thought of marriage scared the hell out of him.

Dislodging that unsettling thought, Collier watched the cascading leaves, reminding himself to enjoy that small pleasure. His blue eyes narrowed on a big red leaf stuck on the windshield. He laughed out loud for the pure hell of it, despite the fact the drizzle had turned into a steady rain, making driving that much more treacherous.

Gripping the wheel even tighter, Collier slowed his speed as he rounded a curve. That was when he saw *her*. Or at least he thought it was a her. With the rain, he couldn't be sure. What he was sure of, however, was that someone was walking toward him on the side of the road.

Leaning closer to the wheel and further narrowing his eyes, he decided it was definitely a woman and that she seemed to be in a world of hurt.

She was weaving as if she was drunk or completely disoriented. Either way, the situation was dangerous for both of them. Collier's heart raced, and his palms turned sweaty. If he hadn't slowed down, he might not have seen her until it was too late.

He could have struck her down.

Cool it, he told himself, breathing deeply to control his erratic pulse. He hadn't hit her. But what the hell was she doing on this stretch of highway at this time of the evening? And alone, to boot?

He was sure it wasn't by choice, a thought that made the hair stand up on the back of his neck. Something terrible must have happened, because no one in her right mind would be afoot in these hills in this rain at dusk.

What should he do?

Keep on going, pretending he hadn't seen her? Stop? He blew out a pent-up breath. Numerous reasons why he shouldn't stop flooded his mind. He ignored them and pulled off the road. Even though she was bound to have heard the noise behind her, she didn't so much as turn around. She kept moving forward in that same dazed, weaving motion.

Aiding a stranger was the last thing he needed to be doing, yet how could he just drive away and leave her?

He drove past her onto the shoulder, then opened the door and stepped out, flinching against the bone-chilling rain that struck him in the face. Controlling his growing anxiety and frustration, he caught up with her, stopping short of touching her. "Ma'am?"

Only after he spoke did she halt and turn slowly around.

Collier swallowed a gasp and a curse. Even though the elements were against him, her features were visible. Two things were immediately evident: she was young, and she was hurt. Gut instinct told him she'd been physically assaulted. One side of her face was bruised and swollen. And visible through her torn clothing were signs of other scrapes and bruises on her chest.

If she'd been in an accident of some kind, there would be a vehicle around. As it was, the two of them were alone, the cold rain becoming more of a problem by the second.

The fact that she was shivering and couldn't seem to stop jolted him into action. He had to get her into his car, then to a hospital. Shock had apparently set in, and that put her in more jeopardy than her wounds.

He suppressed another curse and motioned toward his Lexus. "Come on. Get in my car."

She didn't argue, but she didn't move, either.

"Please," Collier said, hearing the coaxing note in his voice, something that didn't come easily to him. "I can help you if you'll let me."

She remained motionless. Rounded eyes that seemed to take up more of her small face than necessary were centered directly on him, though he would have bet she wasn't seeing him at all.

"Please," he said again, reaching out and lightly touching her arm.

She flinched, and his lips tightened. "Sorry. But you have to get in my car. You need help."

Though she still remained mute, she took a step toward his vehicle. Careful not to touch her again, he rushed to open the door. Once she was seated, he slammed it shut and strode back to his side, releasing his held breath.

Too close to call. What if she'd refused to get in? What would he have done then? Since that was a moot point, he didn't have to go there. Now all he had to do was get her to the hospital and his responsibility would end.

Immediately he turned to her. She sat rigid, staring straight ahead. "I have a cell phone," Collier said in an awkward tone. "Is there someone I can call to meet you at the hospital?"

He had no idea if his words had penetrated, but he had to try. He would have to leave her, the thought of her fending for herself even at the hospital suddenly pricked his conscience, which in turn made him furious at himself.

What the hell was the matter with him? She wasn't his problem. He'd best remember that. But she was so pitiful, like a helpless, wounded animal or worse, a wounded child.

"Please..."

Her voice, in that broken plea, jerked him back to the moment at hand. "Please what?"

"Don't take me to the hospital."

So she wasn't totally catatonic after all. Or in total shock. Both good signs that filled him with relief. At least it didn't appear she was going to collapse on him, a fear he hadn't heretofore wanted to address.

"That's where you belong," he stressed, disturbed anew that she would even hesitate.

"I'm not going."

While weak and trembling, her voice held conviction, increasing his alarm and frustration.

"You—"

"If you try to make me go, I'll get out."

"And do what?" He knew his sarcasm was lost on her, but he couldn't stop the words.

"Keep walking."

"And die?"

"That wouldn't be a bad thing," she said, her voice breaking.

Now what? Collier thrust his hand though his hair. "Look, you need medical attention. But then, I obviously don't have to tell you that."

"I'll be all right. Please, take me home."

Curbing his growing anger, he asked, "Where is home?"

"Chaney."

That was a small town twenty miles north of Haven where he lived, which meant turning around and driving farther back than he'd already come. "Is anyone there?"

"No."

"Then I'm not taking you home."

"You…you have to."

"The hell I do," he muttered. "Besides, the weather's getting too bad to be on the highway." While that wasn't quite truth, it was as good an excuse as any.

She began sobbing quietly.

Cursing, Collier shoved the car into gear and drove off. He was about to make an incredibly stupid and dangerous move. He was taking her with him to the cabin. But what choice did he have?

Two

Collier peered at his watch.

She'd been in the shower far too long to suit him. He hoped she was all right, but he was concerned. She'd seemed so fragile, so breakable, when they had arrived at the retreat that he had again questioned his judgment in not taking her straight to the nearest hospital whether she wanted him to or not.

She'd seemed so weak that he'd been tempted to offer to help her undress and get into the shower, but the words had stuck in his throat for more reasons than one. Now he was wondering what to do. Check on her? Would that be appropriate? Hell, he didn't know. He'd never been in a situation like this before. This woman was a total stranger. He didn't even know her name, yet she had suddenly become his responsibility.

Not for long, he told himself, a grim expression changing his features. Come morning, they would both be headed back toward civilization, although that would of course put a kink in his plans. Once he left, he doubted seriously if he'd return to the cabin, despite how much was resting on the case. It demanded copious research, meaning he needed time alone without interruption, something he couldn't get at the office or at home.

Her timing couldn't have been worse, dammit.

How had she gotten herself into such a nightmarish

situation, anyway? He was loathe to travel down that mental path on his own or with her, but he knew the journey was inevitable. At some point she had to talk to him. She owed him that. He was curious. And sad. And angry. Not just because of her but for her. No woman deserved to be treated in such a vile manner.

The bastard who had done this to her should get his just deserts. But that certainly wasn't his responsibility, and he wasn't about to assume it. He wanted her out of here ASAP. That was his objective.

Collier stared at his watch again, then, frowning, looked at the closed door across from his room. Although hers was the smallest of the five bedrooms, he'd chosen it because of its location. He felt compelled to be near her so he could keep an eye on her.

He'd been afraid to put her upstairs, where most of the guests stayed. Until Jackson's tragic accident, Mason had often used the cabin for entertaining special clients of the firm. Now, for the most part, it remained empty, except for rare times like this weekend when a member of the family was lucky enough to sneak off and head for these hills.

For some reason, Collier had never entertained the thought of bringing Lana here. He almost laughed, trying to picture her wandering aimlessly through the large airy rooms looking to find something to occupy her time. She would hate the peace and quiet the hideaway offered. She always had to be busy making a statement, whatever the hell that meant.

Enough of Lana. His plate was full without bringing her into the equation. Suddenly he felt the urge to do something. His pent-up energy needed another outlet. When they had first arrived, he'd started a fire in the huge rock hearth and left it crackling and spitting, which effectively broke the sharp silence. But now he needed something else, another project.

The kitchen. Once there, he paused. Coffee or hot chocolate? He opted for both, thinking he'd need the caffeine fix long after she'd settled in for the night. And she just might drink a cup of the chocolate. Maybe that would help calm her fractured nerves. Disposing of that chore in record time, Collier made his way back into the great room, coffee in hand. After taking two sips, he set his cup on the nearest table.

She still hadn't made an appearance.

Deciding that his ''guest'' had definitely had enough time to take care of her personal needs, he strode to her door and knocked. No answer. He knocked again. More silence greeted him. Concern driving him, he knocked again. ''Are you okay?''

''I'm…fine.''

When her breathy voice reached his ears through the door, he went weak with relief. He'd had visions of all sorts of things having happened to her, all of them bad—and under his roof, too.

''May I come in?'' he asked, feeling like a stranger in his own house and not liking it.

''All…right.''

He didn't know what he'd expected when he saw her again, but it wasn't what he got. She'd been such a mess when he'd picked her up—wet, bedraggled and hurt, physically and emotionally—that he hadn't really looked at her. And once they had reached the cabin, he'd shown her straight to her room and left her there. It seemed as though neither of them had been comfortable in each other's presence.

Now, though, she was standing directly in his line of vision, and some vision *she* was, too, despite the nasty bruising on the side of her face, where it looked like someone had slapped her good and proper. For a second he couldn't get any farther than her delicate but perfectly cut features, especially her white, translucent skin and heart-shaped lips. And her lush black hair. He couldn't escape that. Even though the tousled curls were still damp, they looked like silk.

Her figure was perfectly cut, as well. Barefoot and wearing nothing but a terry robe that had been hanging behind the bathroom door, she stood tall and willowy, with a small waist, full breasts and long legs. A man couldn't ask for a better package. If he were interested, that is. And he wasn't. He couldn't believe he was standing there like an idiot and cataloging her assets.

He coughed. "By the way, I'm Collier Smith."

"I'm Brittany Banks."

Before he thought, he almost said the trite words "pleased to meet you." Under the circumstances, they would have sounded absurd. But then, this whole scenario was absurd.

It was at that moment that her robe gaped open and he saw the nasty cut above her left breast. His throat constricted at the sight. "That needs attention."

Brittany pulled the sash a little tighter, closing the gap somewhat. Then, as he watched, blood seeped through the material and stained it a bright red. His stomach revolted. Where else was she damaged? Had her attacker raped her? From the get-go, that thought had teetered on the edge of his mind, but he hadn't let himself go there.

"How 'bout you sit on the side of the bed and let me take a look-see?" He had forced himself to speak in a flat, unemotional tone so as not to further spook her. But he was determined to tend to her wounds, whether she liked it or not.

"If you have some salve, I can take care of it."

"I don't think so," he said stoically. "You look like you're about to pass out."

He wasn't lying. Even though she was rational enough, he knew she was still in shock and could crash at any time, and that time appeared imminent. He saw her hand on the doorjamb, her knuckles white from clinging to it. She was barely able to stand on her own.

It wasn't too late to go with his gut instinct and take her to the emergency room, he reminded himself, walking toward her. "I still think you ought to be in the hospital."

She gave her head a shake, her silky hair caressing her cheeks.

"Then you ought to be in bed," he said in a strained voice, thinking how personal, how intimate, that sounded, as his blood pressure pounded like thunder through his veins.

"It does look inviting."

She almost smiled, which sent another disturbing pang shooting through him. Ignoring it, and without asking permission, he took her lightly by the arm and eased her down onto the side of the bed.

"Hold on while I grab some medicine and gauze," he said grimly and left her there.

Minutes later, he was back. She was still where he had left her, but her eyes were closed and her head sagged to one side, though he sensed she wasn't asleep. For a brief second he stared at her, feeling another disturbing pang. Tightening his mouth, he reached the bed. Easing down beside her, Collier gently touched her arm.

Her eyes popped open, and their gazes met and held. Something hot and instant leaped between them, a heat that defied all logic and explanation. Swallowing hard, Collier was the first to look away, though his heart was beating much too fast. Something was happening, something he'd never experienced, and it was scaring the hell out of him.

He fought the strong urge to get up and run like the devil himself was chasing him. Curiosity on his part and need on hers clearly won the battle raging inside him, forcing him to stay put.

"I'll try not to hurt you," he said more brusquely than he had intended. But he was shaken, which left him no recourse but to try to protect himself as best he could. Knowing that she was naked under the robe made his mouth go bone-dry.

"You don't have to do this," she said in a breathless tone.

"Yes, I do."

The intoxicating scent of roses assaulted his senses as he eased the terry robe off a creamy shoulder, further exposing the nasty scrape. Without looking at her, he squeezed a generous amount of salve onto a finger, then placed it on her bare flesh. And rubbed. Instantly he went hard, his erection pushing against his zipper.

Had she picked up on his reaction? More than ever, he dared not look at her. He almost couldn't move that finger over the wound. Again the urge to flee was almost too tempting to ignore. Yet he wasn't sure he could even stand, mortified by his own behavior.

She seemed unaware of his dilemma, because she didn't pull away, for which he was thankful. She needed medical attention, and, for the moment, he was the only one who could provide it.

"Who did this to you?" he asked in a steely tone.

"I'd rather not say."

He peered up at her, his lips tight. "Why would you want to protect such an animal?"

"You wouldn't understand."

"Why don't you try me?"

She licked her lower lip, then whispered, "Please."

Please what? he wanted to shout. *Please don't kiss you senseless?* Sweat drenched him; he was losing it.

He forced himself to look at her, he hoped without showing any of his chaotic thoughts. "Did he rape you?"

Her face paled. "No."

"Did he try?"

"Yes, but he didn't succeed."

"Don't make me pull the details out of you. You owe me that much."

Tears welled up in her eyes as she focused on him. "I…we were in his car when he attacked me. We'd gone out to dinner—" Her voice broke, and she wiped at the tears.

That gesture was almost more than Collier could take. He wanted to lick those tears away, to soak up all her pain and heartache and make it disappear. Instead he forced himself to say, "Go on."

"When I wouldn't let him…touch me, he became angry, then mean."

"How did you get out of the car?" Collier suspected he knew the answer to that question. Nonetheless, he wanted to hear her say it. He was no shrink, but he knew she needed to talk about this.

"He…pushed me."

"That sonofabitch!" He'd like nothing better than to break the man's neck for damaging her perfect skin and body, not to mention her mind. What kind of animal did these kinds of things? He knew. A sicko. In his profession, he'd dealt with more than his share.

"I have no idea how long I'd been walking when you stopped."

"I'm assuming no other cars had passed."

"If they did, they didn't bother to stop."

Silence ensued while he gritted his teeth and placed the bandage over the scrape. Without asking permission, he gently pushed her robe completely off her shoulders and checked for other injuries that might require his attention.

Having her full, pointed breasts so close, barely hidden, almost begging to be touched, was almost his undoing. His erection pinched that much harder as he continued on his mission, all the while trying to ignore what was happening to his body.

Finding no other wounds worthy of medication, he covered her, then moved out of harm's way to the rocking chair near the bed. "Tell me his name."

"No."

He gave a start. "No? Why not?"

"It's none of your business," she said in a small voice.

"As an attorney, what if I want to make it my business?"

Her mouth worked. "Why would you do that?"

"Does it matter?" His tone was tight.

He wished he knew what was going on behind those lovely eyes. Even in her vulnerable state, she seemed a master at guarding her secrets.

"I have to handle this in my own way, in my own time."

Boy, had he heard that one before. "You're not going to file charges." His words were a flat statement of fact.

"No, I'm not," she said, though she kept her gaze averted.

Feeling his attorney modus operandi kick in, he wanted to fire more questions at her, weaken her resolve until she agreed to make the scumbag pay. But he sensed that tactic wouldn't work with this woman, that underneath her fragility was a strong will, so he kept his mouth shut. Besides, she was right. It *wasn't* any of his business.

"Would you like a cup of hot chocolate?" he asked, changing the subject.

"No, thanks. I just want to go to bed."

"No problem." He took a deep breath, then stood. "Are you sure there's nothing else you need?"

"I'm sure." She paused, locking her gaze on his. "Thanks for taking care of me."

"You're welcome," he lied, then turned and strode out of the room.

A short time later, Collier's frustration continued to rise along with the water. With too much rain, the bridge up to the house became impassable. Under normal conditions that wouldn't be a bad thing, since he had tons of work to keep him occupied.

However, Brittany Banks had put a whole new spin on things. After the way she'd affected him, work remained the furthest thing from his mind. What was there about her that had his gut in such a mess? That ignited his libido? Hell, he was practically engaged to a woman with whom he had everything in common.

With Brittany, it was just the opposite. It was a given from the way she was dressed that she didn't have much money, much less move in the same social circles he did.

Disgusted with his thoughts and with himself, Collier turned back to the stack of papers piled on the coffee table. Man, did he need to be busting his butt. Defending a bigwig from a large energy company on sexual harassment charges brought against him by one of the female employees would not be a piece of cake. He had to be prepared. There could be no mistakes on his part, especially with the federal appointment in the offing.

Still, his mind was cluttered with the woman occupying the guest room. Running a close second to that thought was another equally as chilling. What if someone got wind of this incident—like the press, for instance? What would happen? They'd have a field day coming up with all kinds of inappropriate sexual connotations. With him under consideration for the federal judgeship, that would be the worst possible scenario.

Shuddering, Collier stared out the window and watched a bolt of lightning rip across the sky.

Three

Brittany found it hard to believe she'd actually slept. Opening her eyes, she peered at the clock on the table bedside her. Six o'clock. Time to get up, only she wasn't at home, in her bed. For a moment she lay unmoving, the events of the previous evening suddenly leaping to the forefront of her mind in living color. When she thought of Rupert Holt's groping hands and slimy lips on her body, she couldn't bear it. Groaning, she squeezed her eyes shut again, fighting off the queasiness in her stomach.

Following several deep breaths, she felt her nausea finally subside, but tears took its place, clogging her throat. Was it still raining? She listened, her sore body tense. Yes, it was still coming down, though seemingly not with the same fierceness as last night. But more rain of any kind could not be good, not on the side of this mountain.

She had to get home.

Hot tears continued to drench her face, but Brittany didn't try to stop them. She hadn't cried, not even when she'd been alone with her rescuer. She'd been so exhausted, she'd fallen into a deep sleep, too tired to cry.

Now, however, with a new day staring at her, reality hit like another of Rupert's blows. She winced, feeling the tears jam her throat. For a second she feared she might choke.

How could something so awful have happened to her? How could she have let it happen? She almost never went out with a man. Following one disastrous love affair long before her brother Tommy was incarcerated, she'd sworn off men. Since then, she'd held herself aloof, making sure no one approached her.

But Rupert Holt had been so attentive, encouraging her to talk, especially about Tommy. He'd seemed genuinely concerned about her brother's plight, even hinting that he was willing to help seek his release, until he'd caught her in a weak moment.

He was one of Haven's leading businessmen, chairman of the board of his wife's high-end furniture manufacturing company, which did business all over the world. On top of that, he was the travel agency's most lucrative client, and she'd been reluctant to offend him, since she needed her job.

Still, she should have known he was setting her up. When things sounded too good to be true, they usually were. But he'd been such a gentleman, she'd been fooled. The fact that he was a married man with grown children, and so much older than she was, had lulled her; anything other than friendship between them had never occurred to her.

How stupid and gullible she had been.

Yet never in her wildest imagination would she have picked him to be an abuser of women. That kind of man fit in the category with her drunken stepfather, who'd been a lowlife scumbag from the time he'd married her mother until his death several years afterward.

Rupert was good-looking and charming. He was a big man, with steel-gray hair, crisp blue eyes and more than his share of charm. Although he'd rarely mentioned his wife, she hadn't attached anything significant to that. His behavior toward her just didn't make sense. Why had he resorted to violence?

A renewed sense of fear coiled tightly in the pit of Brittany's stomach, only subsiding when she told herself that he couldn't hurt her anymore. She was safe. But for how long? When she returned to her job at the travel agency...

She wouldn't think about that now. She had to put Rupert and what had happened out of her mind, bury it deeply in a secluded part of her heart and forget it. Since she couldn't do anything to get back at him, that was the only logical thing to do.

Pretend it never happened.

Life would go on. She would continue with her classes at the college. Work at the travel agency during the week. Slave at the diner on weekends. Business as usual.

But logic told her that wouldn't work. All she had to do was look in the mirror. The emotional damage she could hide; the physical she could not. She'd been a mess last night. This morning she'd probably be downright frightening.

If only she had a way to get back at Rupert for taking advantage of her. For hurting her. Even her vile stepfather had never struck her in the face, though he'd raised many a welt on her back and legs when her mother hadn't been around.

Rupert wasn't drunken trash like Cal Rogers, but there must have been that same evil glint in Rupert's eyes, though she'd obviously missed it.

Big mistake.

Maybe, if she'd seen it, she could have stopped him from assaulting her. Instead, his change of personality had come out of the blue, as if he'd suddenly snapped, becoming a different man from the one she'd known.

He'd taken her to one of Haven's most upscale restaurants, which was a treat for her, since she'd never been there. Following a couple of glasses of wine, the meal had been served. Over dinner, he'd been attentive, asking about her classes at the college, which he knew was her passion. Then they had discussed her weekend job at the diner, waiting on tables. She wasn't proud of that second one, but it was all she could find that didn't conflict with her hours at the travel agency.

"You shouldn't have to wait tables, you know," he'd said in a low, kind voice, bringing up the topic.

She'd flushed, then looked away, uncomfortable discussing her personal life with him or anyone else. "I guess Sissy told you," she finally responded. Sissy Newman was her boss, who had a big heart as well as a big mouth. She and Rupert were good friends, which wasn't going to help her situation. In fact, Sissy thought Rupert and his wife could walk on water.

"Does it matter how I found out?"

"No," she said, stifling a sigh. "I'm not ashamed of it."

"What if I found you another part-time job? Would you be interested?"

Brittany suppressed her sudden excitement. "What did you have in mind?"

"Nothing yet." He paused with a chuckle. "But with my connections, I'm sure I could come up with something more suitable."

"That would be nice." Brittany paused, then added, "You know where to find me."

His eyes probed. "That I do."

She averted her gaze, shielding herself from the intensity she saw there, unwilling to look a gift horse in the mouth. If he could wangle her another job, she would be forever grateful. Standing on her feet into the wee hours of the morning was not something she looked forward to, nor was putting up with obnoxious customers and their rudeness.

"So, about your brother..."

Brittany gave an audible sigh. "Nothing's changed. He still maintains his innocence, and he's still begging me to get him out."

"I'm willing to help you out there, too, you know. Only you've never given me the green light."

"Maybe that's because I don't understand why you'd want to." She knew her words sounded much more suspicious than she'd intended, but she hadn't done anything special for this man, which made his sudden generosity a bit suspicious.

Rupert shrugged and smiled. "Let's just say I have the connections and like to help where I can. Besides, Sissy tells me how hard you're working to get your degree, and how tough it is."

"It has been hard, but that's the only way I can help Tommy."

"We'll talk more about that later," Rupert said, turning to the waiter, who was hovering, and ordering a mixed drink.

He hadn't stopped with one, either. By the time they left the restaurant, Brittany could have sworn he was drunk, though his actions never confirmed that, not even when he got behind the wheel.

Only after they had been driving for a while and he pulled off the road did she grow alarmed. And she'd had reason, because he'd immediately reached for her and begun kissing her, hard and deep, trying to force his tongue into her mouth, while running his hands up her legs to her panties.

"No!" she cried, desperately trying to push him away.

But he was too strong and determined. When she wouldn't comply, he'd slapped her. The more she'd struggled, the more violent he'd become, until she blacked out.

The next thing she remembered was being shoved out of his car onto the side of the highway, cold rain assaulting her bruised body.

Suddenly Brittany pulled herself into a fetal position on the bed and sobbed quietly into the pillow. If the stranger in the other room hadn't come along, she shuddered to think what would have happened to her. She couldn't have walked much longer. Worse, some other sick, violent person could have come along and finished her off.

Still, she hated the thought that she was at another man's mercy. For all she knew, he could turn out to be worse than Rupert. Her instincts resisted that thought, though. She barely remembered what her rescuer looked like, but she sensed he would never hurt a woman.

The way he'd touched her had told her that.

Brittany's breath caught as she thought about how she'd inhaled the subtle yet expensive scent of his cologne, how manly he'd smelled. But it was the way his hands had felt on her bare flesh that lingered. Stop it, she told herself, panicking. The fact that he would never touch her again was what was important.

As soon as she got up and dressed, she could return home, she assured herself. She could escape from this nightmare, then figure out how best to put herself and her life back together. No matter what Collier Smith advised, she had no intention of reporting Rupert to the police for fear of repercussions, both professionally and emotionally.

She had no confidence in the justice system, especially against an adversary like Rupert Holt. Who would believe a nobody like her, whose brother was a jailbird?

What about Tommy? Another hard shudder went through her, and Brittany panicked. She was due to visit him in a couple of days, on Sunday, but she couldn't go with her face all bruised.

Suddenly she wished she could get her hands on Rupert, first for hurting her and second for dashing her hopes of getting help for Tommy. Every time she visited him in that awful place, her heart broke anew.

What a difference there was between her circumstances and those of the man who had helped her. From what little she had noticed of her surroundings, it was obvious he was someone of means, the complete opposite from her. She and Tommy had been left to fend for themselves after the death of their mother when they both were young. Her drunken stepfather and Tommy's father had contributed little to their upbringing; most of the time they hadn't even known where he was.

Brittany had struggled all her life to get where she was today, which still wasn't where she wanted to be. At thirty, she was still trying to get her degree so that she could become financially secure, something she had never known. After that, she would like nothing better than to flee her hometown and live somewhere else. Anywhere else.

But leaving Chaney wasn't an option, not until she was able to hire an attorney and start working to get Tommy released from prison.

Because of her brother's one terrible error in judgment, she might as well wear a scarlet letter on her chest. Even though the accident had happened three years ago, she was still shunned and talked about. Long before the mishap, her family was considered trailer park trash. Now she had no chance of earning anyone's respect in the town where she'd grown up.

The fact that Tommy was in prison would never be laid to rest, especially since he had permanently injured the son of the town's most prestigious family.

Yet Brittany loved her brother and felt responsible for him, though she definitely saw his faults. He'd caused her more than her share of heartache during his teenage years, even joining a gang for a short time and getting arrested, though she'd believed him when he told her someone had set him up in order to get even with him. Still, it was the accident that had done the real damage.

Following the accident, they had hauled him down to the police station, since he hadn't had a scratch on him. Once there, Tommy had called her almost in hysterics. Clamping down on her own hysteria, she had gone to him immediately. She never would forget the desperate look on her brother's face when she'd walked into police headquarters.

"Sis," he'd told her, "I swear I didn't know my head wasn't clear when I left the party."

"Come on, Tommy, surely you felt something."

"Not until I turned onto the highway, then, wham, it hit me. Suddenly I didn't know where I was or what I was doing." He paused, his voice cracking when he spoke again. "Hell, I don't even remember hitting the guy's car. My drink was doctored. I know it was. Someone's out to get me."

"Tommy—"

"Say you believe me," he pleaded, grabbing her hands and clinging to them. "I know I've been in my share of trouble, but you know I've never driven drunk. You know that."

And she did. Yet there was always a first time. Still, she wanted to believe him—for her own sake as well as his. "Oh, dear Lord, Tommy, what are we going to do?"

"Make this go away, sis," he sobbed. "You always make things right. I know you won't fail me now."

But she *had* failed him, and miserably, too. Because she'd had no means to hire adequate counsel to represent him, Tommy had been assigned a court appointed attorney who failed to substantiate his claim that he'd been drugged. As far as she could tell, the man had hardly bothered to try. That was why, when Rupert had offered to champion her cause with an attorney, she'd dropped her guard.

Never again.

Deciding she'd wallowed in self-pity long enough, Brittany forced her sore limbs to move into a sitting position, then upright. Soon she would be dressed and on her way home.

Four

Stranded.

No other word adequately described the situation. During the night, the rain had come down in buckets. Without even having to walk outside and take a look, Collier knew the bridge was impassable. Whether he liked it or not, he wouldn't be taking his guest anywhere. And whether she liked it or not, she wouldn't be going anywhere.

Through the years, Mason had kept saying he was going to do something about the bridge, get a crew up here to rebuild it, so this kind of problem wouldn't rise every time the water did. But he hadn't followed through. Collier figured it was because the retreat wasn't used all that much anymore, which was a shame, since it was a great place for R & R.

And work.

He began to pace the floor again, as he had been on and off for hours. Good thing the floors were hardwood; otherwise, he would have worn a trail in the carpet. Lord knew he'd tried to work—all night, in fact. Yet he hadn't made a dent in the case. Instead he'd been consumed with thoughts of the woman in the next room and his bid for the judgeship.

Though far apart in reality, they seemed closely related in his disjointed mind. He shouldn't be holed up in this cabin with a lovely woman with an obviously shaded past. *With secrets*. The worst kind of woman to get involved with.

The hell of it was, he *wasn't* involved. So why was he getting himself all worked up over something he hadn't done? Loaded question. Loaded answer. When he'd touched Brittany Banks, it had been like tossing gasoline on an open flame. And that flame was still smoldering in his gut.

He'd never reacted to a woman as strongly, certainly not Lana. He could go for days, even weeks, and not touch her, and it wouldn't bother him.

But he knew the woman in the nearby room was a different story. He would bet that underneath her aloof exterior were seething emotions that, when tapped in the right way, would run as hot as molten lava. Of course *he* would never find out. He didn't intend to touch her again.

If only he could stop thinking about how good she'd smelled, as if she'd just bathed in a tub of roses. How her soft bare flesh had felt under his fingers, how he'd ached to caress her full breasts and suck her dark, pink nipples.

Collier drew air through his dry lungs, once again feeling that unwelcome tightening of his groin.

He'd been tempted to check on her during the night. Thank heaven his good sense had overruled that crazy thought.

He needed to get out of here. He needed to get *her* out of here. If she knew how he felt, how he had reacted to her body, she would be more petrified than she already was. He froze. Had she guessed? Had she picked up on the raw hunger gnawing inside him? Had she seen it in his eyes? He hoped not, for both their sakes.

She must never suspect how deeply she affected him.

When she awakened, he would be the perfect gentleman and host—cool but polite. And accommodating. Somehow they would get through this day. Hopefully, by tomorrow morning, the rain would have stopped and the bridge would be passable.

Until then, he had to think with his head and not his libido.

His thoughts suddenly brightened when he turned them back to the judgeship. He still couldn't believe his good fortune. However, he wasn't going to rely on his hopes, because nothing was certain and plenty could still go wrong. Granted, he had a lot going for him. He was a prestigious attorney who rarely lost a case, and he came from a family that was highly visible in the political arena. When it came to working for and contributing to the party, he could hold his own.

"No one has the record or the credentials you have, boy," Mason had said when the call came from one of the senators. "You'll be a shoo-in."

"Now, Dad, don't count the chickens before they hatch."

"The hell you say." His father's white bushy eyebrows drew together, forming a frown. "As much time, energy and money as this family has poured into Washington's coffers, you should be a sure thing."

"Well, I'll do my part. You know I want this appointment as badly as you want me to have it. But then, so do the other guys who made the cut to the final four."

"I'm not worried about them," Mason said with his typical air of self-confidence. "You're the best man for the job. No doubt about it."

"You wouldn't be a bit prejudiced, now would you?"

Mason almost smiled. "Maybe, but it's the truth. Because I'm so sure of it, I'm going to have a precelebration party.''

''I don't think that's a good idea.''

''Why the hell not?''

''What about Jackson? He seems more depressed than ever.''

''That's one of the reasons I'm going to do it,'' Mason countered fiercely. ''Maybe it'll get him out of that room of his.''

''Don't bet on it.''

''You let me worry about your brother. You just worry about keeping your nose clean and not stepping on anyone's toes.''

As much as he would have liked to do that, Collier feared he'd already pulled the pin out of one grenade when he'd agreed to defend the energy company on the sexual harassment charge. That could become a real sticky situation if some feminist got in on the action. But he'd given his word, and he had no intention of backing off, regardless of whether his dad approved or not.

As far as Brittany Banks went, no one would ever know that he'd been alone up here with her. She would remain a secret. He hadn't done anything wrong—not yet, anyway—which meant he had no reason to feel guilty. Still, to the press and anyone else interested in probing into his life, a sure thing with the potential appointment, someone would make something of the matter, especially with Lana and her high-profile family in the picture.

Hearing a sound, Collier paused in his thoughts and whipped around. She was standing just barely inside the room. Their gazes met, and an unwanted jolt went through him. ''Good morning,'' he managed to say through a throat that sounded like it had been shredded with razors.

"Good morning," she responded, her voice sounding soft and a bit uncertain. The side of her face seemed more swollen this morning, the bruising more pronounced. His blood boiled hot again. Damn that bastard. One of these days...

He reined in his renegade thoughts and asked, "Did you sleep okay?"

"Actually I did, which surprised me," she said, moving deeper into the room. "I guess I was totally wiped out."

"I'm sure you were."

Suddenly an awkwardness fell between them, followed by a tense silence. Maybe it was because when she moved her robe had loosened far enough that the upper portion of one breast was exposed. He groaned inwardly, his breath spiking.

As if she sensed where his gaze was targeted, she flushed and pulled the sash tighter. "I looked for my clothes, but..." Her voice trailed off, and she swallowed hard.

No doubt she felt the hot tension, too. He didn't know why that made him feel better, but it did. "I hung them in the laundry room to dry," he forced himself to say around his elevated breathing. "But I'm not sure they're wearable."

"I'll have to wear them anyway."

He rubbed the five-o'clock shadow on his chin in frustration. She was right. As far as he knew, there wasn't one article of women's clothing on the premises.

"Are you hungry?" he asked, deliberately changing the subject.

"I hadn't thought about it."

"Come on and I'll make us some breakfast." He had to do something to ease the tension, needed to keep busy. His insides felt ready to explode.

Once he had freshly dripped coffee on the small kitchen table, along with bowls of oatmeal and plates of toast, he finally sat down across from her. He kept his eyes averted for fear she would pick up on his raw and growing hunger for her, which could only make the situation even more uncomfortable.

He grimaced, then focused his attention on the oatmeal. It reminded him of a glob of cement. He almost got up and dumped it into the sink. If only he hadn't given in to the urge to play the Good Samaritan.

"When can you take me home?"

The sound of her soft, Southern voice pulled him up short. Oh, boy. His grimace deepened. "I can't. At least, not today."

Her face lost what little color it had, making her eyes appear deeper and darker than before.

"The bridge is impassable," he added flatly.

Her lower lip quivered, which was almost more than he could handle. "What if..." Again her voice faded into nothingness.

"I know what you're thinking, but it's supposed to clear. As soon as it's safe, trust me, we'll be out of here."

Brittany bit down on that deliciously plump lip, stopping the trembling. Though she didn't say so, he sensed she was terribly upset by the turn of events. Hell, so was he. But he couldn't do anything about it, and neither could she.

"I have to get back to my job."

Her dark brown eyes implored him, and he stifled a curse. "I'm sure you do, but that's not going to happen. Not today."

"There's...nothing you can do?"

He shoved the bowl away, dropping all pretense of eating. "Nope, except wait." He paused, angling his head. "Where do you work?"

"At a travel agency in Haven. I'm also taking classes at the college. Tonight, however, I have to be—" She stopped midsentence. "Never mind. It's not important."

He frowned. "If there's someone you need to call, feel free."

"It doesn't matter," she said in a forlorn voice. "I can't go to the diner looking like this anyway."

"Diner?"

Her chin seemed to lift a notch as she met his gaze. "I work on weekends as a part-time waitress."

A waitress.

He didn't know why that bothered him. There was nothing wrong with that job. Maybe he was more of a snob than he realized.

Finally collecting himself, he said, "Like I said, make any calls you want."

"Thanks," she said tightly.

He wanted to bombard her with questions, asking why the hell someone who looked like her had to sling hash. More to the point, he wanted to know everything there was to know about this lovely creature who had dropped into his life.

But his throat felt suddenly paralyzed, especially when that lower lip started to quiver again. For a long moment he couldn't take his eyes off it, imagining his tongue running across its soft inner lining.

"Don't."

He gave another start. "Don't what?"

"Look at me like that," she said in a slightly cracked voice.

Distress spilled from her eyes, which made him feel more like a heel than ever. Realizing he was on the verge of falling off a very high cliff, he stood and muttered roughly, "Sorry."

When she didn't respond, he added, "Look, stay and finish your breakfast. I've got work to do."

Rupert Holt slammed the paper down on the desk in his study so hard that his cup rattled in his saucer. Coffee sloshed on the wood. "Damn!"

He ignored the mess his burst of temper had made, continuing to seethe. Let one of his maids clean it up. He paid them enough.

The last thing he wanted was for Collier Smith to get that appointment to the federal bench. No son or stepson—it didn't matter—of Mason Williams would succeed in any political arena if he had his way. And as long as he had the money to back up his mouth, he usually got what he wanted.

But then, so did Mason. He had as much clout, prestige and money as Rupert himself had. Yet Rupert was determined to best him. Besting his contemporary had become one of his most sought after goals. He felt justified, too, since the law firm of Williams, Smith and Rutledge had represented him on a lawsuit that had gone sour, costing him a bundle of money.

While that was bad enough, Mason's superior attitude rankled just as much. The fact that he hailed from an old Southern family, with roots going back before the Civil War, didn't make Mason any better or his shit smell any sweeter.

Rupert would have given his left ball to have the same social clout Mason and his family had, but no matter how much money he made, no matter how many of the rough edges he whittled off his personality, his efforts never seemed to be enough.

In the social circles of Haven and the surrounding county, he was always going to be one down simply because he didn't have a family tree of distinction.

A crock of crap. That was his thought on the subject. He had news for the snobs: he could hold his own when push came to shove. And with this federal appointment wide-open, the shoving had started.

Hell, he was a staunch Republican, in good standing with the party muckey-mucks, and he had his own man in the race for the judgeship, a man who was much more qualified than Smith.

Before he could mount an attack against the William and Smith armies, however, he had to fix a more pressing problem—Brittany Banks. Somehow he had to make up for the damage he'd done to her before she returned the favor and damaged *him.*

Sweat dampened his shirt as the ramifications of his poor judgment hit home. He couldn't remember when he'd gotten that drunk or lost control so completely and so quickly.

But when she'd told him no and looked at him as if he was some reptile that had just crawled out from under a rock, he'd lost it. He remembered slapping her hard at least once. What happened after she cried out remained fuzzy, except for when he shoved her out of his vehicle.

If she blabbed and his wife found out... Sweat covered Rupert's entire body as he suddenly lunged up from the table and walked to the window. The grounds of his mansion were a sight for any eyes, especially when the leaves were at their peak. Now the beauty of his estate held little fascination for him. His mind was too cluttered with neutralizing the damage.

He'd already ordered two dozen long-stemmed red roses to be sent to the travel agency that afternoon if Brittany showed up for work. Suddenly his entire system threatened to shut down.

What if she was dead?

Although it hadn't been freezing last night, it had been cold and raining. And he'd just dumped her on the side of a highway like a piece of garbage. Someone could have come along and run over her, or worse.

His sweat turned into a chill, making him shake. He'd already called the local hospitals to see if she'd been admitted. So far, so good. If she didn't show up at work in a few days, he would have to hire a private eye to find her. If she was dead...

He almost lost the contents of his stomach. He shouldn't have gotten so stinking drunk. He knew he couldn't handle it. Angel, his wife, would have his head on a platter, not to mention what would happen to his position in the company. She would strip him of all power. He thought he'd conquered his drinking problem, or at least had it under control, but apparently he hadn't.

The thing was, he hadn't wanted a woman in a long time. And he couldn't remember ever wanting one as badly as he wanted Brittany, even if she was trailer trash.

And to think she'd rejected him. No one thwarted Rupert Holt and got away with it. This time, though, he feared he'd taken his rage and vindictiveness too far. Until he knew for sure, he had to back off.

His only hope was that Brittany was a survivor. Considering what she'd been through already, she would bounce back. When she surfaced, he would make amends, take care of the problem. Her brother was her Achilles' heel, so he'd keep hammering on his willingness to help Tommy. Before long, he would wear her down and get back into her good graces. She would never say a word to anyone.

Suddenly feeling better, Rupert turned his attention back to Collier. He eyed the cordless phone on the buffet and reached for it. Might as well start the dice rolling against Smith.

He punched out a number and waited.

Five

Would this mess ever end? The rain had been falling all day and into the night, which meant the bridge was completely submerged. They were truly marooned.

It had to quit. It just had to. The day had been long and not really profitable, though he'd remained in his room for most of it. When he was lucky enough and got a respite from thoughts of Brittany, he'd actually gotten a little work done. Not nearly enough, however. He'd used most of his energy debating what to do about *her*.

Absolutely nothing, his common sense had told him. As soon as they were able to get back to civilization, Brittany would no longer be his responsibility. So why did he feel so responsible? Go figure.

It was apparent she'd wanted to avoid him as much as he had her. Still, he'd forced himself to knock on her door a couple of times and ask if she was all right, telling her to help herself to anything in the kitchen she might want. Once he'd heard her rummaging around in there and been tempted to join her, but he hadn't. He knew he wasn't playing the gracious host, not anywhere close to it. But this entire situation was so bizarre that he had no real idea how to behave.

Brittany Banks made him uncomfortable. That was the stark truth. She made him want something he couldn't have. Her. Every time he was around her, he got a hard-on. He wasn't proud of his urges, but he *was* proud that he'd stayed away from her.

As it was, she'd been to hell and back. He had no intention of sending her back there again, which was what would happen if he touched her. Just that thought knotted his stomach even tighter. He wasn't thinking like a rational man but like a teenager in heat.

Actually it was worse. Instead of tending to business, he'd spent his time lusting after a woman who, under normal circumstances, he wouldn't have looked at twice or given the time of day.

Well, maybe that was going a bit too far. He probably would at least have noticed her. With her beauty, all she had to do was walk into a room and heads would turn. Especially men's. She transmitted sexual signals with her every move, yet she seemed totally unaware of them.

That was what made her so intriguing.

Enough, Smith. Brittany Banks had taken up enough of his time. He had to forget her and turn his attention to what counted in his life. Tomorrow. Surely the rain would cease then and they could leave. She would go her way and he would go his. If she chose to let that scumbag who attacked her get away with it, then so be it. He wasn't going to beg her to do the right thing and turn him in.

Now all he had to do was get through the remainder of the night.

Collier shifted his gaze toward the bed bathed in lamplight. While it certainly looked inviting, he knew that once he lay there, his eyes would stay wide-open as if they had been glued.

What would his mother's advice be? His insides stilled. Why had the late Hannah Smith Williams come unexpectedly to mind? The answer was a no-brainer. He missed her. Despite the fact that she had died when he was only thirteen, he remembered every detail about her.

She was the prettiest, sweetest woman he'd ever known. And she always smelled so good, like roses. Maybe that was why Brittany's scent had captivated him. Hannah had been perfect in every way, or at least he'd thought so. And still did.

Unwittingly his mind slid back to that awful day when he'd come home from school and rushed into the parlor where his mother would wait for both him and Jackson. On that particular day he'd been alone, with something important to tell her.

Hannah had been sitting in her usual chair, close to the fireplace, where the burning wood hissed pleasantly in the hearth. Her eyes had been closed, and she'd looked peaceful and beautiful, even more so than usual. He'd dashed to her side, expecting her to open her eyes, smile, then hold up her cheek for a kiss.

"Hey, Mom, I'm home."

No response.

"Mom!" he called again, kneeling beside the chair and poking her. "Wake up."

Still no response. He shook her shoulder gently, grinning, thinking she was playing a trick on him. "Come on, I know you're just playing possum." He shook her harder.

When she didn't respond, he frowned, rose to his feet and hollered for Maxine, the housekeeper, who was like a second mother to him. She stormed into the room. "What on earth, boy? You're yelling like a banshee."

"It's Mom!" he cried. "She...she won't wake up."

He moved aside as Maxine ran to Hannah and began to shake her gently. "Miz Hannah, wake up. Collier's home."

She placed her fingers on his mother's throat, feeling for a pulse. It wasn't what Maxine said afterward but rather the sudden terrified expression on her face that told him something was wrong. Horribly wrong.

"What's the matter with Mom? Is she sick?"

"Come with me," Maxine said, not looking at him. "Let's go into the other room and call your dad."

"No, I'm not leaving Mom." Collier's tone was belligerent. "She'll want me here when she wakes up."

"Please do what I say."

Collier stiffened. "Why?"

"Because your mother's not going to wake up," Maxine blurted, then covered her mouth with her hand, as if she knew she'd spoken out of turn.

Collier's eyes suddenly filled with tears, and he backed up toward his mother. Once there, he whipped around, dropped to his knees beside her and placed his palm against her face. "She's not dead!" he sobbed in a fierce tone. "Don't say that!"

"Collier, please," Maxine whispered, touching his shoulder.

He shrugged her hand away. "No! I have to make her breathe again. You have to help me."

"Collier, don't," Maxine whispered again in a broken voice.

"No!" he screamed, leaning over and beating on Hannah's chest. "Wake up, Mom. Please don't die. Please don't. *Please.*"

But no amount of pleading on his part had changed the hard, cold fact that his mother was indeed dead. What happened immediately afterward became sketchy. Until this day, he couldn't remember the details of Mason's arrival, the funeral or the days following. All he remembered was knowing that his life as he'd known it was over, that nothing would ever be the same again. And it hadn't been.

Hannah had been his greatest protector, his biggest champion and his fiercest disciplinarian. For the longest time after she'd died, he had been so angry with God and everyone around him that he'd been unbearable. Looking back, he actually felt sorry for Mason, who had been left with two teenage boys to rear alone.

Mason had married Collier's mother when he had been only two years old. Mason's son, Jackson, had been six. Both his mother and Mason had been divorced. Collier's birth father hadn't wanted anything to do with him after his mother had caught him with another woman and left him. Even so, as a result of the nasty divorce that followed, his father had refused to give his permission for Mason to adopt him.

Despite that, Mason was the only father Collier had ever known. And while Mason had been good to him, certainly treated him like his younger son, Collier knew that he wasn't and nursed deep insecurities.

That feeling had worsened after his mother's death. Hannah had represented the softer, gentler side of the family. Mason was hard-edged and expected too much from his sons. That worsened, too, once they became his total responsibility. He hadn't a clue how to handle the needs of two boys. A succession of nannies was the order of the day.

Yet he and Jackson had survived those difficult years, both becoming successful attorneys any father could be proud of. Even so, Collier felt he hadn't quite made the grade yet, that he still had more hurdles to jump.

In many ways, though, he was just like Mason despite the fact that no blood linked them. Collier was smart, ambitious and driven, all the attributes that had launched

Mason to the top of his profession and earned him the bucks and respect that went with it.

Despite the similarities, Collier continued to feel that he still didn't measure up, that he had something more to prove. That was why he had to get that appointment to the bench. Maybe then he would finally feel like Mason's son in every respect.

If Jackson hadn't had that accident, he wouldn't feel quite as much pressure. It wouldn't dog his every waking moment, this need to succeed because the eldest son hadn't. Too, he yearned to take away some of the pain that Jackson's misfortune had put in his father's heart.

Mason harped constantly on the injustice of it all, making closure impossible. He grieved daily over Jackson's unwillingness to continue to practice law. Instead Jackson seemed content to simply sit in his room at the mansion and nurse his bitterness and anger. And become weaker by the day.

As a result, Collier often felt pangs of guilt for remaining upright and whole, something that Jackson would never be again. He had always idolized Jackson, positive he was smarter, wittier and more likely to succeed. When the accident occurred, Collier had felt his own heart and spirit break.

Now, however, though Jackson refused to make a new life for himself, Collier refused to give in to his brother's despair. He was determined that sooner or later Jackson would be productive again. On that point, he and Mason were in total agreement.

Thinking about his mother's untimely death and his brother's plight left him more depressed than ever. "Ah, to hell with it," he spat aloud, crossing to the bed and plopping down on it. Perhaps if he lay there long enough, he would fall asleep, regardless of his restless mind and heart.

He awakened with a start, totally disoriented for a moment, then realized where he was. He couldn't identify what had interrupted his sleep. He peered at the clock. Midnight. His rest had certainly been short-lived.

Collier heard the noise then. This must be what had awakened him, and this time he recognized it. Someone was sobbing. *Brittany* was sobbing. Before he had time to think, he lunged off the bed and headed for her room. Without hesitation, he opened the door, then eased onto the side of her bed, scared shitless that she had internal injuries only a doctor could fix.

"Brittany," he whispered, hearing the note of panic in his voice but unable to control it.

The small lamp burning in the corner gave him access to her face. When she gazed up at him, the stark sadness in those eyes opened an emotional floodgate inside him. It was all he could do not to grab her and hold her tightly, aching to absorb some of that pain.

Instead he ignored that need and concentrated on his fears, growing more alarming by the second. "Are you in pain?" he rasped.

She blinked back tears. "No. I...guess I was dreaming. I'm sorry I disturbed you."

"Hush," he said gently.

As if they had a will of their own, his hands began wandering over her body, searching for broken bones, signs of something, anything, he might have missed.

Only after a sob suddenly caught in her throat and her big brown eyes locked on his did he pause, realizing one hand was covering her breast.

For the longest time, neither one of them moved. The

feelings clamoring through him were so raw, so all-consuming, so terrifying, that he could only stare back at her while her nipple budded in his palm.

"Collier," she breathed, placing a hand on his cheek.

Further indulging himself in this moment of madness, he lowered his mouth to hers. At first he simply grazed her lips. But when she answered his groan and pressed her mouth closer, his need increased to a feverish pitch. He drank from the sweetness she offered him, kissing her with a deep and frightening intensity.

All the emotions that had been smoldering inside him since that first night exploded. Only after he had no more air in his lungs did he let her go and pull back.

Mutual shock seemed to paralyze them both for several seconds, the sound of the rain barely drowning out the rapid beat of their hearts.

"Dear God," Collier said in a strangled tone before easing her back onto the pillow, horror washing over him.

Before she could respond, he got up, turned and walked out the door.

Six

"What on earth is going on?"

Brittany tightened her grip on the phone. "You did get my message, didn't you?"

"Yes," Sissy Newman, the owner of the travel agency, responded. "But I didn't like the vibes I got. You sounded different, like something was wrong. Is it?"

"Yes," Brittany admitted, "but I can't go into it right now." She had left a generic message and the phone number on Sissy's machine after Collier had given her permission to use the phone. She had called the diner, as well. She hadn't wanted to lose either of her jobs.

"As long as you're okay." Sissy paused. "I'm assuming you're not coming in today."

Sissy sounded a bit out of sorts, since Brittany often worked on Saturdays, but Brittany took no offense. The older woman was her friend and had been for years. She knew Sissy had her well-being at heart. She was the only person Brittany felt like she could count on in a time of crisis.

But because Rupert was Sissy's biggest client, his involvement made for a sticky situation. While she couldn't entirely keep what had happened from Sissy, she wasn't about to go into it on the phone or tell her who had hurt her.

"No, I'm not," Brittany hedged.

"When are you going to tell me what's going on? It's not like you to miss work."

Brittany willed the tears back. "I know."

"Are you sick? Why don't you just say so?"

"Please, Sissy, I'll explain later. I promise. Just trust me, okay?"

"All right," Sissy said with a sigh. "I know when to back off. You take care now, and let me hear from you."

Once the phone was back in its cradle, Brittany sat still for a minute. That was when she realized how quiet it was. Had it stopped raining? Crossing to the window, she opened the blind. Peeping out from behind the clouds was the sun. Relief washed through her.

Did that mean they could leave? She dared not get her hopes up, but she couldn't help it. After what happened between her and Collier Smith last night...

For a second her mind simply closed down and she couldn't get enough air through her lungs for a decent breath. Feeling dizzy and slightly queasy, she tried not to think about that soul-depriving kiss.

Crazy.

That was the only word for it. She was shocked and mortified at her own behavior. Long after he'd lurched off the bed and torn out of the room, she had lain awake, thinking that the trauma she'd suffered had affected her mind, made her so weak and vulnerable that she hadn't known what she was doing.

Liar. She'd known, all right.

Not only had he kissed her, but she'd kissed him back. This time fresh tears burned her eyes. Furious with her inability to control her frayed nerves, she made her way into the bathroom, flipped on the light and looked in the mirror.

She still looked the part—an abused woman. Another

sick feeling washed over her. If there was a positive note to this, at least only one side of her face had born the brunt of Rupert's fist. She dug her nails into her palms, not even wincing against the pain.

Damn him. Damn herself for letting him do this to her. He shouldn't get away with it. He should have to pay. Collier was right about that. But turning him in wasn't the answer, either. She knew Rupert and his connections. He would find some way to make everything her fault, deal her more misery than she could handle. With Tommy, two jobs and college, her plate was full.

Rupert had the money and the power to squash her. She had neither. Because she was without means, young and alone, she had been an easy target. However, when the time was right and she knew she had a chance to get Rupert, she would. Her gentleness was often perceived as weakness. But that wasn't so. She was smart enough to pick the battles she could win. One of these days, Rupert would pay.

Turning away from her bruised face, Brittany made her way back into the bedroom, her eyes going immediately to the bed. Collier's image rose to the forefront of her mind, bigger than life. Who was this man? Other than the fact that he was an attorney, she didn't know anything about him. Yes, she did. She knew he had class and money, and that he was good-looking, though not magazine good-looking. His angular jaw and slightly crooked nose prevented that.

Still, he had plenty of entries in the plus column. He was tall and slender, with just the right amount of well-defined muscles and lines in his face to give him character. His dark hair, free of any gray, accented his deep blue eyes and long sooty lashes.

She wondered if he was married. Probably. The good

ones always were, and she judged him to be in his late thirties, too old to still be single. He wasn't wearing a ring, but that didn't mean anything these days. If he wasn't married, he was certainly involved.

Suddenly she pictured him easing down beside her, taking her gently into his strong arms, his potent male scent enveloping her as his lips lightly brushed her sore cheek before claiming her lips as though they were his for the taking.

Her body quivered with emotion.

She'd felt safe and warm, like nothing could ever hurt her again. She ached to feel that way again, to have his arms around her, his hungry mouth on hers, his hand on her breast. Feeling the blood rush to her cheeks, Brittany covered them with her hands and swallowed a cry of dismay. Even so, the image wouldn't go away, nor did she really want it to.

That was what frightened her the most. Those seething emotions he'd stirred in her left a hard, aching knot in the pit of her stomach.

What was he thinking? Her face flamed brighter. She couldn't imagine. He'd had every opportunity to take advantage of her, to make her a victim again, but he hadn't, thank God. As horrifying as the thought was, she didn't know if she would have stopped him if he'd tried to make love to her.

While that admission almost brought Brittany to her knees in remorse, she couldn't change how she felt. But she vowed he would never know. Once he took her home, this chapter in her life would end. She found strength and comfort in that fact. No matter that she would never forget him, never forget he'd saved her life.

Yet she dreaded seeing him again, didn't want to feel that sudden rush of sexual awareness when he came near her. But since she had no choice in the matter, she brushed that thought aside and slipped into her clothes, clothes that would be discarded the minute she got home.

Home.

That sounded like heaven. While it didn't have much in the way of amenities, it was hers. And she couldn't wait to get back there. Then and only then would she begin to heal and pick up the pieces of her shattered life.

In the meantime, there was Collier to face. In the daylight.

He was out of here. *They* were out of here, he corrected mentally.

First thing that morning, he had put on his boots and trudged down to the bridge. Apparently it had stopped raining shortly after he'd left Brittany's room, which had given the water plenty of time to subside.

Now all he had to do was tell Brittany the good news and they would be off. Amazingly, the words stuck in his throat, while a shock of guilt ran through him. He rubbed the back of his neck, feeling the coffee he'd just drunk sour in his stomach.

He'd kissed her, for god's sake.

No, it had been much more than that. It had been another assault, only this time motivated by a desire to arouse pleasure, not pain. Still, there was no excuse for his loss of control. After what she'd been through, how could he have done such a thing? Had he no shame?

But there was something about her that had tapped into his sexual reservoir, creating a raw hunger inside him that nothing would appease except her. And even though he'd indulged himself and given in to that hunger, it hadn't fixed his problem. Instead it had made it worse. If he had his way, he would kiss her again and again. In fact, he wished he never had to *stop* kissing her.

It had been lust at first sight.

He ignored the blood pounding through his body, settling into his loins, and concentrated on tying a knot in his runaway thoughts. But recognizing his lust for what it was didn't seem to slow his hammering pulse or keep his mind off her.

The phone rang, and for a moment he was tempted not to answer it. But maybe a dose of reality was what he needed to get him back on track. He reached for the receiver.

"What it is?" he demanded.

His top-notch investigator, Kyle Warren, chuckled. "I see you're still your same sweet self." Then his tone sobered. "Get any work done?"

"Tons," Collier lied.

"I was hoping you'd say that. So when are you heading back?"

"ASAP, now that the bridge is passable."

"I was afraid you were marooned, which wasn't a bad thing, not with as much work as you had to do."

"Anything pressing I need to know about?" Collier asked, changing the subject. He was tempted to ask about his brother, but he knew there wouldn't be any change there, much to his regret.

"Yeah, that's why I'm calling. Otherwise, I swore I wouldn't bother you."

"Let's hear it." Collier heard the tired note that had crept into his voice. He was back on track, all right, the fast one.

"You need to stop by Ashton on the way in."

Ashton was the prison in the next county. Collier frowned, his thoughts jumping back to Brittany. He could hardly stop by the prison with her in the car. "Whatever it is, can't it wait?"

"I don't think so. It's Jim Sauterwhite. He tried to kill himself last night."

"Shit," Collier muttered. Jim was one of his old school buddies. He had been convicted on attempted murder charges, with his wife the target. Though he maintained his innocence, he had been convicted nonetheless and was serving a twenty-year sentence. Collier made it a point to visit him from time to time.

"What the hell happened?"

"I don't know," Kyle admitted. "The details are sketchy. I just thought, since the prison's on your way in, it would save you a trip."

"Look, I'll see him, but not today."

There was a short silence, then Kyle said in a puzzled tone, "Suit yourself."

"I'll see you later."

"Yeah, later."

Collier hung up and headed for Brittany's bedroom door. His gut instinct told him that she would be ready and waiting. He paused, his hand on the knob, sweat lining his upper lip.

Apologize. That was the first order of the day. But he knew he couldn't bring himself to do that, because he wasn't sorry. Not for the right reasons, anyway. His chest felt like it was caving in. He paused, took a deep breath, then let loose a few expletives under his breath.

He opened the door, nipping his circling, self-hating thoughts in the bud.

Seven

"So what's the verdict?" Kyle asked.

Collier faced the door and watched as the investigator strode in, a stack of papers in hand. "Man, you and Dad. Give you a whip and your torture chamber would be complete."

Kyle was of medium height and weight, with medium brown hair and eyes. Everything about him was medium, except his intelligence. There was nothing medium about that. He was one of the sharpest men Collier had ever worked with. He shuddered to see the day Kyle took a notion to leave.

Since he wasn't married and had no ties that bind, he had a reputation for getting bored and moving on to greener pastures. Because of that, Collier worked hard to make sure he was one happy—and busy—employee.

He gave Collier a pointed look. "Learned it from the chamber master."

Collier snorted, then rose behind his desk. "Somehow I don't think that's a compliment."

"Sure it is," Kyle muttered offhandedly, then grinned.

"Sit your ass down."

Kyle chuckled. "I need something to get me going. You got any coffee? I didn't even take time to stop by the kitchen."

"I've been here since dawn-thirty. I'm working on my second pot, so help yourself."

"Man, you must be wired and ready to go."

"I'm wired, all right, but not ready to go. Not with that harassment case, if that's what you mean."

Kyle didn't respond. Instead he crossed to the coffee bar in a far corner of the opulent office, where he poured himself a generous cup. Once he was seated directly in front of Collier's desk, he said, "I was thinking about the appointment."

"You're rushing things. I'm one of four in the pot."

This time Kyle snorted. "You'll get the appointment. I'm not worried."

"Well, I am," Collier countered flatly.

Kyle swallowed a mouthful of coffee, then set his cup down. "Why? From what I know of the other candidates, you're far superior to any of them."

"Are you forgetting I have no, quote, 'political experience,' unquote, under my belt?"

Kyle shrugged. "So?"

"So the others have, especially Travis Wainwright."

"That prick. He won't get to first base."

Collier frowned. "Are you forgetting he's Rupert Holt's choice? You know what power that guy wields with Senator Riley."

"The senator's backing you, right?"

"That's the impression I got, but you never really know."

"Ah, you're just borrowing trouble."

"Don't think I'm not going to fight for the job, because I am," Collier stressed. "I want it, and Dad wants me to have it. I can't, *won't,* disappoint him."

"That's not going to happen," Kyle responded, his tone confident.

"We'll see. But it'll be tough. If I get anywhere close to being the top choice, the FBI's going to jump in and scrutinize me closer than a bug under a microscope."

"So?" Kyle said again. "You don't have any skeletons in your closet."

"We all have skeletons." Collier sighed, then rubbed his chin. "But now's not the time to go into that."

"If anything will give you trouble, it'll be this upcoming case."

"I've thought about that, and so has Dad. He's not happy I took it."

"As far as the firm goes, it's damn lucrative and good for business. It never hurts to have a bigwig like Luther Brickman in your pocket."

"Only if I win his case." Collier took a heavy breath. "You know how tricky harassment cases are. I probably wouldn't have taken it if I'd known I'd be up for the judgeship."

Kyle grinned. "Doesn't matter. You can have both."

"Yeah? Then you'd better get cracking on your end. The woman who's his main accuser is one tough cookie. This could get nasty. And there are other cases awaiting my attention." Collier raised his eyebrows. "Are you forgetting that?"

"Nope. Just tell me what I need to do and it'll be done." Kyle paused. "By the way, did you get through all those depositions?"

"No."

Kyle's jaw went slack. "No? How 'bout some of them?"

"Didn't do that, either."

"What the hell does that mean?"

"Exactly what I said," Collier said impatiently.

"But that's why you went to the cabin." Kyle's tone

was incredulous. "I thought you said you got a lot of work done?"

Collier knew he should cut the other man some slack, but he was reluctant to talk about Brittany. Just the thought sent cold chills through him. Not that he had to give Kyle any of the juicy details, he reminded himself with a trace of sarcasm. Yet he felt it necessary to tell him the bare facts, just in case the incident came back to bite him on the butt. Under the circumstances, he was probably overreacting. But with the stakes being so high, he couldn't take that chance.

"What's wrong?" Kyle's words were as blunt as his tone.

"Nothing's wrong, exactly."

"Hell, man, stop hedging. Something happened, and of all people who should know, it's me."

Collier took a deep breath. "I picked up a woman."

"Where?"

"On the side of the highway."

"Holy shit," Kyle said under his breath. "I think you'd better pretend I'm a priest and you're in a confessional."

Collier told him the gist of what had happened.

"Holy shit," Kyle muttered again, getting to his feet, his eyes narrowed on Collier. "That was about the craziest-assed stunt you could've pulled."

"You would've stopped, too, and you damn well know it."

"Not if I had as much to lose as you," Kyle shot back.

"Well, it's a done deal, so there's no point in arguing about it now."

"Does Mason know?"

"Hell no, and he's not going to, either."

"Then you'd better pray nothing comes of this. If that little tramp decides to accuse *you* of trying to rape her..."

Fury choked off Collier's voice. But when he spoke, his words were cold and hard. "She's not a tramp. Don't ever say that again."

Kyle was taken aback by his tone. His face drained of color. "Sorry, boss, didn't mean any offense."

"Just forget it, okay?"

"No problem for me, as long as it isn't one for you. Just keep the dangers in mind, that's all."

Kyle's refusal to back down made Collier respect him even more. Right now, he needed someone to keep him on the straight and narrow.

The mere thought of Brittany melted his bones and gave him a hard-on. No matter, there could never be a repeat performance. No more self-indulgence.

"It's not like I'll be seeing her again."

"I hope that would go without saying."

"Well, I'm saying it. I have no intention of jeopardizing anything."

"That's music to my ears." Kyle reached for his cup, then took a sip, only to frown. "Damn, nothing's worse than cold coffee."

Collier nodded toward the bar. "Make a fresh pot, then."

"Nah. Gotta get to work. My desk is piled almost as high as yours."

"Let me know when you dig up something on Virginia Warner." He frowned as he said the name of the woman who had brought suit against Brickman. "She can't be as lily-white as she appears."

"No one is. We just have to find her skeletons."

"Get on it."

"Will do." Kyle rose and headed for the door. "I'll check in later."

Collier nodded, his thoughts turning inward as he felt a sudden prick of conscience. What was the matter with him? He'd never let going for someone's jugular bother him before, though he never veered from the law. He'd never had a grievance filed against him, and he enjoyed a reputation for being honest and above reproach in his work.

But he didn't like to lose and rarely did. However, he'd never tried anyone on sexual harassment charges before, and, as he'd told Kyle, he fully expected things to get nasty.

If anything would catapult him to the top of the judge-ship list, it would be his integrity and his dogged determination. All the more reason why he couldn't let this soul-draining attraction to another woman cost him everything he held near and dear.

Suddenly Collier went numb all over, Kyle's words coming back to haunt him. Then he dismissed those words as crap. Brittany wouldn't accuse him of being the one to assault her. She wasn't that type of woman.

How do you know? a little voice asked.

He didn't, nor did he want to. He didn't want to know anything about her. He just wanted her; he wanted her body. He wanted only to taste every morsel of her delicious flesh, then bury himself inside her.

Shit!

Sweat saturated his entire body, while his mouth went as dry as cotton. He had to stop thinking like that. He had to stop thinking about her. When they left the cabin, she'd spoken very little. In fact, she'd told him how to get to her trailer and that was it. Only after he'd pulled up at the curb in a run-down part of Chaney did she speak. She'd thanked him in her gentle, husky-toned voice, keeping her eyes averted. It had been all he could do not to grab her, the desperate feeling gnawing inside him threatening to override his sanity.

But he'd quelled that sexual urge and just nodded, then watched as she'd walked up onto the rickety porch and disappeared inside. He'd gripped the steering wheel so hard he thought his knuckles would surely crack while his stomach pitched.

Finally he'd rammed the Lexus into gear and driven back to Haven, back to his upscale condo with the words "from two different worlds" seared on his brain with a red-hot branding iron.

Now, as he blew out a ravaged breath and tried to regroup, his phone jangled. He automatically punched the lighted button and listened to his secretary, Pamela Nixon, say, "Ms. Frazier's on line one, sir."

Lana, he thought, despising himself because he had no desire to talk to her.

"My God, what happened to you?"

Sissy Newman stood inside the door of Brittany's living room with her mouth gaping and her cloudy green eyes wide, something Brittany didn't often see. Usually Sissy was unflappable; that was why she made such a good travel agent. The public rarely rattled her.

Though she was slightly overweight, with gray hair she refused to color, she had a lot going for her. She wore stylish clothes and had a great personality. Childless and widowed, having lost her husband a few years ago right after she turned sixty, Sissy's whole life was wrapped up in her work and her friends. Brittany considered herself fortunate to be part of both.

"It's a long story, so you'd better come on in and sit down." Brittany paused. "You have time, right?"

"After seeing your face, you bet I do."

"Want some hot chocolate?" Brittany asked, once Sissy was seated.

"That does sound good."

Brittany thought so, too, since it was a cold, drizzly day, more characteristic of winter than fall. She had the space heater in the room up as high as it would go, and still she was cold. But she knew it wasn't altogether the weather that kept her chilly. Her heightened nerves were responsible; it was like they were sitting on the outside of her skin.

"Are you sure you're all right?" Sissy asked, her eyes tracking Brittany as she returned from the kitchen and sat on the sofa, folding her legs under her.

"Drink some of your chocolate," Brittany said lightly, dreading the next few minutes, when she would have to rehash the horror she'd endured. Sissy wouldn't rest until she told her, though Brittany had no intention of telling her the whole story.

"To hell with the cocoa. I want to know whose fist you ran into. I can't accuse Tommy—"

"Sissy!"

"Just kidding."

A short silence ensued while both women sipped the steaming cocoa. Then Sissy put her cup down and said pointedly, "I'm waiting."

"It's not an easy thing to talk about," Brittany said, still hedging.

"Did...he rape you?"

"I don't think so. I blacked out, but..."

Sissy swore, which was so out of character it almost made Brittany smile.

"Other than your face, do you have other injuries?"

"Some cuts and bruises."

"So what happened?"

Brittany explained, but without mentioning Rupert's name—or Collier's.

"What a horrible experience," Sissy said in a numb-sounding voice. "It's a miracle you survived, and it's another miracle someone came along to pick you up. Even though you won't tell me who's responsible, I hope to hell you told the police."

"No."

"Dammit, Brittany, why not?"

"I'd rather not talk about it."

Clearly frustrated, Sissy snapped, "That's not smart. Hell, I didn't even know you were seeing someone, much less that he would turn out to be a violent creep."

"Please, Sissy, don't ask me anything else. I've told you all I'm prepared to."

"Fine, but if that bastard touches you again, I won't let you off the hook so easily."

"You know how I feel about depending on the law," Brittany said by way of another excuse. "After the way Tommy was railroaded, you, of all people, should understand."

"I understand, but in this instance, I don't agree. But you have to do what you have to do."

"Thanks for your support." Brittany tried to smile.

"Can I do anything for you?" Sissy asked. "I feel so helpless."

"Nothing except give me a few more days off."

"What about your classes?"

"I'll go to those and work in the diner."

"Can't you forget the diner? I'll advance you—"

"No," Brittany interrupted. "I'll be okay."

Sissy stood, her mouth stretched in a thin line. "When you come to your senses, I'll be here for you. Meanwhile, take care and heal." She leaned over and brushed Brittany's other cheek. "And that's an order."

Brittany gave her a watery smile. "Thanks."

"I'll see myself out."

Once Brittany was alone, her head hit the back of the sofa, though it wasn't all that comfortable. A spring jabbed her in the back of the neck, forcing her to shift positions and making her wince again. Her body was just now beginning to feel the effects of her ordeal. But at least the bruising had paled somewhat, and she no longer scared herself when she looked in the mirror.

Maybe Tommy wouldn't even notice. Ha. She knew better, but right now, she didn't have to think about that. Nor did she have to think about Collier Smith. That problem was solved. He was out of her life.

Though she would never forget the hot, physical attraction that had crackled between them, it had been his special way of cutting through her shield and finding her tender spots that made him unforgettable. He was the type of man she had searched for all her adult years and never found. Until now. But she could never have him.

He had gone back to his world and left her in hers.

Eight

"**H**ey, Dad."

"Son, you're just the person I wanted to see."

Son.

Collier's heart always beat a little faster every time Mason called him that. He didn't remember reacting like this when he was younger. He guessed that back then he'd just taken it for granted he belonged to Mason. But since he'd become an adult and learned the cold truth, that word had taken on new meaning. If only Mason could have adopted him...

"What's going on?" Collier finally asked with a smile, something that didn't come often or easily of late.

"I've set the date for the party," Mason said without preamble.

Collier propped his foot on the bottom stair, almost wishing he hadn't stopped by the mansion before heading for the office. It had been a while since he'd seen his brother, and he felt like a heel. Though officially retired, Mason maintained an office at the firm and spent a lot of time there. Not so with Jackson. If Collier wanted to see him, he had to make an effort.

"Your silence tells me you don't approve."

Collier blew out his breath. "No. I wish you hadn't done it."

"It's the right thing to do."

"I don't agree," Collier countered. "It makes me uncomfortable. We have to face facts. I might not get the appointment. Nothing's for sure, you know."

Mason gestured impatiently. "All the more reason to start tooting your horn now, especially since a friend called and told me Rupert Holt's out lobbying strongly for his candidate, Travis Wainwright. I refuse to let Rupert get the upper hand."

"When are you two going to stop taking punches at each other? This has been going on far too long. You ought to call a truce."

"He's the one with the ax to grind," Mason said doggedly. "The one who keeps the pot boiling."

Collier suppressed a sigh. "Regardless of how you feel about Rupert, Wainwright's a credible candidate. He's got a good chance of getting the presidential nod."

"Over my dead body. No one associated with Holt's going to kick your ass."

Mason's thick white eyebrows bunched together, giving him a fierce look. Collier understood why his mother had fallen for him. Not only was he downright handsome—tall and robust, with white hair and blue, blue eyes—he was highly intelligent and filled with boundless energy. And at sixty-six, he was blessed with good health.

Yet, since the tragedy that had befallen his eldest son, there was another side of Mason that had risen to the surface. He'd developed a vindictive, angry streak. Before, he'd been personable and levelheaded. Now, almost anything, insignificant or not, could set him off like a rocket.

No matter, Collier loved him and wanted to find favor in his eyes in everything he did. Sometimes, though, he thought that was an unattainable goal.

"Did you hear what I said?" Mason demanded.

"Uh, no."

"Dammit, boy, where's your head?"

Deliberately ignoring Mason's irritation, he asked, "What were you saying?"

"That you need to give me a guest list for the dinner."

"I can't talk you out of it?"

"No," Mason said with force. "I'm convinced it's the right thing to do."

"All right," Collier conceded with a sigh. "At least Lana will love it."

"Speaking of Lana, when are you two going to tie the knot? Hell, her old man can do as much or more than anybody to help you get that appointment. This would be a perfect time to announce your intentions. The news might even make the front page of the paper." Mason's face suddenly brightened. "Why not do it at the dinner party?"

Collier's stomach bottomed out. "Whoa! You're getting way ahead of things. Besides, that's something personal between Lana and me."

"Well, don't lollygag much longer." Mason's chin jutted. "It's high time you were married with a family."

"Dad, can we change the subject?"

"Yes, but only because I have an appointment. Will I see you at the office?"

"I'm heading there after I look in on Jackson."

Mason's features tightened. "I'll warn you. He's in more of a funk than ever, and not very pleasant to be around."

With that, he walked out the door. Collier remained motionless for a moment, trying to regain his momentum, feeling as though he'd been hit by a mini hurricane.

Shaking his head, he finally turned and bounded up the

stairs to Jackson's suite. Following the accident, Mason had had an elevator installed in the house so Jackson wouldn't be confined to his quarters. He'd also added a full gym and all the amenities, including a trainer and physical therapist.

At first Mason had done everything in his power to make sure his son walked again. But when it became clear that that wasn't going to happen, he'd focused on making him as comfortable as possible. But nothing, no amount of money or attention, had been able to help Jackson's attitude.

Forcing himself to be upbeat, Collier tapped on his brother's door. Only after he got no response did he ease it open. Jackson was sitting in front of the smoldering fireplace in his wheelchair, sound asleep.

Collier was tempted to wake him, thinking he could sleep most anytime. But for some reason, he refrained from doing so. Perhaps it was because Jackson looked so peaceful, so at ease, something he never was when he was awake.

Even though his lower half was no longer functioning, his upper half was in fine form. Before the paralysis, he'd been a tall, fit, good-looking blond man with piercing blue eyes, so like Mason's. Now, at forty-two, his upper body had become the focus of his attention. He'd honed those muscles to perfection, in contrast to his wasted lower body.

Too bad he didn't work that hard on his attitude, Collier thought. Lately, it had sucked. As Mason had pointed out, Jackson had been even more bitter than usual, feeling unusually sorry for himself. Collier hoped his bid for the federal judgeship hadn't been the catalyst.

Collier would gladly give that up to have his brother whole again.

He continued to look at Jackson, guilt pounding him once again. He was unable to get over the idea that he'd somehow let his brother down.

He hadn't been there for him when the accident occurred or right afterward. He'd been in the Soviet Union on a case that had represented a golden opportunity for the firm. He'd wanted to come home. He'd made his plans to do just that, only to have Mason demand that he remain in Russia, claiming Jackson didn't want to see him or anyone else.

He'd gone with Mason's call, but he'd never forgiven himself for it, thinking that if he'd come home, he might have been able to break through the barrier Jackson had erected between himself and the world. But hindsight was twenty-twenty, and now he had to live with the fact that he hadn't gone with his heart.

Suddenly Collier jerked his mind back to the present and noticed that the coverlet had slipped slightly to one side, exposing one of Jackson's legs. It was terribly thin and stiff, as if it was artificial. Collier's heart turned over, and he felt the sting of tears behind his eyes.

Blinking them back, he crossed lightly to the chair, reached down and replaced the crocheted afghan. When Jackson still didn't stir, he stepped back. Such a waste of such a brilliant mind. Before the accident, Jackson had been a crackerjack attorney, and he still could be. Unfortunately, he'd chosen not to practice law any longer. Instead, he seemed content to sit and brood behind these walls.

Something had to give soon. But what? Although Collier had asked himself that question numerous times, he still had no answer. Nothing seemed able to shake his brother out of his depression. If by some chance Collier did get the appointment to the bench, there would be a big void in the office. Maybe then Jackson would come to his senses.

Collier clenched and unclenched his fingers. Dammit, it wasn't fair. *Life* wasn't fair.

What a morning.

Collier had been busier than a cranberry merchant, though he couldn't say he'd accomplished all that much. He *had* stopped by the prison to see his friend, though. He'd done that immediately after he'd left the mansion.

Afterward, it had taken him a while to get his head back on straight. First Mason, then Jackson, and finally Jim's sad plight, had started his own day off on a down note. Not that he'd needed a reason. Ever since he'd left Brittany in her sparse surroundings, he hadn't been able to settle down.

His insides felt like jumping beans had set up shop there. He'd flitted from one case to another. It was a continuation of the night, when he'd lain awake, his mind ping-ponging between Brittany, wondering what she was doing, what she was thinking, and the judgeship, asking himself what dirt his opponents would uncover on him.

He'd counted every slow turn of the ceiling fan in his room before daylight had forced him out of bed.

Forget her.

He might as well. He sure as hell couldn't see her again. It would be political and emotional suicide. He might as well get a gun and shoot himself in the head and be done with it. If he didn't, Kyle would, he reminded himself brutally. Despite that, thoughts of Brittany refused to die a natural death, regardless of how many drinks he took or how often he saw Lana.

It was inconceivable that it had only been a week since

he'd left Brittany. It seemed an eternity already. Lust for her gnawed constantly at his gut.

"Good, you're here. Since Pamela wasn't manning the desk, I thought I'd take a chance on catching you."

That was the only reason Darwin Brewster had made it into Collier's office. Pamela knew better than to let that happen.

Still, Collier was glad of the interruption, even if Brewster was the only attorney in the entire firm he had trouble stomaching. The guy badly needed an attitude adjustment, and, on several occasions, Collier had obliged him.

"What's up?" Collier asked, pushing his folder aside and peering at his uninvited guest.

While not handsome, Darwin did have a gift of gab that seemed to charm his clients, especially the women. His deep brown eyes, thick hair and perfectly groomed mustache apparently made up for his lack of stature. He was short, and thin almost to the point of gauntness. Collier suspected his arrogant attitude stemmed from the "little man syndrome."

When in a group, Darwin's demeanor proclaimed he was the best, brightest and most intelligent one in the room. If you didn't believe him, you could just ask him. He would admit it. That arrogance irritated the hell out of Collier. If he'd had his way, he would never have taken the man on board the firm.

But Mason had been Brewster's champion, something Collier failed to understand, especially since he had been the court-appointed attorney for that Rogers kid who was responsible for Jackson being in a wheelchair.

Shortly after the scumbag was sent to the pen, Mason had insisted on hiring Brewster. Ever since, Brewster had been in like Flynn. And though Mason's high regard for him stuck in Collier's craw, he had to admit that the man knew the law and had won some tough cases.

He hoped Darwin's track record would carry over to the personal injury case they were working on together. Darwin was second chair.

"There's something I want to talk to you about." Darwin looked up from the folder in front of him. "We go to trial next week."

Collier hadn't needed a reminder. "I know." To his knowledge, the details had been pretty much worked out, and he was ready. Apparently Darwin wasn't. "So what's on your mind?"

Darwin cleared his throat, though his eyes didn't waver. "I want to be lead counsel."

Collier didn't so much as flinch. "Oh, and why is that?"

"For one thing, I feel like I've put in more work and know the facts better. Also, the last few weeks, I've really bonded with our client. She's the one who asked that I be in charge."

"So you asked."

Darwin looked a bit confused. "And?"

"The answer is no," Collier responded in a smooth and controlled tone.

"But—"

Collier stood. "No buts, Brewster. Consider yourself lucky to still be on the case. Now get the hell out of my face and out of my office."

Nine

Would her life ever get back to normal? Would she ever get her energy back?

Since the accident, she'd not only been exhausted but restless, edgy, as if something else terrible was about to happen. For one thing, she kept waiting for Rupert Holt to come through the door of the agency. To date that hadn't happened, and maybe it wouldn't. With any luck, he was running scared, not because of her and what she would do, but because of his wife.

According to Sissy, Angel Holt's family was the money behind Rupert. So why had he taken the chance of cheating on her? Maybe his wife didn't care. Maybe she did her thing and Rupert did his, which was to take advantage of unsuspecting women like her. How many other notches did Rupert have on his sexual belt?

Despite the warmth in her Honda, Brittany shivered. She couldn't get out of her mind just how close she'd come to losing her life that night on the lonely stretch of highway. The resurgence of that thought made her breakfast congeal in her stomach.

A part of Brittany had been tempted to throw caution to the wind, make a phone call and rat on the sleazebag. If she told Rupert's wife what her husband had done, surely that would bring him to his knees. But she couldn't. That wasn't the way she operated. When and if she got the chance to nail Rupert, she wouldn't use his wife as the hammer.

She simply wanted never to see him again and to get on with her life. A bitter smile erupted. She could have done that if she hadn't met Collier Smith. He had her mind so fractured, her insides so tangled, nothing made sense anymore.

Did she want to see him again? Was that what all her stewing was about? Apparently so, or she wouldn't be in such a mess. She thought about him constantly, when she was in bed, in class, at the diner, at the agency. It didn't matter; he seemed to have attached himself to every aspect of her mind and body.

She'd even gone so far as to envision Collier walking in one day with a lovely bouquet of flowers and asking her to dinner. After he'd wined and dined her, he would take her to his place and make slow, leisurely love to her, his lips and hands acting out her fantasy.

Ridiculous.

She told herself that over and over, but to no avail. She couldn't seem to close the door on him. Shifting positions, Brittany took a deep breath, then let it out. Just as it had been for her outer wounds, time was the perfect healer for the mind, she reassured herself. It would take care of her heart as well as her face. When she didn't see Collier again, he would soon fade from her mind and become nothing but a sweet memory.

Meanwhile, her goal had not changed. She'd been sidetracked, for sure, but she would get her degree, no matter how many tables she had to wait on or how many creeps like Rupert she had to deal with at the agency.

But no one would ever violate her again.

She wouldn't put herself in a vulnerable situation again.

Regardless of who promised to help her or Tommy, she wouldn't fall for it. Her brother was her responsibility, always had been and always would be. As soon as she got her degree and a decent job, she would be able to help him.

Thinking of Tommy made her realize she was near the prison. Suddenly her anxiety increased, not because she was about to go behind prison walls, but because of how she looked.

Tightening her lips, Brittany shifted her concentration back to the highway. At least the sun was shining, she thought, trying to buoy her spirits. Where she was headed might be depressing, the beauty surrounding her certainly wasn't. Fall in the South had a way of cloaking itself with such bursts of brilliant foliage that it took a person by surprise.

Brittany soaked up that beauty, feeling its serenity comfort her like a balm. It wouldn't last long, this feeling of peace. As soon as she was seated in that stark room and saw Tommy in his drab prison garb, looking lean and strained, that black, hard core of grief would settle in the pit of her stomach once again.

One of these days, he would walk out of that miserable place.

Realizing she was on the prison grounds, Brittany whipped into the nearest parking space and got out, the immense size of the plain brick buildings further intimidating her. Gritting her teeth, she made her way inside, refusing to acknowledge the smells, the sounds, that were part of this drab world.

Soon she was through security, seated, and waiting for her brother. When she saw him coming, she plastered a smile on her face, though she had to catch her lower lip between her teeth to keep it from quivering. Now that she was here, she realized anew how difficult it was going to be to keep the truth from Tommy.

Once he was seated behind the glass directly in front of her, they both picked up their phones simultaneously, though Brittany hated touching those phones with a passion. She'd been tempted to bring a can of Lysol and spray the receiver, except that she knew it would make her brother feel worse than ever.

"Hey, sis," he said, then narrowed his eyes and added, "What the hell happened to you?"

"Hello to you, too, brother dear," she said in a light, forced tone.

"Who hit you?" he asked coldly, his brown eyes narrowing to slits.

Hesitating on purpose, Brittany perused him closely, as she did every week when she saw him, checking to make sure he wasn't run-down or ill. Before his incarceration, he'd been thin and small boned, like her. But he was tall, which made up for his lack of weight, and very healthy, rarely sick until he started smoking pot. At one time he might have been considered good-looking, with his dark wavy hair, dark eyes, tanned skin and sullen-slanted mouth.

Now, after three years behind bars, his entire face had become sullen, which made him anything but good-looking. He appeared much older than his twenty-three years. She noticed right off that he'd lost some weight, which didn't help his appearance. Had he been ill?

She voiced that thought. "Are you okay?"

"Don't try and change the subject."

"Okay, I was involved in a minor auto accident," she lied. "I ran off the road and hit a tree."

A smirk tightened his lips. "It looks like your boyfriend might've worked you over."

Brittany winced, then said in a dull tone, "I don't have a boyfriend."

"Well, you should. Do you ever have any fun?"

"I'd rather not talk about me." But then, he wasn't really interested, anyway. He hadn't even bothered to ask for any details. While she should have expected his self-centeredness, it still smarted. She wondered what he would do if she really had been in an accident and couldn't come see him.

"Okay, we'll talk about me," he said bitterly, "and all the fun I'm having in here."

"Tommy, please—" Her voice broke. "I know you hate this place, and I hate you being here. But right now, there's nothing more I can do."

"What if you went back and tried to find Renee?"

"Oh, Tommy, she's long gone. You know I went to her trailer and tried to find her right after it happened."

"I know, but maybe she's come back." He moved the receiver closer to his mouth. "What about knocking on that shithead lawyer's door again? The one who sold me down the river. Maybe he's had a change of heart." Tommy finished with a sarcastic smile.

Heaven forbid, Brittany thought, hiding her dismay. She didn't relish the thought of facing Darwin Brewster again. "You know better than that," Brittany responded in a tired voice. "He'll never admit to any wrongdoing. You're just grasping at straws."

Tommy thrust a hand through his hair. "But you don't understand. You *can't* understand. Some days I think I won't survive if I have to stay here. It's making me nuts."

Brittany fought back tears. "You're making it harder on yourself."

"Don't preach to me," he said angrily. "I get enough of that shit in here."

Some days there was no pleasing Tommy. Today was one of those days. It appeared that no matter what she said or did, it would be wrong. Something had happened to ignite his temper, though she didn't dare ask what.

"Is there anything you need?" she asked instead.

"Yeah, but you obviously can't hack it."

Another low blow, which she didn't deserve, but she took it, nonetheless. If only she didn't feel so responsible for her brother, so responsible for everything that concerned him—good, bad or indifferent. She continually berated herself for not having taken better care of him, for not keeping a tighter rein on him. If she had, then maybe he wouldn't have ruined two lives—his own and Jackson Williams'.

Realistically she knew she couldn't hold herself responsible for his behavior on the night of the accident or any other night. Considering the way they'd been reared, she'd done her best. And while she remained loyal to him and really did believe in his innocence in this particular situation, she wasn't blind to his shortcomings.

Tommy had done a lot in the past to bring shame on both of them.

Still, she loved him and would continue to work diligently to get him released, back into society where he could get counseling for his problems.

"How 'bout some money, sis? Maybe a little extra for this week. What you gave me two weeks ago didn't last. Cigarettes keep going up."

"Sure." Although she didn't have any extra money, she fished what she did have out of her purse and clutched it in her hand. Before she left, she would stop by the office, where the cash would be put in his account. "I wish you'd try and stop smoking."

"Yeah, yeah."

Paling under his insulting tone, Brittany stood. Enough was enough. She'd had all of his ill-temper she wanted for today. Maybe next time he would be a little more considerate.

"Where are you going?"

"Home."

"What's your hurry?"

"Your attitude."

"How the hell would you like it if you were innocent," he lashed back, "and no one believed you?"

"I believed—believe—you."

"Then get me out of here."

Brittany suppressed a tired sigh. "I'll see you next week."

Collier found Jackson in his suite, parked in his usual place, in front of the fireplace, staring into it. Although he could only see his profile, he knew Jackson was brooding. "I hear you're under the weather, big brother."

"So?"

Collier barely held on to his temper. When Jackson was in one of his moods, which was all the time lately, he could be as trying as hell. After Mason had told him that Jackson was suffering with a bout of the flu, he'd detoured by the mansion on his way home from a Sunday in the office to check on him, hoping to cheer him up a bit. So much for his gesture.

When the silence became stifling, Collier made another attempt to carry on a normal conversation. "Once you're up to it, I could sure use your help on this sexual harassment case I'm working on, or that's working on me, I should say.''

''I think you have enough attorneys on staff to assist you,'' Jackson muttered darkly.

Collier lost it. ''Dammit, Jackson, you won't give an inch, will you?''

''If you're going to start—''

''Start what?'' Mason asked, walking through the open door.

''Same old shit,'' Jackson said petulantly, rolling his wheelchair toward the window, turning his back to both men.

Collier looked at his stepfather and shook his head in frustration, loving and hating his brother all at the same time.

As if he could read Collier's mind, Mason spoke to Jackson's back, ''Son, you're not being fair.''

Jackson turned his chair abruptly and glared at the two of them. ''Look, since I feel like hell, I'd prefer to be alone.''

Without a word, Collier headed for the door with Mason in tow, his features set like concrete, then swung back around. ''I'll concede this battle, big brother, but you're not about to win the war. Sooner or later, you're going to have to give the outside world another shot.''

''Don't bet on it.''

Later, in the foyer, Mason balled his fists and said, ''What are we going to do? We can't just let him keep going this way.''

''He'll snap out of it,'' Collier said with more confidence than he felt, concerned for his dad as well as his brother. Jackson's attitude was taking more of a toll on Mason each day. ''Maybe you should cancel the dinner party, though.''

"No." Mason's tone was obstinate. "Somehow I'll get him out of that room. I refuse to give up on him, dammit. You've got to help me."

Mason's desperation was almost palpable. Collier reached out and squeezed him on the shoulder. "We'll think of something."

"Such a goddamn waste," Mason said, looking away, talking more to himself than to Collier. "Even if he is in a wheelchair, he could be in the running for a judgeship."

Collier flinched inwardly. "You're exactly right."

Mason whipped around, his mouth working. "Look, Collier, I didn't mean that the way it sounded. I—"

"Forget it," Collier said in a bleak tone. "I understand, and I couldn't agree more."

A few minutes later, he drove off, feeling as if he'd just been gutted.

Ten

Collier was about to get out of his vehicle when he heard a noise behind him. He peered into the rearview mirror and cursed. Lana had pulled into the driveway.

He should be ashamed for not wanting to see her. But then, he didn't want to see anyone right now except... Cursing again, he shut that thought down and tried to improve his mood. What was the matter with him? He should be thrilled to see Lana. After all, he was thinking about marrying her. He must have strong feelings for her.

Her timing was bad. That was all. After his encounter with Jackson, he was in a pissy mood and wanted to be alone, get a hot shower, down a couple of beers, then hit the sack.

So much for that plan.

"Hey," he said, after getting out and watching her exit her sleek Jag and walk toward him. No doubt about it, she was a looker. Tall and model thin, with highlighted brown hair, gray eyes and a full lower lip. That lower lip gave her a petulant look that matched her personality perfectly. If things didn't go Lana's way, there was hell to pay. But then, things rarely *didn't* go her way. Her daddy saw to that. He had more than his share of money and clout in this country. And he doted on his only child.

Lana smiled back at him, then grazed his cheek with her scarlet lips. "Hey, yourself."

"What brings you here this time of day?"

She poked him in the chest with a matching nail. "You."

"That's nice."

Lana gave him a suspicious look. "You sure don't sound like it."

"Sorry, it's just that it's been a helluva day and I'm beat."

"All the more reason why you're coming with me."

"Where?"

"To dinner."

"Not tonight. I'm only fit for bed."

She gave an angry toss of her head, then complained, "You're not being fair. I haven't seen you in ages. If you won't have dinner, then at least have a drink with me." That same long nail made its way slowly and deliberately up and down his chest. "Please."

Usually such a blatant gesture raised the hair on the back of his neck. Not tonight. Maybe not ever again, he thought with alarm.

"Collier, darling."

He forced another smile. "Uh, sorry. You name the place."

"Get in."

He shook his head. "I'll follow you, so you won't have to bring me back home."

"Maybe that's exactly what I had in mind."

He leaned over and kissed her lightly. "I'll be right behind you."

A few minutes later they were facing each other in the bar area of one of the nicer hotel restaurants, a favorite haunt of Lana's and her women friends. For what was considered happy hour, the place was fairly deserted,

Collier noticed, perusing the area. He was glad. He wasn't in the mood to make small talk with anyone.

"I've missed you," Lana said, her voice dropping to a husky pitch as she laid her hand on the back of his.

"Me, too."

Her eyebrows lifted. "You sure?"

He sighed, withdrawing his hand. "Of course, but like I told you, it's been crazy at the office."

"Well, things will change after you become a federal judge."

"You're awfully confident."

"Daddy says it's going to happen."

Collier gave her a lopsided smile. "And that makes it so, huh?"

"You can make fun all you want, but you know better. Once Bill Frazier makes up his mind about something, it's a done deal."

"You won't hear any complaints on my part. Sitting on that bench would be a dream come true for both me and Mason."

"Good."

He took a sip of his drink and watched her over the rim, thinking he could do a lot worse than Lana. Yet...

"So?" she asked.

"So what?"

"When are we going to set a wedding date?"

Collier's stomach suddenly bottomed out. "I don't think this is the time to talk about that."

"I think the timing's perfect."

"Lana—"

She ignored him. "Daddy wants that, too. For us to get married soon, I mean."

"I thought we might wait until I'm either in or out of the running for the judgeship. My name could be scratched any day. Besides, I've taken on a case that could eat my lunch. I don't need to be distracted."

She leaned her head to one side and smiled coyly. "Are you saying I'm a distraction?"

"You betcha," he declared with forced enthusiasm.

"Mmm, maybe I'll let you off the hook a bit longer, but only if you'll promise not to neglect me like you have been lately."

Collier finished his drink in one swallow and signaled the bartender for a refill. "I'll give it my best shot."

"You drive a hard bargain, Collier Smith." Lana reclaimed his hand, then pressed another of those long, blood-red nails into his palm.

He winced.

"Just don't wait too long," she added with false sweetness. "Daddy wouldn't like that, not one iota."

"Are you threatening me?" Although he kept his tone light, the steely edge was there.

Flushing, she said, "You know better than that." She paused and gave him her most engaging smile. "So do you want to talk about your case?"

"You know I can't do that."

She smiled. "Good. That stuff's boring anyway. Let me tell you about my latest charitable project. I know it's going to be a huge success."

Collier sipped his drink and listened.

A short time later, his torture finally ended. He accompanied Lana to her Jag, then looked on as she took off, full speed ahead, the way she did everything. Whenever he left her, he often felt as if he'd been caught in a whirlwind.

He headed for his condo. Once there, he grabbed his briefcase and made his way inside, only to stop in his tracks. For some reason, spending an evening alone no longer interested him. In fact, the emptiness ahead made him feel like a stranger in his own home.

Suddenly he whipped around, and got back into his Lexus, knowing that what he was about to do would merely make matters worse.

Still, he cranked the engine and backed out of the driveway.

Another day without Rupert walking through the door.

Lately that was how Brittany had come to measure the success of her days at the agency. She knew that was absurd and no way to live, but she couldn't help it. Every time the door opened, her heart lodged in her throat until she peered from under thick lashes and saw who it was.

The flowers were what kept her on edge.

They continued to arrive. The smell and the thought were both sickening. She'd always loved flowers, but at the moment she wouldn't care if she ever saw another one again.

How dare he think he could win her over with flowers after what he'd done to her? Just the thought made her furious.

As soon as she got off from work, she took them by the local hospital and left them at the nurses' station. So far, she'd gotten by with that ploy because Sissy had been out of town. Otherwise, she would have demanded to know what was going on.

If Rupert didn't call a halt to this madness soon, she would have to take measures on her own. That thought made Brittany's skin crawl. That was why she always shed her clothes the second she arrived home and took a hot bath.

Anything associated with Rupert Holt made her feel dirty.

Now she was in her robe, her face devoid of makeup, a cup of decaffeinated coffee in hand, ready to study for the remainder of the evening. She had two hard tests coming up, and she wanted to ace them. Concentrating, however, was difficult. Her recent visit with Tommy had left her feeling more depressed than usual, which cluttered her mind. He seemed to be on a downward spiral, and she didn't know how to stop it.

She couldn't believe he'd asked her to try to find Renee again. Worse was his mention of Darwin Brewster. The one and only time she had talked with him alone, it had been an awful experience. After the trial and Tommy's sentencing, she'd marched into his office, demanding to know why he hadn't called Renee to the stand.

"I didn't believe her story," he'd told her in a condescending voice.

Her temper had flared. "How can you say that, when she backed up Tommy about his drink being spiked? She said she saw Chad Creekmore spike it."

"I don't think that happened, Miss Banks. I think she just made it up, hoping to get your brother off."

Brittany had been horrified. She agreed with Tommy. At the last minute, Darwin Brewster had indeed hung him out to dry, and there had been nothing she could do about it after the fact. Still, with that horror driving her, she had gone to see Renee, only to find her trailer deserted.

She hadn't stopped there, although she hadn't told Tommy that. A few days later she'd paid Chad a visit. He'd been in a rival gang. Even though Tommy no longer participated in gang activities, old enemies died hard.

Chad worked as a mechanic in a local garage. He'd been alone that day, working under a car.

When she'd called his name, he'd rolled out, then risen

to his feet, grease covering him from head to toe. A big glob was matted in his hair. Still, that grime failed to hide the tattoos covering his hairy arms. He was husky and dark complexioned, with dirty, shoulder-length hair.

"I'm Tommy Rogers' sister," she said, forcing herself not to show how revolted she was by him.

He spat tobacco on the dirty concrete, his eyes raking over her, a glint in them. She cringed inwardly.

"Whatcha' want?" he finally asked.

"The truth."

He gave her an ugly grin, revealing stained teeth. "I don't know what you're talking about, lady."

"That stuff you put in my brother's drink," she said boldly. "That's what I'm talking about."

He took a step toward her, clutching a wrench in his hand. "You got balls, I'll have to hand you that. But I suggest you git your sassy ass back where you came from. I don't know nothin' about no drink."

Brittany backed up, the foul odor coming from his body taking her breath away. "It's your fault he had the wreck, and I can prove it."

"Lady, you can't prove Jack shit." He slid the wrench back and forth across his palm, giving her a leering grin. "But if you'll make it worth my while, I'll say anything."

"Go to hell," Brittany spat, then spun on her heel and headed back to her car, her heart pounding.

Forcing her thoughts away from that awful day, she shuddered, still amazed that she had pulled such a stupid stunt. But she'd been so desperate she hadn't used good judgment. Another shudder went through her. He could have raped her, or worse.

Thinking of that brought Collier back to the front of her mind, not that he had ever gone far, she reminded herself ruefully. Sometimes she thought his hands on her and that heart-stopping kiss had been a figment of her imagination, or simply a dream.

She wondered if he ever thought of her.

To think that he did somehow brought her a strange kind of comfort. When the knock sounded on the door, she gave a start, thinking it was Sissy. When she reminded herself that Sissy was out of town, she frowned.

Rupert?

No way. He would never be bold enough to show up at her home. Or would he? Her heart upped its beat, and for a second she considered ignoring the knock. But when it turned more insistent, she hurried toward the door.

Her hand curled around the knob, but not before switching on the dim porch light. "Yes?"

"Brittany, it's Collier."

At first she was so stunned she couldn't respond. She simply stood there, her tongue stuck to the roof of her mouth.

"Brittany, please, let me in."

What on earth was *he* doing there? All sorts of crazy explanations flooded her mind. None of them made any sense. While she couldn't comprehend the reason for his presence, she wasn't about to look a gift horse in the mouth. Hadn't this been what she'd wanted? What she'd been wishing for?

Without further thought, she jerked open the door, knowing her eyes were wide and questioning. So much for her vow not to become another name in what she knew must be the Collier Smith army of women.

For a second he continued to stand on the porch, unmoving, staring back at her. His dark eyes seduced her on the spot, causing her stomach to flutter and her heart to beat out of sync. And though there was a cold, damp breeze whistling through the trees, it couldn't stop the current of heat that flared to life between them, setting them both on fire.

Brittany drew in her breath and held it, her gaze moving to his lips, remembering how they had felt against hers.

Collier cleared his throat, finally breaking the heavy silence. "I shouldn't be here, you know." His voice sounded hoarse, as if he'd swallowed a rusty nail.

Did she ever. But she didn't voice that thought. Instead she stood there and waited. "You're going to freeze," she finally said in a soft tone, her teeth starting to chatter, more from nerves, she suspected, than from the chill.

"So are you."

She stepped aside. That was when he swore under his breath, then strode across the threshold. For what seemed like eons, they stood silently in the middle of the small living room, its warmth enveloping them. Still, she couldn't seem to stop shivering.

"This is insane."

His voice had that rusty edge to it again. Coming here had apparently not been easy for him. So why had he done it? Dare she hope he simply wanted to see her again?

"Then why did you come?" she asked with a tremor.

Their eyes met again. Another flare of heat surged between them.

"You know why," he muttered, his jaw clenched.

She licked her lower lip.

His eyes darkened. "I had to see you, make sure you were all right."

"I'm…fine."

"I can see that. Your face is healing."

Suddenly it hit her how pale, how awful, she must look without any makeup.

As if he sensed what she was thinking, he shook his head. "You look lovely just the way you are."

Those huskily spoken words sent a shaft of longing though her, so intense that her knees almost buckled. "Is that why you came?" she asked inanely. "To check my face?"

"No...yes, I mean—" His voice failed, then he cursed again, "Hell, I just wanted to see you."

She didn't say anything, choosing to stare at him, to appease the hunger gnawing inside her.

"I shouldn't be here." Despite the words, he didn't move.

"You've said that already."

He rubbed the back of his neck. "I know."

Exhaustion was written in the irregular planes of his face; he looked as if he hadn't slept in days. Suddenly it was all she could do not to reach out and ease some of those lines away. Any excuse to touch him.

Realizing where her thoughts had taken her, Brittany felt her face flush with high color. God, this was madness—him being here, her letting him stay.

Yet he still made no effort to leave.

"Would you like some coffee?" she asked at last, for lack of anything else to say.

His features seemed to clear somewhat, become less tense. "That'd be great. Anything you have."

"That's it, I'm afraid," she added by way of an apology. She loved wine but couldn't afford it. Oh, every once in a while she would treat herself to a bottle of the cheap stuff and sip on it. But mostly, if she had it at all, she kept it on hand to have when Sissy stopped by. Having been reared in an alcoholic's home, booze was something she was careful not to abuse. "I have some milk."

He smiled.

That action was so unexpected that she was totally caught off guard. The wattage was so high-powered, it took her breath away.

"I'll settle for the coffee."

She forced her heart rate down. "Please, have a seat."

"Are you sure?" The intensity had returned to his eyes and his voice.

"No, I'm not sure at all."

"Me, either," he rasped.

Eleven

Brittany forced herself to downplay her confused emotions and ignore the uncomfortable silence that seemed to have become another person in the room. Standing in front of him, watching the light play over his deeply masculine features, emphasizing the dark stubble on his face, she inhaled the faint aroma of his cologne, making her senses spin.

With very little encouragement, she could lose total control and give in to the need that was stampeding through her.

"I should put on some clothes," she said breathlessly, shifting away from the laserlike intensity of his eyes, suddenly conscious of how scantily she was clad, positive he could see through the material of her robe. But then, he'd already seen her flesh, she reminded herself.

"No, please," he said. "I won't be here that long."

"I'll...get the coffee," she said, almost desperately, escaping to the kitchen. Once there, she leaned against the counter and struggled for a decent breath. After she finally got herself together enough to prepare a tray, she made her way back into the small living area, where she was struck again by the way his commanding presence seemed to dwarf the size of the room.

He looked so out of place here, like a misplaced modifier. He was meant for much bigger and better things than a trailer. No doubt about it, he was out of his element in her shabby surroundings.

Though obviously not as neatly dressed as when he'd left the house that morning, he could still hold his own with anyone. His gray sports jacket and charcoal slacks looked great with his longish dark hair. Actually, the fact that he was slightly disheveled made him that much more attractive.

Inhaling another shaky breath, Brittany placed the tray on the scarred coffee table, conscious again of just how few amenities she had. She wondered what he was thinking. She shouldn't care, but she did. While she might only have the barest of necessities, at least what she did have was neatly arranged and spotlessly clean.

"The coffee's good."

Brittany gave him a startled look, then colored. She hadn't even realized he'd filled their cups. "Sorry."

"For what?" he asked warmly, his eyes probing.

"For…" Her voice failed under the smothering feeling in her chest. Please Lord, let him stop looking at her like that, aggravating a treacherous intimacy already present in every word, every look, making each a caress in itself.

"I can't believe you're not coffee-logged." She tried to inject some light humor into the room, hoping to erode some of the crackling tension.

"Close to it," he admitted with an endearing half smile, easing his long legs out in front of him.

She couldn't stop her gaze from dipping to the intense flexing of his leg muscles as they rippled under his pants. She dared not raise her eyes any further for fear of what she might encounter at the apex of his thighs.

Good Lord! After deliberately reaching for her cup and taking a swallow, she averted her gaze off him entirely.

Had she gone stark-raving mad or what? She was behaving like some man-hungry tramp.

"Brittany."

The low, raspy sound of his voice jerked her back around. "Have you changed your mind?"

"About what?"

"Filing charges against that bastard."

Her cup shook before she placed it back on the table. "No."

"Is there anything I can say that would persuade you otherwise?"

She shook her head.

"You know he might do the same thing to someone else."

Brittany cut him a look. "God, I hope not."

"You know he might."

She licked her dry lips. Was it her imagination, or did she hear a slight groan part his lips? "I know," she admitted reluctantly, determined to keep her mind focused and not pay attention to every detail about him. And while she didn't want to discuss the near-rape with Collier or anyone else, at least they were on somewhat settled ground.

It was those heated looks and suffocating silences that agitated this madness.

"I just want to see that he gets what's coming to him."

"Please..."

"Okay, I'll shut up."

She felt herself smile. "That would be nice."

He chuckled, which sent another shaft of longing through her.

"Do you want a warm-up on your coffee?" she asked suddenly, too suddenly, knowing she shouldn't say or do anything to encourage him to stay. Yet she wanted him to do just that. As for the reasons behind such a crazy notion, she refused to delve into that subject. It bordered on insanity.

"I'm already wired, so a little more won't matter."

This time she beat him to the pot and filled his cup. They sipped in silence for a long moment, though the silence itself remained deafening.

"It looks like I stopped you from studying." He cut his gaze toward the pile of books on the opposite end of the couch.

"I'm always looking for an excuse not to open them." She paused, then added, "That's not true. I actually love going to school, though it's hard."

"I know. Although it's been a while since I was in law school, I haven't forgotten how tough it was. And it's still tough. Actually, attorneys, if they're worth their salt, spend as much time studying the law as upholding it."

"That makes sense."

"So what are you planning to be when you finish?"

"Don't you mean when I grow up?"

His chuckle deepened.

"You have to think it's a bit odd that I'm thirty and still going to school."

"Not hardly. As many adults are enrolled in college nowadays as kids."

"True. It's just that sometimes I feel really self-conscious."

"Well, you shouldn't. You should just keep on keeping on."

Brittany couldn't believe they were sitting there talking—with her wearing nothing but a robe, for heaven's sake—carrying on an almost normal conversation, as if they actually *knew* each other and had something in common.

Dumb and dangerous.

Still, she was tempted to flood him with questions about himself. Personal questions. Yet she didn't dare, more for her own protection than his. The more she knew, the more she would want to know. And why? Nothing would ever come of their relationship. Her instinct told her that, and it had served her well in the past.

As if he suddenly realized the same thing, Collier held his silence. Brittany wanted to tear her gaze off him, but she couldn't, especially not when his eyes were locked with hers.

The air was immediately recharged with electricity. Brittany swallowed hard and watched as he rose abruptly to his feet. "I should go."

She stood as well, tightening the sash on her robe, a gesture he apparently didn't miss, because she watched his darkening gaze drop, then settle at the V where her breasts came together.

"Brittany…"

Her name came out sounding rough but gentle, though his features were a mixture of torment and uncertainty.

"You're…right, you should leave."

Without waiting for a reply, Brittany crossed to the door. She knew he was right behind her; she could feel his breath on her neck, which made chills cover her body.

It was in that moment that they both reached for the knob, their hands touching. Instantaneously they stiffened and stared at each other, their breathing suspended.

Brittany's lips parted on a muted cry, which seemed to be all he needed to do the unthinkable. He grabbed her and crushed her mouth against his.

Lust, hot and lethal, shot into her stomach, then lower.

At first she could only cling to him in desperation while his hot, moist lips plundered hers, as if trying to suck the very life out of her.

But he didn't stop there. His hands ran possessively over her body, parting her robe, where he covered a pulsating breast. It was only when that same hand made its way down to the valley between her legs that she cried out.

Collier, looking dazed, turned her loose and stepped back, his breathing coming in hard spurts. "You don't have to kick me out," he muttered harshly. "That honor belongs to me."

Despite how busy the agency had been, Brittany wasn't all that tired. On the contrary, she was glad to be busy, wanted to be overwhelmed with work. That way she wouldn't have time to think.

Sissy's return had been delayed, which made the responsibility of the agency sit squarely on Brittany's shoulders and those of a part-time employee. Today, however, Liz, had also been out, sick with the flu. It was a good thing she hadn't had class. Otherwise she would have had to put a Closed sign on the door for a few hours.

Missing class was not an option.

However, not studying apparently was. Since the night of Collier's unexpected visit, it seemed her mind had been on hiatus. She hadn't been able to do one thing sensibly, especially study.

However, she didn't think she'd messed up too badly on either test. Unfortunately she hadn't gotten her grades yet, so she would have to stew a bit longer. Realizing that the agency was empty for the first time that day, Brittany got up and stretched her aching back muscles, then walked into the bathroom, where her eyes strayed to the mirror.

Slowly but surely, her bruises were fading. At least she no longer felt like a freak when customers walked in and exclaimed in an astonished voice, "What happened to you?"

She'd told the same untruth so often that now it just rolled off her tongue without hesitation. And though she felt guilty about her little white lie, there was nothing she could do about it.

What she could do something about, however, was Collier and the way he dominated her thoughts. Twice now, he'd brought her to the brink of ecstasy, leaving her heart emptier than ever.

The buzzer sounded as the door opened.

Her head came up, and she froze. She wanted to move, though. She wanted to get up and dash out the back door. Only sheer force of will kept her still.

With a bouquet of flowers in hand, Rupert Holt strode farther into the room, his big stride eating up the distance between them. It was all Brittany could do to stand and not flinch.

"I was hoping you'd be here," his said, his blue eyes narrowing on her.

Too bad such a perverted person lurked beneath that pose of confidence and good looks, she thought. For a man well into his sixties, with his steel-gray hair and blue eyes, he would never fail to be noticed, especially not by a woman. But underneath that outward charm was a vicious streak, one she'd experienced firsthand.

"What do you want, Rupert?" she asked, her tone colder than icicles.

"To apologize in person."

"I don't want your apology."

He laid the flowers down and perched on the edge of her desk. "I had too much to drink. I know that's no excuse."

"You're right. It's not."

"It won't happen again."

She laughed, but with no humor. "You're right about that."

Though he flushed, he peered more closely at her face, then reached out a hand.

She recoiled visibly, and for a moment she saw a flicker of that hidden menace reappear in his eyes. Renewed fear coursed through her when she realized she was alone. Panic gripped her.

"You don't ever have to be afraid of me again," he said with a smile, apparently reading her thoughts. "I'll make it up to you, I promise."

"What about your wife, Rupert?" she asked with blatant scorn. "Are you going to make it up to her, too?"

Though his smile fled, his tone remained unchanged. "Let's leave her out of this, shall we? She has her life, and I have mine."

"Fine. Then you go about yours and leave me with mine."

"I want to see you again, Brittany," he said, his voice dropping. "I can't let our relationship end on this note."

She gave him an incredulous look. "Relationship? Are you crazy? The only reason I went to dinner with you was because you conned me into thinking you were going to help my brother."

"And I aim to make good on my word. That's a promise, too."

"Yeah, right."

His flush deepened under her sarcasm. "You see me again, and I'll prove it."

"I don't think so."

Rupert got up and crossed to the door, where he stopped, then turned back around. "This isn't over, Brittany. Meanwhile, I suggest you talk to your brother. I bet he'd have another opinion. Think about that."

Once the door shut behind him, Brittany fell against the chair, feeling as if someone had deflated her. No way would she let that bastard near her, yet he'd used Tommy like a carrot again, dangling him in front of her.

She buried her head in her hands. What was she thinking? She would be insane to believe anything Rupert said or go anywhere alone with him ever again. Suddenly Tommy's pinched, agony-filled face filled her vision.

"Damn you, Rupert Holt," she snapped. "Damn you!"

Twelve

Jackson rolled his wheelchair out of the bathroom and into his living area. As usual, he locked it in front of the fireplace. Yet he could still see out the French doors to the balcony and grounds beyond.

Sometimes he sat for hours and stared at the gardens behind the estate, watched a squirrel jump from branch to branch, then nibble on an acorn. Fidgety little fellow, he'd often think before his gaze moved on. On nice days, he would even roll out onto the balcony in order to get a taste and smell of the outside world. Today, however, was not a nice day.

It was another of those cold, damp days, typical of early fall. At least the trees were still strutting their colorful cloaks of leaves which made for a lovely scene, especially if nothing else was going on in a man's life.

A deep sigh filtered through Jackson as he brought his eyes back to the fire. Bad weather seemed to be harder on him mentally and physically. Understandable. Arthritis had settled into some of his good joints, though he tried to ignore that fact.

Still, he was strong as an ox in his upper body, which was something, anyway. His trainer always worked him hard. But lately his therapist, whom the family didn't know he'd hired, had also put him through some grueling paces, promising Jackson he would eventually see results.

Fat chance.

Despite his piss-poor attitude, he'd hung tough. Another sigh parted his lips. Mentally he was lower than a snake's belly, so low he couldn't even stand his own company. He'd dismissed his valet, Harry, told him to take a much-needed day off. Harry hadn't wanted to leave, Jackson could tell, but he hadn't given him any choice. He hadn't wanted anyone underfoot.

Maybe his lousy frame of mind had something to do with the dinner party his dad was giving tonight in honor of Collier's bid for the judgeship. He knew Mason would have a fit if he didn't attend. Guess what? He wasn't about to let himself in for that kind of abuse from well-meaning friends. He'd been there and done that. Besides, he'd retired from any kind of social life.

He had all he needed in his suite on the second floor and was perfectly content to remain behind these walls. He was surrounded by books he loved, priceless oil paintings he'd collected on past trips abroad, and a state-of-the-art gym in which to keep his upper body fit. He had all he could ask for.

Except the use of his legs.

Jackson muttered a dark curse as the past seemed to rise out of nowhere and blast him with memories of that horrible day when he'd awakened in the hospital and found out he couldn't move his legs. The pain that had hit his heart had been much worse than the pain wracking his body.

"No!" he'd cried in gut-wrenching anguish, determined to show the doctor he was wrong, that he could indeed walk.

"Mr. Williams, you can't," Dr. Tatum had told him, jumping up and trying to restrain him.

Jackson had knocked his hand away, then jerked back

the sheet and tried with every ounce of strength he possessed to move his limbs. They remained lifeless. Facing the truth that he was only half a man had been the darkest moment of his life.

Jackson drew a deep breath, jerking himself back to the moment at hand, at the same time trying to calm his racing heart, knowing what had put him in such a foul mood. Confrontation was imminent. Before much longer, Mason would come charging into his room, demanding to know what time he planned on coming down this evening.

Maybe he ought to bite the bullet and attend, make his dad and brother's day. No way. He simply wasn't up to facing the stares of pity or the well-meaning questions he would get asked. Shortly after the accident, he'd had hopes of being part of the normal, functioning world again, but it hadn't worked out. He hadn't given it a chance; he realized that. But the fact that he would never walk again was a horror that haunted him daily, that he couldn't get past.

He hated himself and what had happened to him.

Still, he was glad for Collier. If he had to have a stepbrother, he couldn't have asked for a better one. Collier was the cream of the crop. And he knew Collier still looked up to him, though he also knew his little brother would like to throttle him for shutting himself off from the world.

Well, Collier would have to get over it, just like his dad. Collier was more than capable of taking up the slack. If the appointment came through, all the better. He deserved the honor and would make a damn fine judge. Even though he wasn't blood kin, lawyering was in Collier's veins the same as it was in Mason's and his own.

Used to be in his, Jackson corrected.

He never intended to practice law again, though he continued to keep up with the changes in the codes and statutes, and stay on top of recent court opinions. But that was his secret, one he had no intention of sharing with his family. If his dad had any inkling he remained interested in any aspect of the law, he'd never give up trying to get him back into the office.

Not going to happen.

He couldn't face rolling himself around the firm, in and out of the courtroom. Ironside he wasn't and never would be. Now, if he could *walk* into a court of law...

Jackson jerked his mind off that thought just as he heard the tap on his door. His features darkened; he figured it was Mason, his verbal arsenal loaded and ready to fire.

"Yes," Jackson responded in a crisp tone.

The door opened, and Maxine's head eased around it. "I know you don't want to be disturbed, but—"

"But what, Maxine?" Although he sometimes lost patience with the housekeeper, just as he did with everyone else, he adored Maxine and she adored him. Most of the time she didn't take any crap from him, either. She would stand up to him when no one else would.

Today, however, even she seemed on edge.

"You have a visitor," she said in a near-whisper.

"You know I don't do visitors."

"I know that, sir, only she refuses to take no for an answer."

"She?"

"Yes, sir. It's a woman, and she says she's your friend."

He snorted. "I don't have any women friends." He waved his hand. "Tell her I have the flu, that I'm contagious. Tell her anything you want to. Just get rid of her.''

''But, sir—''

''Maxine!''

''Oh, for heaven's sake, Jack, give a poor woman a break.''

Jackson froze. No one called him Jack except— Before that thought could mature, a tall, striking woman skirted around Maxine and breezed across the threshold.

''Haley!'' he said in a shocked tone. ''What—''

''What am I doing here? That should be obvious.'' She grinned. ''I came to see you.''

Jackson closed his eyes, then opened them quickly, positive they were playing a trick on him, that Haley Bishop, the only woman he'd ever considered marrying, wasn't standing in front of him, looking better than he'd ever seen her look.

Had it been five years since he'd seen her? If so, she didn't look a bit older or worse for wear, though he knew she was thirty-five. Apparently life hadn't dealt her any severe blows.

She had always been tall—five-ten, to be exact—though now she seemed even taller. Maybe that was because before his accident he'd peered down at her, instead of the other way around.

Her hair was still a dark auburn and worn in a shoulder-length bob. Her light brown eyes and freckles remained highly visible and were as winsome as ever. But more than her wholesome beauty, it was her personality that was the clincher. It was magnetic and drew people to her like bees to honeycomb.

''Cat got your tongue?'' she asked with a grin, showing off her perfect set of white teeth.

"You might say that," Jackson muttered darkly.

"Hey, don't be such an old fuddy-duddy. I know you didn't want company—Maxine made that quite clear—but—"

"You don't play by the same rules as everyone else, right?"

Her grin widened. "Right."

"What are you doing here, Haley? Really?"

"I told you, I came to see you. Do you mind if I sit down?"

"Would it matter if I said yes?"

"No."

Jackson simply shook his head and gestured toward the sofa nearest his wheelchair. For a moment after she was seated, silence filled the room, both of them staring into the flames.

"You're looking well," Haley finally commented in a sober tone.

"Bullshit."

She laughed, that impish glint returning to her eyes. "It sucks, doesn't it? Being in that chair, I mean?"

No one else would have dared say that to him, but then again, Haley really did play by her own rules. He would rather have it that way. He didn't like to be mollycoddled. People could pretend all they wanted that he wasn't in a wheelchair, but he was. And that fact wasn't going to change.

"Yeah, it sucks. Big time."

"I heard about what happened, and I was tempted to come to the hospital, but I knew that wouldn't be smart."

"You're right. I refused to see anyone, even my family." He paused, switching the subject. "So what brings you back to Haven? Are you still with the same insurance company?"

"That I am, and they've transferred me back here. This office had gone to pot, and the powers that be thought I was the one to straighten it out."

"I'm surprised you'd leave Dallas."

Haley shrugged. "I was getting tired of the rat race, the traffic, the whole nine yards. It's a pain in the butt."

Jackson smiled, much to his surprise. He'd thought his lips had forgotten how. "I'm sure your mother's glad to have you back."

"Yeah, she is. And my sister, too. She wants help with those brats of hers."

"Speaking of brats, do you have any?"

"I'd rather have a husband first," she said pointedly, tilting her head to one side and giving him a direct look.

He shifted his gaze, feeling a slight flush steal up his face. Hell, he hadn't been the one who had walked out. It had been her. They had been together for nearly two years when she told him she was taking a promotion in Dallas. He'd been dumbfounded and devastated. But he hadn't wanted to stand in the way of her career, so he'd held his pain inside and wished her good luck.

Later, he'd considered going after her, thinking he'd let her off the hook far too easily. Then the accident happened, and he'd thanked Fate he'd left her alone. No way would he have wanted her to live in hell with him. He couldn't have handled that.

"So you're not married?" he said into the growing silence.

"Nope." Her gaze trapped his again. "And no prospects, either."

Dammit, what did she want? For sure he was out of the running. So why was she here? If it was for old times' sake, then to hell with that. To hell with her!

"I find that hard to believe," he said, wishing she would leave.

"Why didn't you ask me to marry you, Jackson?"

Her softly spoken words hit him with the force of a bomb. He jerked his head back and narrowed his eyes. "That's beside the point now, don't you think?"

"No," she said bluntly. "I know you loved me, and I definitely loved you."

"You had a strange way of showing it. All of a sudden you decided to choose your career over me."

"That's not true! I wanted to marry you, but you showed no signs of giving up your bachelorhood for me or anyone else."

"Dammit, why didn't you tell me?"

"Why should I have had to?"

They stared at each other fiercely for what seemed like an eternity, then Jackson let go of another expletive before saying in a dull tone, "What difference does it make now? You should be rejoicing you're not tied to a cripple."

"Stop it!"

His eyes widened. "It's the truth. I'll never walk again. There's no way to pretty that up."

"I'm not trying to. It's just that you could still lead a productive life."

Jackson's expression soured. "Don't you start that shit. Since the accident, that's all I've heard, especially from Dad."

"You're not practicing law?" She sounded appalled.

"No."

"So what *are* you doing?"

"Feeling sorry for myself."

Haley laughed. "At least you're honest."

Another silence descended over the room.

"Will you let me come see you again?"

"What's the point?"

"I'm still your friend. I was that even before I was your lover."

His face lost its color. "Dammit, Haley, do you always have to say what's on your mind?"

She smiled. "You used to like that."

"Not anymore," he said crossly.

She got up, walked to his chair, leaned over and kissed him on the cheek. He sucked in his breath and held it until she straightened. "You really need to get a better attitude. We're going to have to work on that."

"What's this 'we' shit? I don't want to see you again."

"I'm sure you don't, but that doesn't matter."

"Haley—"

"I'll be back—and soon, too," she said, grabbing her purse before squeezing him on the shoulder. "Meanwhile, give Mason and Collier my best."

"Haley, I—"

His words fell on deaf ears as he heard the door close firmly behind her. If he'd had an object handy, he would have thrown it against the wall, needing an outlet for his pent-up frustration and anger. Instead he remained sitting stiff as a rod, seething, his pulse pounding in his temples.

How dare she just waltz in here, as if she had a right, and interfere in his life? He wasn't interested in being her friend or anything else.

He rolled his chair to the front window, where he peered outside. That was when he got a glimpse of her getting into her car. He winced, suddenly wishing he could call her back. It was okay that she'd come this one time. He'd been glad to see her; he would admit that.

He just couldn't let it happen again.

Thirteen

Collier surveyed the scene in front of him. The mansion was ablaze with lights. Flowers adorned every table, candles sweetened the air, the Waterford sparkled, and the music vibrated.

Everything was perfect.

So why didn't he feel perfect as well? The supposedly small party given for him had turned into a giant gala, just as Collier had feared. Mason didn't seem to know how to do anything on a small scale, certainly not when it came to politics.

And this evening, politics had top billing. Several high-ranking members of the Republican party hierarchy were on hand, including United States Senator Newton Riley, who was openingly supporting him for the position. He couldn't have asked for a sweeter deal, though he still thought the shindig was premature and too presumptuous.

Not Mason, though. From the way he was blustering, he appeared to think the appointment was a done deal. At times throughout the evening Collier had fought the urge to caution his dad to go a little easier, to tone down the rhetoric. But he'd known it wouldn't do any good. Mason was in his element and loving every minute of it.

And for the most part Collier was, too, except that Jackson had stuck to his guns and refused to join them.

At first Mason had been livid, but Collier had finally calmed him down enough to reason with him.

"Dad, you've got to stop badgering Jackson."

"Dammit, he can't spend the rest of his life rotting in that room."

"Yes, he can, if that's what he chooses."

Those words drew a glare from Mason. "Since when did you change sides on the issue?"

Collier rubbed his chin and squelched a sigh. "I haven't changed sides. But what else are you going to do? Forcibly lift his chair and haul him downstairs?"

"Of course not," Mason snapped, red-faced.

"Well then, back off."

"And let him just waste away to nothing, like he's done for the past three years?" Mason's tone had grown fierce again.

"No. We're not giving up. We're merely picking our battles. On this one, Jackson's dug his heels in, so you might as well admit defeat." Collier paused. "Oh, by the way, he had a visitor."

Mason was clearly shocked. "Are you serious?"

"Yep. Haley Bishop. Remember her?"

"Of course. He almost married her."

"According to Maxine, she showed up unannounced and walked right into Jackson's room."

"I bet she didn't stay long."

"You're right. She didn't."

Mason's features dimmed again. "Well, I'm not about to get my hopes up."

"One of these days he'll come around and be your son again." Collier squeezed Mason on the shoulder. "You wait and see."

"If that day happens, I figure I'll be dead and buried. Meanwhile, it's up to you to make me proud."

"I'll do my best," Collier said with a sinking heart. Talk about pressure...

"I know you will. And tonight's the first step toward that."

And what a night it had been so far, Collier reminded himself again, one that political dreams were truly made of. And to think he was the center of attention, a fact that filled him with anxiety and excitement.

As he continued to stand off to one side, Lana and her father caught his attention. They were working the crowd, talking to the bigwigs in the party who had the money and the clout to influence both the senator and the president himself.

In fact, everyone in attendance was in his corner and had promised to work on his behalf. Mason had made sure of that. Still, nothing was a given, he reminded himself.

Earlier in the evening, he and Senator Riley had had a private visit, which had certainly been encouraging, but it had also stirred some unrest in him, since the senator had gone straight for the jugular.

Even without his straightforward manner, the man himself would have been intimidating from sheer size alone. Not only was he tall, he was thick, especially his neck and shoulders. He could have once played linebacker for a professional football team or been a wrestler.

He had a thatch of white hair, bushy brows, and green eyes that didn't seem to miss anything. Longevity in the senate alone had given him power. Yet he'd apparently earned it, too, the old-fashioned way, by showing up on the Hill and doing his job. He had gained respect from both parties, another plus for Collier.

The only criticism most associated with Riley was his penchant for the bottle. Although Collier had never seen him have more than a few drinks at a time, Riley had a reputation for getting stinking drunk. Because his face stayed flushed and he spoke in a bourbon-edged voice, Collier suspected there was some truth to that rumor.

No matter. The man's personal life was his own business.

"Have you ever done anything you're ashamed of, young man?" he'd demanded, after having come up behind Collier and slapped him on the back.

For a moment Collier didn't know which caught him off guard the most—the blow or the bluntness.

Having assumed it was the latter, Riley chuckled. "You'd better get used to questions like that."

"If you say so," Collier responded with a smile and in a smooth voice, having jerked himself back on target. "There's a lot more where that one came from."

"Were you wanting an answer to yours now, Senator?"

"Nope. Just wanted you to be thinking about your past. It wouldn't hurt to try to remember every time you took a crap."

"Oh, shit," Collier muttered.

"Literally, my boy, literally."

They both laughed, then the senator sobered. "This could be a tough, dirty fight, since you've got such stiff competition. But then, I guess you're aware of that."

"Oh, you bet I am. I don't think Mason is, though."

"He will be."

There was an ominous note in Riley's voice that sent a cold chill through Collier. "It could get that nasty?"

"With Rupert Holt lobbying for Travis Wainwright, you bet your sweet ass. My phone's been ringing off the bloody wall, both on your behalf and his."

"And Wainwright's got the political experience," Collier pointed out in a concerned tone. "As you well know, I'm not part of the 'political mash potato circuit,' so to speak."

"Doesn't matter. You've got an unblemished record as an attorney, which is one of your biggest assets."

"I hope that still holds true in a few weeks."

The senator made a face. "What does that mean?"

Collier explained about the sexual harassment case he'd taken on.

"Hell, man, out of all the clients who come through that door, why did you have to choose an explosive one like that?"

"I'd already made the commitment before I knew I had a snowball's chance in hell of getting in the top four."

"Well, do whatever it takes to make sure none of the shit that hits the fan gets splashed on you." Riley paused and sipped his drink. "Your biggest ace in the hole is that you and your family have tossed big bucks and big chunks of time into the political arena for years. That, along with your distinguished career, will count big on your behalf."

"Let us pray."

"Meanwhile, keep your nose to the grindstone and stay out of trouble."

Collier took his outstretched hand and shook it. "Will do, sir. And thank you."

"Don't thank me yet, boy. Wait till the president gives you the nod, then you can thank me."

Now, as Collier forced his mind off that conversation and back to the present, he realized he should be circulating, shaking hands and making small talk. Suddenly he felt weary rather than pumped. Strange, distracted, as if his body was there but not his mind. Definitely not his heart. Brittany had that. What if she were here…?

His spirits took another nosedive. Had he lost his mind? Hadn't the senator just told him to stay out of trouble? And Brittany was definitely trouble.

"For heaven's sake, get that look off your face."

"What look?" Collier asked innocently, staring down into Lana's upturned features.

"Like you want to turn tail and run."

"Relax, I'm not going anywhere."

She squeezed his arm. "Oh, yes, you are, darling, straight to the federal bench, then who knows where from there."

"Whoa, you're going too fast for me."

She kissed him on the cheek, then winked. "But not too fast for us. Together. As a team."

"Lana—"

"By the way," she interrupted, batting her eyelashes at him, "you haven't said anything about my dress."

"It's smashing." And it was. Collier didn't think he'd ever seen Lana look more beautiful than in the jet-black beaded dress that made her look as if she was covered in thousands of diamonds when she moved.

"Well, I wanted to look my best for you tonight." She paused, her features brightening even more. "Ah, here come Daddy and Mason."

"Quite a party in your honor, young man," Bill Frazier said, giving Collier his big, famous grin that showed off a mouthful of slightly crooked teeth.

"That it is."

Bill nudged Mason's arm. "Think this night might do the trick? Kick our boy here into the top spot?"

"The only thing missing is the press." Mason drew

his brows together in a concentrated frown. "I could kick myself for not inviting that reporter friend of mine."

Lana's grip on Collier's arm tightened. "That would've been the icing on the cake. I can just see the headlines now."

"I hardly think I'd make headlines," Collier said tightly. "Anyway, I'm glad we saved the press for another time."

"Stop being so modest, darling. You've got to get used to being in the limelight."

"You'd better listen to my daughter," Bill said in his robust tone. "And speaking of my daughter, when are you going to make an honest woman out of her?"

"That's right, son," Mason said.

Collier cursed silently before flashing a brittle smile. "Soon, gentlemen, soon."

"Is that a promise?" Bill asked, pinning Collier with bold gray eyes.

Collier smiled. "Come on, give me a break. Lana, too."

"Speak for yourself," Lana said, grinning. "I'm loving it. I was beginning to think I'd have to hog-tie you to get a commitment."

"Well, we all just heard him," Mason said in a jubilant voice before adding, "Guess I'd better excuse myself and circulate. You, too, Collier. Make sure you say a personal word to everyone."

"Don't you worry," Lana said, pulling on Collier's arm. "I'll see that he does all the right things. Come along, darling."

Collier plastered another smile on his face and fell into step beside her.

* * *

Collier stared at the clock on his bedside table. It was only midnight, but he was beat.

Yet he'd enjoyed the party, at least for the most part. He wanted the federal job, wanted it with a passion, though he wasn't looking forward to all the brouhaha that apparently went along with it.

Had he always felt that way? Or did his sudden impatience with the process have anything to do with his involvement with Brittany? He flinched against that unvarnished thought. Involved? Was that what he was?

He pushed back the panic. Perhaps the word involved was a bit strong. Obsessed. Somehow that seemed to fit his feelings much better. No matter. He couldn't ignore the fact that he couldn't get Brittany off his mind, or that she was a factor in everything he felt and did these days.

The idea that he'd thought about her with Lana by his side was disturbing, to say the least. The time he'd spent at her trailer hadn't helped. It had made him want to return there, created an ache in his gut, and not just because he had the hots for her body, either. She had a calming effect on him, as if he'd just been given a reprieve from the fast track he lived on.

Nor was she pretentious at all, so unlike Lana. Being the center of attention didn't seem to interest Brittany, though it was something Lana thrived on. Different women. *Different worlds.*

Maybe if he saw her just one more time, never mind the reason. Then his conscience taunted him. Why string out the inevitable? Why risk Lana finding out about her? Why risk political suicide for a woman with whom there was no future?

To appease that raw hunger in his gut, he told himself. To see her, to smell her, to touch her, just one last time, God help him. Then he would walk away, cold turkey.

That was a promise.

Fourteen

Collier still couldn't believe Brittany was sitting across from him in the restaurant, that she had agreed to go out to dinner. But she had, and for the time being he wasn't about to analyze her reasoning. Or his. It didn't matter that it was risky taking her out in public. The only thing that mattered was that she was here, in the flesh, in all her quiet beauty.

When he'd arrived at the office this morning, he had lollygagged around until he thought it was all right to call her, though when he'd reached for the phone and punched out the number, he was unsure what to expect. Would she tell him to go to hell, hang up in his ear, or be cordial? Even though he hadn't wanted to admit it—and still didn't—he'd been as nervous as a kid about to experience sex for the first time. His mouth had been dry and his palms clammy.

As luck would have it, he'd caught her at home, which had made it easier, because he wouldn't have liked calling her at work. The name of the travel agency would have been easy enough to find out, along with everything else there was to know about her, *if* he'd chosen to do so.

It seemed as if the less he knew about Brittany Banks, the safer he would be. Common sense told him that if he kept her at arm's length personally and emotionally, he had a better chance of getting out of this sexual abyss with his sanity and his soul intact.

Otherwise...

The sound of her soft, husky-toned voice when she answered the phone had suddenly stabbed him in the gut like a sharp knife. For a long moment he'd held his breath before releasing it. "Brittany?"

"Yes."

The tiny catch in her voice didn't escape him, meaning she recognized him. "It's Collier."

"I know."

Silence.

"Did I interrupt anything?" he asked inanely, not caring if he had or not. Just hearing her voice and having her remain on the line was a gift from heaven.

"No."

She wasn't about to make this easy for him, he realized, digging deeply for another breath. "I'd like to take you to dinner."

Another silence.

"Are you still there?" Two stupid questions in a row. Boy, was he making progress.

"Yes."

"Well?"

"Collier...I..."

He could feel his control slipping. Bottom line, he didn't know what she was about to say, what excuse she was about to give, but he didn't give a shit. He didn't want to hear it. He only wanted her to acquiesce.

He squelched the rising panic inside him and said, "Please."

Another heartbeat of silence. "When?"

"Tonight."

"Tonight?" she echoed in a dazed voice.

"If not tonight, then tomorrow night." He knew he sounded pushy and rash, but he didn't care.

"I have class then." She paused. "Tonight's about it for me."

Though she didn't sound overjoyed at the prospect of spending an evening with him, she didn't make him beg, either, for which he was grateful. If his churning gut was any indication, he would have done that and more in order to see her again.

One last time.

Now, as he stared at her across the table, having just been served coffee and dessert, he thought she was the loveliest thing he'd ever seen, though everything was so simple. She had on a plain long-sleeved black knit dress that hugged her slender curves just right and complemented her translucent skin, which bore little makeup. A pair of silver studs in her delicate earlobes and a watch were the only jewelry she wore.

Simple elegance.

Those words fit her to a tee. So different from Lana. So different from any woman he'd ever been with. In a class by herself. As he peered at her over the rim of his cup, he couldn't understand why she was still single, why someone hadn't snapped her up.

Secrets.

Those lovely, expressive eyes held secrets, secrets he would give his eyeteeth to know without having to ask. "You're not eating your dessert," he said, putting his cup down.

She smiled. "It looks delicious, but I'm stuffed."

"You didn't eat all that much."

"Oh, yes, I did." She paused and tilted her head. "You're not eating yours either."

"I know."

Their eyes met and held, as they had during most of the meal. When that happened, it was as if they'd been zapped by a volt of electricity. He felt it, and he knew she did, too. The same sexual awareness that blazed in his insides was reflected in her eyes.

"The meal, this place, everything was lovely."

"I'm glad you enjoyed it. I wanted you to."

"Why?"

Though the question was quietly asked, it packed a wallop. More to the point, it nailed his butt. But he didn't try to worm his way out of it. "I wanted to see you." He was tempted to reach out and cover her hand, but he refrained, taking another sip of coffee instead. "Isn't that what you wanted, too?" His gaze trapped hers again, and, as usual, his insides went haywire.

Her eyes clouded; then she said in a soft, troubled tone, "When it comes to you, I have no idea what I want."

"We're on the same page, then," he admitted brusquely, turning away and letting go of a sigh.

Throughout dinner, very little conversation had taken place. But somehow that hadn't seemed to matter. It was as if small talk between them wasn't necessary. They had simply enjoyed the good wine, the good food and the good coffee. *And each other,* he reminded himself almost painfully.

He'd had a long, difficult day at the office and in court. He had needed some quiet time, and being with Brittany bought him that luxury. Dining with Lana, on the other hand, would have been anything but soothing. She would have chattered nonstop about her busy day, then grilled him about his.

Collier cursed silently, telling himself he had to stop comparing Brittany to Lana. Lana was the woman he was going to marry, not Brittany, dammit.

Now it seemed their time together was nearing an end, yet he couldn't bear that. He didn't want to take her home and say goodbye. He hadn't had enough time to soak up all the special movements, smiles, gestures, that were exclusively hers. He needed much more time. His gut clenched. Time was a luxury he didn't have. He was crazy to keep seeing her. Yet that was exactly what he wanted to do, more than anything.

"Are you about ready to go?" he asked abruptly.

"Yes."

He loved the fact that she wasn't a nonstop talker, that her answers to questions were brief and to the point. He'd first picked up on that in the cabin, but he'd attributed her quietness then to the bizarre circumstances. The other times he'd been with her had borne out that fact, though, and tonight was no different. He signaled for the check.

"I know why you brought me here," she said into the silence.

He faced her, narrowing his eyes on her. "Here? To this restaurant?"

"Purposely away from Haven is what I mean."

There was suppressed hostility in her voice and eyes. And something else, too—pain. He had hurt her. His gut clenched even tighter.

"You were embarrassed to be seen with me in town, weren't you?"

"Dammit, Brittany—" Further words dried up in his throat. She'd caught him red-handed. He could lie to her, but she would see through that just like she had seen through his ploy.

"Are you married?"

Another mental jab in the solar plexus made him wince visibly. "No."

"Engaged?"

He opened his mouth to deny that, then thought better of it. "Not officially," he admitted dully.

"At least you're honest," she responded tersely.

He felt like a first-class ass. "But she's not the reason—"

The waiter chose that moment to arrive with the check, which brought him a reprieve. Still, he didn't have a clue how he was going to get out of this mess. If he'd had any idea she was so astute, he wouldn't have pulled such an asinine stunt.

Nothing he could say would make up for the harm he'd done. She damn sure deserved better than she'd gotten. It wasn't that he was embarrassed to be seen with her—far from it. It was just that it wouldn't be smart, but not for the reason she thought.

Once the check was taken care of, they left, a heavy silence walking between them. That silence remained the entire way to her trailer. Only after he shoved the car in Park did he break it. "It's not what you think."

"Then what it is?" she asked, staring straight ahead instead of looking at him.

The night was crystal clear; a big moon and lots of stars beamed from overhead, allowing him carte blanche to study her profile. And what a lovely profile it was, too, he thought, drinking in the tilt of her nose, the fullness of her lower lip, the graceful curve of her neck, the jut of her breasts....

"You're ashamed of me, aren't you?" she asked into the silence.

Her words yanked his mind back to the moment of brutal reckoning. "Dammit, that's not true!"

Without warning, she began groping for the door handle. It was when she pulled it up that his reflexes responded. His hand clamped down on her arm. She swung around and stared at him out of round, tear-filled eyes.

Suddenly all the air seemed to woosh out of the vehicle as their eyes met and held. Collier groaned as he jerked her against him and ground his lips down on hers. It was a raw, hungry kiss that communicated his desperation in a way no words could have.

She whimpered under the assault. But then when he eased the pressure of his lips and began playing tag with her tongue, he felt her rigid body relax and give way under his.

When breathing was no longer possible, he pulled his mouth off hers, transferring it to her neck, where he licked and nibbled a path down to the vee of her dress.

"Collier," she moaned, placing her arms around his neck and pulling him closer. Frantic to feel and taste more of her delectable flesh, he moved his hand down her hips, then back up under her dress, to the warmth between her legs.

Although her panty hose kept him from making direct contact with that warmth, he wedged his hand there nonetheless and stroked back and forth, creating a friction that increased her moans. Realizing he'd made her wet and that she was about to orgasm, he pressed his lips to hers once again, at the same time increasing the pressure between her legs. Momentarily she threw her head back and cried out. Moisture dampened his hand, and he cupped her mound tighter until her shudders had passed.

He couldn't believe how easily, but how hard, he'd made her come. Though he was rock-hard and hurting, he was willing to sacrifice his own desire for her, something he'd never been willing to do with any other woman.

He'd always been a selfish lover. Until now. Until this fragile woman had come into his life.

"It's okay," he whispered after watching the shocked, dazed look come over her.

"Collier, my God," she began, then her voice played out as she stared at him wild-eyed.

"I loved making you come." He wiped a tear off her cheek with a thumb. "Don't be ashamed."

"Please," she said in a broken and mortified voice, turning her head away.

"Please what?" he whispered.

"Please let me go."

"Of course you can go. I would never make you do anything against your will, Brittany. Always know that."

"Where do we go from here?"

He had to strain to hear her strangled words. "I don't know," he said in a tortured voice. "I wish to hell I did."

Without responding, she opened the door and got out. This time he didn't try to stop her. Still, he didn't crank the engine. He sat there for the longest time, unable to move, feeling like a boulder was lodged in the pit of his stomach.

"Good morning, my dear."

Rupert laid the paper aside and watched as his wife walked over to the buffet and helped herself to coffee and the sweet rolls the housekeeper had put there just for her. A frown marred his face when she heaped two of the goodies on the plate before taking a seat adjacent to him.

"I don't know why you insist on eating that junk."

"Because I happen to like it," she said in an even tone.

He scowled. "It's not good for you."

"Don't you mean it's not good for *you*, because it makes me fat and you don't like that?"

His scowl deepened.

"I don't intend to have this conversation every morning for the rest of our married lives, Rupert. You're going to have to accept the fact I'm putting on weight in my old age and be done with it."

He would never accept it, though he wasn't about to tell her that, not when she controlled the stock in the company he ran, and quite successfully, too, he might add. He didn't have the guts to tell her point-blank that he was appalled at how she looked, embarrassed by it.

The only saving grace was that they weren't together much in public. While she supported his love of politics, especially when it came to money, she rarely attended the functions. Hell, she was too busy attending church, the first love of her life.

That was why, if she ever found out he'd been unfaithful to her, she would send him packing in a heartbeat. He'd become too used to the good life, even if it didn't carry the social standing he coveted. While her old man had left her rich and he himself had added millions to the family coffer with his sound business practices, his dream of being on the same rung of the social ladder as Mason Williams continued to elude him.

Angel didn't give a fig about that. And even though she didn't want him to make love to her anymore, she would be mortified if she knew he was getting it on the side, under the influence of alcohol.

If she ever found out he'd hit a woman...

The thought of that happening sent his breakfast surging up the back of his throat in the form of hot bile. He swallowed with difficulty, then felt himself relax. She wouldn't find out. He'd do whatever it took to make sure that didn't happen.

In order to pursue Brittany, he had to have deep pockets, which he did. And if he played his cards right, which he intended to, then maybe he could leave Angel's fat ass one of these days.

Meanwhile, he didn't intend to let up until Brittany was at least in his bed.

"My, but you're quiet this morning."

"I have a political matter on my mind."

"The federal appointment?"

"Right."

Angel bit into the first roll, then sipped some coffee. "I understand Collier Smith has a leg up in the race. That must really stick in your craw."

Blood rushed into Rupert's face. "Travis Wainwright will get the appointment," he said tersely.

"How can you be so sure?"

"Because I won't have it any other way. I wield as much power in the party as Mason Williams, and Senator Riley owes me a favor, which I intend to collect on this deal." Rupert peered at his watch. "Which reminds me, I'm supposed to meet Travis in my office shortly. He's driving up for a strategy session."

"Good luck," Angel said with her mouth full.

Disgusted, Rupert stood, then turned and walked out of the room. One of these days he was going to walk out of the house and never return.

Fifteen

"Tommy, what's wrong?"

"Nothing," he said in his tight but petulant tone.

Brittany had made her usual midweek phone call to her brother, but the instant she'd heard his voice, she'd known something wasn't right. Since she'd been responsible for Tommy for so many years, she could pick up on the most minute details.

"Something's happened. You can't fool me. Are you sick?"

"No."

A chill darted through her. "Are you in trouble, then?"

"It wasn't my fault." That petulant whine had thickened.

Brittany's heart plummeted. Since he'd been behind bars, Tommy had already had several scrapes with other inmates. After the last one, when he'd been sent to the infirmary, she'd thought he had learned his lesson. Apparently not. She began to wonder if her brother had it in him to become a responsible and polite citizen.

"Tommy, you—"

"Dammit, sis, it wasn't my fault. Why won't you believe me?"

"It doesn't matter what I believe," she responded with

as much calm as possible. "It's what the guards and the warden believe that counts."

Another muffled curse filtered through the line. Brittany bit her lip to keep from making a sharp retort. She didn't need another crisis in her life. For the moment, Collier was enough. Now Tommy had to go and pull another stunt.

"Look, if you don't hold on to your temper, you're going to get badly hurt." Her voice broke, and she paused to regroup. "You know how that thought makes me crazy, how it makes me worry."

"Then get me out of this hellhole, sis."

"Tommy, for god's sake, don't you think I'm trying? I'm working two jobs, going to school and pinching what few pennies I have in order to hire you a decent attorney."

"But that's not going to happen anytime soon," he said bitterly.

A weary sigh escaped. "You're right. I won't lie to you about that."

"If only you had a man. A rich man."

"That's not fair, and you know it." Her voice broke again, this time from rage. How dare he want her to get involved with someone just so he could help him.

"And this *is* fair?"

"Even if I had a man, there's no guarantee he'd be willing to come to your rescue."

"What the hell," Tommy muttered, "you don't have one, so what's the point? Hell, you don't even like men."

"I don't like you when you're in this kind of mood."

"So hang up."

Brittany gritted her teeth, suddenly wanting to get her hands on him and throttle him. But the other side of that coin was that she wanted to put her arms around him and love him. Such a young life, wasting away behind bars. It wasn't fair. Continually beating up on herself, however, wasn't going to solve the problem. If only she had the means of proving Tommy was indeed telling the truth, then maybe...

"Sis?"

"Yes?"

"I got beat up again."

She had a death-grip on the receiver. "Oh, Tommy," she said in a terrified voice, "please, from now on, just mind your own business. Don't do anything that will call attention to yourself. Promise me."

"Sis, you don't understand."

"Promise me!"

"All right already. Just calm down. You're screaming in my ear."

Brittany made a valiant effort to gather her scattered wits. "One of these days, I'm so afraid you're going to get—" Her voice stopped. She couldn't say that word.

"Killed. Even if you can't say it, I can."

"Tommy, please."

"Look, I gotta go. I'll see you this weekend."

"Wait. You never told me how badly you're hurt."

"Does it matter?"

The next sound she heard was the dial tone buzzing in her ear.

After slamming the phone back in its cradle, Brittany folded her arms, bent her head and sobbed. When the crying jag ended, she didn't feel any better, just spent, as if she'd been put through a wringer washing machine.

"Oh, Mamma," she whispered with longing. "If you were here, you'd know what to do. You'd know how to help Tommy."

Her mother, Harriet, had always known what to do

about everything until her drunken stepfather completely broke her spirit. Until then, she'd been the most loving, gentlest person Brittany had ever known.

Despite the fact they were poor, they had never lacked for the essentials—food and clothing. If Harriet had been aware that Cal Rogers was a closet drinker, she wouldn't have married him. She'd told Brittany that over and over, which had been one of her many ways of apologizing for bringing such pain into their lives. But once Harriet had made the commitment, she'd been determined to hang in, to make it work, to change Cal.

Ha.

That never happened. What *had* happened was her mother had finally kicked him out after coming home from work one day and finding him whipping Brittany with a belt. Tommy, just a toddler at the time, had been next in line, cringing in the corner of the kitchen, too terrorized to move.

As long as she breathed, Brittany would never forget the horror of that moment when her mother had walked through the door, dead on her feet after cleaning houses all day. She had run to her mother, blood oozing from her legs from the harsh blows of Cal's belt.

The next day her stepfather was gone, and Brittany never saw him again.

Shuddering, she slid her mind off that awful time and rose to her feet. What a day, but at least it was over. It was time for her bath and bed. But once Brittany's head hit the pillow, she couldn't sleep. For one thing, heavy winds and rain, accompanied by thunder and lightning, pounded the roof and shook the trailer.

That wasn't the real reason, though. Thoughts of Collier and their latest fiasco had plagued her relentlessly. She'd had difficulty concentrating in class and at the agency. Even now, as she lay staring at the dreary ceiling, her face turned crimson.

Mortified. And appalled. Those words best described the feelings churning inside her. If only she hadn't hesitated. But his hand had clamped down on her arm so unexpectedly, so quickly, she hadn't had time to think. Only feel.

Some feeling it was, too.

She wondered what he thought about her?

Placing her hands against her hot cheeks, Brittany moaned. What difference did it make? She would never know. He wouldn't be back. Even though he'd all but denied it, he hadn't wanted to be seen with her in public, at least not in Haven where he lived and worked. She suspected his unofficial fiancée wasn't the only reason. No matter what he said, she wasn't good enough for him.

That cut to the core.

She removed her hands from her face and clutched the sheet.

He wanted a fling.

Any idiot could figure that out, and she was no idiot. Just vulnerable and gullible. And she actually liked him. As screwy as that sounded, it was the truth. She wished circumstances could be different, that he would be interested in her as a person rather than a sex object. Yet she couldn't cry wolf. She was as much to blame as he was.

For the first time in her life, she had the hots for a man.

Brittany whimpered against that unadulterated truth. But she wouldn't deny it. She had wanted him as badly as he'd wanted her. And still did. She could still feel the texture of his skin, smell his sweat, *taste him*. Fighting against the heat and stark misery that washed through her, she turned her face into the pillow and squeezed her eyes shut.

Regardless of the need raging through her, she refused to be used. She didn't want to become any man's side dish.

"We need someone in that firm who's on our side."

Rupert carefully eyed Travis Wainwright, the man from Nashville whom he was backing for the federal appointment, who was occupying the chair in front of his desk.

"That's a solution, for sure," Rupert acknowledged, "but I think going that route's pretty dicey."

Wainwright fiddled with a button on his expensive jacket. "Why? There's bound to be someone there who's willing to be bought."

Rupert pitched his head back and laughed. "You're going to do just fine, my man, just fine and dandy."

Wainwright leaned forward, his full lips thinning unnaturally. "I want this appointment, Rupert. And by all rights I should have it. After all, I have the credentials and the experience. Smith doesn't have either one."

Rupert scowled. "Even if he did, I don't want that bastard to have it."

"So any ideas whose shoulder in the firm we can tap to get us some dirt on Smith? Just a hint of impropriety and Smith's screwed."

Rupert's scowl eased into a chuckle. "Whether he's guilty as charged or not."

"Right. And with him handling that sexual harassment case, which I think is suicidal, he's setting himself up to take a fall. There's bound to be some trash under his rug he'd like to keep hidden."

"Absolutely," Rupert agreed wholeheartedly. "If not his, then his old man's."

"Whatever. Just as long as Senator Riley ends up recommending *me*." Wainwright's heavy chest extended a little further.

"Consider it done, my boy. I think I know just the person." Rupert stood and extended his hand. "Now, you'd best get yourself back on the job and let me do the same."

After giving Wainwright time to leave the premises, Rupert followed suit. A few minutes later he walked through the door of the travel agency. The gods had given him a break. Brittany was working, and she was alone.

"Sissy's not here," Brittany said, her eyes wider than usual.

Fear. That was what he saw. Rupert grimaced inwardly. He would have to do something about that. He'd have to work that much harder to regain her trust. He couldn't stop thinking about her, lusting after her. The idea that she didn't want him with equal lust made him crazy. And more determined than ever to have her.

No one said no to Rupert Holt and got by with it, except his wife. And he didn't want *her*. It had been years since he'd touched Angel except in a perfunctory manner. She had her charities and her church to keep her warm, and that was all right by him.

"I didn't come to see Sissy," Rupert finally responded.

Brittany sat stiff as a block of wood. "I...we don't have anything to say to each other."

He aimed for his usual spot on the edge of the desk and perched there. Although Brittany didn't so much as flinch, she recoiled nonetheless; he could see it in her eyes. Dammit, apparently he had done more damage than he'd thought. But then, he'd been so stinking-ass drunk, he couldn't really remember the details of that night. They remained as fuzzy as a bad nightmare.

"Oh, that's where you're wrong," he countered smoothly. "We have a lot to talk about."

"Your ploy, whatever it is, isn't going to work."

"Why don't you wait till you hear me out?"

She glared at him. "You're wasting your time."

Her unbending attitude fueled his anger, but he suppressed it. He had to go easy, treat her like an injured animal who was gun-shy and ready to bolt. Thank God only the remnants of the blows he'd dealt her remained. Still, she seemed paler than usual. On closer observation, her eyes were slightly swollen, as if she'd been on a crying jag.

He bet that little creep of a brother was responsible.

"Is Tommy in trouble again?"

When he had first started wooing Brittany, getting her to warm up to him, he'd encouraged her to talk about her brother, manufacturing sympathy when she had told him about the boy's plight. Now he had to reinforce that sympathy. If anything would lure her into his bed, it was that no-good half brother of hers.

However distasteful it was for him to help that piece of shit, it would be worth it if Brittany were nice to him again. Thinking about his hands and mouth on her young, ripe body made him ache. Maybe she would even come to like him slapping her around a bit, to enhance the pleasure. He'd become real adept at that, or so he'd been told.

"I don't want to talk about Tommy."

"Sure you do," he countered with ease. "I told you I would help, and I'm willing to do exactly that. All you have to do is say the word and I'll have an attorney out there to talk to him just like that.'' Rupert snapped his fingers, then waited.

He sensed her hesitation rather than saw it. His breathing quickened. She was tempted, which was a start. And while she hadn't yet taken a bite of the carrot, she'd at least leaned toward it. Meanwhile, he had to have some assurance she wasn't going to do anything stupid.

"Please leave,'' she said, hate radiating from her eyes. "And don't come back.''

He forced a smile, then leaned closer. "You know, my offer can work the other way, too.'' He paused for effect. "If you so much as think about ratting on me or stop being nice to me, I can hurt your little brother. Real bad.''

Brittany gasped, her face growing even paler. Before she could make a comeback, however, he turned and walked out.

Sixteen

"I won't take no for an answer."

"Come on, Lana, can't you see I'm up to my ears in work?" Collier flung his hand toward the mess on his desk, emphasizing his point. "I'll take you out on the town another time."

"I'm not asking to go out on the town," she countered dramatically, "only to get a quick cup of coffee, for heaven's sake, on a Friday night. We don't have to go far. There's a diner close by that will have coffee. Please," she continued in a wheedling tone. "I have to tell you, though, I'd much rather have a glass of wine, a wonderful dinner, then a long night in bed." She paused, then toyed with her lower lip. "With you, of course."

"Lana…"

"I know, I know. You have to work."

"I'll make it up to you."

"I know you will—and soon, too. Meanwhile, I'm willing to lower my expectations in order to spend some time with you."

Collier blew out a frustrated breath, leaned back in his chair and stretched. It wouldn't kill him to humor her, he told himself. In fact, it would probably do him good to get out of the office for a while, clear the cobwebs from his brain. So why was he so reluctant to go? Why was he making such a big deal out of such a little thing?

It was Lana herself.

He didn't want to be with her. While that thought didn't make him feel any better about himself, it was the truth. He couldn't tell her that, though. She would think he'd lost his mind, and in truth, he was afraid he had. If he couldn't be with Brittany, then he would just as soon work. Crazy. But then, he'd been thinking like a crazy man lately.

"Collier, you're acting like an ass."

He shook his head to clear it. "You're right, I am."

"So come on, let's hit the road," she quipped, her mood brightening considerably. "It's not often I'm in the treating mood."

Collier stood, reached for his sports jacket and slipped into it. "This has to be a quickie. I go to trial in a few days."

"Speaking of trial," Lana said with a frown, "Daddy's not happy about you taking that harassment case."

"That's too bad," Collier responded, letting his irritation show.

"Since I obviously stepped on a nerve," she said in an equally irritated tone, "we'll finish this conversation over our coffee. Maybe a shot of caffeine will put you in a better frame of mind."

Don't count on it, he almost said, then caught himself. Lana was right. He was acting like an ass, and she hadn't done anything to deserve his ill-humor. Except bug the hell out of him, of course. Maybe he should end things between them tonight, he told himself, his emotions skidding off into uncharted waters. Then sanity reasserted itself. What was the matter with him? He cared deeply for Lana. He must. He planned to marry her, make a home and family with her.

Brittany was just a sexual fantasy, a sexual rush that would soon fade. Sex alone was never enough glue to hold any relationship together.

"You're awfully quiet," Lana commented after they were in her car and she was skillfully maneuvering her Jag down the street. "Still nursing your foul mood?"

He cut her a lopsided smile, feeling more put out with himself by the second. "You're not about to cut me any slack, are you?"

"Should I?"

"Nope."

She giggled, then reached over and trailed her long red nails teasingly up his leg. "I can't believe you won't forget about work for a little while and come home with me. I can't even remember the last time we fucked."

He flinched at her use of that crude word, something that had never seemed to bother him before, since it was a regular part of her vocabulary. "Lana, how 'bout giving it a rest?"

"One of these days you're going to tell me that and I'm going to tell you to go fuck yourself."

"Maybe a cup of coffee will put *you* in a better mood."

Lana killed the engine, then cut her gaze toward him. "No matter how much of an ass you are, I'd never leave you."

Collier leaned over, kissed her on the cheek, then muttered, "Let's go get drunk on coffee."

Although he was certainly no connoisseur of diners—he could count the times he'd been in one on a single hand—this one seemed incredibly busy. They had to sit in a dingy far corner.

Perhaps that was why he didn't see her right off. When he did, he visibly sucked in his breath and held it. He knew he must look like someone had hit him in the gut with a crowbar.

Brittany? Here? Dressed in a uniform? Waiting on tables? So this was the diner where she worked part-time. Had Fate sent him here? He shut his eyes, then opened them again.

She was no illusion. She was here, in the flesh, across the room, taking some guy's order. And looking as lovely as he'd ever seen her look. But weary, as if she could drop on her feet at any moment. He swallowed the hot bile that rose up the back of his throat.

"Collier, what on earth's the matter with you?" Lana hissed, reaching out and clasping his hand. "You're not having an attack of some sort, are you?"

He twisted his head and stared at Lana, only it was Brittany's face and body that filled his vision. "What did you say?"

"Oh, for chrissake, you heard me."

"I'm fine."

"Could've fooled me," Lana said with sarcasm.

He forced his gaze to stay off Brittany. That was the only way he was going to keep his emotions in check. Thank God she wouldn't have to wait on them. He didn't think he could have handled that.

"What made you go berserk all of a sudden?" Lana asked, unwilling to let the matter drop.

Good question. He had known Brittany waited on tables on weekends. She'd told him that. And there was nothing wrong with that, per se. It was a perfectly legitimate and decent job. Just not for Brittany.

"Collier, the waitress is here," Lana said, not bothering to disguise her impatience.

"Uh, I'll have just coffee, please. Black."

"I'll have some cappuccino."

Once their waitress had shuffled off, Lana narrowed her eyes on him. "Don't ever scare me like that again. I swear I thought you were having a heart attack, or worse."

"Sorry."

Lana gave him an incredulous look. "Is that all you have to say?"

"Yes." Collier didn't blink. "I'm okay, so let's just drop it."

Lana tightened her lips, which meant she wasn't happy and would like to pitch one of the tantrums that usually got her what she wanted, at least from her father. But he wasn't her father, and she seemed to know just how far she could push.

Forcing his mind off Brittany and the fact that she was within touching distance, only he couldn't touch her, he forced himself to say the first thing that came to mind.

"So your dad's not happy I'm defending that energy company executive." Collier really didn't give a shit what her father thought, but he knew that sooner or later she would get around to reopening that can of worms, so he might as well get it over with. Too, it was something to talk about, something to get his mind off Brittany.

And pigs fly.

"Not at all. In fact, he asked me to ask you to reconsider."

"Can't do that."

"Yes, you can. Your firm can do anything it wants and get by with it."

"That's a crock, and you know it."

"What if it blows up in your face? What if you lose? That's what concerns Daddy."

"I won't lose," Collier replied with much more confidence than he felt. "If it's any consolation, Mason feels the same way, but I've made a commitment, and I'm going to honor it.''

"Even if the man you're defending is a grab-ass scumbag?''

"That hasn't been proven,'' Collier said coldly.

"Yeah, right,'' she snapped.

Their coffee arrived at that moment. When Collier looked up at the waitress and smiled, he caught a glimpse of Brittany. She was staring at him. He wanted to shift his gaze, pretend he didn't see her, *didn't recognize her,* but he couldn't.

He did see her. He did recognize her. And he still wanted her. It had been days since that episode in the car, and he'd hoped that some of his frantic, tangled emotions concerning her would have abated. That hadn't happened.

And to make matters worse, she had seen him. And was returning his stare with a shocked look on her face. As their eyes held from across the room, he could barely breathe.

Brittany was the first to shift her gaze, but not before giving Lana the once-over. Then, with a look of contempt on her face, she turned her back. It was all he could do not to bolt out of the booth, close the distance between them and grab her.

Then what?

"Your coffee's getting cold.''

Collier swung back around and forced himself to pay attention to Lana.

Brittany's heart was pounding, and her hands were shaking so hard she could barely carry the empty tray back to have it refilled. She couldn't believe he was here, in the diner, of all places.

Impossible.

Of course it was. Her mind had merely conjured him up. She eased her eyes back around. He was there, parked in a booth in life-size reality. In truth, she had noticed him the second he'd walked in. She just hadn't wanted to admit it. A person couldn't miss him. *Or her.* They stood out like sore thumbs in this place.

Brittany closed her eyes for a second, trying to regain her composure. Why in heaven's name had they chosen Sam's Diner? Although it wasn't a dump, it was no first-class joint, either, not by any stretch of the imagination. Certainly not a place that either one of *them* would be likely to frequent.

So why was he here?

A wave of panic upped her heart rate another notch. Had he chosen to come here because of her? Had he somehow found out she worked at this particular diner? Once those thoughts darted through her mind, she realized how absurd they were, how ludicrous. He didn't care enough about her to poke that deeply into her personal life.

He only cared about her body, she reminded herself painfully.

If she'd had her choice, she would have just disappeared on the spot. But she didn't have a choice. She had to have this job. Collier Smith wasn't worth losing it over. She would simply have to do what she'd done so many times in the past when confronted with awful situations. Suck it up and endure.

Get through it.

She could chalk up this invasion of her territory as one of those freakish coincidences that just happened and wouldn't ever happen again. However, getting through it was going to be tough, especially with his unofficial fi-ancée in tow.

Looks. Class. Money. The list could go on. She had it all, but then, so did Collier. They were a different breed from her and the rest of the patrons in the diner. In fact, the beautiful couple had become the center of attention, especially the woman. Out of one corner of her eye Brittany saw some of the men rubber-necking, their mouths slightly gaping, as if they were salivating.

Trying to ignore the envy pinching her stomach, first that Collier was with the other woman, and second because she was so lovely, Brittany quickly averted her gaze.

"'Bout damn time you got here to git the grub."

The cook's harsh voice refocused her attention, and she reached for the plates, though her hands remained far from steady. By the time she made it back to the table, her customer was glaring at her.

Oh dear, she'd seen that look before, and it wasn't good.

"Lady, what the hell took you so long?" the man bellowed.

Brittany cringed inwardly before responding in a low, tense voice, "I'm sorry, sir."

"Well, I ain't eatin' no cold shit." His voice grew louder.

"I'll be happy to take care of the problem if you don't like it." She could smell the liquor on his breath and suspected he was half-drunk. She knew every eye in the diner was stuck on her.

"Damn straight you will."

"I'll wait while you check it," she said, holding her tone as low as possible.

He picked up the piece of chicken with his large, beefy

fingers, then bit into it. Instantly he threw it down, then spat it out. "Not only is it cold, the sonofabitch ain't done."

Horrified at the sudden turn of events, Brittany reached for the plate. That was when it happened. The man chose that moment to slam the glass he was holding down on the table, shattering it.

"Oh!" she cried, jumping back, but not soon enough. A piece of glass pierced the top of her hand, and blood spurted. Feeling sick, Brittany quickly stuck her hand down in her apron pocket.

"You bastard, you owe the lady here an apology."

Brittany gasped, then lifted horrified eyes to Collier, who was looming over the man like a thundercloud ready to erupt.

"Please, Collier," Brittany pleaded in a tight voice, "go back and sit down. It's all right."

"The hell it is," he spat, his eyes still on the man, who was cowering against the back of the booth.

The owner suddenly stepped into the picture, his eyes on Collier. "Is there a problem, sir?"

"You bet there is. This man—"

Brittany interrupted Collier. "Don't worry about me, Winston," she pleaded in a trembling voice. "We need to get my customer some more food."

"We can take care of that," Winston said, his gaze still on Collier, clearly intimidated by Collier's presence and the cold fury that emanated from him.

"Please, Collier," Brittany pleaded again, for his ears only.

"Dammit," he snapped. "You're bleeding."

Brittany followed Collier's eyes and saw that her pocket was stained crimson. The sight of her own blood was almost her undoing. To keep from fainting, she took several deeps breaths.

That was when she felt Collier's hand encircle her arm. "I'm taking you to the emergency room."

"No, let me go."

"Brittany," Winston ordered in a contrite tone, "go to the washroom and take care of that. I'll handle things here."

Before Collier could argue, Brittany pulled free of his hold, turned on wobbly legs and walked away.

Seventeen

"I'll see that you get inside."

Brittany shook her head at Winston Tanner, who looked as uncomfortable as a fish out of water. "Thanks, but I can make it. I'm just fine. The doctor fixed me right up."

"Are you sure?" he asked anxiously, his thin face appearing even thinner under the streetlight.

She forced a smile. "I appreciate you taking me to the emergency room. You didn't have to do that."

"Yup, I did. And I'll get your car back to you, too." He shoved a hand over his balding head, then rubbed his day's growth of whiskers. "You aren't planning on suing me, are you?"

Brittany blinked. "Sue you? Whatever for?"

"You got hurt in my place, that's what for."

"But it wasn't your fault. That man was drunk. There's nothing else to say."

"I'm sure there's a lot more," Winston added glumly, "but I'm glad you ain't saying it."

Brittany reached over and patted his arm. "I'm just glad you're not firing me."

"Lordy, that thought never crossed my mind."

"Well, then we're even." She made herself smile. "Thanks again for taking care of me. I'll see you later."

That conversation had taken place a little over an hour

ago, and Brittany still hadn't been able to settle down. She'd had to take a sponge bath, because of the bandage on her hand. But thank goodness the cut hadn't been as bad as she'd first thought. Even so, if she'd had her way, she wouldn't have gone to the hospital. But when Winston had come to the back and taken a look at her hand, he'd ordered her to climb in his pickup.

The doctor hadn't stitched the wound, because it was more of a puncture than a cut. Still, she had lost a lot of blood, and it hurt like the devil. But at the moment, more than anything, she was exhausted.

Before that animal had pitched a fit about his food, business had been booming. The cool, crisp evening seemed to have brought the customers out in numbers. As a rule, Friday nights were busy, but not that busy.

Until the unfortunate incident, she hadn't been complaining. She'd made a lot of money in tips, which was the reason she was there. Her male customers, especially her regulars, tended to tip generously. The guy who broke the glass was a stranger; he'd never been in the diner before.

But then, neither had Collier.

Groaning, Brittany plopped down on the sofa and closed her eyes. His image wouldn't go away. She still couldn't believe he'd been there. More unbelievable was that he'd witnessed the incident.

She had never been so embarrassed, not because of what had happened, but again because Collier had been there. Cranky, out-of-sorts customers were common in the diner. She was used to dealing with them, even the belligerent ones. What she wasn't used to dealing with was having someone around whom she cared about.

Forbidden fruit.

That was how she saw Collier, and she was oh, so

tempted to take a bite. But she'd never get the chance. Even if he'd entertained the notion of seeing her again, tonight would have nixed that.

A waitress. Come on. He was more than likely thanking his lucky stars he'd walked in and blindsided her. Yet he hadn't pretended not to know her, which earned him high marks. He could have just ignored the brouhaha and not stepped in. Even so, she couldn't afford to attach any significance to his actions.

He remained forbidden fruit.

Forbidden fruit or not, he'd made her aware of her sexuality as no other man ever had. She'd never really enjoyed having a man's hands on her body; she had more or less endured. Not so with Collier. He had shown her what making love was supposed to be like between a man and woman.

And when he'd charged to her rescue in the diner, that sexual high had kicked in once again, despite her pain and embarrassment. For a second, she'd wanted to give in and let him take control, take care of her. But that second had passed quickly, especially after she saw the look in his eyes. He'd been ready to tear that creep from limb to limb.

Which would have bought him a trip to the police station.

Still, it had made her proud that he'd wanted to defend her, for whatever reason. But that feeling, too, had been short-lived when she remembered he was with a woman, obviously the woman he intended to marry.

Unwanted tears slipped from under Brittany's closed lashes. She brushed them aside, knowing that wallowing in self-pity and what-might-have-beens would be futile.

Like it or not, she had to move on.

* * *

"Are you upset with me?"

"Of course not. Why would you think that?"

"Because you haven't said two words since we left that place." Lana gave an angry toss of her head, which sent her long hair swishing across her face.

Collier was still in her car, though they were back at his office, where he'd been trying to get out of the Jag for a while now but without success.

"It's been a long day," he responded in a tired voice. "And remember, I still have work to do." He realized that was a lousy excuse, but it was the best he could do at the moment. That pile of papers on his desk was the furthest thing from his mind, and he had no intention of looking at them anymore tonight.

Lana didn't have to know that, though. He just wanted her to leave him be. But, unwilling to be rude and send her off with hurt feelings, he'd held his tongue. However, his patience was fast dissolving.

"You're pissed because I took you to that dump." Her words were a flat statement of fact as she peered at him from under long lashes, thickened with mascara.

"You know better than that."

"Well, it was an experience, anyway." She smiled, then rolled her eyes. "What a creep that guy was. And that poor waitress. If that had been me, I'd have taken the plate and tossed that pile of crap in his fat face."

"It was all I could do not to put my fist in his fat face."

Lana was quiet for a moment, then she said in a strained voice, "You know that woman, don't you?"

He didn't respond.

"I kept waiting for you to say something about the incident, about her, but so far, you haven't."

"There's nothing to say," he said in a clipped tone. "You saw everything that went down."

"Right, but I still get the feeling I'm missing something."

He leaned over and kissed her lightly on the lips. "Forget it. It was just a bad experience. Go home, take a bath and crawl into bed."

She ran the tip of her tongue across her lower lip in a provocative manner. "So how 'bout you joining me later, darling? Crawl into my bed with me." She repeated the movement. "Daddy's out of town. First we could indulge ourselves in a bottle of champagne, then play a while in the hot tub…" Lana let her voice trail off.

Collier got the message, but he wasn't biting. At one time, before Brittany, he would've taken her up on her offer in a heartbeat. Now he could barely stand to touch her or be touched by her in return. What had he done to himself? What had he gotten himself into?

"Another time."

"Damn you, Collier. You're turning into a real bastard."

He got out of the car, then turned and peered back at her. "Take care."

"And you go to hell!" She jammed the car in gear and spun off, leaving a trail of rubber behind.

Collier didn't wait for her lights to disappear before he dashed to his vehicle, jumped in and took off. He had to get to Brittany. He had to assure himself she was all right, that she'd taken care of that nasty cut. Dammit, he should already have been there instead of humoring Lana.

What he *should* have done was take her to the hospital.

Furious with himself, Collier pounded the steering wheel with a fist, then released a shuddering breath. He knew what he was doing was not smart. A sudden and bitter laugh erupted from his throat. When had he done anything smart of late? He had no business whatsoever showing up at her door.

He didn't even know if she would let him in, although it wasn't all that late. No matter, he had to try to see her. Where Brittany was concerned, it was as if his emotions were on a feeding frenzy. He couldn't stay away from her, and when he was with her, he couldn't keep his hands off her.

Cool it, he told himself, feeling the blood literally pound in his temples, fearing he was going to have a stroke. But when he'd seen that blood on her apron, he'd gone berserk. If the owner hadn't been standing in his way, he would have jerked that big, beefy guy out of his booth and rearranged his ugly face.

He didn't get mad often, but when he did, he didn't always think straight, which had been the case tonight. In one way, he was thankful the owner had been in between. In another, he was sorry he hadn't gotten the extreme pleasure of teaching that piece of scum a lesson.

Another bitter laugh erupted. He could see the headlines now. God, his dad would have had a heart attack. As to the federal appointment—well, he could have kissed that goodbye.

Was Brittany worth that?

Sweat poured off him, though it was chilly both inside and outside the vehicle. He should turn around and head home. No, he should turn around and head to Lana's. At least, with her, he recognized himself. When he was around Brittany, he became a different person, someone he didn't know.

Suddenly he longed for his old rational self, the rat race of the life he had grown comfortable with, had come to depend on. Yet the thought of not seeing Brittany again was unthinkable.

Collier wiped the sweat off his brow seconds before he pulled against the curb in front of her trailer house. It appeared she was at home and not in the hospital. Lights were on. Shouldn't that satisfy him? Absolutely. All he had to do was put the car in Drive and go.

No way.

While the lights gave him some comfort, he couldn't settle down until he saw her face-to-face. Feeling like a foreign substance was stuck in his throat, he got out and walked up the rickety steps, then knocked on the door.

And waited.

Eighteen

Brittany opened her eyes with a start, her widened gaze quickly surveying the room. Something had awakened her, though she hadn't even realized she'd fallen asleep. She sat still and waited to see if she heard the sound again.

A knock. Someone was at her door.

Was it...? Her heart raced with excitement. Stop it! Don't set yourself up for more pain. Of course it wasn't him. More than likely Collier was making love to his lady friend about now. She winced at that thought, then put it out of her mind. Winston had probably returned to check on her.

Then her heart raced with fear. What if it was the man who had pitched a hissy fit at the diner? It wasn't him, either, she told herself, irritated with this stupid game she was playing. He didn't have a clue where she lived. Besides, he was probably passed out in his car or some alley.

Simple solution. Why didn't she just get up, go to the door and find out who was there?

"Brittany?"

Her heart stopped along with her legs. Just hearing his voice and knowing he was on the other side of the door filled her with both renewed excitement and sheer panic. Calm down, she told herself. She had to stop making mountains out of molehills. He might not even opt to come in. He might just have stopped by to check on her.

Still, that was something, much more than she'd ever thought he'd do.

Once her knees had quit knocking, she closed the distance to the door and grasped the handle. "Collier?" She had no idea why she said his name, maybe to buy herself more time to get a grip on her emotions.

"May I come in?" He paused. "Or would you rather I didn't?"

Loaded question.

"It's okay," she said, realizing she had on the same robe she'd had on the other time he'd surprised her. Naked underneath. Should she go change?

"Brittany?"

She heard the urgency in his voice and decided it made no difference one way or the other what she had on. Nothing had changed. He'd already seen her body. *And touched it.* Thrusting those memories aside, as well, she took a shuddering breath and unbolted the door.

"Are you all right?" he asked right off, his eyes traveling over her body before coming back to meet her gaze.

As always, they stared at each other for several precious seconds before sanity seemed to return and jolt them back to reality.

"Come in," Brittany said in a breathless tone, feeling hot all over, as if the heat from his eyes had scorched her body. As much as she would have liked to deny what was happening between them, make it go away for her own peace of mind, she couldn't.

If only she could look at him and not see him naked.

She shut the door behind him, then leaned against it for support. He took two steps and swung around, his features tormented. He looked as if he'd been the one who'd gotten hurt, not her. His hair was mussed. He needed a shave. And the lines around his incredible eyes were deeper. He'd gotten rid of his tie, which left his shirt open at the neck, exposing a sprinkling of dark, crisp hairs. What would it be like to run her hands through them?

"You never told me if you were all right."

"Can't you see I'm okay?" she responded in that same breathless tone.

"What happened after I left the diner?"

She hesitated, hating to tell him she had gone to the E.R. She didn't know why, except it might make him feel bad because he hadn't taken her. Even though he shouldn't be here, and they both knew it, she didn't want him to feel bad about anything. She wasn't his worry or responsibility. Just because they had an unspoken craving for each other's bodies, that didn't mean they had to include the rest of the package.

"Brittany?"

"Winston, the owner, took me to the E.R.," she reluctantly admitted.

His features contorted that much more. "Dammit, I knew I should've gone with my gut."

"How would you have explained that?"

Though softly spoken, her pointed words hit their target. He lost what little color remained in his face. "That would've been my problem," he muttered harshly.

She didn't respond.

"How badly were you cut?"

"Puncture wound, actually. No stitches."

"Thank God." Collier paused and shoved a hand through his hair, leveling his pain-filled eyes on her once again.

"Hey, stop beating up on yourself." She forced a

smile, though it was weak, at best. She yearned to reassure him that she was okay, but short of physically touching him—which she couldn't let herself do—there didn't seem to be a way. "You came to my rescue, and I'm grateful."

"If I could've gotten my hands on that scumbag, I—"

"Don't, Collier," she pleaded, stepping closer.

"It's just that I can't stand the thought of any man ever damaging your lovely skin again."

"Why did you come here?" she whispered, almost choking on the words.

Several heartbeats later, he said, "I couldn't stay away."

"Oh, Collier…"

"Please don't send me away," he said in a broken voice, stopping just short of begging.

Later, she didn't know how it had happened. Perhaps her trembling legs simply refused to support her any longer. She only knew his arms were around her and they were clinging to each other as if they would never let go.

"Oh, Brittany, Brittany," he whispered, showering her face with tiny, moist kisses before claiming her mouth in a deep, long one, his tongue seeking, then mating with hers.

Lust. Gift wrapped in pure magic.

She thought her lungs were going to rupture from the sheer ecstasy hitting her in waves. She didn't care if she never saw him again after tonight. She intended to make the most of their time together, of *him*, and savor it for a lifetime.

"I want you," he rasped. "I've always wanted you."

His hands had untied her robe and were wandering over her body, lingering long enough in all the right places to force a cry from deep within her.

But it was when a hand settled between her legs and two fingers slid inside her wet warmth that she went into a frenzy. She crushed her mouth to his, then latched onto his lower lip, sucking it.

"Touch me," he begged.

Without waiting for her to take the initiative, he grasped her hand and placed it on his crotch. For an instant Brittany's fingers remained still; she was filled with the breathless wonder that she was actually touching him *there*. But her inactivity didn't last long. He was already rock-hard, and she began to rub him with her palm before taking the liberty of unzipping his slacks.

A deep moan erupted from him and his eyes glazed over as she continued to massage his erection, especially the tip, where droplets of moisture wet her fingers.

"Oh, Brittany!"

Her name seemed ripped from him as he grabbed her and sank to the floor. Without removing his clothes, he eased her back on the worn carpet, spread her robe and knelt over her. With his hands covering her breasts, he parted her legs and thrust high and deep inside her.

They both froze.

The exquisite shock of their bodies finally coming together rendered them useless for a moment. Then, with his dazed eyes locked on hers, Collier began to move fast and with raging intensity. Every nerve, every muscle in her responded to his desperate hunger.

Seconds later, their cries penetrated the silence simultaneously.

Just watching her sleep stirred his sexual appetite.

Propping himself up on one arm, Collier soaked up every detail of her lovely face, long swanlike neck, creamy shoulders and breasts. But it was her nipples peeping above the sheet that brought him to another slow boil. They were perfectly rounded and rosebud pink.

He was tempted to lean over and lick them, then take them between his lips and suck until they were pebble-hard. He shifted, his erection making him uncomfortable. She was sleeping so peacefully, he hated to disturb her.

After they had made love on the floor, he'd carried her to the bed, where he'd pulled her against his chest and held her. She'd gone to sleep almost instantly. Rest was what she needed. She'd been through so much lately, the assault and near-rape, then the wound to her hand.

She also continued to hold down two jobs and go to school. She was bound to be exhausted. His heart went out to her, but realistically, there wasn't anything he could do to change her circumstances.

She wasn't his responsibility. But if she was, and he could change things, would he? He held his breath for a moment while that thought took on a life of its own. The idea of sharing a home with Brittany, of waking up in the same bed with her every morning, was actually chilling.

Horrifying.

Yet wonderfully enticing.

Impossible.

Although their lovemaking on the floor had been quick and desperate, it was the most incredible sex he'd ever had. He had no qualms admitting that. Still, sex was all it was. Sooner than later that would cease to be enough, especially when so much was at stake: his career, *his life*.

A night's romp in the sheets wasn't worth that.

Lana. A groan escaped him. The fact that he wasn't ready to commit himself to her for life didn't mean he could deliberately and continually cheat on her. He could excuse tonight. He'd acted on pure, hot adrenaline, appeasing the raw hunger that had turned him into a wild man.

But when he walked out of this trailer, he'd be a wise man not to return. He'd had his dose of Brittany Banks, and that would have to suffice.

"What are you thinking about?"

The sound of her soft, raspy voice gave him a start. "So you're awake."

"Did you sleep?" she asked in an almost shy tone.

"No. I watched you."

Her face was bathed in color. "Oh."

Collier chuckled. "I can't believe you're blushing."

Her color deepened. "I'm not."

"Sure you are," he responded with a tenderness he'd never felt for another woman. But there was something about Brittany that tapped that emotion inside him, made him want to protect her, shield her from further pain and heartache.

Including him.

Still, he ached to know everything there was to know about her, what her hobbies were, what she liked to eat, what she liked to read. He wanted to buy her nice things, rid her closet of all those inexpensive clothes, dress her in the finest the stores had to offer. He wanted to shower her with the finest in jewelry, as well, and he pictured diamond studs in her small earlobes.

Everything. He wanted it all. Therein lay the danger. The more he knew, the more he wanted to know, which made it impossible to walk away.

"What time is it?" she asked.

He peered into her sweet upturned face. "Time for me to go," he said heavily.

"Don't. Please."

Following her strangled plea, she reached up, pulled

his head down, then fluttered her lips against his, sucking the tip of his tongue, then biting her way across his neck.

"Don't stop!" Her unexpected touch was like gasoline on an open flame. A deep burn spread through him, and in one swift move he rolled her on top of him, lifting her so that her softness swallowed his hardness with perfect precision. As he placed his hands on her breasts, they began to move, slowly at first, once again savoring the fact their bodies were united, then faster, the friction building to an unbelievable pitch.

"Oh, yes, Brittany!" he cried out.

She answered his cry at the same time he spilled his seed into her. A hard shudder followed; then she collapsed on top of him.

Rupert had noticed the vehicle when he'd pulled up and parked on the dark, deserted street across from Brittany's trailer. Was she entertaining? If so, male or female? It was hard to tell, though, if the visitor was even hers. The homes were jammed so closely together in the park that cars were always lining the curb. Still, he'd never seen a Lexus there before, and it made him uneasy, though he knew Brittany wasn't seeing a man.

He would know it if she were.

Since he couldn't have her in his bed, watching her comings and goings at odd hours had become one of his greatest pleasures. And obsessions. He didn't know how long he'd been here this particular evening—several hours, for sure, though he'd obviously dozed off for part of that time.

That must have been when the car arrived.

Now he had no alternative but to wait. Until he knew whether the overnight guest belonged to Brittany, he wasn't budging, even though daylight was threatening to peep over the horizon.

The thought of anyone else making a move on Brittany made his blood curdle. She belonged to him. He wasn't about to let anyone come along and take his place. He had plans for her. For *them*.

Rupert shivered suddenly, the chilly air from outside finally making its way inside. Rather than crank the engine and turn on the heat, he reached for the bottle beside him and took another generous sip. He hadn't been able to drink much lately. Too dangerous. He'd had a lot going on at the office that demanded his undivided attention.

Also, no one must suspect his love affair with the bottle.

Closing his bleary eyes, he savored the feel of the booze invading his system. It was only after he finally opened his eyes again that he noticed the Lexus had pulled away from the curb, its taillights winking back at him.

"Sonofabitch," he muttered.

If the owner of that vehicle had been at Brittany's, he'd missed seeing him or her leave. There would be another time, he told himself. If Brittany was cheating on him, he'd find out.

The booze suddenly soured in his stomach. He opened the door and upchucked.

Nineteen

Haley Bishop ran her finger around the rim of her cup and stared out the window at the tall trees drenched in their coat of multicolored leaves.

"What's bugging you, darling?"

Haley gave her mother, Odessa, a less than enthusiastic smile. "Oh, just stuff."

She had dropped by her mom's house just for a second to check on her and grab a quick cup of Odessa's delicious hot chocolate. For so long Haley had been robbed of that pleasure, since she'd worked and lived out of town. But now that she'd returned to Haven, her mother's house and goodies were readily accessible.

Haley knew Odessa was delighted she had returned, especially as Odessa had not being feeling well, her weak heart acting up. Still, Odessa wasn't sickly, not by any means. Tall, with more gray in her hair than red, she was an older version of her daughter. And almost as active, too, Haley thought with relief. Only when she had a spell with her heart did Odessa slow down. For someone in her late seventies, that was a blessing.

"What kind of stuff?" Odessa asked into the lengthening silence, her gaze pinned on her daughter.

Haley shrugged her slender shoulders. "You know, just life."

"Haley Elizabeth Bishop, stop beating around the rosebush. Out with it, child."

Even though Haley was thirty-five, Odessa still referred to her as a child. But then, she guessed that was how mothers were. She wouldn't know, she reminded herself sadly, never having had that pleasure.

"That sigh proves something is bearing heavily on your mind," Odessa commented. "Is it your work?"

Haley picked up on the anxious note in her mother's tone and hastened to reassure her. "Absolutely not. I love my new job. But what I love more is not being on the road. Now that I'm head adjuster, it's the people under me who have to hit the highways."

"You have no idea how relieved I am about that. I worried about you every minute." Odessa paused, taking a sip of her chocolate. "So if it's not work, then what?"

Haley let go of a deep sigh. "I went to see Jackson the other day."

"Jackson Williams?"

"Do you know another Jackson, Mom?" Haley asked.

"No."

Her mother's lips had narrowed. "Oops. You don't approve."

Odessa put down her cup. "I didn't say that."

Haley smiled. "You didn't have to."

"He broke your heart," Odessa pointed out in a soft but concerned tone.

"That he did," Haley said flatly. "Though in truth, part of that was my fault."

"Has there been any change in his condition?"

Another sigh. "Unfortunately, no."

"Haley, dear, talk to me. Stop making me use tweezers to pull out what's bothering you."

Still Haley hesitated, perusing the cheerful kitchen and

breakfast nook done in yellow, green and white. Such a wonderful, cheery room, filled with light and hope. "He…he seems so lost, so depressed, sitting in that awful chair." Her voice cracked, and for a moment she couldn't go on.

Odessa reached over and placed her hand on top of Haley's. "I'm so sorry, honey."

"I know, Mom. So am I. I just wish I could help him."

"As a friend only?"

The question took her aback and made her think. "I don't know. Perhaps I still love him."

Odessa put pressure on her hand while her eyes turned troubled. "Don't confuse pity with love. That's never a good thing for the person on the pity end."

"Don't you think I know that? It's just that when I saw him, something inside me changed. I…felt like I'd come home."

"Dear—"

"I know what you're thinking, that I've lost my mind, that he's no longer a whole man and won't ever be. But that didn't seem to matter to me." Haley paused, her mouth taking a downward slant. "Besides, I've never found anyone else."

"Oh, honey, that's no reason to think you won't. You're so young."

"Mom, I'm thirty-five."

Odessa rolled her eyes. "And that's old?"

"It is if you want to have a—" Haley stopped midsentence, feeling the color drain from her face.

"A baby. Was that what you were going to say?"

Tears clogged Haley's throat. She could only nod.

"Oh, honey," Odessa said again in a distressed voice, "that's all the more reason why you can't…shouldn't get involved with Jackson except as a friend. Somewhere out there is Mr. Right. You wait and see.''

''What if it's Jackson?'' Haley maintained stubbornly.

The lines on Odessa's face deepened. ''What was his reaction to you?''

''Pissed off.''

If her mother was shocked by her choice of words, she didn't show it. Haley suspected she was too upset by this entire conversation to worry about one word. No doubt her mother wanted her to marry and have a family. What mother didn't? But she knew Odessa would never make her feel badly one way or the other. She'd always been supportive of whatever Haley undertook. That was why Haley had ended up spilling her heart to her, something she hadn't planned on doing.

''He wasn't glad to see me,'' Haley added into the silence, ''but he didn't kick me out.''

''I wouldn't think so,'' Odessa said in a slightly mollified tone.

''I'm going back, though.''

''Do you think that's smart?''

''No, but it's something I have to do. I have to figure out some way to get him out of that room, out of that shell he's built around himself.'' Haley balled her fists. ''He's wasting his life.''

''But it's his life,'' Odessa reminded her softly.

Haley's chin lifted defiantly. ''Maybe not. Maybe he just thinks because he's a prisoner of that chair, he has no choice.''

A deep sigh escaped Odessa. ''Oh, Haley, darling, you were always an impetuous child. As an adult…well, you haven't changed all that much.''

Haley gave her head a shake. ''Don't worry, Mom, I'm not about to do anything stupid.''

"Since when?"

Seeing the mischievous twinkle in Odessa's eyes, Haley felt herself relax, then chuckle. "If the shoe fits, wear it. Right?"

"Right.

They both laughed, which seemed to take the heaviness out of the air.

"Finish your chocolate," Odessa ordered gently. "It's bound to be getting cold."

Haley downed the last little bit, then licked her lips. "I'd forgotten just how good that was." She paused, another shadow crossing her face. "Jackson always loved your hot chocolate."

"Yes, he did," Odessa responded lightly, getting up and taking their cups to the sink.

"Would you mind if I brought him here?"

Odessa hesitated, which told Haley what she needed to know. Her stomach bottomed out. She could never become seriously involved with anyone her mother didn't approve of. She just couldn't. They were too close. Yet she couldn't live her life entirely by Odessa's standards, either. She had always been too stubborn, too strong-willed, for that.

So what was the answer? Should she leave Jackson alone? Was her mother right? Was she only interfering where she wasn't wanted, ultimately doing more harm than good? After all, there were so many more complicated factors than him just sitting in that room—his manhood, for one.

"When you get quiet, something's amiss," Odessa said, turning around and leaning against the counter.

"Mom!"

"It's the truth. It was never wise to turn my back on you. Your father never let me forget that, either."

Odessa's eyes turned dreamy for a second. "He absolutely adored you."

"And I adored him," Haley said. "And, like you, not a day goes by that I don't miss him."

Walter Bishop had succumbed to cancer a number of years ago. Although her mother had had several opportunities to remarry, she hadn't, maintaining that if she couldn't have Walter, she didn't want anyone.

Haley had felt much the same, positive no one could ever take her daddy's place. Perhaps that was why she'd never married. She was looking for someone with the same qualities as her beloved dad. Jackson had come close, only he hadn't asked her to marry him.

If only...

"Haley?"

She shook her head. "Yeah, Mom?"

"I'm not trying to rush you, but isn't it time you went to work?"

"Oh my God!" Haley yelped, peering at her watch. "That's an understatement." Even though she wasn't on a time clock, she had no intention of taking advantage of her new position. And strolling in an hour late would definitely be taking advantage.

"See you soon." Haley kissed her mom on the cheek, grabbed her purse and dashed for the door. "Thanks for the morning treat."

"Haley?"

Odessa's soft but firm voice pulled her up short. She swung around, and her heart sank. Her mother suddenly looked old and frail. Was their conversation responsible? She opened her mouth, but nothing came out.

"I just don't..." Odessa's voice seemed to just fade away.

"Oh, Mom, don't you worry, you hear? Jackson probably won't let me get near him again, even if I wanted to.''

"I don't want you to stay away from him, my dear," Odessa countered in a chastising tone. "I just don't want you to try to run his life."

Suddenly Haley laughed, then sobered. "Yes, ma'am."

"Go on, child, and get to work before I turn you over my knee." Odessa smiled and pointed a finger at her. "Don't think you'll ever get too old for that."

Haley blew her a kiss and walked out the door, knowing she should take her mother's advice. But she wasn't about to. If ever anyone had ever needed someone to run his life, it was Jackson Williams.

And she was definitely up to the task.

Collier stood at the window of his office and stared out. The longer he stood there, the sicker he became.

Picketers.

Women picketers, at that, picketing against *him*. Collier closed his eyes and rubbed his forehead, but when he opened them, the demonstrators hadn't gone away, nor had his headache. Man, but he was a mess—a pounding head and an upset stomach.

Kyle had been the one who had alerted him. Collier had been poring over another case, since he wasn't due in court on the harassment case today. The judge was ill with the flu.

"Have you looked outside?" Kyle had demanded, charging in.

"No, why?" Collier had asked, irritated at being disturbed.

"Take a look-see."

"Why can't you just tell me, dammit? I'm up to my ass in work here."

"You need to see for yourself," Kyle had said, his tone insistent.

It was then that Collier realized his investigator was upset, that his face was drawn tight. Muttering a curse, Collier pushed his chair away from the desk and crossed to the window. Although the official protest hadn't yet begun, the feminists were organizing, piling out of their cars with signs in hand. One poster caught his eyes right off.

Women Are No Longer Seen But Not Heard, Smith!

Color in the form of fury filled his face. "Great. Just fucking great."

"Isn't it, though?" Kyle said as Collier swung back around.

"So what do we do?"

"Not a damn thing except endure." A muscle ticked overtime in Kyle's jaw. "I'm sure they've got all the legal permits necessary to take your name in vain."

Collier swore.

"Look, just try to ignore it. You might as well. There's nothing we can do. Right now, I have to go. We'll talk more later." Kyle paused. "And don't worry."

Don't worry? Collier scowled. Like hell he wouldn't worry. He'd be a fool not to. Collier rubbed his jaw, turned once again from the window and went back to his desk. What a way to start the day.

His sexual harassment case had gone to trial a week ago, and he'd thought everything had been going pretty smoothly until now. Wonder what the committee would think when they got wind of this?

Nix his name?

What about his one-night stand with Brittany? He might as well toss that question into the mix. If the lid ever flipped open on that sealed jar, it would be another strike against him, especially with Lana and her old man in the picture. Just the hint of scandal was all that was needed. He could just hear the rumor mill now.

Collier's frown deepened as he peered down at all the legal mumbo jumbo in front of him. Suddenly he longed to tear out of the office, grab Brittany, drive up to the cabin and spend the day making love to her, buried inside her sweet fire.

Just the thought made his mouth dry and his palms sweaty. He couldn't think about her right now or he'd never make it through the day. Actually, though, that was all he'd thought about since he'd spent the night in her bed, in her arms.

But he'd stayed away. He hadn't seen her since then, though he'd picked up the phone countless times, then slammed it back down. He'd driven by the diner and the travel agency, but he hadn't gone into either of them.

"Well, son, what do you think now?"

Collier's head jerked up as his stepdad strode through the door, tossing his hat and coat across the nearest chair. "Hello, Dad."

"Don't you wish you'd listened to me?" Mason asked tersely. "I told you not to take this case."

"Calm down, Dad, and sit down."

"Dammit, this isn't going to look good," Mason ranted. "Not good at all."

"If you keep this up, you're health is going to pay for it. Calm down."

Mason glared at him. "So how can we put this fire out?"

"We can't," Collier replied evenly. "I'm committed to try the case, and that's that."

Mason's glare turned fiercer. "You mean you're not going to bow out?"

"Would you?"

"Hell yes."

"Well, I'm not," Collier declared.

Mason's lips turned white and his voice shook. "If you let this or anything else cost you the bench, I'll never forgive you."

Twenty

The walls of the small trailer house were closing in on her. Usually her tight, dismal surroundings didn't bother her, but today they did. She knew why. She was soon to visit Tommy at the prison. On the one hand, she couldn't wait to see her brother. On the other, it was so depressing, so degrading, for both of them. He'd been in such a foul mood the last few times she'd seen or spoken to him.

Resentment. That selfish emotion was wreaking havoc with her conscience. Brittany hadn't wanted anything to interfere with the feeling of euphoria that was her constant companion. Since Collier had spent the night there, nothing had been the same. *She* hadn't been the same.

Everything around her looked different. She felt different. The leaves on the trees seemed more vivid. Her college work had been easier. And she hadn't seen Rupert.

At first she had been on an incredible high. A sexual high. She attributed her weird behavior and feelings to that. When he'd had his arms around her, and especially when he was inside her, she'd never felt so treasured, so wanted, so needed.

So alive.

And while she knew it was only temporary, that *she* was only temporary in his life, she had milked every moment of their time together like a miser with ten new pennies. She had relived the numerous times he'd made love to her with his hands, his lips, his tongue.

She blushed just thinking about how easily he could make her come, especially with his tongue. No one had ever touched or tasted her body like Collier. When it came to making love, he knew all the right buttons to push.

But then, the same could be said for her, though she didn't have near the skills he had. Still, she knew she turned him on with equal fervor. It didn't matter that she wasn't as artful. His inexplicable but intense attraction to her was her best weapon. And she'd used it.

In her heart of hearts, she had nursed the hope that she'd hear from him again, that he wouldn't be able to stay away from her. But after a week her hopes had begun to fade, leaving her feeling empty and without purpose. It had seemed to hit her square in the face this morning, when she'd awakened, that he wasn't going to come around again.

He had gotten what he wanted, and he now was back with his beautiful fiancée. She made a distasteful face, hating the thought of his being with someone else. Jealousy stampeded through her, an emotion heretofore foreign to her. Then a prick of conscience followed. She was the intruder, not the other woman.

Blame rested on her own shoulders for giving in to her physical needs, for throwing sane caution to the wind and going with those needs. If she had it to do all over again, would she opt to place her heart in jeopardy and spend the night in his arms?

Yes.

For a while he had pulled her out of her drab, dreary existence and plunged her into a fantasy world. Too bad she couldn't hang on to that world for a bit longer. Unfortunately the close confines of her rinky-dink home and the upcoming trip to the prison had brought her back to reality with a hard knock.

Realizing she'd squandered precious hours of her one day off, she kicked herself mentally. It was almost time to head for the prison, and she hadn't done anything constructive.

She was about to put some clothes in the washer when the phone rang. For a second her heart leaped, as it always did when her initial reaction was that it might be Collier. When it wasn't—because it never was—her heart immediately sank.

This afternoon it was Sissy. "Hey, what are you doing?" she asked.

"I'm about to leave and go see Tommy."

"That's right. This is your day."

"What's up?" Brittany hoped Sissy wasn't planning on leaving town again. Cramming in extra hours at the agency was great for her pocketbook but hard on her classwork. She had some tough labs coming up in the next few weeks that would require extra time and effort.

"Not much. When will you be back?"

"Not late," Brittany responded. "Why?"

"That's good. Since your bad experience, I worry about you when you're on the road."

"It's nice to know someone does."

"How 'bout lunch tomorrow?"

"With you?" Brittany didn't know what made her ask that question. Perhaps it was the way Sissy issued the invitation, much more formally than usual, that made her inquire.

"Yes, and Rupert Holt."

Brittany stiffened and bit down on her lip to keep from shouting not just "No!" but "Hell no."

"You don't want to go." Sissy's tone was flat. "Look, you know I believe in sucking up to our best customers...." Her voice trailed off.

Brittany got the message. "I know that," she responded tightly, "and I understand." And she did, but she wasn't having any part of that outing. The fact remained, though, that she couldn't tell Sissy the truth. She felt as if she was walking on thin ice.

"And since he thinks we do such a great job for him," Sissy added, "he's asked us to lunch."

"You go, and I'll mind the shop."

"No, no. He insists on you coming, too."

"I'd rather not," Brittany said cautiously, feeling the ice begin to crack under her feet.

"Oh, come on," Sissy said in a coaxing voice. "You never have any fun. And this will be fun. You know what a great guy he is."

Brittany clamped down on the hysterical laughter that bubbled to the surface. "What about his wife?"

"Angel? She won't care. Why should she? It's business."

"Tell him I appreciate the offer, but I really don't want to go. You know how antisocial I am."

"If you hadn't been through some tough times lately, I'd browbeat you into going. But if you really don't want to, then I won't insist."

"Good girl," Brittany replied with great relief and forced humor.

"I'm hardly a girl," Sissy said dryly. "But we'll let that slide for the moment. Anyhow, you be careful and give Tommy my best."

"Thanks. I'll see you tomorrow."

Glancing at the clock, Brittany noticed that she'd run out of time. After giving herself a quick once-over in the mirror, she grabbed her purse and left the mobile home, trying to get a handle on the fury that Rupert's under-handed dealings had evoked.

The sneaky bastard! It seemed he would stop at noth-ing, would stoop to any level, to get his way.

That was what frightened her the most.

"I'm glad to see you're feeling better."

Tommy shrugged. "I've been forcing myself to eat the slop they serve in here."

Brittany's relief was almost palpable. The second she'd seen her brother she'd sensed that something was differ-ent, but she hadn't been able to put her finger on it. She wouldn't have guessed it was the few extra pounds that made the difference, but stranger things had happened. Besides, she'd take any good news she could get these days.

"You've had me worried," she said at last.

"You worry too much."

Brittany forced a smile. "It comes with the territory. After all, you're my responsibility."

He didn't respond to that. Instead, he averted his gaze, which made her suddenly uneasy. When Tommy couldn't look at her, something was usually amiss. What was he trying to hide?

"I've been going to chapel."

Brittany barely stopped her mouth from gaping. "To chapel?" she repeated in stunned disbelief. "As in church?"

"Yeah. Kinda shocks you, doesn't it?"

"Are you serious?"

"Yep."

Clearly disconcerted by this news, but jubilant, Brittany struggled to find the right words to respond. "That's…wonderful."

"The other day this guy started talking to me. At first I tried to dodge him, thinking he was just coming on to me. But after he did me a favor and asked for nothing in return, I started talking to him some." Tommy paused and took a breath. "Come to find out, he's a goddamn preacher."

Brittany paled. "I wish you wouldn't use that word, especially not when you're talking about a man of God."

"Sorry, sis, but this is all new to me."

"No, it isn't. Mother took us both to church."

"Well, it didn't stick," he countered, sounding irritated.

Careful not to fan that irritation or put a damper on his news, she smiled warmly. "I'm glad you found someone who you can at least talk to."

Although she didn't doubt that Tommy's change of heart was sincere, she didn't think for a moment it was permanent. But if it helped him through this rough patch, she would be thrilled.

"If I get in any more trouble," he said darkly, "they've said I'll never get parole."

Panic rushed through her. "Oh, no, Tommy!" she cried. "You…we can't let them do that."

"Then get me out."

"Don't start, please. Nothing has changed. I'm still doing everything I can." Short of accepting Rupert's help, that was. She squirmed against a sudden prick of conscience. Maybe…? Never! There had to be another way to help her brother. There just had to be.

"Sis, what's wrong?"

She shook her head. "Nothing."

"You looked kinda weird for a second."

Brittany forced another smile. "It's just your imagination. I'm fine."

"If things work out, I might get to help in the chapel office."

"Tommy, that's great news. Praise the Lord."

"I'll start praising Him when I get outta this joint."

Before she could respond, the guard indicated that their time was up. With a heavy heart, Brittany said her goodbyes, and shortly afterward she walked out into the blinding sunlight. It was while she was searching her purse for her sunglasses that she realized she wasn't alone.

She lifted her head, and her eyes widened. Collier was standing in front of her. For what seemed the longest time they just stared at each other, a devouring stare, as though both of them were remembering the last time they'd been together.

Brittany's hands began to tremble. She shoved them into her pockets before he noticed.

"What in heaven's name are you doing here?" Collier finally asked, his voice sounding scratchy.

"I could ask you the same thing," she responded in a breathless tone.

"I have a friend who's here."

"I'm sorry," she said lamely, licking her lip.

"Brittany, I..." His voice faltered as his eyes once again seemed to devour her.

"You asked me why I'm here, right?" she asked suddenly, shattering the erotic spell that had fallen over them.

He gave a start. "Right."

Deciding it was time he knew the truth about her, the good, the bad and the ugly, she blurted out, "I came to see my brother. He's an inmate."

It was obvious Collier was taken aback, though, to his

credit, he rebounded quickly. But as an attorney, that was what he'd been trained to do—think on his feet. "That's too bad. I'm sorry."

"Thanks," she murmured, shifting her gaze. How had this happened, this chance meeting out of the blue? She'd ached all week to see him, to be within touching distance of him. But not here, not like this, she cried silently. Not on prison grounds, one of the places she hated most in the world.

He cleared his throat. "Is there anything I can do? I mean—" He shoved his hands through his hair, then muttered, "Hell, I don't know what I mean."

"Thanks for asking, but I doubt there's anything you can do."

Silence.

"What's his name?" he pressed in a tortured tone.

She met his gaze head-on. "It's Tommy Rogers, but—"

Collier flinched visibly, as if she'd struck him. This time *she* was taken aback. Had she missed something? "What's wrong? Do you know him?"

"Oh, yes," he said in a cold, harsh voice, "I know him, all right."

"But...how?" she stammered, stepping back, uncomfortable with that look in his eyes, that same vengeful look he'd given her when he'd demanded that she press assault charges against Rupert.

"How?" He laughed mirthlessly. "He's the little bastard who hit my brother and put him in a wheelchair for the rest of his life."

Twenty-One

By sheer force of will, Brittany made it to her car. Once there, she laid her head back against the seat and took deep, heaving breaths, feeling as if she'd been socked in the stomach.

Mentally she had been. After Collier had delivered his knockout punch, he'd turned away and walked to his car, leaving her standing alone and defenseless in the wake of his destruction. Now, as she struggled to come to terms with what he'd told her, she was finding that impossible. Her heart and mind were rejecting the despicable truth.

Suddenly she felt sick to her stomach. But, following several more deep breaths, the queasiness eased. Still, she was shaking and weak all over, as if she'd come down with a nasty virus.

If only that were the case. Unfortunately her plight wasn't that simple or easy to get over. Her malady was permanent.

Collier Smith. Collier Smith. Collier Smith.

His name ran through her mind like an endless freight train, until it finally made the right connection. He was the Smith in *Williams, Smith and Rutledge.* But how was she to have known? To her knowledge, Collier had never been at the trial, though it would have been easy to have missed him. After Tommy's accident, she'd been in such a terrified state that a lot of details had escaped her.

Throughout the court proceedings, she'd barely hung on to her sanity, much less anything else.

Jackson Williams, the high-powered attorney whose life Tommy had wrecked, was Collier's brother. Another jab of pain to the stomach forced her upright in the seat.

Unbelievable. Impossible. Unfair.

Those words and more pelted her brain, keeping her breathing abnormal and her stomach in an upheaval. Angry tears marred her vision. Maybe if Jackson and Collier had had the same last name, she might have put two and two together. But since they were apparently stepbrothers, no way would she have made that connection.

The point was moot now. The damage had been done, and beating up on herself was fruitless and detrimental. But she couldn't stop her self-flagellation any more than she could stop breathing.

Tommy must never find out what she had done. Hysteria suddenly took the place of tears, and she almost laughed out loud at the irony of the situation. *God, what had she done?* She had slept with a man who would love to see her brother spend the rest of his life rotting behind bars.

The sudden tap on the window sent another shock wave through her. Brittany darted her head around, thinking the unthinkable. Hoping for the impossible. It was a man, all right, but it wasn't Collier.

She rolled down the window.

"Ma'am, is something wrong?"

Brittany realized by his uniform that he was an employee of the prison, probably a watchman. "No, sir. It's…" Her voice failed.

"I didn't mean to intrude, but you've been sitting here for a while. I thought maybe you might be having car trouble."

"Thanks for checking on me," she said in a distracted tone, "but everything's okay."

Once he'd gone, she started the car, backed out of the parking space and headed for home, that old sick feeling washing through her once again. Even though she hadn't expected Collier to have a change of heart and to follow her, her heart had cried out for him to do that very thing.

Now that cry was silenced. She would never be bothered by Collier Smith again, except maybe in a court of law if there was an appeal or when her brother came up for parole.

And that hurt. God, that hurt. She hadn't wanted it to end like this, not on such a harsh, bitter note.

By the time she'd made it home to her dismal surroundings, Brittany's face was saturated with tears, because she hadn't wanted it to end at all.

"I didn't grab her ass. I don't give a damn what she said."

"She's not the only one who said it, Luther," Collier responded in a mild, even tone.

His client in the sexual harassment suit, Luther Brickman, had called and asked him to stop by his house following their day in court. As he watched the sixty-year-old executive take a long pull on his drink, it was obvious why the man felt confident he could have any woman he wanted.

With a thick head of steel-gray hair and penetrating green eyes that remained clear despite his penchant for the bottle, he presented a fine specimen. Twice divorced, with no children, he had a reputation for womanizing in and out of the workplace.

"I don't give a shit what they said, this time I'm not guilty. She's lying through her teeth."

"You don't have to keep telling me that. I'm on your side."

"Then why the hell did you let that runt of an attorney talk to me like that?"

To say the least, their day in court had been a volatile one. Luther had been fiercely cross-examined and was obviously still reeling from the beating he'd taken.

Collier wished he hadn't indulged Luther. Instead he should have gone home to his condo. He was in a worse mood than his client. But since he was getting paid big bucks to cater to the man, he'd given in.

"I warned you this would be nasty," Collier said at last. "That you'd get pummeled on the stand."

"That's a fucking understatement."

Collier sat with drink in hand and watched Luther pace like a madman. "If you don't settle down, you're going to have an attack of some sort."

"That might just solve all my fucking problems."

"Man, you *are* on a rampage," Collier said, striving to keep his tone even. However, he was fast losing patience.

"Do you think I'll get out of this with my hide intact?"

"I believe we'll win."

Luther's relief was obvious. "So you still think I'm innocent?"

"In this particular case, I do. But that's beside the point. I've agreed to represent you, and I'll give it my best shot."

"But you don't like me, do you?"

"That's also beside the point."

"Not to me it isn't."

Collier downed the rest of his drink and stood. "Look, Luther, don't expect me to be your buddy or to hold your hand. You're a skirt chaser, a fact you've never denied. But sooner or later, when a man gets his pussy and his paycheck in the same place, he's going to get in trouble.''

Luther flushed; then his eyes narrowed. "I told you—"

"I'm not saying you screwed Virginia Warner. I happen to agree with you. She wants your job, and she sees this suit as a way to get it. Having said that, we both know you've slept with several other women in the office, which is exactly why your balls are now in the wringer."

"Just as long as you get them out."

"I'll do my best."

Luther reached into his pocket and pulled out a white linen handkerchief, then mopped the sweat off his face. "I hope you've got your guns loaded for her."

"I keep them loaded. Isn't that why you hired me?"

"You're damn straight it is."

"Then give it a rest, and let me take care of things."

Luther paused and angled his head. "You haven't given thought to jumping ship, have you?"

Collier went still. "What made you ask that?"

"All the adverse publicity this case has generated. Like those picketers, for instance. I know that can't help with the judgeship you're vying for."

"You let me worry about that," Collier said tersely.

"I don't want to be pawned off on anyone else."

Collier set his glass down harder than he normally would have. "I'm out of here before you piss me off."

Luther's flush deepened. "Sorry, it's just that—" He stopped, as if he didn't know what to say.

"Forget it. Just remember what I said from the get-go. Keep your mouth shut and your pants zipped."

Luther opened his mouth, then snapped it shut.

Collier reached for his overcoat. ''If there's nothing else—'' He broke off, his gaze and tone pointed.

Luther growled, then strode over to the bar and began to mix another stiff drink. Collier merely shook his head as he walked out.

What a miserable bastard.

He wasn't in much better shape, he reminded himself a while later when he let himself into his empty condo. After his conversation with Luther, he hadn't really wanted to come home, yet he hadn't wanted to go back to the office, either.

Maybe he should have stuck around Brickman's house and gotten belly-crawling drunk with him. Was that the answer to ridding his thoughts of Brittany? Right now, he'd do almost anything, whatever it took, to make her stop haunting him.

Although it was chilly outside, Collier could have sworn it was chillier inside. He shivered as he strode to the fireplace filled with gas logs and switched them on. Instantly the flames seemed to reach out and lick him. He loosened his tie, made himself a drink, then collapsed on the sofa.

Had it been a week since that god-awful day? Since he'd last seen her?

He'd felt like a turkey that had just gotten its head chopped off when she'd told him who her brother was. He still found that incredible. How could he have been so blind?

How could he not have known, for chrissake?

He'd go one better than that. Why the hell had he ever gotten involved with her in the first place? He'd known it would be trouble, even if not what particular kind of trouble. His sexual hunger for her had consumed him, that was why.

Disgust rose like bile up the back of his throat, nearly strangling him. He took another swig of his drink. If he took many more swigs, his pain would simply disappear. Tempting? You bet. Only he knew when he awakened, he would still be crippled with the same pain.

He put his glass down and sank back against the pillows, feeling his head pound. Thank God he'd found out who Brittany was before his father and brother learned about his little liaison.

Needless to say, Mason would have disowned him. And Jackson—well, he couldn't begin to imagine what his brother's reaction would be. But Fate had done him a favor, allowing him to dodge both those lethal bullets and giving him a chance to get his head on straight and his life back in order.

Then why was he as miserable as that sonofabitch whose house he'd just left? Simple. The brutal truth had done what he couldn't do himself, and that was sever their relationship. He still ached for her.

What did that say about him?

The answer to that question further disgusted him. He got up and made his way back to the bottle of booze. Going on a binge just might be what he needed to get through the night after all.

If not, he was likely to do something he would regret for the rest of his life, and that was haul his ass back outside, jump in his car and head for Brittany's trailer.

"To hell with it!" He shoved the glass aside and raised the bottle to his mouth.

Twenty-Two

"Hello, Senator, it's great to see you again."

Collier's stomach had clenched when Pamela told him Newton Riley had stopped by. He'd had mixed emotions, realizing that a visit from the high-powered senator, who held his future in his hands, could bode either good or bad. He preferred to dwell on the former. For the time being, he didn't need any more bumps in the road.

"Same here," the senator responded, shaking Collier's outstretched hand vigorously, his beefy size seeming to shrink the large room.

If nothing else, Collier noted, that size alone commanded respect. "Have a seat and I'll get you some coffee or whatever."

He suspected Riley would pass on the whatever, since it was still too early in the day to hit the booze. But one never knew.

"Thanks, but no thanks. I don't have but a sec."

"So what's on your mind?" Collier asked in as casual a manner as possible, since his stomach remained clenched.

"You've made it to the top two."

At first Collier didn't grasp the meaning of the words. The senator had spoken them so nonchalantly, as if he was commenting on how nice the day was.

"Pretty heady stuff, huh?" Senator Riley went on.

"It sure as hell is." Collier blew out a breath, the reality of the situation finally sinking in. "And I can't thank you enough."

The senator chuckled. "You sound shocked, but you shouldn't be."

"Well, I am. And honored and humbled."

"The committee is who actually narrowed the list."

While that might be true, Collier knew Riley had his eye on every move that committee made. He had helped to appoint it, and so in one sense they were responsible to him.

"If I may ask, who's my competition?"

Riley told him. Collier winced inwardly. Travis Wainwright, Rupert Holt's man, had made the cut. Mason wouldn't be happy, but then, neither was he.

"However," the senator continued, his green eyes piercing, "there *is* a problem."

"With me?"

"With you."

Collier's stomach bottomed out. *Terrific, here comes the bombshell.* "Let me guess." The two most controversial problems facing him were Brittany and the harassment case. He hoped and prayed Riley was referring to the latter. Sweat broke out on his upper lip. He wanted to wipe it off, but he didn't. Instead, he remained unflinching under Riley's intent gaze.

"It shouldn't be hard to figure out."

"The sexual harassment case," Collier said, a little embarrassed by the relief in his tone.

"You nailed it."

"I'm in trouble because of the publicity it's garnered." Collier's words were a flat statement of fact.

"Let me put it this way," Riley said, leaning forward, as though to better make his point, "it would be to your advantage if nothing else like that happened again. In fact, it would be even more to your advantage if it was settled out of court or ended quickly.''

"I can't guarantee either, Senator.''

Riley scratched his perfectly shaven chin, then narrowed his eyes. "If someone should come to you and ask for a favor, would you comply?''

Collier stiffened, not liking the sudden tone of this conversation or where it was heading. "Might that someone be you, Senator?''

"Maybe, maybe not.'' Riley paused and scratched his chin again. "Perhaps I should put it this way, if you'll pardon my slang. If you were asked to dance with the one who brung you, what would you say?''

Collier didn't flinch. "I'd say it's too bad he's looking for a whore.''

The room turned eerily quiet.

Collier squirmed mentally, though he didn't let his unsettled emotions show. He'd already made it clear he would do everything he could to win the appointment to the best of his ability, no matter what. But that "no matter what'' didn't mean prostituting himself to anyone. He would never do that.

Suddenly Newton Riley laughed heartily, then got to his feet. "I have to admire you for sticking by your guns, young man. So few do that nowadays.''

Collier rose, as well, and squared his shoulders. "That's who I am, Senator. I don't see that ever changing.''

A short silence descended over the room. Collier could hear the clock ticking on his desk, or was that the sound of his heart? Had he passed the test? Or could he still get the proverbial kiss-off?

"That's why you're still in the running,'' Riley said

with conviction. "The bench needs men like you. Men with integrity."

Collier figured his relief was visible, but he didn't care. He'd just jumped another hurdle. "So I was being tested?"

Riley merely laughed again, then said, "Before I go, answer me one more question." The senator's eyes were narrowed on him once again.

Collier swallowed hard. "I'll do my best."

"Why did you take that case? Other than the money, that is?" The senator's sudden smile softened his bluntness.

"I think my client's innocent."

"You do, huh?"

Collier didn't so much as blink. "In this particular case, yes."

"Brickman has a reputation with women, always has. I know, because he's been a friend for years."

"True," Collier replied carefully, "but despite that, I believe in this particular case, he's innocent."

"Well, good luck, young man." Suddenly Riley's eyes twinkled. "In the midst of all this controversy, it wouldn't hurt for you to be seen out somewhere kissing babies. It might even warm those feminists' hearts toward you."

Collier's lips twitched. "Yes, sir. I'll see what I can do about that."

"I'll be in touch. Oh, and give Mason my regards."

"I'll do it, and thanks for coming by."

Once they shook hands, Riley left and Collier was alone. He sat back down, feeling as if he'd gone down for the count, only to be revived at the last minute. But he wasn't out of the woods yet, he cautioned himself.

Now was not the time for smugness, though he did feel Riley was definitely in his corner.

Still, if this case took another unexpected turn or word got out about his affair with Brittany…

Feeling the sweat spread to other parts of his body, Collier nipped those thoughts in the bud posthaste, especially that last one.

Suddenly he felt the urge to see his brother. Whenever he felt sorry for himself, visiting Jackson seemed to jerk him back in line, put things in perspective, renew his deep sense of responsibility.

Though the guilt over his affair with Brittany was certainly part of that package today, he still needed to be grounded, to keep his eye on the target, which was the federal appointment. Nothing must stand in the way of that.

Collier gritted his teeth and got up.

"Anything else you need, sir?"

Harry, his valet, seemed to be hovering more today than usual, which irritated Jackson no end. Some days he could actually tolerate Harry's mollycoddling, but today wasn't one of them. He wanted to be alone.

"No, thanks."

As if he sensed Jackson's mood, the hefty middle-aged man, who had been a weight lifter before he came to work part-time for Jackson, said, "I'll be in the gym setting things up for your workout and therapy. When you're ready, just buzz."

Jackson nodded. Moments later he heard the door close, and he suddenly regretted being left alone. What the hell was wrong with him? He knew the answer, and he didn't like it one damn bit.

She never should have come and upset his applecart.

He'd been fine the way he was, content to wallow in self-pity and remain apart from the outside world.

Haley's unscheduled visit had changed that, though he hated to admit it.

Would she come back?

Jackson cursed inwardly as he turned his chair away from the window and rolled it toward one of the bookcases that bordered the fireplace. He hadn't read in a while. Maybe that would be a good thing to do. He turned his head toward the French doors, noticing how perfect the day was, thinking how nice it would be to sit outside.

Only if he had some company.

Don't! He had to stop doing that to himself. Haley was the last person he should want to see again. There wouldn't be any point. He still didn't want her pity, although he hadn't seen any of that in her eyes. He'd have to give her that much. If she had pitied him, she hadn't let it show. Most people were not that considerate.

Still, he couldn't start hankering for something he couldn't have. And that was a woman. Despite himself, he smiled when he thought for at least the hundredth time how lovely Haley was, how vivacious, how full of life.

"Hey, big brother."

Jackson snapped his head around. He'd been so lost in thoughts of Haley that he hadn't heard the door open. "You should knock," he said in a quarrelsome tone.

"Only to have you tell me to take a hike? I don't think so."

Jackson frowned, but down deep, he was glad to see his brother. Actually, he sometimes felt sorry for Collier, having to carry the burden alone of living up to their father's expectations and dreams, a tall order for anyone to fill.

"Besides," Collier added, "I wanted to see you."

Jackson cut him a look. "As long as you don't lecture me."

"Come on," Collier countered in a cajoling voice, "give me a break. You know I don't hassle you all that much. Dad does enough of that for both of us."

"For the whole damn world," Jackson muttered.

Collier chuckled.

Jackson pulled at a loose thread on the throw covering his legs. "So what's on your mind?"

"What isn't?" Collier responded.

"I heard about the picketers, of course, from Dad. He was about to blow a gasket."

"Well, I do have some good news amongst all the bad." Collier hesitated.

"Go on, spit it out."

"Senator Riley came to see me. I haven't even told Dad yet."

"Have you moved up another rung on the ladder?"

"How did you know?"

Jackson shrugged. "That's a no-brainer. The senator likes you."

"It's Mason he likes, because of all the money he's contributed."

"Hell, you've put in almost as much. And look at your record. It's without blemish."

"Was, don't you mean?" Collier said down in the mouth. "This trial is threatening to nix that."

"Is there something else bothering you?"

Collier gave him an odd look, then said with a hedging note in his tone, "What makes you think that?"

Jackson shrugged again. "I know you, little brother. You look drawn, like something's eating at your gut."

"Nah. It's just your imagination."

"Sorry if I'm interrupting."

Jackson's heart dropped to his toes at the sound of the lilting voice. He whipped his head around simultaneously with Collier's. They both stared at the figure standing on the threshold of the open door.

Collier was the first to respond. "Why, hello, Haley." He crossed to her and held out his hand. "It's great to see you."

"Same here," she said, her eyes darting around him to Jackson.

He saw the question in those expressive eyes and wanted to tell her to get the hell out of there, that she was definitely interrupting and wasn't welcome, to boot. However, those harsh words locked in his throat. In truth, he was thrilled she had returned, though he was angry at himself for that weakness.

"Come on in," Collier was saying, stepping aside.

She never moved. Her gaze continued to hold Jackson's. "Is that all right?"

"Since you're here," he muttered more gruffly than he'd intended, "you might as well stay."

Haley flushed, though she didn't let his surly attitude stop her. She visibly squared her shoulders as though prepared to do battle and walked into the room, not stopping until she was close to his wheelchair, close enough for him to get a whiff of her perfume. He held his breath, suddenly feeling a crazy notion that his lower body had reacted. God, but she was messing with his mind in a bad way. He had to get rid of her.

"Are you back in town to stay?" Collier asked her.

Jackson picked up on the humor-laced curiosity in his brother's tone, and it irritated him, though he couldn't say why.

"As far as I know," Haley said, her vibrant red hair swirling softly around her neck.

For a second Jackson was spellbound by that. Spellbound by her. He cursed silently.

"That's great."

Haley smiled. "My mom thinks so, too."

Jackson thought her smile seemed forced, but then, so did her voice. Still, she showed no sign of leaving. But she'd always had more than her share of sweet, reckless gall. The intervening years hadn't changed her one iota.

"Look, I'm going to go and let you two visit," Collier said, an obvious glint in his eyes.

Damn his brother, Jackson thought, his ill humor festering. The bastard couldn't be happier about Haley's presence.

"Don't let me run you off," Haley said, frowning.

"You're not. I need to get back to the office. I'm in court this afternoon." He turned to Jackson. "Later, bro."

Jackson nodded.

Once Collier was gone and the door had closed behind him, silence shrouded the room like a heavy mist.

"I know I shouldn't keep dropping in like this," Haley said, "but..."

"You're not sorry," Jackson said, finishing the sentence for her.

Haley's delightful chin tipped defiantly. "That's right."

Another silence.

"What do you want, Haley?" Jackson asked in a strained voice.

"Nothing more than to take you for a ride." She paused and peered outside. "It's a lovely day, much too lovely to be indoors."

"I like being indoors."

"You don't mean that."

"Dammit, Haley, why aren't you at work?"

"I'm about to be. I have to check on an adjuster in the field for the first time. I thought maybe you'd like to go with me."

"What if I told you to leave me the hell alone?"

She was silent for a long moment. "I wouldn't do it."

Jackson let go an expletive.

"So?"

"So, all right, I'll go. But if you think I'm going to make a habit of this, you're wrong."

"Whatever you say."

"Yeah, right," Jackson countered darkly. "Don't forget, I know you."

She laughed, then sobered, her bottom lip suddenly quivering. "Please, just don't shut me out, okay?"

"Haley…"

"Jackson…" she mimicked, her hands on her hips, her head tilted.

"I'll call Harry," he said in a terse but resigned tone, at the same time that he shifted his gaze off her lovely face. "He'll put me in your car."

"You won't be sorry, I promise."

Oh no, he would be sorry, all right. Still, he found himself pressing the buzzer, unwilling or unable to deny her.

Twenty-Three

Brittany always dreaded going inside the prison. This afternoon, that dread seemed worse than usual. The instant she walked through the doors, its particular smell hit her with a vengeance. She paused and leaned against the wall.

If only Tommy were allowed to go outside to visit. Unfortunately that wasn't the way things worked in the penal system. Though she hated to breathe, she had no choice. She couldn't hold her breath much longer.

She couldn't imagine how her brother dealt with being caged like an animal day after day. God, was she ever morbid. It was moments like this when she considered taking Rupert up on his offer and becoming the consummate unselfish sibling.

Forget that. With a disgusted shake of her head, that insane thought disappeared. While she loved her brother dearly, she refused to degrade herself that way or put herself in further jeopardy. Being alone with Rupert would do both.

She would just have to stay on her plotted course, which was to finish college and get a fabulous job. In the meantime, she would continue to work her fingers to the bone and save money. Maybe, with some luck, she'd have enough to hire an attorney before she got her degree, an attorney who believed in Tommy's innocence and that he was imprisoned unfairly.

For the moment, however, she had to cast those thoughts aside and get in a better frame of mind. When she saw Tommy, she didn't need to be down in the mouth. It was her place to buoy his spirits, a burden that continually weighed heavily on her.

That wasn't all, either. Since her run-in with Collier here, on these grounds, she hadn't been herself. She had gone about her daily routine while completely unraveling on the inside. But she would get over him. *She would.* It had only been a week. What did she expect? Apparently too much. Collier had gotten under her skin, made her think and feel things she couldn't forget. During the short duration of their affair, she'd become addicted to him.

While she hadn't fallen in love—though just that thought almost caused her knees to buckle—she missed him terribly. What she missed were his arms, his mouth, his tongue....

Dear Lord, she begged, she didn't want to think about Collier right now. Her time and attention belonged to Tommy. At the moment, however, Collier and Tommy were tied together. On an equal plane with her desire to see Collier was her guilt for wanting to do so. She felt as though she was consorting with the enemy. Her brother would have a fit if he had an inkling of what was going on. *What* had *gone on.*

Tommy must never know. She must keep her secret at all costs.

He was waiting behind the partition, staring at the door, an anxious expression on his face. She forced a smile as she picked up the phone.

"Hey, sweetie."

"Hiya, sis."

Her eyes took in everything about him, making sure he was taking care of himself as best he could. She didn't want his weight to drop again. That frightened her. "What kind of week have you had?"

He shrugged. "Same as all of 'em."

Her spirits fell. He didn't seem as upbeat as he had last week. Something must have happened with his job in the chapel.

She voiced that thought. "Did the chapel job come through?"

"Not yet."

"I was so hoping it would."

"Me, too."

"What does your minister friend say? I thought he was spearheading it?"

Tommy picked at a scratch on his hand. "That's the problem. I haven't seen him. I asked, but no one would tell me anything."

"Do you want me to check?"

Panic darkened his eyes. "No, don't say anything to anyone."

"If you don't want me to, I won't, but—"

"Forget it. It'll either happen or it won't."

"Just don't lose faith," Brittany encouraged, grasping for anything that would put hope back into those bleak eyes.

"What's been going on with you?" Tommy asked, abruptly changing the subject.

"Work and school," she hedged, looking away.

"Sis...?"

Brittany whipped her head back around, alerted by the changed tone of his voice.

"Have you been able to pay back any of the money you borrowed?"

"No, why?"

"I was just hoping you might have, so we could borrow some more for an attorney."

Another kind of dread spread through her, even more potent. "Tommy, we've been over this before. That's not possible. I simply can't go back for more. As it is, I'm barely managing to pay my college tuition. And remember, we have a mortgage on the trailer."

She hated this, hated hearing that desperate, almost begging, note in his voice and being unable to do anything to help him.

Suddenly Rupert and his promise jumped back into her mind. She cringed inwardly. No. She simply wouldn't give in to that kind of blackmail. Besides, there were no guarantees she could trust him to deliver. Trust was not what Rupert was all about.

"I was just hoping."

Unbidden tears filled her eyes, and a sob caught in her throat. He looked so forlorn, so lost. And she felt so damn guilty. That renewed sense of guilt was almost crippling. While he was rotting in this hellhole, thoughts of Collier had consumed her, how much she missed him, how much she wanted to make love to him again.

Had she no shame?

"Hey, sis, I didn't mean to make you cry."

"I know," she gulped, taking a tissue out of her purse and dabbing her eyes. "It's not you."

"Then what is it? You look like you've been sick. Have you?"

"No."

"So what's wrong?"

She knew it upset him to see her lose control. He depended on her to be the strong one, to be there for him.

But oh, how she wished she had someone strong to lean on herself. Someone like Collier...

"I've done something awful, Tommy," she blurted out. "I've been sleeping with Jackson Williams' brother."

Dear God, what had she done? The horror of her unplanned, unwanted confession turned her as rigid as stone. She couldn't think. She couldn't breathe. She couldn't do anything but stare into Tommy's stunned eyes, waiting to see his love for her turn to hate.

"Hey, that's great news, sis!"

"What?" she managed to screech.

Tommy's eyes and face were animated. "Way to go. That's just great, the best news you could've given me."

Brittany was too flabbergasted to speak. She opened her mouth, but nothing came out. It was as if paralysis had suddenly gripped her throat.

"Yeah, that's just great," he repeated, a grin having removed the sullen look from his face.

Brittany rubbed her head as if to clear it. "I don't...understand."

"Think about it and you will." Tommy lowered his voice until it was hardly more than a hush. "Man, can we ever use this to our advantage. What a stroke of luck."

She simply stared at him incredulously, not believing what she was hearing. "Have you lost your mind?"

"No. He's got the hots for you, right? So use it. I betcha if you refuse to put out anymore, he'll be glad to do anything you want. If I'm guessing right, his brother'll suddenly take second banana to his pecker."

"Tommy!" she cried in horror. "That's crazy!"

"It's brilliant." His eyes seemed on fire. "Use him, sis, to help me. Don't you see? It'll work. It just has to."

Speechless once again, Brittany could only sit and stare at her brother, sick to her stomach.

"You mean he actually went with her?"

Collier nodded at Mason. "I hung around to see for myself."

"Maybe there's hope for your brother after all, though I would never have guessed that any woman, even Haley, could accomplish what we've been unable to do for three years."

"Miracles do still happen."

"We'll see," Mason said in a sobering tone. "I'm not going to get my hopes up again, only to have them shot down."

His stepdad had barged into his office unannounced shortly after Kyle had come in. Before they settled down to business, Collier had wanted Mason to know about Haley and Jackson, certain Jackson would not have told him. He'd been right in that assumption.

"I didn't think he could—" Kyle broke off midsentence, his face turning scarlet.

"He can't," Mason replied bluntly.

"I repeat, miracles do happen," Collier said, almost to himself. Maybe that was what he was hoping for with Brittany—a miracle that would get rid of all the debris that lay between them, enabling them to be together again.

"Dammit, boy, you haven't heard a word I've said."

Collier gave a start. "Sorry."

"You should be," Mason responded, a fierce expression on his face.

"What did you say?"

"That I found out you made the next cut, only not from you."

Collier flushed.

"I was going to tell you. How did you find out?"

"I just happened to run into Newton Riley. He said he'd been to see you."

"I guess he also told you that the committee's not happy about the picketers."

"Sure did. He also said he told you to kiss some babies and make the women happy. Think you can do that?"

Collier didn't bother to answer that question. When Mason hit his office, he'd been itching for a fight, and Collier didn't see that changing. Nothing he'd done lately seemed to please his dad.

"What's with you?" Mason demanded. "Suddenly you don't seem interested in the appointment or anything else, except maybe that goddamn harassment case you should've dumped."

Collier sighed as he glanced at Kyle, whose eyebrows were raised in a knowing manner. He knew what that look meant: his investigator was siding with Mason.

"That's crap. Of course I'm interested in the appointment, but—"

"But what?" Mason interrupted.

"But until I've been appointed," Collier said with stressed patience, "I'm going to continue to practice law, which means representing Luther Brickman. End of discussion."

"I just hope you don't live to regret that."

"Me, too," Collier said tightly.

"Meanwhile," Mason said, seeming to have recharged his enthusiasm, "we have to watch our backsides. With Holt's boy Wainwright still in the hunt, it's going to be hard going."

"He's a tough opponent," Kyle added in his easy-going voice.

"Any ideas how we can spike his guns?" Mason asked, his gaze nailing Kyle.

"Let's hold off on going that route," Collier said. "If we start slinging dirt, then so will they. So far, it's been civil. I'd rather keep it that way if we can."

Mason kept his eyes on Kyle. "You agree with that?"

"Yes, sir, for the time being. But I'll keep my ears and eyes open. That way, if anything changes, we'll be prepared."

"Good." Mason peered at his watch. "I'm due on the golf course. I'll be in touch."

A long silence followed Mason's exit. Finally Kyle said, "I'm on the same page with your dad. What's up with you, anyway?"

"Both of you are imagining things."

"I don't think so," Kyle said in that same easy tone, pushing himself out of the deep leather chair and crossing to the window. From there, he faced Collier once again. "You're distracted as hell, have been for days."

"It's the case."

"Bullshit."

A smile of sorts tempered Collier's lips. "Why don't you say what's on your mind?"

"Why don't you level with me?"

"Confession's good for the soul." Collier smiled sarcastically. "Is that what you're saying?"

"Whatever it takes to get your head out of your ass." Collier muttered an expletive.

"Tell me it's not that woman."

Collier felt his face burn with unnatural color.

"Holy shit," Kyle spat, his features saying even more than the words.

"It's worse than you think," Collier said in a strained voice.

Kyle groaned. "Let's hear it."

When Collier finished, Kyle looked as if he'd been gutted. For a long moment, silence dominated the room.

"Man, oh, man, what a fucking mess."

Collier averted his gaze. "I know."

"Say that with more conviction, dammit! If anyone gets wind of this, you're screwed in more ways than one."

"You think I don't know that?" Collier lashed back.

Kyle drove his hands through his short hair, forcing it on end. He looked like a porcupine. Any other time, the picture he portrayed would have garnered a chuckle. Not today. Collier was fresh out of chuckles.

"Look, let's both settle down," Kyle suggested, "and think this through rationally. Does anyone else know about her? About the affair?"

"Not to my knowledge. Unless—" He aborted his words.

Kyle stiffened. "Unless what?"

"Unless she told someone, which I doubt she did."

"If that's the case, then you're home free. As long as you stay away from her, that is."

"What choice do I have?" Collier responded bleakly.

"None," Kyle emphasized. He paused. "Have you considered the possibility she might decide to blackmail you, since you've dropped her like—" He stopped, as if he'd been about to step on a grenade.

Like a piece of trailer trash, Collier added silently, sick to his stomach. "She wouldn't do that."

"Are you sure?"

The tension in the room suddenly swelled along with the tension inside his chest. "Dead sure," Collier muttered harshly. "So drop it."

"Not a problem. But just to be on the safe side, I

suggest you make it a point to be seen in public with Lana, even kiss some babies like the senator suggested."

"Next you'll be telling me to set a date with Lana," Collier said with intended sarcasm.

"Not a bad idea." Kyle's normally stoic face brightened. "In fact, I think that would probably nail the bench for you, especially since her old man has almost godlike status among the party's rank and file."

When Collier didn't respond, Kyle went on. "Tell me you'll think about it, at least."

"Okay, I'll think about it," Collier said in a dull tone, turning his back on Kyle and staring outside with unseeing eyes.

The door closing alerted him that he was finally alone. He slumped against the wall.

Twenty-Four

The frozen dinner she'd popped into the microwave tasted like sawdust. Making a face, Brittany forced herself to take one more bite before getting up from the couch and discarding the remains of her meal. She wasn't hungry, but she should be. She'd had a glass of orange juice and a muffin early that morning, and nothing since.

Since her last visit with Tommy, her stomach had been perpetually upset. As long as her brother remained incarcerated, she didn't see that changing. However, this evening her queasiness stemmed more from emotional upheaval than lack of food.

Even now, several days after that traumatic visit, she was at home, listening to the rain pound the roof, unable to wipe their conversation from her mind. Rather than dwell on spilled milk, she had a million other things to do—mainly study. But she couldn't concentrate. She still found it hard to believe she'd actually confessed to Tommy. That confession and its repercussion haunted her relentlessly.

She had no idea what had possessed her to blurt that out. Just thinking about that moment robbed her of her next breath. Guilt. She supposed that had been the driving force behind such insanity. Tommy was the last person she would ever have planned to confide in. In fact, she hadn't planned on confiding in anyone. It was to have been her best-kept secret.

More mind-boggling had been his reaction. She'd expected him to lash out at her, to be furious with her for betraying him, for joining the ranks of the enemy. Instead he'd wanted her to use the affair to help himself.

What a guy.

Sarcasm didn't help. Nothing helped. Brittany closed her eyes and rubbed them. She'd tried to delete that awful time from her mind, but she couldn't. Like the Energizer bunny, it went on and on.

When Tommy had praised her for getting involved with Collier, she'd been so shocked, so outraged, that she'd remained mute while every ounce of blood drained from her face. All she'd been able to do was stare at him, her mouth open.

"I take it you don't agree." His tone had reeked of hostility. "Hell, you look like I just kicked you in the gut."

"You did," she whispered in a strained voice, still trying to come to grips with the bizarre and unexpected turn of events.

"Can you help me? *Will* you help me? I don't believe you can't see the advantage to me, to you. You're just being selfish, sis."

"Tommy..." Again her voice failed her. How was she supposed to respond to such self-centeredness, such total self-absorption? Granted, he was desperate, but this insanity went far beyond that.

"Hell, just forget it," Tommy said with disgust, his knuckles whitening around the receiver. "I thought I could count on you for anything, anytime. It looks like I was wrong."

Wounded by his unfair words, Brittany groped to defend herself. But it was hard to collect her thoughts when she was still reeling from shock. What kind of twisted mind could have come up with such a plan? The answer to that question was too frightening to pursue.

Yet she couldn't afford to ignore it. His behavior had to be faced and dealt with. The idea that her affair with Collier could benefit him would never have occurred to her. In her wildest imagination, she couldn't have conjured that up. But then, she wasn't behind bars, fighting for any hope that would change her situation.

If anything, her affair with Collier would work to her brother's disadvantage. For some reason, though, that thought had apparently never occurred to him. Of course, he wasn't thinking straight. He didn't care about anything except himself. She couldn't forget that, though she had to assume her share of responsibility. She'd helped make him the way he was.

"He's not even speaking to me, Tommy," she said into the lengthy silence.

He gave a start. "So you're not sleeping with him anymore?"

Brittany flinched at his blunt wording before gritting her teeth and saying, "No, I'm not."

He glared at her. "What happened?"

"I told him you were my brother. That's what happened." She gave that statement time to soak in before she added, "So you see, your idea that he'd choose me over his family is not only ludicrous, it's just not true."

"Aw, hell," Tommy muttered. "I thought I'd hit on a gold mine."

"You thought wrong," Brittany said, fury changing the tone of her voice.

His glare turned to curiosity. "How'd you get hooked up with him in the first place?"

"That no longer matters," she replied tightly, fighting the urge to get up and bolt. She didn't want to talk about Collier. She didn't want to think about him. It was too painful.

Tommy continued as though she hadn't spoken. "That family's rolling in dough. I would've thought he was a bit out of your league."

His words cut to the quick, but she ignored them. "Will you just forget I said anything, please?" she demanded, her suppressed fury boiling over. "Like I said, it no longer matters."

"It does to me. There still might be a way—"

"That's not going to happen," Brittany interrupted harshly, her impatience winning out over her frayed nerves. "Collier Smith is history."

"There's nothing you can do to plead my case, to make him see that I was set up?"

Despite the ever-present desperation in his voice, enough was enough. She gave her head a violent shake. "No, Tommy. No! Forget it. It's not going to happen."

Tommy's lips formed a thin, bitter line. Suddenly his face brightened and he snapped his fingers. "Hey, I got it! If he's out of the picture, then how 'bout trying to get some bucks out of him?"

"As in blackmail?" Brittany screeched, horror washing through her.

"Yeah, why not?" His voice was revved. *He* was *revved.* "What have you got to lose? If he's dumped you, why not go for his jugular? Hell, I bet he'd rather fork over than let himself and that highfalutin firm be dragged through the mud in a scandal. At least it's worth a try."

"For god's sake, Tommy!" she exclaimed. "Listen to yourself. That's sick. You were raised better than that."

His features turned mean. "You just don't give a shit."

"I'm not even going to respond to that."

"Then it looks like I'll continue to rot in this stinking hellhole."

Before Brittany could make a comeback, the guard indicated that their time was up. With a heavy but at the same time grateful heart, she rose. Tommy rose, as well, then turned his back without so much as saying goodbye.

By the time she reached her car, she was shaking all over.

Now, as she forced her mind back to her surroundings, she listened to the thunder boom, forcing her mind off that horrifying conversation.

However, there was no rest for the weary. Her thoughts switched to Collier, which was equally disturbing. Her heart suddenly felt like a chunk of lead in her chest. Shivering despite the warmth of the room, Brittany reached for the afghan and covered herself.

Shivering again, Brittany wrapped the coverlet tighter. She ought to consider going to bed. With this being Friday, tomorrow would be a long day. She had to work at the travel agency and the diner. She would be at the diner until midnight or later if she had to stay and help clean up.

Brittany had tossed back the afghan when she heard the knock. She froze outwardly, though her insides turned to putty. Collier? Her thumping heart suddenly rivaled her melting insides. If it was him, how did she feel about that?

She scrambled off the sofa, stood, and took several deep breaths. Then she moved hastily toward the door where she flipped on the porch light.

"It's Collier."

His tone sounded muffled, either from the chill or the

blinding rain. With that in mind, she didn't hesitate, opening the door and stepping aside. Wordlessly he crossed the threshold and instantly shed his wet topcoat, letting it fall to the floor.

Brittany moistened her lips and waited, speech impossible.

"I know I shouldn't be here," he said in a tormented voice. "I know that sounds like a broken record, but…I couldn't stay away." He drew a harsh, ragged breath, his gaze locked on hers.

"What do you want me to say?" Brittany responded in a whisper, every nerve ending in her body on fire and screaming for relief that only he could provide.

"Please, just don't send me away."

He made no effort to mask the pleading note in his voice. That fact alone rendered her breathless, as though she were suddenly smothering. Demanding he leave would be the rational, smart thing to do, but when it came to this man, all rationality fled. She wanted him, and he wanted her. At the moment, nothing else seemed to matter.

"Oh, Collier," she cried softly, tears gathering in her eyes.

"Brittany, don't cry. I'd cut my heart out before I'd hurt you. But I know that's exactly what I'm doing." He paused, his eyes more delving, more tortured, than ever. "Forgive me, but—"

Another muted cry escaped her lips, and her arms reached out. Then she was in his, held tightly against his pounding heart, her fingers digging into the back of his neck.

For a brief time they simply clung to each other. Then, with heat flaring in his eyes, Collier took her lips in a frantic, driven kiss that made her tremble with anticipation and longing.

"God, Brittany," he whispered against her lips, his fingers undoing her robe. When they came in contact with her bare flesh, her breath caught, especially when he cupped her buttocks and pulled her against his erection, moving up and down, creating a friction that made her instantly wet.

He seemed to sense that, running a finger down the crease in her buttocks to the hot warmth between her legs.

She cried out, feeling as if he'd torched her insides with that erotic move. Only after he eased that same finger inside her, sensing she was about to climax, did he make another move, a more dramatic one.

Silently, and without taking his heated gaze off her, he removed his finger, clamped down once again on her buttocks and lifted her. Instinctively her legs circled his waist at the same time he unzipped his pants. Seconds later, he entered her with one hard thrust.

"Oh," she cried out, her lips seeking his.

Two harder thrusts later, they both groaned, then held each other in weakened relief.

Remaining inside her, he immediately carried her to the bed. In that same frantic mode, he removed his clothing along with her robe and joined her—flesh against flesh.

"It's my turn," Brittany whispered, pushing him back onto the bed and leaning over him, taking him into her mouth, tasting herself on him.

"Oh, sweet baby," he moaned, fondling her breasts while her mouth made him hard once again. When she sensed he couldn't take any more without coming in her mouth, she raised a leg and guided him inside her.

With him nestled high and hard in her, she moved back and forth, creating a friction that threatened to take the top of her head off. She knew he felt the same way as his glazed eyes rolled back in his head as he emptied himself inside her once again.

She must have fallen asleep, for when she awakened, she was on her back and his head was between her legs. This time he was tasting *her*. Another wave of heat washed through her, only to intensify when she realized his tongue had taken the place of his erection, stroking in and out of her warmth at leisure.

Her hips bucked as she thrashed on the bed, finally grabbing a handful of his hair, thinking she would surely die from this sweet assault on her body. She hadn't thought she could climax again, but she was wrong. He only had to touch her and she was wet, ready, aching for more.

Because she knew this might be the last time she saw him, Brittany let herself go, basking in the exquisite pleasure of his mouth and tongue. Her sharp cry rent the air just as he entered her.

Flesh into flesh, and they became one. Again.

Twenty-Five

How could he let her go?

Collier peered down at Brittany, who was nestled close against him, sleeping peacefully. He knew he should leave. It would soon be daylight. Yet he didn't move, didn't want to disturb the euphoria that surrounded them.

The smell of sex filled his nostrils. It had been a night of marathon lovemaking. He'd had no idea he could come that often, and with the same intensity each time. He shouldn't have been surprised. Brittany had wrung him inside out from the first time he'd seen her. One look and he'd been a goner.

Neither time nor circumstances had changed that. Emotions he couldn't begin to identify charged through him as he continued to stare at her perfect profile, listen to her gentle breathing, all the while fighting off the urge to turn her over, ease her legs apart and take her once again.

Even though he felt himself grow rod-hard, he didn't disturb her. She was bound to be exhausted, since she'd put as much energy into their lovemaking as he had. Besides, he figured she had a long day facing her, especially since she had to finish it off working late at the diner.

He frowned, suddenly cursing the thought of her going back to that place, enduring the verbal abuse that went along with the job. Collier lowered his gaze to the hand that had been injured. It was outside the sheet, giving him clear access. It had healed nicely on the top, though he would bet that underneath the skin, it was still tender. For a second he was tempted to lean over and kiss it.

Instead he remained unmoving, though his mind continued on a roll. Maybe he could help her find another job, one more suitable to her personality and needs. Hell, what did he know about her needs? he asked himself scornfully. Outside the bed, he didn't know much about her.

Except that her brother was responsible for ruining *his* brother's life.

Beautiful.

His chest suddenly tightened. He lifted his head as though he was smothering. If it weren't for Jackson he'd... What? Continue to see her? Stop hiding the fact he was sleeping with her? Yes. No.

Collier's jaw clenched. He felt frustrated enough to bite a ten-penny nail in two. He wasn't the only one in this equation. He still had his family, his job, his obligations, to consider. His life was planned, for chrissake, and that plan didn't include sharing it with a woman from the wrong side of the tracks.

Even though he despised himself for that snobbish thought, it was the truth. Yet in his heart, he knew that didn't really matter. To some extent, it was just a cop-out. The truth was, he was scared shitless of Brittany and her ability to turn him inside out, to make him lose sight of what was important to him.

Since he'd met her on that lonely stretch of road, his life hadn't been the same. He was beginning to fear it never would be again.

However, the thought of bringing her out of the closet, so to speak—he winced inwardly at that terminology—

and introducing her to Mason and Jackson was too overwhelming to contemplate.

Suddenly his conversation with Kyle jumped to mind. If he ever made his vow to stay away from her stick, would she turn vindictive? The hair lifted on the back of his neck but only for a moment. Then he relaxed. No. He was holding firm to his gut instinct. Regardless of what happened between them, Brittany was not that kind of woman.

Lana. What about her? She remained on the outer fringes, niggling at his conscience, wanting more than he was prepared to give. He couldn't entirely blame her for that. He'd been content to pacify her, to go along with her demands.

Until Brittany.

Now he was playing in a different ballpark. His gaze rested on Brittany once again, and he felt a giant squeeze on his heart.

Had he fallen in love? Panic gripped him, tightening that squeeze. How could he even think such a thing? He didn't know her well enough to love her. Their relationship was based on pure lust, nothing more. Suddenly his panic subsided.

His constant ache for Brittany would pass, he told himself. Soon he would tire of her.

Once this sexual storm had spent itself, he could resume his life and no one would be the wiser.

No, he knew better than that. No matter how much he might want to, he couldn't keep Brittany a secret forever. Time was running out, and pressure was mounting from several different directions. On top of that, it wasn't fair to her. She deserved better.

That strategy simply wouldn't work.

He shifted his position. Instantly Brittany's eyes opened and sought his.

For a long moment their gazes held.

He watched as Brittany licked her lips, leaving them moist with a light sheen. He swallowed hard, staving off the urge to feed his addiction and crush his lips against hers, tasting that sweet nectar once again.

Her words stopped him, a troubled look marring her lovely face. "It's time for you to go, isn't it?"

"Yes."

Silence.

"Will I see you again?"

She averted her gaze which told him that question had come hard. He struggled for a decent breath. "I—"

"You don't have to say anything," she interrupted. "I already know what the answer is."

"Then tell me, because I don't."

Her eyes widened. "I don't expect I'll see you again."

"Is that what you want?" he rasped.

"No," she responded in a shaky voice, "but that's the way it has to be."

He didn't say anything, though he knew he was passing up a golden opportunity to end the affair, to put their lives back on the right track. Yet the words wouldn't come. They jammed in his throat, almost choking him.

"I didn't think I'd ever see you again," she whispered, pulling that lower lip between her teeth.

"I didn't think you would, either." He paused and drew a harsh breath.

"Then why did you come back?"

"You know the answer to that," he muttered in a strangled voice.

"So you don't hate me after all?"

"Hate you? God, no. I never hated you."

She smiled without humor. "That's not the way I read it when you left me at the prison."

He grimaced. "It was just that I was so goddamned shell-shocked."

"Me, too, but I wouldn't have turned on you like that."

He flushed under the gentle reprimand. "I was pissed, too, pissed that Fate had dealt us such a dirty blow."

"Yet here you are."

He grazed one soft cheek with a finger, then cleared his throat. "Are you sorry?"

"No," she whispered. "Just confused."

He sighed and removed his hand. "So am I."

Several beats of silence followed his words; then he said, "Tell me about yourself. I want to know everything there is to know about you."

Suddenly he found that he meant that. He *did* want to know what had made her the person she was, what was going on inside her head, and not just about him, either, but about everything. While delving into her personal life was another suicidal move on his part, he didn't care. At the moment, nothing mattered except her and the fact that she was in his arms.

"There's not a lot to know," she said in a hesitant tone.

"Oh, I bet there is."

"I live a pretty dull life, actually."

"There's nothing dull about you," he whispered, rubbing his foot up and down her leg, which sent a current of electricity shooting through him. He knew she felt it, too, because her breath came out in a soft gasp.

"I'd rather hear about you."

He ignored her. "Was the man who hurt you ever important to you?"

"Absolutely not."

The conviction in her voice reassured him. "Has there ever been anyone? Maybe what I'm asking is, have you ever been in love?"

"No, I haven't."

The idea of another man touching her the way and in the places he'd touched her didn't bear thinking about. He was glad he didn't have to.

"What about your parents?"

"My dad died when I was young. A few years later, my mother remarried."

He felt a slight shudder go through her. "I take it that wasn't a good move?"

Surprisingly, she was forthcoming, telling him about her stepfather, who was a mean drunk, and how her mother had the responsibility of keeping food on the table and the family together. "My peers had a high old time making me the brunt of their jokes, especially since we were so poor."

It tore his heart out to think of what she'd had to endure through no fault of her own, especially from that stepfather. "Unfortunately our peers tended to be the cruelest judges of all."

"How would you know?"

Although her tone held that same gentleness, the hint of another reprimand was there. "You're right, I don't," he admitted, "but that doesn't keep me from imagining how you must've felt."

"It was awful," she said in a dull tone.

He leaned over and gave her a quick, hot kiss, their tongues mating for a second. Forced determination made him remove his mouth and resist making love to her again. But while she was willing to talk, he wanted to listen.

"When will you have your degree?"

"One more year, if—" She broke off.

"If what?" he pressed.

She shifted her gaze. "Never mind. It's not important."

"If you can hold up under the pressure," he said, using her chin to turn her face back toward him. "Is that what you were going to say?"

She gave him a surprised look. "Is it that obvious?"

"Two jobs and college. That's a heavy load for anyone to carry."

"Well, I have no choice," she said flatly. "I have obligations."

He knew her sorry brother figured into those obligations, but he didn't say that, gathering from her tone that she didn't want to expand on the subject. And he didn't want to break the tenuous thread that bound them, so he held his tongue.

"What about you?"

Her turning the tables caught him momentarily off guard. Talking about himself had never been easy, but, in all fairness, he couldn't expect to have it all his way.

"I'm a workaholic," he said in a light tone.

"I bet you're a crackerjack attorney."

His lips twitched. "What makes you think that?"

She answered with a question. "I'm right, aren't I?"

"Some people must think so," he admitted modestly, "since I'm in the top two being considered for a federal judgeship."

Her eyes got bigger. "That sounds like an awesome responsibility."

"Trust me, it is. I lie awake night after night and ask myself if I'm up to the task. The thought of holding someone's life in my hands is mind-numbing."

"The fact that you feel that way means you'll do well."

Her confidence made him feel good. "I hope so, but I haven't gotten it yet. I have stiff competition, plus I'm working on a controversial case, which isn't to my benefit." When she held her silence, he touched on the sexual harassment suit.

"You'll do fine," she stressed with that same easy confidence.

"We'll see," Collier responded on a heavy note.

Another silence ensued, during which his mind continued to churn. He should go. He was due in court, and time was running out. Even though they had talked, where they went from here hadn't been settled.

"I wish Tommy had had a lawyer with your values."

Once she'd spoken her brother's name, he felt her stiffen, as if waiting for the explosion she was sure would follow. "You love your brother, and I love mine. And though we are definitely on different sides of the fence, I don't want it to come between us."

"But it *is* between us, Collier. You have to know that Tommy's the reason why I'm working myself to the bone. He got a raw deal, and I'm determined to get him a new lawyer and prove it."

"Brittany, don't go there," he said in a voice filled with agony.

"I have to. I know you don't believe it, but Tommy was set up. I'm convinced of that, and I intend to prove it."

Before he could interject, she went on and told him Tommy's side, about how someone had put a narcotic in his drink, which hadn't taken full effect until after he'd gotten behind the wheel.

Collier once again held his tongue, unwilling to enter

into a verbal slanging match with her and drive the wedge deeper between them. Of course she would side with her brother. Most sisters would. And while he didn't hold her allegiance to Tommy against her, he didn't believe that garbage her brother had fed her, not for one minute.

She wouldn't lie. But Tommy would—and did.

"So now that the line has been drawn in the sand," she whispered, her voice quivering, "where do we go from here?"

"I don't know," he responded, that old desperate feeling clawing at his gut. "All I care about now is how good I feel when I'm inside you."

"Oh, Collier," she whispered, circling his neck and bringing his lips to hers.

That was when he tasted her tears.

Twenty-Six

Rupert reached for the bottle in the seat beside him and took another swig. When the strong booze hit his stomach, it burned for the first time ever. He frowned, hoping he wasn't getting an ulcer.

He knew he should stop drinking so much, but with so many things going wrong in his life right now, liquor was his comfort, especially when he sat outside Brittany's trailer. And watched. It was such a cold, lonely and boring endeavor, yet he couldn't make himself stay away. He admitted it bordered on the sick side, but he didn't care. Besides, what he did was his own business, including this kinky pastime.

Until the other night, when he'd seen the fancy Lexus parked close by, he'd been certain Brittany had no man in her life. Now he wasn't certain at all.

That same Lexus was back, and this time it was parked right in front of Brittany's trailer.

Who the hell was her mystery lover? Who was getting the nooky that belonged to him? That was the big question. The thought of anyone else infringing on his territory made him see red. He wasn't budging until he saw the guy. Neither was he going to fall asleep, as he had last time.

With daylight approaching, her visitor was bound to leave soon. Rupert didn't know the exact time, and he didn't want to take the chance of turning on the light for fear he would be seen—which was ludicrous, of course. Who in this shabby mobile home park gave a shit about an extra car parked on the street?

No one, he assured himself. Still, he didn't do anything to call attention to himself. Thank goodness it was chilly but not cold. Most times he only sat for an hour or so and that was all. Tonight, however, he intended to remain for the duration.

A belch escaped while he loosened his tie and unbuttoned his coat. Thank goodness Angel was out of town on one of her church retreats. Otherwise, he wouldn't have the luxury of staying here. He could have told her he was away for the night on business, and she wouldn't have questioned that. But if he was accidentally seen, then it could cost him. He wasn't ready to chance that.

If he could just dump Angel's narrow-minded ass, a big part of his problem would be solved. One of these days, he swore, he would. First, though, he had to find a way to sneak more money out of the business and hide it. So far, he'd done a damn good job of that and no one had been the wiser. Still, he didn't quite have the funds to retire on and keep Brittany and himself in the style he wanted.

Too, he'd promised to hire an attorney for that sorry brother of Brittany's, something else that would take money, more than normal, because it was going to have to be on the sly. Angel must never find out about that, either.

And he couldn't forget about his obligation to Travis Wainwright. He had to get that appointment to the bench, and that meant adding even more funds to the Republican party coffer. At least that was something Angel didn't mind.

Ordinarily he wouldn't have given a shit who got that federal appointment, but since Mason Williams' boy wanted it, he had no choice but to get involved. Anytime the opportunity presented itself to battle Mason, he took it.

The way it was looking now, Travis had a strong chance of being named. To date, Rupert hadn't had to do anything underhanded, although that remained an open option. If it looked like the committee was going to openly recommend Collier Smith, he would make his move. Until then, he'd just keep pressure on Riley, reminding him of how much money he'd given his campaign.

Suddenly tired of his thoughts and tired of waiting, Rupert eased his head back against the seat, promising himself he would only close his eyes for a few minutes. Later, he didn't know what awakened him. Maybe it was the porch light that suddenly came on in the mobile home adjacent to his vehicle. He would never know, but it didn't matter. Whatever the reason, he was grateful.

Because it was shortly thereafter that the door to Brittany's trailer opened and her guest walked out. At first Rupert was so stunned he was certain he was hallucinating, that the booze was messing with his mind again.

Because he was looking straight at Collier Smith.

Rupert blinked several times to clear his vision. Nothing changed. The upstart stepson of Mason Williams strode to the Lexus, climbed behind the wheel, cranked the engine, then drove off into the silence.

Dumbfounded and livid, Rupert gripped the steering wheel until he heard his knuckles pop.

He vowed Collier Smith would pay for this. And dearly, too.

* * *

"Daddy's gone," Lana said, a sultry edge to her voice. "So we have the entire house to ourselves—except for the servants, of course. And, as you know, they will disappear on command."

Collier leaned over and grazed Lana's cheek with his lips, then stepped back. He hadn't wanted to join her for the evening, but since it was imperative that he talk to her, he'd accepted her invitation. However, he dreaded every second that was to follow.

"Is that all?" Her smile turned into a pout.

Collier frowned. "I don't know what you're talking about."

"Just a peck on the cheek. Is that all?" she asked again, eyeing him with a glint.

He felt his face heat. "Sorry."

"No, you're not, but you will be if you don't make it up to me."

"Lana—"

"It's all right, darling, I'm willing to cut you some slack. I'm sure you've had a rough day in court. After you've had a drink or two, you'll be in the mood." She smiled and winked. "And the drinks are ready and waiting."

Somehow Collier managed to get through the cocktails and dinner. When Lana wanted to, she could be something other than the social butterfly who flitted from one meaningless function to the other. In reality, she was extremely intelligent. That was one reason he'd been attracted to her.

Lately, though, it seemed nothing was important to her but superficial things. She had changed. Or perhaps he was the one who had changed. *Brittany had changed him.*

Once coffee was served in the parlor, Lana took a sip

of hers, then cut her eyes toward him. "You didn't eat much dinner. Was something wrong?"

"Absolutely not. The pork tenderloin was perfect."

She scrutinized him. "As a matter of fact, you look like you've lost weight." She paused and tilted her head. "Of course, I haven't seen you without your clothes in so long, I can't say for sure."

If she intended for her barb to hit its mark, it did. Only he didn't let on. He steeled himself not to show any emotion. He'd come on a mission, and he wasn't about to be sidetracked.

"No comment, huh?" she said, reaching for her cup again, then staring at him over the rim.

"We need to talk."

"You might, but I don't," she snapped. "Unless it's to set a wedding date."

"That's why I'm here."

Lana's eyes widened. "You mean—"

Damn, he was messing this up. He had known talking to her was going to be difficult; he just hadn't known how difficult. He wished he could tell her the truth, but he couldn't. That just wasn't possible.

"No, that's not why I'm here."

Her face tensed. "So you're still not prepared to set a wedding date?"

"I don't love you, Lana."

Finally. He'd been wanting to tell her that for weeks now, ever since he'd met Brittany. In all fairness to Lana, this conversation was long overdue, but he'd been such a mess emotionally, it was as if his life hadn't been his own.

She shrugged. "I don't care."

He gave a start, and his eyes narrowed. "What the hell does that mean?"

"It means exactly what I said." Lana shrugged again. "It's not important to me whether you love me or not."

Collier's mind was reeling. "That's crazy."

"To you, maybe, but not to me," she responded in a matter-of-fact tone.

He bounded off the sofa and walked to the window. He hadn't known what to expect when he'd delivered what he considered to be the deathblow to their relationship, severing it completely, but it certainly hadn't been this reaction.

"I'll marry you anyway."

Letting go an expletive, Collier swung around. "You don't mean that."

"Sure I do." She paused and licked her red lips. "Just out of curiosity, is it another woman?"

He averted his gaze, unprepared to unburden his soul to her or anyone else. But he had come to grips with the reality that he wasn't going to stay away from Brittany, *couldn't* stay away. That was why he had to end his relationship with Lana, so she could move on without him.

"It's okay if you have someone else on the side."

Collier opened his mouth, then slammed it shut. He knew Lana could be a cold bitch, but in his estimation, this went way beyond that.

"It's *not* okay with me."

"Look, Collier, after we're married if you want to have flings on the side, as long as you're discreet, I don't mind. Truly I don't."

He shook his head violently. "I'm not going to marry you, Lana."

"Are you sure about that?" she asked, her voice growing more sultry. He wasn't fooled. Underneath, he heard that core of steel and knew she wasn't going down without a fight. His hopes of an easy out faded. Yet he wasn't about to back down or back off. Still, he had to try and settle this with as much civility as possible. "After I've told you how I feel, you'd go through with it? Marry me anyway?"

"Without question."

"Why?"

"Maybe I don't love you, either. Have you ever thought of that?"

"No." How had this conversation gotten so damned derailed?

"Well, I do, but probably not in the way most people love their spouses."

"God, Lana, you're not making any sense."

"Oh, yes, my darling, I am. Much more than you are."

He didn't say anything. Frankly he didn't know what to say.

"Have you forgotten what's important to you?"

Only Brittany. "Of course not," he said harshly.

"Oh, I think you have," she countered, once again licking her lips.

He withdrew his eyes from that gesture, knowing she was trying to turn him on and, in the end, lure him into her bed. Suddenly he was repulsed by her, and by this entire dialogue.

"Make your point," he said in a weary voice.

"The federal bench. That's my point. You want to become a judge, right?"

"Yes," he said tightly.

"Then marry me, and *voilà,* you'll have it."

"Sure." Collier didn't bother to mask the sarcasm in his tone.

This time her eyes flared, and she rose to her feet. "Have you forgotten my daddy and how much influence he wields, especially with Senator Riley?"

"No, but so does Mason."

"Trust me, you and me tying the knot would seal it." She paused as if to let that tidbit settle in. "Are you willing to give that up?"

He shook his head. "You think I'd marry you just to get ahead?"

She stiffened. "You could do worse."

"Sure I could, because you have a lot to offer. I can't imagine why you'd want to waste your life marrying a man who doesn't love you the way you deserve to be loved."

"Love has nothing to do with it."

"It does to me," he said flatly, heading toward the door. Once there, he swung back around. "And so does the sanctity of marriage."

"Collier," she snapped, "don't you dare walk out on me."

He softened his features. "We'll talk later, when you're thinking more rationally."

"Damn you!" she yelled. "No one walks out on me."

He stared at her for a long moment, then said, "Take care of yourself."

Mason peered at his calendar.

He had thought he had a golf game that afternoon, but he'd been wrong. Somehow he'd gotten his dates mixed up. But that was all right. He would go to court and hear Collier argue the case.

Though he still had strong reservations about what his stepson was doing, he had to admit that he was something to watch in the courtroom. Even though he wasn't blood kin and hadn't gotten the attorney genes from him, it didn't matter. He was a natural at what he did.

Mason supposed he ought to tell Collier that, but

somehow the words always seemed to stick in his throat. Now, if it had been Jackson... God forgive him for feeling that way. But he couldn't help it. He wanted his blood son to excel, to be the brilliant litigator in front of a jury and judge. But that was not to be, he reminded himself bitterly.

Still, he was luckier than most men. He had another son, albeit a stepson, who was apparently destined for great things. Collier getting that appointment to the bench would go a long way toward making all their lives worth living again.

Ever since Jackson's accident, he'd fought to overcome his own demons of bitterness and hate. While he'd come far, he wasn't there yet, even though he'd felt an easing in his gut of late.

He hoped Collier wouldn't do anything stupid to put a kink in things. But with his stepson, one never knew. Collier was his own man. Jackson had always been much more predictable, especially when it pertained to the job. If Mason had advised him against taking a controversial case, Jackson wouldn't have taken it. Not so with Collier. He did what *he* thought was best.

A sigh filtered through Mason. Despite that independent streak—maybe even because of it—he was proud of his younger son, and once he got that appointment, he would tell him. That pat on the back was long overdue.

The phone rang suddenly, jarring him out of his thoughts. He reached for it.

"That you, Williams?"

He recognized the voice right off, and his blood pressure rose. His old adversary, Rupert Holt, rarely called him. When he did, it was always bad news. He steeled himself.

"Hello, Rupert," he managed to say in a civil manner,

though he wanted to slam the phone down in the other man's ear.

He was the last person Mason wanted to talk to in light of the fact that Rupert was supporting his own man for the judgeship. And that worried Mason for more reasons than one. Even without Rupert's backing, Wainwright was a formidable candidate. He had figured it would come down to choosing between Wainwright and Collier, and it had.

"Have you got any free time today?"

Mason's hackles rose instantly. "Why?"

"I'd like to meet you for coffee."

"I'm busy," Mason said coldly.

"I think you ought to reconsider."

"What the hell do you want, Holt? If it's that important, you can tell me over the phone."

"But I'd rather not. What I have to say, you'll want to hear face-to-face." Rupert paused. "Meet me at the Townhouse Coffee Shop in an hour." He paused again. "Oh, and trust me, you'll be sorry if you don't."

Twenty-Seven

"**W**hat's with you, kid? One minute you're blowing hot, the next cold."

Sissy was grinning broadly when she made that statement, though Brittany read the curiosity in her eyes.

"Maybe I'm going through the change," Brittany quipped lightly.

Sissy cut her a look. "Sure you are."

Brittany toyed with a pencil on her desk. It was after lunch, and she'd just gotten out of class and come to the agency. She hadn't expected Sissy to be there, since she hadn't seen much of her lately, which she was glad of. She didn't want her friend and boss to probe. That made her uncomfortable.

"If I didn't know better, I'd say you had a man in your life." Another grin followed those words.

Brittany's head bobbed up, and her eyes widened.

"I *am* right."

"No, you're not," Brittany sputtered, only to feel a slight prick of conscience. But Collier wasn't "in her life," not in the way Sissy meant. For the most part, he was more out than in. Right now she had no idea where he was or where things stood between them.

When he'd left her bed two days ago, nothing had been settled, though he'd said he would call her and she believed him. However, she was anxious for obvious reasons. Collier was a tempting piece of fruit that Fate kept dangling in front of her, baiting her to take just one more bite.

And bite she had, even though she knew she was only fooling herself into thinking that fruit would eventually belong to her.

She was no Cinderella.

"Care to share?"

Sissy's indulgent tone brought her back to the moment. "What?" she asked innocently.

"That stuff churning inside your head."

Brittany flushed. "You wouldn't be interested."

"Oh, yes, I would, especially if I'm right and you've got a man."

"Sissy, would you stop it?" Brittany forced a grin, but she was serious. Even if Collier hadn't only been hovering on the perimeters of her life, she wasn't ready or willing to share him. She was too busy savoring him herself.

"Oh, all right. Have it your way, but I know you pretty well, Brittany Banks, and something's not quite right."

Brittany felt her flush deepen and was irritated that she couldn't hide her feelings better. Collier had probably read her just as well.

"You're just not yourself lately," Sissy pressed, her tone now sober. "If it's not a man, then it has to be Tommy. Or school. Lord knows, you have enough going on." Sissy paused, narrowing her eyes. "Your mood doesn't by chance have anything to do with that 'incident,' does it?"

Brittany picked up on the hesitation in Sissy's tone. It was as though the older woman sensed she was treading on sensitive ground. Sissy still didn't know what had happened or who was responsible, and Brittany was determined she never would.

"It's something I'll never forget," Brittany admitted honestly, "but I've come to terms with it."

"I still say whoever worked you over should definitely pay."

Brittany made a face. "Can we change the subject?"

"In a heartbeat." Sissy rubbed her chin. "When you graduate, would you consider running this place full-time?"

Brittany blinked. "Where are you going?"

"I just want to stay home."

"You're not ill, are you?"

"No, I just want to retire."

Brittany shook her head, then smiled. "Sissy, you beat all. You'll never retire, not for a minute. You're too full of energy to do that. Besides, you don't work all that much as it is."

Sissy chuckled. "True on that last one, anyway. But I do have the worry and responsibility of the business side. If you took over, you could handle it all."

"Oh, Sissy, I don't know. By the time I graduate, I have no idea what'll be happening in my life."

"I know, but just keep that thought in the back of your mind, okay? I know you've always said you were getting out of this town as soon as you could, but I'd sure make it worth your while to stay."

"I appreciate the offer, believe me. And I'll certainly keep it in the back of my mind."

"Good, now down to business."

A little while later, Sissy was gone and Brittany was alone. She had four tours to book, which was enough work to keep her busy without the phone calls and drop-ins. Yet she didn't want to work, she wanted to day-dream. About Collier.

Their last time together had been an added delight, especially as he'd been interested in more than just having sex. He'd been interested in *her*.

What that meant, exactly, she had no idea. But as long as Collier was willing to see her, she would see him. How long he would feel that way was something else she had no idea about.

So what about pride? Where did that come in?

Collier wasn't about to make their affair public, especially not after he'd found out who she was, who her brother was. And what about his supposed fiancée? That issue remained unaddressed. The thought that she was still in his life, *in his bed,* was unthinkable.

She had no choice but to think about those disturbing facts, any one of which could bring about the downfall of their relationship. Yet she didn't care, which meant the pride she'd always held dear had apparently gone on hiatus.

He'd whisked her up and taken her to a world she'd never known before, a world where the heady magic filling her heart took precedence over everything else. Which was not good, she told herself savagely.

Still, she wasn't ready to let him go unless he wanted to go. Somehow, she doubted that was the case. When they were together, he couldn't seem to leave her alone any more than she wanted him to. Their hold on each other was undeniable and unyielding.

So why hadn't he called?

Brittany peered at the phone, willing it to ring, but only if his voice was on the other end. It defied her and remained silent. Suppressing a sigh, she turned to the stack of folders on her desk.

The day wasn't over yet. She would hold on to that.

Fool.

When all was said and done, he was worse than that, Mason told himself as he got out of his car and strode into the coffee shop. He paused inside the door and looked around. Rupert hadn't made it yet. Was that a sign he should leave?

Meeting Rupert Holt was the last thing he wanted to do. When he'd hung up the phone, he'd had no intention of showing up. But a niggling in the back of his mind wouldn't go away. While not overtly threatening, Rupert's words were to be reckoned with.

Rupert himself was to be reckoned with. Even on his best days, he was a snake in the grass. As far as Mason was concerned, that man had no saving graces. And the fact he seemed to have something on Mason or his family scared the hell out of him.

If Collier hadn't been in such a precarious position, he wouldn't give a shit, but Rupert's involvement with the federal appointment added a deadly poison to the mix, so Mason had listened to his gut instinct and come.

Cursing the delay, he followed the waitress to the out-of-the-way table he'd requested. He didn't want anyone to overhear anything said between Rupert and him. Maybe his careful planning would all be for naught. Maybe the bastard had just been blowing smoke and wouldn't show up after all.

That thought had barely jelled when he looked up and in walked Rupert. It had been a while since he'd seen his one-time friend, and he noticed that the man hadn't changed all that much. Perhaps his girth was a little larger, indicating that he was hitting the bottle more than he should. Otherwise, he was his usual handsome, robust and cocky self.

"You made the wise decision," Rupert said without preamble, not bothering to extend his hand.

Mason didn't respond right off, because the waitress showed up to take their orders. Both opted for coffee, though Mason feared he might choke on his. No telling what Rupert had up his sleeve.

The cups arrived almost immediately, which cleared the way to get straight to the point. Mason voiced his thoughts. "What do you want?"

"Not ready to mend any fences, I see."

"No more than you are," Mason replied in a tart-edged tone.

"You're right. I still think you screwed me over on that case."

Mason reached for his coat. "If dredging up the past is why you brought me down here, then you're wasting both our time. I'm gone."

"Hold your horses."

It wasn't so much what Rupert said as the way he said it that sent another warning shot through Mason. In spite of his loathing of this man and his desire to leave, he held his ground. He'd come this far; he might as well stay the course.

"Let's hear it," Mason said coldly.

Rupert deliberately took a slow sip of his coffee, as though enjoying every second of watching Mason stew. "You don't keep very close tabs on your son, do you?"

This time a chill filtered through Mason's entire body. He was right; Collier and the judgeship were the reason for this get-together, which didn't bode well at all.

"He's a grown man," Mason responded, his tone

dropping another degree, "but that's beside the point, and we both know it."

"I thought he was about to marry the Frazier woman. Bill's daughter."

Mason barely spoke. "He is."

Rupert took another sip of his coffee, then reached for a pack of artificial sweetener. Watching another calculated stalling tactic play itself out sent Mason's blood pressure soaring. However, he didn't say anything, knowing that was exactly what Rupert wanted.

Rupert was playing a child's game and enjoying it to the hilt. But Rupert was no fool. In order for him to have had the gall to set up this meeting in the first place, something had to be amiss. Under those circumstances, Mason couldn't afford to tell him to go to hell.

He was between the proverbial rock and a hard place, and Rupert knew it, damn him.

"Mmm." Rupert rubbed his chin. "He sure isn't acting like a man who's about to be married."

"How the hell would you know?"

Rupert chuckled, though his eyes were hard and unsmiling as he reached for another sweetener. Unwittingly Mason's hand shot across the table and clamped down on Rupert's wrist.

For an instant neither moved, the tension thick and heavy.

"Get your goddamn hand off me," Rupert snarled.

"Then you get to the goddamn point. You're playing a dangerous game here, Holt."

Before Mason could withdraw his hand, Rupert shook free, his eyes narrowed and glaring. "Don't ever touch me again."

A new frisson of uneasiness forced Mason to shift positions. Still, he didn't show his seething emotions, realizing Rupert intended to drag this game out to the bitter end, make it last for as many innings as he could. That being the case, Mason had little choice but to cool his heels, let Rupert have his day in the sun.

Later, when his time came up to bat, he'd knock Rupert out of the park.

"Seems Collier's gettin' himself some nooky on the side."

The back of Mason's head pounded. "You're full of shit."

"Why don't you ask him?"

Clamping down on his temper and his tone, Mason said, "I'd rather you tell me all about it. It'll be much better coming from you since you've obviously been spying on my son. Or maybe you had someone else do your dirty work."

His sarcasm wasn't lost on Rupert, whose features turned an angry red. He wasn't pleased that Mason was no longer bucking him, lowering the stakes of the game considerably.

Rupert scowled. "I saw him leave a woman's trailer in the wee hours of the morning."

Mason's heart almost stopped beating, but once again he steeled himself to guard his feelings. If what Rupert said was true, then Collier had messed up big time.

"Aren't you curious to know who she is?"

"Not really, but I know you're going to tell me anyway."

"She's a looker, all right. But she's also trailer trash, goes to school, works two jobs, one as a waitress at a local diner." He paused with a cold grin. "But then, I guess when the pussy's hot, none of that other stuff matters."

It was all Mason could do not to grab the sonofabitch

by his tie and knock his gloating head off. "Now that you've dropped your bombshell, I'm out of here."

"Not so fast," Rupert said with an easy smile. "The best is yet to come—her name."

"I'm waiting." Mason's tone was both harsh and weary.

"It's Brittany Banks."

While that name obviously was supposed to have been a slap in the face, it wasn't. Mason had heard it before; he would admit that. But at the moment he couldn't say why or from what source.

Rupert's grin widened, and Mason's heart sank even further, realizing Rupert smelled blood and was about to move in for the kill. He hardened his heart and his nerves, preparing for the lethal blow.

"She's Tommy Rogers' sister." His gloating, Cheshire cat grin took on new meaning. "Yeah, my friend, he's playing footsie with the enemy. How 'bout them apples?"

Mason's temper flared to stroke level. "You bastard, you're a damned liar. You'll stoop to anything just to get even with me and my family."

Rupert gave him another sly grin. "Your son's the one who gave me the ammunition to shoot him with."

"I'm warning you to keep your mouth shut." The look on Mason's face matched his temper. "If you so much as breathe one word of that malicious rumor about my son, you'll be sorry."

Rupert laughed. "You're venting your anger on the wrong person. It's Collier you need to rake over the coals."

Mason lunged to his feet, then hissed, "Oh, I intend to. Then he'll be slapping a slander suit on you. And you just wait till he's a judge."

Rupert's grin held, but his voice turned savage. "If I have anything to do with it, Collier *won't* sit on that bench. Now get the hell out of my face."

"If it's a fight you're itching for, then you'll get it." Mason's eyes didn't flinch. "And make no mistake, it's a fight you won't win."

Twenty-Eight

Jackson peered at the doctor in stunned amazement. "I—" He stopped cold, unable to form a coherent sentence.

Dr. Ted Ames chuckled. "Sometime medical miracles come about. Not often, mind you, but they do happen. I'd say yours is a combination of factors. One is the result of your therapy. You've been so disciplined and regimented in that area. Another is the type of spinal cord injury you sustained."

"Still, I never thought—" Again Jackson broke off, too shell-shocked to go on.

"Remember, I told you from the beginning SCI's are divided into two types of injuries—complete and incomplete. I had diagnosed yours as incomplete. However, since you've never had any function from the waist down, I'd about decided I was wrong. Now, however, this latest blessing proves I was right."

The doctor paused with a grin. "Just consider yourself one fortunate bastard, my friend."

Jackson was still having difficulty speaking after receiving the second biggest jolt of his life, right after waking up and finding out he was paralyzed and would never walk again.

"You mean I can make love to a woman?" Jackson

gave his old friend and neurosurgeon another disbelieving stare.

"Yes, Jackson, you can have intercourse—at least physically. Making love's a mental effort, too. But then, I don't guess I have to tell you that."

"Yes, you do. It's been so long since I've had any feeling in that part of my body that just about all of life's pleasures have disappeared."

"It doesn't have to be that way, you know," Ted said in a firm but unaccusing tone.

"That's easy for you to say," Jackson lashed back.

The doctor sighed. "We've had this conversation numerous times since the accident. I guess one more time won't matter, not that it will do any good. But you don't have to sit in your room all day simply because you're in a wheelchair."

"I don't need another lecture," Jackson muttered churlishly.

Ted grinned. "In light of your great news, I agree. You just need to savor the moment."

Silence filled the room while Jackson groped to come to terms with the astounding medical facts he'd just learned. He'd suspected that a change had taken place in his body, especially after he'd felt a strange sensation following Haley's touch. Still, he'd believed it had been his imagination and tried to talk himself out of going to the doctor. Finally, though, he'd given in, both fear and hope driving him.

"Is there someone special who will benefit?"

Jackson felt his face turn red. "Not really."

"There will be."

Jackson gave him an intense look and asked the question that had been burning a trail through his brain, although he hadn't had enough courage to ask it before now. "What…about my legs? Is there a chance I'll regain use of them?"

Ted sighed again. "At this point, I don't know. Yesterday, before you came to see me, I would have said no, without any qualms." He paused. "But today, after examining you, I have to acknowledge that someday it may happen."

"Only not now."

Ted patted Jackson's shoulder, then walked to his desk and perched on it, folding his arms across his chest. "They're making new strides everyday in SCI, so you mustn't give up. Hope is the key word here."

"It's hard to hang on to that kind of hope, Ted, when you're trapped."

"I won't argue with that, nor will I pretend to know what you're going through, what you've been through, because I don't."

"No one does, unless they've been there."

Ted smiled sympathetically. "But things aren't nearly as bleak as they were, so rejoice in your good news. Call your woman friend and ask her to dinner."

"That sounds well and good," Jackson mumbled, down-in-the-mouth, feeling the old depression sink its claws into him again. "But no woman in her right mind wants to tie herself to a man who's married to a stinking wheelchair."

"You don't know that, Jackson. Besides, for now you don't have to worry about anything permanent. Just savor the moment and see what happens."

"I guess you're right."

"I want to see you back in about three months. Until then, enjoy life a little. You deserve it." Ted paused, his features sobering. "Are you going to share your good news with anyone? Say Collier or Mason?"

"Not on your life," Jackson said with vigor. "It's none of their business whether I can screw or not."

Ted laughed, then slapped Jackson on the shoulder. "Too bad you're not putting that fire that's still burning in your belly to good use in the courtroom."

Jackson glared at him. "That's not ever going to happen, not as long as I can't stand."

"That's too bad," Ted responded in a light tone, opening the door to his office.

Jackson signaled for Harry. "Thanks, Ted. I'll be in touch."

Since that conversation had taken place earlier that morning, Jackson had spent the chilly but sunlit afternoon in his room, trying to decide if he should shock the devil out of Haley and call her.

He wanted to. God, did he ever. Her vibrant smile, wild red hair and sassy mouth were just the medicine he needed, though he was reluctant to admit that even to himself. And with the feeling returning to that part of his anatomy, he was no longer a total loss as a man. Still, neither Haley nor any other woman would want a lasting relationship with him. So why bother? His heart would just get brutalized once again.

Fear.

Fear of more rejection kept him from reaching for the phone and calling her. Damn! Deciding he couldn't stand being alone with his thoughts for another second, Jackson rolled to the elevator and pushed the button. He hadn't seen his dad today. If he was home, he'd shock him with his unexpected presence, something he ought to do more often.

He knew both his dad and his brother grieved for him and his condition every day. Yet he didn't want their pity, couldn't stand it. What he wanted was his life back as he'd once known it. Cursing silently, he maneuvered his wheelchair down the hall.

Jackson heard Mason's voice long before he realized the study door was open. His dad was on the phone and apparently not happy. In fact, he was livid.

"That's exactly what he told me, Kyle," he said, his voice shaking with fury. "It wouldn't do for me to get my hands on him about now."

Jackson reached the threshold at the same time that Mason saw him. His father's eyes widened in surprise, then he said, "Look, I have to go now. I'll call you back."

Once the receiver was in place, Mason took several deep breaths as though trying to regain control. "This is a surprise," he said.

"What's going on, Dad?" Jackson demanded, rolling deeper in the room. "If you don't calm down, you're going to have a heart attack."

"Are *you* all right?"

"Does something have to be wrong for me to come downstairs?"

"Yes," Mason said bluntly.

Jackson felt the blood drain from his face. That was a low blow, but he deserved it. "What was that conversation all about? I haven't seen you this upset since—" He broke off, unwilling to mention the accident.

He figured Mason picked up on that and chose to let it go, as well. Besides, he had something else eating at him.

"It's your brother," Mason said in a weary but harsh tone.

"What about him?"

Mason hesitated, then looked away. "I'm not sure I should tell you."

"What the hell does that mean?"

"Just what I said."

"Hogwash!"

Mason seemed to go limp, his shoulders drooping. For the first time, he reminded Jackson of a tired old man. Fear dried out his mouth. He had to swallow several times so he could speak. "Dad, talk to me, dammit!"

"I don't know if I can," Mason replied, his Adam's apple working overtime.

"Collier's not hurt, is he?"

"No."

"Did he get passed over for the bench?"

"Not yet."

"Then whatever's happened or whatever he's done can't be that big a deal."

Mason laughed mirthlessly. "Oh, yes, it is."

"Will you stop crawfishing and spit it out before you choke on it?"

"It concerns *you,* Jackson."

"So?" he responded with forced casualness. "Whatever it is, I can handle it."

"All right, you asked for it."

"So shoot."

He listened as Mason recounted his entire conversation with Rupert. By the time he finished, Jackson's fingers were trying their best to make dents in the hard plastic arms of his chair.

For the longest time, silence dominated the room.

Mason was the first to break it. "Do you think it's true? Do you really think he's screwing Rogers' sister? God…" His voice seemed to fade into nothingness.

Jackson was fighting his own demons, wondering if his brother had completely lost his mind, if what Holt had said was true. And in Jackson's eyes, that was a big if. On the other hand, how could he fabricate such a wild tale and think he could get away with it?

"Something's rotten," Jackson said at last. "You can bet on that. And it may be Rupert, so before we jump Collier, let's just ask him."

"What's with you?" Mason demanded. "How come you're taking this so calmly? I thought you'd be ready to fillet him like a fish."

"Why are you so quick to believe Rupert? You know what a piece of shit he is. Why not give Collier the benefit of the doubt?"

"Because something's going on with him." Mason balled both fists. "It's like he's in another world. No, it's like his head's up his ass," he added fiercely.

"Hey, don't get yourself riled up again. If it is true, then we'll deal with it."

"It'll ruin him," Mason said in a dull, resigned tone. "It'll coldcock his chances for the bench for sure. Kyle thinks so, too. He's about to have a shit fit."

"Where's Collier now?"

"In court, I imagine."

Jackson's lips thinned. "I'll call and leave word for him to stop by here on his way home. We'll ask him about it then."

Mason's eyes were bleak. "This can't be happening. It just can't."

"Give it a rest, Dad," Jackson urged gently. "The appointment's not worth having a coronary over."

"It is to me."

Watching his father in total despair over having his hopes and dreams hang in the balance yet again brought on a new onslaught of guilt. If only he hadn't been in the wrong place at the wrong time. If only that kid hadn't been on the road high...

Shutting those destructive thoughts down abruptly, Jackson rolled toward the bar in the study. "Sit down while I make you a drink. You need it." He paused. "We both do."

When she said hello, his knees went weak. Good thing he was sitting down. "It's me."

"Hi," she said in her lilting, husky voice, which produced an instant erection.

Collier hadn't planned on calling her. Instead he'd had every intention of showing up at her place on his way home from work. But when he'd gotten the message from his brother, he'd changed his plans. Talking to her on the phone would have to suffice for now, but it was nowhere near as satisfactory. He ached to hold her.

"Did I catch you at a bad time?"

"I was just studying."

He picked up on the slight husky catch in her voice, and it made him grow harder.

"In what?" he rasped.

"My robe."

"Naked underneath?"

"Yes."

This time his breath caught. "I wish I was there."

"Why aren't you?"

He groaned. "Obligations."

"I see."

"It's not what you think," he assured her tightly, then, lowering his voice, he added, "I haven't touched another woman since I met you."

"Oh, Collier," she whispered. "I miss you."

"God, I miss you, too."

"When will I see you again?"

He gripped the receiver, envisioning her perched on

her tattered sofa with her dainty feet curled under her buttocks, toying with her bottom lip, her robe gaping just enough to expose a full, jutting breast.

Groaning silently, he tried to ease his burgeoning erection by shifting positions. When would this insanity end? Just hearing her voice made him hard, something that had never happened to him before. But then, Brittany had redefined the word erotic.

"Collier?"

"Mmm?"

"Nothing."

"Look, if I can get loose, I'll see you later."

"Tonight?"

"God, yes."

"I'll be waiting."

A short time later Collier bounded up the steps of his childhood home, wondering for the first time what Jackson wanted. Rarely did his brother call him, so it must be important. Suddenly he felt uneasy. Was it possible he had found out about Brittany? No. Kyle wouldn't have betrayed his confidence. More than likely it had something to do with the appointment.

But since it was Jackson, that didn't ring true. Oh well, Collier told himself, shrugging off his forebodings. He would soon find out.

"Hey, it's me," he called out, after letting himself in. Apparently Maxine had retired to her quarters for the evening.

"Dad's in the study," Jackson said, appearing seemingly out of the blue.

Collier frowned. "Is something up, bro?"

"We'll see," Jackson muttered, rolling toward the study.

Collier had no recourse but to follow him. Mason was

standing by the gas fireplace, his features grim. Jackson positioned himself alongside their dad. Both men faced Collier, who suddenly felt as if he were standing in front of a firing squad.

"Sit down, Collier," Mason demanded.

"No offer of a drink first?" Collier countered lightly, trying to diffuse the tension.

Mason ignored him, then asked bitterly, "Is it true? Are you sleeping with the enemy?"

Twenty-Nine

Collier felt all the color drain from his face and fought for a decent breath. How had they found out? He still didn't think Kyle had betrayed him, though he knew his dad could be persuasive when he wanted to be. After all, it hadn't been long since he'd been one of the best criminal lawyers in the state.

"Well...?"

Mason's tone and eyes remained hostile, as if he were staring down his bitterest enemy. Collier's chest tightened as he switched his focus to his brother, whose posture didn't seem quite so hostile. But it wasn't welcoming, either. Far from it.

He hadn't wanted it to come to this. He'd wanted to tell his family. Suddenly he panicked. Tell them what? That he was pussy-poisoned? That he was involved with a woman he couldn't leave alone, no matter the price? Hell no, he couldn't say that. Mason and Jackson simply wouldn't understand. *He* didn't understand himself, so how could he expect anyone else to?

"We've got all evening, if that's what it takes," Jackson said in his lawyerlike tone, something Collier hadn't heard in a long time.

"Who told you about her?"

"Hellfire, boy," Mason lashed out. "That doesn't matter."

"It does to me."

"Is it true?" Mason almost shouted the question.

"Yes, it is."

For several heartbeats no one said another word. Only the grandfather clock in the corner of the room bonged into the slippery silence.

"How could you?" Mason choked out.

Suddenly concerned, Collier stepped toward the old man. "Dad, why don't you sit down?"

"Stay the hell away from me."

Collier pulled up short, feeling about as helpless as he'd ever felt in his life. His world was spinning out of control again, and there wasn't anything he could do about it. Striving to regroup, he inhaled deeply, swinging his gaze once again to his brother, whose eyes were filled with confusion.

"Why would you deliberately involve yourself with that scumbag's sister? Of all the women in this town, it doesn't make any sense."

"I can't argue with that," Collier replied, his voice strained.

"Does Lana know you're screwing around on her?" Mason hammered brutally.

Collier knew he deserved every verbal bullet fired at him. Still, it hurt to see his family turn against him without due process. But hadn't he lambasted himself for the same thing? How could he fault them? He'd pulled some crazy stunts in his thirty-eight years, but his liaison with Brittany topped the list.

"I want an explanation, dammit!"

"Dad, give it a rest," Jackson said in a low but steady tone. "This can all be sorted out, I'm sure, if we don't let our emotions and our tempers get the best of us."

Mason turned on his elder son and spat, "Whose side are you on, anyway?"

"I didn't know we were taking sides," Jackson responded, his voice strained.

"Look," Collier put in, "I realize what a blow this has been to you both, and I'm sorry, sorry as hell. First, I never intended for it to happen, and second, I never intended for either of you to find out."

"Did you really think you could keep something like that a secret?" Mason snorted. "Especially in this town, where the rumor mill rivals D.C.'s."

"She's a fine person, Dad. Just because her brother—"

"Don't you dare sing her praise!"

Collier clamped his lips together, never having seen Mason so livid, so out of control. His concern heightened, forcing him to scramble for something that would diffuse the situation. "Do you want me to say I'm sorry? Is that what you want?"

"What I want is for you to get your head back on straight and focus your time and attention on what's important. Getting that appointment, for starters. Surely you know this kind of irrational behavior could cost you dearly." Mason paused and rubbed his forehead. "Has that occurred to you?"

"I'm kind of wondering that myself, little brother," Jackson put in.

Collier blew out his breath, continuing to hedge, because his own emotions were in such turmoil. "Of course it has," he finally snapped.

"Combined with that damn case you're trying," Mason added, "this kind of scandal could muddy the waters past the point of no return. The senator and the committee will judge you harshly. Count on it."

"I agree with Dad," Jackson said.

Feeling as though he was being treated like the despised stepson who could do no right, Collier's resentment suddenly flared. Dammit, he was a grown man who didn't need others dictating how he should live his life, even if those others were his dad and brother.

Mason spoke again. "As it is, Travis Wainwright's at the top of the list, right along with you."

"And may get the nod regardless of anything I say or do," Collier pointed out.

"By the way, Rupert Holt's the one who told me."

Collier gave Mason an incredulous stare. "How did—"

"I didn't bother to ask. What I did do was accuse him of lying and warned him if he spread that garbage any further, I'd have his hide." Mason laughed bitterly. "Seems I'm the one who didn't know his ass from his elbow. My own son played me for a fool."

Collier's face was suffused with color. "You know better than that."

"I do?" Mason's eyes speared his.

"I'll talk to Senator Riley," Collier said.

Mason shook his head. "No, don't say anything to anyone, not until you're forced to."

"Just how badly do you want this job?" Jackson asked, his gaze back on Collier.

"It's what I've worked long and hard for."

"Then maybe it's not too late for damage control," Mason put in, his relief obvious. "Especially if you stay away from her. Promise me—us—you'll do that."

"I'll do what I feel is best," Collier responded as calmly as he could, though he realized his words would probably ignite another explosion.

"Is that a yes or a no?" Jackson asked, his gaze narrowing.

A muscle twitched in Collier's jaw. "I can't answer that question."

"The hell you can't!" Mason shot back.

"What about Lana?" Jackson asked. "Where does she fit into the equation?"

Collier's eyes darted between his dad and his brother. "She doesn't, not anymore."

Another thunderous silence filled the room.

"You mean you're not going to marry her?" Mason's voice reached the high-tenor range again, his face re-heating.

"No, and I told her that."

"God," Mason muttered, lifting his head toward the ceiling as though searching for divine help.

"So where does that leave things?" Jackson asked, his gaze piercing.

"I don't know," Collier admitted in a tired tone. He wished he could reassure them that it was over between him and Brittany, if only to wipe the sick expressions off their faces, but he couldn't.

He wouldn't lie to them, not anymore. Nor would he share his feelings for her.

"I hope you know what you're doing," Mason said in a dull, hopeless tone.

"Me, too," Collier responded with regret. "Me, too."

The day was cold and crisp, the sun so bright it was blinding as it bounced off the bare window in Haley's apartment. Jackson squinted against the glare.

"Too bad," Haley said.

He swung around to face her, something he'd avoided doing ever since he'd arrived, which had been at least fifteen minutes ago. His eyes had touched on everything in the room except her.

"What's too bad?" he asked, letting his confusion show.

She angled her head and grinned. "That you can't leave."

"What makes you think I want to?" he asked in a blustering tone, feeling heat invade his face. He'd forgotten her uncanny ability to read his thoughts. He would have to be more careful or she'd be peering into the depths of his soul and memorizing it.

Her grin intensified. "It's obvious you'd like to be anywhere but here."

"Dammit, Haley," Jackson said fiercely, only to stop short.

She was exactly right. He couldn't believe he was actually sitting in her living room, after Harry had driven him to her apartment. But after that fiasco with his dad and brother, he'd felt more on edge, more like a caged lion, than ever. Without weighing the consequences, he'd picked up the phone and called Haley.

While her shock at hearing his voice had been evident, she hadn't let that stop her from asking to see him, insisting he come to her place. At first he'd told her no; then, when she wouldn't give up, he finally consented, much to his chagrin.

"Dammit, Haley, what?" she mimicked in a teasing tone, drawing him back to her.

She was having a field day at his expense. If she'd been anyone else that would have set him off, but he couldn't get upset with Haley, not when she looked so delightful dressed in a black pair of slim-fitting pants and a lime-green sweater that stressed the luscious curve of her breasts, breasts that had once been his for the taking.

Feeling his lower half respond, Jackson swallowed hard, then once again shifted his gaze. But he couldn't keep from looking back at her, especially the way her hair blazed as if it were on fire and her eyes twinkled. God, she was lovely, down to the last freckle sprinkled across her pert nose.

"You're enjoying the hell out of this, aren't you?"

"Yep," she replied, easing out her tongue and sweeping it across her lower lip. Did she know how much that gesture could turn him on? Accidentally or on purpose, it did. When she chose, she could be a little temptress.

"I hate to admit it," he said, collecting his thoughts, "but I'm glad I came."

"We'll make a habit of it."

He let that slide, knowing he was teetering on a slippery slope as it was, just by coming here.

"I am curious, though, as to what pushed you into calling me. I'd like to think—" She stopped suddenly and bit down on the same lip she'd licked earlier. "Never mind."

"For one thing," Jackson said, filling the silence, "I needed to talk to someone outside the family."

She smiled, though it lacked the same luster as before. He sensed that she wanted more from him, but what, he didn't know. In order to find out the answer, he would have to put his heart on the chopping block. Right now, he wasn't willing to do that, especially since he might be reading her all wrong. Friendship was probably all she was looking for, nothing else. In fact, he was sure of it.

"What's going on?"

He told her about the mess Collier had gotten himself into and Mason's violent reaction.

"How do you feel about the situation? After all, you're the one who's really involved."

"I'm not sure I even knew Rogers had a sister."

"So you're not as bent out of shape about all this as your dad?"

"Let's just say I'm more concerned about my brother and his state of mind than myself. I—" He suddenly broke off as a grin spread across Haley's face. His darkened. "Don't you say it."

Her grin widened. "Say what?" she asked innocently.

"That you're shocked I'm thinking about someone other than myself for a change."

"Well?"

"Okay, so it's about time. But Collier's in bad shape."

"All the more reason why you should take your rightful place back in the firm."

"What does that have to do with any of this?"

"Everything. It sounds like your brother's about to mess things up good and proper, which means Mason and the firm are going to need your expertise now more than ever."

"That's not going to happen."

Her eyes drilled him. "Why not?"

"Look, I didn't come here to fight with you. I did enough of that earlier with my family."

"We're not fighting, sweetie, we're discussing."

Jackson found it impossible to stay angry at her. "I want Collier to get it back together, but he seems to have a thing for this woman. I've never seen him like this."

"And you really don't see that as a betrayal?"

"Would you?"

Haley was quiet for a moment, then said softly, "She's not to blame for what her brother did."

"Collier said the same thing, but if word gets out, it'll definitely hurt his chances for the bench."

"That's a choice he has to make."

"Dad's got his heart set on that appointment. If it

doesn't come through, I don't think he'll be able to take it."

"Sure he will. He'll do what he has to."

"I'm not so sure." Jackson frowned. "It still boggles my mind that something like this could happen. Let's face it, Collier and Rogers' sister meeting and having an affair is too bizarre for words."

"Chalk it up to one of life's quirks."

"Not only is she Rogers' sister, she's dirt-poor and works as a waitress, to boot."

"Are you saying she's playing Collier for a fool?"

"I wouldn't rule out the possibility," Jackson declared grimly. "Although I may be way off base. She might be crazy about him for himself."

A short silence ensued, then Haley said, "Which is all the more reason why you should return to the court-room."

"I've already told you that's not going to happen."

"Your legs are paralyzed, not your mind, for heaven's sake." Suddenly Haley closed the distance between them, placed her hands on the arms of his chair and leaned over.

Jackson sucked in his breath and held it.

"Don't you think you've wallowed in bitterness and self-pity long enough?"

Jackson almost choked on the fury those words incited. "That's a low blow," he said, clenching his jaw so hard the nerves quivered.

She didn't back down. "It's deserved, though."

"The hell it—"

Her mouth landed on his with unerring accuracy. At first Jackson was so stunned he froze. But when the moist tip of her tongue nudged his lips apart, he jerked her to him at the same time she placed a hand on his crotch.

Moments later, she pulled away and stared at him wide-eyed. "Jackson…"

Her voice was filled with awe.

"Haley—"

"Let's get married."

"God, Haley," he rasped, "have you lost your mind?"

Thirty

Brittany opened the door immediately, then stepped aside for him to enter, giving him a tenuous smile. "I was beginning to give up on you."

"Don't ever do that," Collier responded on a husky note. She looked and smelled good. It was all he could do not to grab her, haul her off to the bedroom and lose himself inside her.

Once he'd shed his coat, Collier turned and faced her, feeling as though his heart was in his eyes.

Wordlessly she crossed to him, reached up and brushed aside an errant piece of hair. "You look beat," she whispered.

"I am. Mentally and physically."

"I'm sorry," she said gently, moistening her lower lip before moving her hand to a stubbled cheek and caressing it.

Collier groaned, then trapped her hand, turning her palm to his lips. Without taking his eyes off her, he laved it with his tongue. He felt a quiver go through her at the same time she sucked in her breath and held it.

Then she was in his arms, clutching him tightly, as though she felt his pain and wanted to absorb it. Moments later, he pushed her back. "God help me, but I can't stay away from you."

"I don't want you to," she said, running a finger

across his lower lip. He groaned again, this time trapping her finger and sucking on it.

"Make love to me." She didn't bother to mask the desperate note in her voice. "Now."

Sweeping her up in his arms, he carried her into the bedroom, where she stepped out of her robe while he discarded his clothes. Once he'd joined her on the sheets, he bent over her and sank his lips onto hers, losing himself in their sweetness.

It was in that moment he felt her warm hand surround his erection. He moaned as a bolt of lust struck him so hard, so fast, he almost couldn't contain himself. "Oh, Brittany, yes," he rasped against her lips.

Without answering, she spread her legs, then guided the moist tip of his erection into her. "I can't wait, either."

One thrust and he was inside her. Instinctively she lifted her legs and tightened them around his buttocks. With her breasts crushed into his chest and his head buried against the side of her neck, he drove higher and harder. Seconds later, his seed was inside her and they were both spent.

"Did I hurt you?" he asked bleakly once she was beside him and he was peering into her lovely eyes. Their coming together had been hotter and rawer than ever before.

"No. Never."

He sighed and brushed back a strand of her hair, so like silk, like her body. "I didn't mean to come here and—" He broke off, cursing silently.

"Jump my bones," she finished for him, a sliver of humor in her tone.

His face paled. "Yeah, I guess that was what I was trying to say."

"It's okay, Collier. I wanted you just as much."

"I don't want to stop touching you," he said in a low, tormented voice. "I think about you and how I feel when I'm inside you twenty-four hours a day."

"Oh, Collier," she said softly, tears appearing in her eyes.

"But I don't want you ever to feel like I'm using you."

"Are you?"

Though her question was softly spoken, it packed a punch. "God, no. Don't ever think that. I'm just trying to take you…us…one day at a time and savor every moment of it."

"I can accept that."

"When it comes to you, I'm out of control. The fact that I haven't used any protection should tell you that."

"So far I'm not pregnant," she said softly, touching his face again.

He didn't have to ask if she was on the Pill. Her words had just told him she wasn't. "You know we're pushing our luck with such insanity. It's just that when I see you, touch you, all rationality leaves me."

She smiled. Then it faded, and she looked away. "When you make…love to her, do you use—"

He placed a finger against her lips, silencing her. "The word is *made*. I told you, I haven't touched her or any other woman since I met you. But the answer to your question is yes. I always used protection."

Brittany pulled his head down and kissed him. "Are you feeling better now?" she asked after they could breathe normally again.

He knew she was referring to his state of mind when he'd arrived. "I no longer want to take someone's block off."

She grinned. "That's a definite improvement."

He didn't respond, suddenly feeling weighted down again, as if a chunk of lead was sitting on his chest. Instead of heading here, he should have gone straight to Senator Riley's house and knocked on his door, but he hadn't. First off, it had been too late, and second, it would have been too crass of him.

More importantly, at that moment he hadn't given a damn about the senator or the appointment. His beleaguered mind had needed the sweet, soothing comfort he could find only in Brittany's arms. He hadn't been disappointed. The second he had seen her, the tension inside him had been diffused. Nothing had seemed as impossible or traumatic as it had before.

Unfortunately he couldn't stay hidden away. He had his job and responsibilities, and he had to make peace with his dad and brother. But he had no intention of going into all that with her. It would only hurt her and accomplish nothing.

He had to work through this time in his life, come to terms with how he really felt about her on his own. He sensed she cared about him as deeply as he did her. Still, a future with her didn't look promising. Even if she were to be accepted into his family—which she wouldn't be, he reminded himself brutally—she wouldn't be comfortable in his world, considering her background and the way she'd been reared. She'd never said that, but she didn't have to. Her personality spoke for her.

If only he had the willpower to walk away from her now, they could both start over. But he didn't.

"I'm willing to listen if you want to talk," she said, tangling her fingers in the hairs on his chest.

He went instantly erect. "I'm through talking," he said thickly, covering her lips with his.

She moaned, trapping his erection between her knees and rubbing.

Brittany awakened and peered at Collier, who was still sleeping. Sighing, she simply stared at him again, committing to memory every line, every angle, of his face just in case she never saw him again.

No! She had to stop tormenting herself like this. If this was the time he walked out and never returned, then she could deal with it. She'd had a life before Collier, and she would again. In fact, she'd had everything all planned, and Collier certainly hadn't been part of that plan. Yet when he held her and made love to her, her plans ceased to matter. She felt so complete, so protected, so *loved....*

For a millisecond, her heart stopped beating. How could her mind play such a mean trick on her? He wanted her and needed her, but love her? Absolutely not. That was much too strong a word.

And she didn't love him, either, her heart cried. Yet she didn't want to think of what her life would be like without him in it, though they were as different as two people could be and had so much unopened baggage between them. If he knew Tommy wanted her to use sex to blackmail him, Collier would turn on her for sure. But unless she told him, he had no way of finding that out.

In reality, it didn't matter. Even if there wasn't bad blood between them because of the car accident, she knew his family, his profession, would never embrace the likes of her. Both demanded more than she was and more than she was able to give.

Still, she didn't want to give him up.

"Why didn't you wake me?"

She looked at him and smiled. "Why?"

"Because you were awake," he said, tonguing a breast, then watching the nipple harden.

Her breath caught.

"I can't ever see myself getting enough of you."

"Mmm, I like the sound of that," she said, tweaking his nipple and making it hard like hers.

His eyes darkened. "As much as I want to make love to you again, I want to talk. Or rather, I want you to talk."

Her hands stilled. "Me? I don't have anything to talk about that would interest you."

"Sure you do. You've never told me who slapped you around, then pushed you out of the car."

Those words, out of the blue, blindsided her. For a moment her tongue stuck to the roof of her mouth and she couldn't speak. "What made you think of that?" she finally asked, stalling for time.

"I never stop thinking about it. Not only does it make me crazy, it remains one of the unsolved mysteries about you."

"Maybe I wonder about you, too."

"No one worked me over."

"He's no longer bothering me."

"That doesn't excuse the bastard."

"Let it go, Collier."

"I can't. What happened that night just doesn't fit with your personality. You're too intelligent, too levelheaded, to get involved with such a lowlife. It just doesn't make any sense."

"It doesn't have to," she maintained stubbornly. "At least not to you."

"You're right," he said harshly. "It doesn't. But I can't stand the thought of that bastard hurting you and getting away with it."

"What if I ask you a personal question?"

He stiffened, and his eyes turned leery. "Like what?"

"Like do your father and brother know about me?" She'd been dying to ask that, only she hadn't had the courage until now, when he'd delved into her personal life.

His grimace told her the answer louder and plainer than words could have. Her stomach revolted, but she hide her torment. Her pride came to her rescue.

"I'm not surprised," she said in a shaky voice, unable to control the tremor.

"It doesn't matter," he responded, his voice equally shaky. "You're in my bloodstream. Even if I wanted to leave you alone, I couldn't."

Though he sounded more resigned than happy about that, she wasn't going to look a gift horse in the mouth. She would take Collier any way she could get him.

"Now it's your turn."

She gave a start. "I—"

"I played fair," he said, cutting her off. "I expect the same from you."

She released a shuddering breath. "It was a married man who does business with our travel agency. He'd promised to help Tommy. That's the only reason I agreed to have dinner with him. He caught me in a vulnerable moment, when I was feeling guilty and desperate about Tommy."

"His name, Brittany," Collier demanded in an unflinching tone.

"Rupert Holt," she said in a small voice.

Collier swore, then stared at her out of glazed-over eyes.

* * *

Travis Wainwright kept pulling on his upper lip as he paced back and forth across the carpet.

"Will you sit down?" Rupert told him. "You're making me nervous."

He had driven the hour and a half to see Travis to let him know his chances of getting the appointment had significantly improved in light of what he'd found out about Collier.

Because of Brittany and his feelings for her, he hadn't gone into detail. He'd just said Collier was involved in an illicit love affair that could nix his chances once and for all.

Travis halted, but only for a moment. "I make better decisions when I'm moving."

"Since there's no decision to make, sit the fuck down."

"How can you say that?" Travis asked, his tone incredulous.

"I'm calling the shots, that's why."

"I'm the one who's going to sit on the bench."

"Only because my money and I put you there," Rupert said through tight lips.

Travis's features registered his resentment, but when he spoke, his tone was even, "So why aren't we jumping on the info, using it to our advantage?"

"Because we don't have to."

"Do you know something I don't?" Travis asked, hope replacing the resentment.

"My gut instinct says you'll get the nod."

"But why take a chance when we could shit-can Smith once and for all and be done with it?"

Rupert scratched his chin and looked around Wainwright's office, though nothing made an impression. Unlike the man, everything was average. Travis deserved better, while Collier deserved worse. He would love to hurt Mason directly, but since that wasn't possible, he'd do the next best thing and take his son down. Hopefully that would still be a lethal blow.

"If it's necessary, we will."

"I don't get the reason for waiting."

"Why dirty our hands when we don't have to?"

"No one would know who started the gossip," Travis pressed. "We could make sure of that."

"They'd blame me, but they wouldn't be able to prove it. Even if they could, it wouldn't matter. The harm would be done and Smith would be out."

Travis's face lighted. "Then let's go for it. I've never known you to play fair before."

If it hadn't been for Brittany, Rupert wouldn't have hesitated. Her screwing Collier had put an unexpected kink in his plans. Just thinking about the two of them in bed enraged him all over again. If she told Collier...

That hadn't happened and it wasn't going to, he reassured himself. But if the tide changed, he still had his trump card. He would merely up the ante on his threat to hurt Tommy. That would keep Brittany quiet for sure. It was that backup insurance that had given him the balls to confront Mason. And if necessary, he'd follow through with his threat to start the rumor mill, as well.

"No. I'm going with my gut and holding off. Meanwhile, you keep your ass clean. You hear me?"

"No problem," Travis said on a sigh.

Rupert stood. "I'll be in touch."

When he reached town, he headed straight for the travel agency. It was past time he and Brittany had another chat.

Thirty-One

Collier opened the door of his office and pulled up short.

"Surprised, little brother?"

"That's an understatement," Collier responded, staring blankly at Jackson, whose wheelchair was in front of the window.

Jackson rolled toward one side of the big desk, where he parked, then grinned sheepishly. "You can close your mouth now."

Instinctively Collier did just that, too shocked to think for himself. As far as he knew, his brother hadn't been anywhere near the law firm since the accident, much less inside it. For him to just show up, out of the blue, was unreal. But a great surprise. And did he ever need something to lift his spirits.

His guts had been churning ever since Brittany told him who assaulted her. As soon as he got out of court this afternoon, he planned on paying Rupert Holt a visit.

"I knew you'd be shocked but not pissed."

Collier gave his brother another blank stare. "Pissed? What makes you think that?"

"The look on your face, like something suddenly went sour in your mouth."

"Hey, bro, don't mind me," Collier countered lightly, striding deeper into the room and plopping his briefcase on the desk. "There's just too much going on, not to mention the trial."

"How's that going?"

"Are you serious?"

"Yes, or I wouldn't have asked."

Collier's mind reeled. Two days ago Jackson couldn't have given a shit how that case or any other was progressing. Now, suddenly, he was interested. It didn't make sense. What was going on? It was as though his brother had done a complete about-face overnight.

"I find that hard to believe," Collier added more bluntly than necessary.

Jackson flushed. "I had that coming."

"No, you didn't," Collier said with a sigh. "It's just that I'm about to lose my freakin' mind."

"Something tells me it has nothing to do with the case."

"You're right, it doesn't."

"It's Brittany Banks, isn't it?" Jackson asked in a sober tone.

Collier could have denied it, but he didn't. Since the genie was out of the bottle, what would be the point? He rubbed the back of his neck, feeling his bunched up muscles. "Yeah," he admitted tightly, continuing to rub, trying to work the kinks out, but to no avail.

"I agree you're in a tough spot." Jackson gave him a lopsided smile. "Closer to reality, your dick's in a nut grinder."

"I can't deny that, either." Collier's eyes pinned his brother. "But right now, I want to talk about you, not me. Not only am I stunned you actually came to the office, but that you're even speaking to me."

Jackson was silent for a moment, then he shrugged. "Me, too."

Collier actually smiled. "So why are you? I know you feel like Dad, that I've betrayed you by having an affair with Brittany."

"I've thought long and hard about our conversation." Jackson gave him a sideways glance. "At first I did feel like you'd karate-chopped me from behind, but then I realized you were in that same boat."

"You got that right." Collier heaved a sigh. "Still, I could've pulled out, stopped seeing her."

"So why didn't you?"

Because I fell in love. That unbidden thought jerked him upright. He didn't mean that. He *couldn't.*

"You really care about her, don't you?"

"Yes," Collier said, following another deep sigh. "Much more than I should, that's for sure."

"I would never have thought you'd look at a woman like her."

Collier scowled. "What does that mean?"

"Don't act so outraged. You know what I mean."

"You're right. I do. Under ordinary circumstances, I never would have gotten involved with her—which is not to say I wouldn't have given her a second glance, because I would have."

"She's a looker, huh?"

"Not in the sense you mean." Collier smiled. "She's lovely, all right, but it's more than looks with her. She's sweet and unassuming." When he realized he must sound like a lovesick puppy, he felt color surge into his face.

"You've been bitten bad, little brother."

"Only temporarily," he said, hearing the desperate ring behind his words.

Jackson snorted.

Ignoring that, Collier went on. "Obviously you're not

going to kick me out of the family. But what about Dad? Think he'll ever speak to me again?''

''Not if she costs you the bench.''

Collier cursed, then walked to the window, where he swung around, too agitated to stand still. He felt like fire ants were crawling all through his insides. ''I know what you're saying, but it doesn't have to be that way.''

''It's the idea that you're hiding her.''

''I'm not hiding her,'' Collier said tersely.

''That's a crock and you know it. You're ashamed of her.''

''No, I'm not!'' Collier lashed out, his breathing labored.

Jackson peered up at him. ''Sorry, but your actions speak louder than your words.''

Collier muttered another expletive, feeling as if someone was using a jackhammer inside his skull. ''You don't understand.''

''Oh, I understand, all right, and so do you. If the media were to get hold of the fact that you're having an affair with a waitress whose brother's in the pen for nearly killing *yours,* they'd have a field day. Senator Riley and the committee would scratch your name off the list with a thick, black marker. And we can't forget about Lana, who you're expected to marry. Old Bill may come after you with a gun.''

''That's a cheery thought,'' Collier muttered darkly.

''Is she worth the price?''

Collier's first inclination was to shout, hell, yes. But something held him back. To say that would be tantamount to admitting he loved her, something he just couldn't do. ''It's not that cut-and-dried,'' he said lamely.

''Unfortunately matters of the heart never are.''

Collier cut him a sharp glance. It wasn't so much what

Jackson said, though coming from him that statement was certainly profound, but rather his tone, as if he knew from experience what Collier was going through. Haley suddenly popped into mind.

"Sounds like you might be in the same boat as me," Collier said, relieved not to be the focus of the conversation any longer. "Is that why you're here?"

Jackson didn't respond.

"Something's going on with Haley, isn't it?"

"Yep," Jackson admitted, his mouth turned down.

Collier could barely contain his excitement. If that woman was responsible for the remarkable change in his brother, then he would be indebted to her for life. Yet his gut instinct told him to temper his excitement for fear of spooking Jackson. Collier sensed his brother was having difficulty adjusting to life in his new skin.

"So what's going on?" Collier asked as nonchalantly as possible.

"More than I can digest, that's for damn sure."

"So are you two going to start seeing each other? Romantically, I mean." The moment he asked that question, Collier wished he could withdraw it. Of course romance wasn't in the cards for his brother. How could it be, when he could no longer make love? Friendship was the key here, and that alone was a gift from above.

"It's a bit more than that."

Collier raised his eyebrows. "Oh?"

"Actually we're getting married."

At first Collier thought he hadn't heard him right, but he knew he had. The words had been spoken plainly and from the heart.

Jackson chuckled. "I have to say, your jaw's getting a workout today."

Realizing his mouth was indeed gaping in astonishment, Collier slammed it shut, then swallowed. While this news was definitely another shocker, he was thrilled beyond words.

"I haven't told Dad yet," Jackson said. "I wanted to test the waters on you."

Collier grinned, then crossed to his brother, leaned down and gave him a spontaneous hug. "Man, I couldn't be more surprised or more delighted."

"But you have to be wondering if Haley's lost her mind. And me, too, for that matter."

"Hey," Collier said, backing up and gesturing with a hand, "whatever it takes to get your life back on track. I'm not about to question anything at this point."

Jackson angled his head and narrowed his eyes. "Unbelievable as it is, I can make love."

Collier's eyes widened. "That's about the best news I've heard in ages, but how?"

"Considering I still can't walk, beats the hell out me," Jackson responded, his own voice filled with amazement. "However, the doc wasn't all that shocked, considering the type of SCI I have. He says it happens all the time if the person's involved in intense therapy."

Jackson went on to fill in the details from his conversation with Dr. Ames.

"I couldn't be more thrilled," Collier insisted again. "Just wait till you tell Dad. He'll be beside himself."

"It took Haley to make me realize I still had feeling in that part of my anatomy."

"Well, bully for her. If I'd known she was going to bring about a miracle, I would've tracked her down a long time ago."

"Wouldn't have done any good," Jackson countered. "I was too busy enjoying my private pity party."

Amazement filled Collier's face. "Is this really my older brother talking? Sure sounds like a stranger to me."

Jackson gave Collier another sheepish grin, then muttered, "I knew you'd have a field day with this."

"You're damn right, bro. You've put Dad and me through hell right along with you."

"It wasn't that bad," Jackson said in a huffy tone.

"Worse."

They both laughed, and Collier thought he'd never heard such a great sound, especially coming from Jackson. He'd reached the conclusion he would never hear his brother laugh again.

"So when's the big day?" Collier asked.

Jackson swallowed hard. "I...we haven't gotten that far. I'm still struggling to come to grips with the fact that I accepted."

Collier was confused. "You accepted?"

"Yeah. She asked me to marry her."

Collier laughed out loud again. "Figures."

"And wouldn't take no for an answer."

"Shows she's got good taste and good sense."

Jackson's features suddenly turned bleak. "Actually I think she's lost her mind. I'm still not upright. I still can't walk."

"I know, and I'm sorry. I grieve over what happened to you every day. But like I've told you from the get-go, just because you're in a wheelchair doesn't mean you can't have a life."

"You think you would react any differently?"

Jackson's blunt question threw him a sudden curve. "Maybe," Collier said with a sigh. "And maybe not. Who knows? But that's beside the point, because it wasn't me."

"You're right."

Not only was Collier still spinning from the news that his brother had wedding plans, but the fact they were having this personal conversation was even more astounding. No matter how hard he tried, he'd never been able to get Jackson to talk to him, to discuss his feelings following the accident. Ever since Jackson had come to in the hospital and found out his plight, he'd retreated inside himself and hadn't come out. Until now.

Bless Haley.

"Do you think I'm a fool?"

Collier blinked hard. "What?"

"You heard me."

"You're right, I did. But it's the question I don't understand."

"I keep asking myself why she'd want to saddle herself with a paraplegic when she's so vibrant, so full of life. Hell, she could have any man she wants."

"She wants you," Collier said in a matter-of-fact tone. "She always has."

"How would you know?"

"Everyone knew but you. You broke her heart when you didn't follow her and marry her."

"Did she tell you that?" Jackson shot back.

"She didn't have to. It was obvious."

"Except to me." Jackson released a deep sigh. "I really fucked things up, didn't I?"

"Yeah," Collier left it there.

"But would she have stuck by me after my injury?"

"What does it matter?" Collier asked, giving his brother's rock-hard shoulder a squeeze before he walked to his desk and sat down. "Anyway that's beside the point."

"You're right." A flicker of pain darted across Jackson's face. "I still have a lot of demons pulling on me."

"Don't we all?" Collier muttered, his mind returning to Rupert Holt and the confrontation facing him, a confrontation he was looking forward to. How dare that bastard hurt Brittany and think he would get away with it?

"You're thinking about Brittany, aren't you?" Jackson asked.

"Always," Collier admitted before he thought.

Jackson let out another sigh. "While I'm not overjoyed with the idea of you two together, I can live with it, especially now. And you're right, just because her brother's a piece of shit, that doesn't mean she is." He paused. "I think you love her."

Collier bolted out of his seat. "Hey, I don't want to talk about me. This is your moment. You're the one who's getting hitched."

"Whoa, I told you, we're not in any hurry."

Collier gave him a knowing grin. "Something tells me I'm not the one you have to convince of that."

Jackson's face colored. "You're right. She's ready to just do it."

"I'm all for that. However, I suggest you tell Dad first."

"I also have to tell Dad something else. And you, too."

Collier raised his eyebrows and waited, holding his breath.

"I intend to start practicing law again."

Thirty-Two

How could he be envious of his brother?

It didn't make sense, but that was exactly how he was feeling. Suddenly Collier felt ashamed. He paused and stared down at his limbs. He had full use of his entire body. Nothing within reason was impossible for him to do. He didn't have to depend on others to care for him. Not so with Jackson. He no longer had any of those luxuries, could no longer do the day-to-day things that most people took for granted, himself included.

Collier realized his feelings made no sense, yet what did lately in his life? he asked himself, depression settling over him. Jackson finally seemed to have gotten his act together. While Collier was overjoyed and relieved about his brother's returned confidence and good fortune, it was those factors that were the source of his own envy, deepening his shame.

At the moment his life was in such an upheaval, he didn't know which way to turn. He wanted Brittany, and he wanted the appointment to the bench. And he had no guarantees he would get either. If not, the blame for both failures would fall squarely on his shoulders. Problem was, if he pursued Brittany, it could cost him the bench and his father's love and approval. If he didn't, it could cost him his heart.

"Shit," he muttered, mentally kicking his own backside for letting his thoughts dwell on the negative. His mind was often his worst enemy. Today was one of those days. Besides, he had something more important on his agenda. Rupert Holt. He had vowed to confront him, and nothing was going to stop him. Brittany wouldn't want him to, he knew that. But the idea of Rupert getting away with assaulting her or any woman couldn't be tolerated.

A solid confrontation with Rupert would help put things back in perspective for him.

Peering at his watch, Collier saw he didn't have much time. He was due in court posthaste. He stared at the phone. Maybe he would give Brittany a quick call, yearning for even the sound of her voice. He'd just lifted the receiver when he was interrupted.

"Got a minute?"

His heart sank. Darwin Brewster had once again taken the liberty of walking into his office uninvited. Something really should be done about the man's cocksure attitude, and it appeared he was the only one willing to do it. Right now, however, Brewster was way down on his priority list, even though he got on his nerves big time.

"A minute and not much more," Collier finally said, his agitation up-front.

That didn't seem to bother Darwin, who promptly sat down and crossed one leg over the other knee as if he had all the time in the world. Collier's temper shot up another notch. Maybe he'd have to move Brewster's overdue attitude adjustment up on his priority list.

"When am I going to get what's coming to me?"

Collier almost laughed at the irony of that question. But he kept a straight face in order to get this set-to over with. "I didn't know you were due anything." Cocky bastard, Collier wanted to add but didn't.

"My just deserts, I should say," Darwin explained, when Collier held his silence.

"Just deserts?" Collier scowled. "I have no idea what you're talking about."

"Oh, I think you do," Darwin drawled.

"Dammit, Brewster, I don't have time to play games. Spit it out or get out."

High color flooded Darwin's face, and his eyes narrowed. "I'm tired of you treating me like I'm not fit to wipe your shoes on."

Collier expelled an impatient sigh. "Look, Brewster, I haven't got time to dick around with you. I'm due in court."

"You still have a few minutes. What I have to say won't take long."

Brewster's gall continued to amaze Collier. What Mason saw in this man still remained a mystery. So what if he was a good attorney? So were a lot of others. They hadn't been hired by the firm, something Collier knew was considered a high honor.

"I'm listening," Collier said tersely, deciding to let him have his say. Brewster wasn't worth getting riled over.

"You're not fooling me."

Collier's lips thinned. "My patience is fast running out, so you'd best get to what's eating you."

"Maybe Mason didn't tell you after all."

"Tell me what?" Collier spoke through clenched teeth.

"About our deal."

"You're right, he didn't." Collier's tone was overtly hostile, but he didn't care. The other man's arrogance had finally pushed him over the edge.

Brewster grinned and rubbed his mustache. "While

I'm not sure I believe you, I'll indulge you and fill you in.''

"Please do.''

Though he knew Brewster had picked up on his blatant sarcasm, it didn't rattle him. He continued to milk the scenario for all it was worth. Curiosity was the only thing that kept Collier from forcing him out of his office.

"Because of your brother's accident, Mason and I have been joined at the hip.''

"That's a crock,'' Collier said with a humorless laugh.

"Hear me out and you won't think so.''

"You have five minutes.''

Darwin grinned. "How 'bout some coffee?''

Collier was looming over him before he realized it. "Listen, you little pissant, say what's on your mind or get the hell out of my office. I don't have my father's patience for bloodsuckers like you.''

Darwin's color heightened and his grin fled. For a second Collier thought his words might incite a stroke as the veins in Darwin's temples bulged.

"When you hear what I have to say, you won't be so goddamned full of yourself.''

Collier looked at his watch. "Four minutes.''

"Once Mason learned that Jackson would never walk again, he called and asked to see me.'' Brewster paused, as if waiting for that to jell in Collier's mind.

"So?'' Collier forced himself to speak in an even tone, though his stomach was tied in knots.

"He was a man on a mission, and since I was Rogers' court appointed attorney, he saw me as his missionary.''

Collier felt a sense of uneasiness, but he tried not to give in to it, determined not to rile himself more than he already was. Still...

"Yeah, we met for dinner out of town, and your old

man promised me the moon and even some stars if I'd do him a favor.''

"What favor?" Collier didn't really care, having decided Darwin was merely jerking his chain and enjoying it to the hilt. No longer. What little patience he'd had was gone.

''First off, Mason promised a paid honeymoon cruise for me and my fiancée, whom I no longer have, by the way.'' He smiled. ''However, if and when I marry, I'm going to hold Mason's ass to the fire about that trip.''

"Good," Collier said in an uninterested tone, picking up his briefcase and walking from behind his desk. He'd had it with Brewster and his shit.

"Whoa, hold your horses," Darwin said. "I've saved the best for last."

Collier kept on walking toward the door.

"He also promised me a junior partnership in his firm.''

Collier stopped abruptly, feeling the hair stand up on the back of his neck. He whipped around. "You're a lying bastard."

"Ask him," Darwin said with easy confidence.

Collier laughed mirthlessly. "I'd just be wasting my time and his."

Darwin's features turned menacing. "The cruise and the partnership were my prizes for doing a half-assed job of defending Tommy Rogers, for suppressing evidence." He paused again, that sly grin making an encore appearance.

Collier stopped midstride and cringed inwardly. He should have seen the knockout blow coming, but he hadn't. Too bad. Darwin had just stepped over the line.

He swung back around, his nostrils flared. "By the

time I get back from court, your desk drawers had better be empty.''

With that, he jerked open the door.

Behind him, Darwin snorted. ''That's not going to happen. You see, I don't take orders from you. Mason's calling the shots.''

Brittany hated waiting for the knock on the door, for the phone to ring. She hated living that way. But with Collier still keeping their affair in the closet, that was the way it was.

It had only been two days since they'd made love, but he hadn't called. She tried not to let that fact upset her, yet it did. She hated that weakness in herself, hated the way she let Collier use her. Suddenly she felt a prick of conscience. Wasn't she using him, too, in her own way? Of course she was. She could have ended this affair long ago, only she hadn't wanted to.

And while she probably loved Collier, even though she wasn't ready to admit that even to herself, love couldn't bridge the wide gulf between them. She knew that, and so did he. Why couldn't he have been an ordinary man? Why couldn't he have been an accountant instead of an affluent attorney with political aspirations? Why? Why? Why?

Swallowing a sigh, Brittany forced herself off the sofa and headed for the bedroom to freshen up. It was time for her to head for the prison to see Tommy, a trip she especially dreaded today, certain he would ask her if she'd used her sexual wiles to cajole Collier into helping to free him.

When she told him no, which she would, a row would ensue. Even so, she had no choice but to face him and get it behind her.

Halfway there, she heard the knock. Her pulse quickened, and her heart pounded. Collier? Oh Lord, she hoped so. Feeling as though her feet had wings, she rushed to the door and opened it.

Her breath congealed in her lungs.

"Don't look so surprised," Rupert said, shivering from the chill in the air.

"How dare you come to my house?"

"Let me in."

Despite feeling the cold in her bones, Brittany stepped onto the rickety porch and slammed the door behind her. "No."

Rupert let go an expletive, then said in a low, threatening tone, "I'd hate to make a scene out here."

Although she didn't believe he'd follow through with his threat, she couldn't be sure, not when she smelled liquor on his breath. Still, she hesitated, fear rendering her useless for a moment.

"Go ahead and make a scene," she said suddenly, that same fear giving her the strength to call his hand. She refused to be alone with him again, especially in her own home. "You have more to lose than I do. The neighbors are quite nosy. I'm sure your wife doesn't know you're here."

"Good try, but it won't work. You see, I don't give a tinker's damn about what my wife thinks."

She sensed he was blustering, that he did care, but she wasn't about to argue with him. "Go away, Rupert."

"There's still Tommy, remember?"

Her eyes flared. "You can't hurt him anymore, either. With him being locked up, we're both living our worst nightmare." She paused, shivering, though she wasn't sure from what—the cold wind or his foul breath.

"You're wrong there, sweetheart, but I was hoping it

wouldn't come down to that. You see, I'd much rather help your brother than hurt him. I'm just waiting for the green light from you to go forward."

"Is that why you came here?"

"That, and to see you, to make sure you were all right and didn't need anything."

Brittany stiffened, instinct telling her there was more to this visit than met the eye. Rupert was taking an awful chance by being seen here. Surely he didn't know she'd ratted on him to Collier. If so, he wouldn't be so pleasant. Still, she deeply regretted telling Collier about Rupert.

"Well, you've accomplished your goal. I'm all right, and I don't need anything, so I'm going back inside."

"Whoa." He grabbed her arm.

She shook it off, fighting panic. "Don't ever touch me again."

Rupert muttered another expletive. "I'm fast losing my patience with you. One of these days you're going to push me too far."

"Leave me alone, Rupert. Please," she said in a trembling voice.

"I can't, and I refuse to accept that you want me to."

Trying to reason with him, to make him face the truth, was a lost cause, a waste of her time. She didn't know if the alcohol or his hardheadedness was responsible for her inability to get through to him. But it didn't matter. What mattered was getting rid of him.

"When I get Tommy out of the pen, then you'll change your mind," he said, breaking the silence. "Meanwhile, you be good and stay out of trouble."

Another chill shook her, this time from the underlying message behind his smooth words. He was warning her again to keep her mouth shut or else. For a moment she wished Collier would play the knight in shining armor and ride to her defense. But she knew that wasn't going to happen, even though his outrage had been sincere. To confront Rupert on her behalf would put him in a perilous position concerning his bid for the bench. Collier wasn't about to put himself out on that kind of a limb.

Besides, Rupert was her problem, her fight. She had to take care of him herself. "Don't ever come here again, Rupert." Her voice was more frigid than the wind.

He stared at her for a long moment, then smirked. "You're in no position to tell me that, darling." He paused. "If I were you, I'd keep that in mind, knowing that if I choose to, I can make your life even more difficult than it already is." He ran a finger down one side of her cheek.

She jerked back, repulsed. "You bastard!" she spat. "You'd better keep in mind that if you try to hurt me through Tommy, I'll turn the tables on you. I swear to God, I will."

Before he could find a suitable comeback, she turned, dashed back inside, then slammed the door in his face.

Thirty-Three

Collier felt as if he'd stepped into a boxing ring and gotten the stuffing beat out of him. Even so, he was mad enough to step back into that imaginary ring and take on both Rupert and his dad.

His anger festering, he sat in his car for a moment, trying to get his bearings. First he'd learned about Rupert, then Mason. Though both punches had packed a wallop, it was the second that had knocked him out.

His instinct had been to ignore Brewster's wild accusation, but he couldn't. Darwin was a renegade, all right, but he wasn't stupid. If he was willing to waltz into Collier's office expecting to collect on a promise Mason had made, his argument had to be legitimate.

Dammit all! How could Mason, who lived by the law, stoop so low? How could he wallow in the gutter with the unethical attorneys who made their living by underhanded deals? Not Mason. Never. Sweat collected under Collier's armpits. He couldn't escape the fact that Brewster's accusations had to have some merit. He was ballsy, but not that ballsy.

Collier had wanted Tommy Rogers to get what was coming to him, but only according to the law. Mason had blatantly tampered with the wheels of justice, which now put a whole new spin on things. Suddenly Collier felt cold to the bone.

Brittany.

If she ever found out, she wouldn't throw water on him if he were on fire. His pain cut deeper. But he couldn't dwell on his feelings. Instead he had to hold himself together and find a solution to this mess. To confront his dad right now would be a mistake. At the moment he was too shaken and upended. Mason would have to wait.

Collier slumped in the seat, then rubbed his temples, feeling his head pound as if he'd had one too many. He wished he had. If ever he were going to drink himself into oblivion, this would be the time. But when his hangover cleared, he'd still have to face harsh reality. He'd still have to face both Rupert and Mason.

And Brittany.

A shiver coursed through him. She must never find out. But how was he going to keep her from doing just that? He refused to worry about that now. He still had a date with Rupert, which he intended to keep.

Maybe once that was over he would have worked off some of his temper. Because when he faced Mason, he had to be in tip-top condition.

His dad might be getting on in years, but he was still sharp. And when it came to Jackson and his plight, he was unbending in his bitterness and blame. It wouldn't be easy to reason with him. But right was right and wrong was wrong, Collier reminded himself. If Mason had done what Brewster said, then he was dead bang wrong.

Feeling like a pile driver was having a field day inside his head, he reached for his cell phone. Moments later, he heard her voice and his whole insides mellowed.

"Hey," he said huskily.

He heard the slight catch in her voice he'd come to expect when he called her. "Hey, yourself."

"Are you all right?" He didn't know why he asked that. Maybe it was because he couldn't think of anything else to say. If he couldn't be with her, *touch her,* then hearing her sweet, raspy-toned voice was the next best thing. Right now it represented a balm to his battered soul.

"I'm...fine."

Was there a slight hesitation, or was he imagining it? If he was with her, he could tell if anything was wrong. He gripped the phone tighter. This long-distance shit was a bunch of crap.

"Are you sure?"

Another hesitation. Something was wrong. His blood curdled.

"Have you been crying?"

"No. I'm just tired."

The latter he believed. How could she not be tired, with the schedule she kept? As far as the crying, he was sure she was fibbing. However, if she didn't want to confide in him, he didn't want to push her. Besides, now was not the time to grill her, especially since he couldn't hold her.

"What about you? Are you sure you're okay? You sound like—" She broke off for a second, then went on. "Like you're stressed to the max."

"I'm okay," he lied. "But I'd definitely be better if I were with you." His already low voice dropped another octave, making it sound rougher than usual.

"Something *is* wrong."

Careful, he told himself. Apparently he wasn't as good at hiding his feelings as he'd thought. He had to be careful. She couldn't know the truth until he was ready to tell her, and that wouldn't be until he had all the facts, then a game plan.

He sighed. "I'm just missing you, that's all."

"Me, too," she said in a small voice.

Silence.

"Look, I have to go now, but I'll see you soon." He paused, not wanting to end the conversation, feeling himself shake with need. "Are you on your way to work?"

"Shortly."

"Be careful, okay?"

"I will. You do the same."

A longer silence.

The words *I love you* almost escaped his lips, but he caught them in time, feeling another pinch in his gut. "I'll be in touch," he said gruffly.

Moments later he cranked the engine and headed for Rupert's office, hoping he would catch him there. If not... He refused to dwell on the negative. Whatever it took, he'd find him. Once that task was behind him, he had his dad to face.

One hurdle at a time, he reminded himself.

Five minutes later he was in Rupert's outer office, in front of his secretary's desk. "Mr. Holt's in, but he's on the phone," she said pleasantly.

"I'll wait." Collier smiled at her. "In his office."

An incredulous look came over her face, and she opened her mouth, only to snap it shut. For a second Collier almost felt sorry for her, knowing he'd put her in an awkward position with her boss. Her job was to make people without appointments sit and wait.

In all fairness, when the notion hit him, he could be as intimidating as hell. Apparently she'd picked up on that and decided to leave well enough alone. Smart woman.

After nodding and giving her a smile that didn't reach anywhere near his eyes, Collier opened the door and crossed the threshold. Rupert was just hanging up the phone. When he realized who had barged in, his face drained of color. Then, with blatant hostility marring his features, he rose to his feet.

"Why, Collier Smith, to what do I owe this honor?"

The sarcasm and hatred were right up-front. But Collier ignored that, wanting to say what he had to say and get out.

"I would offer you a seat, but—"

"Skip the bullshit, Holt. This isn't a social call, and you know it."

"Would it by chance have anything to do with the appointment?" Rupert paused. "The one you're not going to get." Snideness now overrode the sarcasm.

"I ought to tear your head off," Collier responded harshly, every muscle in his body on high alert.

Rupert's face turned mean. "If you think you're man enough, then come on. I've never backed down from a fight in my life."

"Especially not when it comes to a woman, huh?"

His lethal barb struck its mark. Collier watched as a gamut of emotions played across Rupert's face, from fear to belligerence to contempt. "I don't know what you're talking about."

"Oh, I think you do. Otherwise you wouldn't be messing in your pants right now."

"Listen, you cocky bastard," Rupert hissed. "You don't know who you're dealing with. If I choose, I can squash you like a cockroach."

"Save your pompous blustering for someone who gives a shit. My only reason for being here is to advise you not to lay a hand on Brittany Banks ever again."

At first Collier had thought Rupert had simply lost his

color. Now he actually looked like he was dead and had been embalmed standing upright. "Why you...you—"

"If I had my way," Collier interrupted, "you'd be in jail for assault and attempted rape."

As if he realized the jig was up, that to deny he'd hurt Brittany would be futile, Rupert smiled a sudden and cruel smile. "How do you know she didn't ask for it?"

Collier saw red. Before he could control himself, he was eye level with Rupert, his hands clenched by his sides, so furious he couldn't utter a word or make a move.

"Is she a good piece of pussy?"

"Shut your filthy mouth, old man, before I decide it's in your best interest to put you out of your misery."

Though undisguised fear clouded Rupert's eyes, he didn't back down. "I saw you sneaking out of her hovel and told your old man."

Unwittingly a hand closed around Rupert's tie and Collier jerked him closer. "Stay out of my business, and don't even think about taking your beef with me out on Brittany." Collier let him go and backed away.

"Get out of my office." Rupert's voice shook uncontrollably. "Now! But before you go, know you'll never see the inside of a judge's chamber!"

Collier closed the distance between them, his breathing as labored as if he'd run a mile up a mountain. "Stay away from her. Otherwise, you'll be sorry you were ever born. Got it?"

Rupert swallowed hard, blood replacing the pallor in his face.

Then, with a finger, Collier jabbed Rupert in the chest. Obviously caught off guard, Rupert went stumbling backward, where he landed in his chair.

Collier jabbed him again. "Remember, you've been warned."

Jackson's eyes wandered leisurely over Haley's nude body, taking in her long neck, her full breasts, her tiny waist, her long limbs. For a moment his eyes lingered on the red curls nestled between her legs, and he felt himself react again. He still hadn't come to terms with the fact that he'd buried himself in that moist hotbed several times already.

Sex. He'd actually had sex. No, he corrected himself. He'd made love, and there was a difference. Suddenly he wanted to shout hallelujah at the top of his lungs. But he contained himself.

He'd had no intention of making love to her until he'd come to grips with the change in his body. Haley, however, had had different plans.

She had come over to discuss wedding plans, even though he was still in stalling mode. Not so Haley. Since she'd asked him to marry her and he'd accepted, she'd assumed it was a done deal and gone full speed ahead.

"What are you thinking?" she asked in a husky voice.

He grinned. "How much I enjoy what I see."

"So you still like my body?"

"Nah, I was just kidding."

Haley poked him in the ribs, then rolled onto her side and snuggled against him. He hugged her close.

"Was it good for you?" He heard the anxiety edging his tone but couldn't control it.

He felt her eyes seek his. When he peered down, he noticed hers were dewy. Squeezing her tighter, he rested his head on top of hers, feeling her silky red hair cushion his chin.

"It was perfect," she whispered.

A sigh was all he was capable of uttering.

"Remember how we used to do this all the time?"

"What?"

"Make love in the afternoon."

"You're right, we did."

"It couldn't have worked out better today, with Harry off and your dad at the office."

He chuckled. "Would it have mattered?"

"No."

He tapped her on the nose. "Don't ever change."

"Change how?" she asked in a sassy tone.

"Don't ever become meek and submissive."

She poked him harder in the ribs. "What you're saying is that I'm assertive."

"What I'm saying is that you're a steamrolling dynamo."

"If I hadn't been," she said on a huffy note, "you'd still be sitting in this room alone, sulking."

Before Haley had come back into his life, he would have taken umbrage to that statement. Now, however, he knew it was the truth. She had forced him to take a closer look in the mirror, and he hadn't liked what he'd seen.

"I missed you so much, Jackson. I didn't realize how much until I saw you again."

"Does that mean you love me?"

"Oh, yes," she whispered. "I've never stopped."

"And I love you, too."

"When are we going to tell your dad?"

He played dumb in order to stall. "Tell him what?"

"Oh, no, you don't." She sat up in the bed and crossed her legs Indian style. "I want to get married tomorrow."

Jackson gasped. "Tomorrow? There's no way."

"Sure there is," she said calmly. "Just gather our families, find a church and a preacher, and it'll be done. We'll be husband and wife.''

He stared at her. "You'd do that?"

Her gaze didn't waver. "In a heartbeat."

Jackson swallowed against the emotion clogging his throat. "Are you sure you want to be saddled with a man in a wheelchair? We've never talked about that."

"That's because there's nothing to talk about. I know what I'm doing, Jackson. I'll take you any way I can get you." She paused, her eyes tearing up. "I love you that much."

He leaned over and kissed a nipple. She moaned. For a while the room fell silent again. Afterward he whispered, "I hate you having to help me."

"Why? I love being on top."

He sighed with a grin. "You always did."

"Now, with that out of the way, we can move on to telling Mason."

"If you're sure."

"Will you stop it? I've told my mother, and she's all for it."

"I know Dad will be, too. He'll be over the moon, especially when I add whip cream to the dessert and tell him I'm returning to the firm."

Haley gave him a spontaneous hug. "Oh, Jackson, we're going to have a wonderful life."

"That we are, darling." He paused and frowned.

"What's wrong?"

"I was just thinking about my brother."

"You mean with that girl?"

"Yep. Right now, he's in the demon pit where I was before you breezed back into my life."

"If word gets out about her and her brother, will it really nix his chances of getting on the bench?"

"Maybe, especially if that juicy stuff finds its way into the wrong hands."

"We'll have to keep our fingers crossed that doesn't happen." She paused. "Do you think he loves her?"

"Yep, only I don't think he knows it, or else he won't admit it."

"And how do you feel about Brittany? That's her name, right?"

"At first I was knocked for a loop, but now that I'm in love, I understand how the poor bastard feels. Besides, his sister shouldn't be held accountable for her brother's sins. Brittany didn't run over me while under the influence."

"What a mess. I bet Mason's about to have a stroke."

"That's putting it mildly."

"Since you've gotten your shit together and rejoined the human race, maybe that will help his feelings."

"I love it when you say what you really mean."

She giggled. "Just part of my charm."

He leaned over and kissed her other nipple. "That and your delicious body."

Her eyes glazed over. "You've made me wet again."

A groan escaped him in concert with an impatient knock on the door. "Jackson, may I come in? I know Haley's here."

At the sound of Mason's voice, they both froze and stared wild-eyed at each other. Thank God he'd thought to lock the door before they made love.

"Uh, we'll be down shortly," Jackson called, managing to maneuver himself out of bed without Haley's help. "Just wait for us in the study."

His dad didn't respond right off, as if trying to figure

out what was going on. "Whatever," he said at last, though his tone was testy at best.

Once they were sure he was out of hearing range, Jackson and Haley looked at each other and burst out laughing.

Thirty-Four

"How long may I stay?"

The tall, robust guard looked at her with sympathy. "As long as you like, actually."

"Thank you," Brittany said, her relief obvious.

"He's in room number three, on the right side."

Brittany murmured her thanks again, then made her way with firm, quick steps toward Tommy's cubicle, feeling as though her heart was in her throat. The prison had called just as she was grabbing her purse, ready to walk out the door. She would already have been gone had it not been for Collier's call.

After the prison spokesperson had identified himself, her first thought was that Tommy had been in another fight. But then she was told he had a bad virus and was in the infirmary. In order to make record time, she'd broken every speed limit possible, without so much as seeing a cop.

Now, as she made her way to Tommy, she noticed that the small hospital was spotless, which made her feel somewhat better. It was terrible to be sick, but being away from home and family made it ten times worse. She hated the fact that she couldn't take him home.

A sudden bout of depression almost overwhelmed her, especially when she found his room and saw him. After tiptoeing to the side of the bed, she sat down and watched as he slept, noticing how pale he looked. Still, under the light sheet, she could see the bulging muscles of his upper arms.

He was obviously fit otherwise, which would be in his favor in shaking off the virus. Still, the fact that he was sick enough to come here frightened her. She wouldn't stop worrying until she talked to the doctor and found out what was going on.

"Hey, sis."

Rerouting her thoughts, Brittany scooted closer to the bed and smiled at him, then reached up and laid her hand on his forehead. It was burning hot. Her fear heightened. "I don't have to ask how you're feeling."

"Like warmed-over piss."

She frowned. "That's really bad."

"I'm glad you're here."

"I wouldn't have it any other way." She paused, swallowing a sigh. "Is there anything you need besides a cold rag on your head?"

"Yeah, I wanna go home."

He sounded so forlorn, so miserable, she fought the sudden urge to cry. Ever since Rupert had showed up at her trailer, her nerves had been shot.

And Collier. Their precarious situation weighed heavily on her, giving her the sensation of being on a wild roller-coaster ride. Sooner or later that ride had to end, either in disaster or jubilation.

"I want you home, too, more than anything," she whispered, forcing her mind off her personal troubles and back on her brother. She brushed his hair back, all the while wondering if she should call a nurse and ask for a wet cloth.

Tommy was facing her with glazed eyes. "Pastor Ed says I should pray. Imagine that."

"Maybe you should try it," she said calmly and carefully, thrilled to hear him talk like that. "So you've actually gone to work in the chapel?"

"Yep. Three days ago."

"That's great."

"At least it keeps me away from most of the creeps all day, unless I lose the job for getting sick."

"You won't. The chaplain wouldn't do that to you."

"He wouldn't, but the warden might. He doesn't like me."

Brittany didn't know what to say. One minute she felt a little glimmer of hope for her brother, who wasn't a bad person, just a misguided one, while the next she felt he would never get it together. He always wanted someone else to blame.

"Every morning when I wake up, I think maybe this is the day I'll walk out of here." He paused and stared through seemingly blank eyes at the ceiling. "But it never happens."

"It will," she said desperately. "I promise you it will."

"Your promises don't mean Jack shit. I bet you haven't even talked to your boyfriend."

Her heart took a dive. "I—"

"I knew it," he said in a listless tone.

She had dreaded this visit, fearing he would ask about Collier. But since he was ill, she had hoped that subject wouldn't come up again. She should have known better.

"You're right, I haven't."

"And you don't intend to," he said in that same listless tone.

"No, I don't."

Tommy turned away, his lips stretched in a straight line.

"Look, darling, you're too sick to worry about that now," she said anxiously. "You just have to trust that I'll do whatever I can to get you out of this place, but Collier's not the answer."

Tommy looked at her again, and she noticed that his face appeared more flushed. Without saying anything, she located the nurse call button and pushed it.

"Smith's the perfect answer," Tommy muttered. "I just know he is, only you won't cash in on it."

She sighed aloud. "Our relationship's not what you think."

"Then it doesn't matter if you use him," Tommy pressed, then began to shiver. "Sounds like he's using you."

Although that barb made her wince, Brittany wasn't about to argue with Tommy, especially not when he was so sick. Besides, she had no intention of asking Collier for any special favors. The idea had been ludicrous when Tommy posed it, and that hadn't changed.

"What do you need?"

Brittany turned around and faced a burly male RN. "It's my brother. He's burning up with fever. Perhaps you should call the doctor."

"It's time for his medication," the nurse said in a gruff but not unkind voice. "If that doesn't do the trick, we'll go from there."

Brittany would have liked to argue, very much wanting to talk to the doctor while she was there. But she didn't push the point.

Turning back to Tommy, she placed her hand on his arm. "He's going to bring you something to make you rest."

"I heard him."

Brittany wanted to shake him and hug him at the same

time. If only he didn't make *her* feel so guilty for something he had done. She clenched and unclenched her fingers. One of these days he was going to have to assume some responsibility for his actions, though now was not the time to bring that up.

"While I still think Smith's my best way out, I guess I'll have to pursue Plan B."

Dumbfounded, Brittany simply stared at him. "Plan B? I don't understand."

"He's probably just blowing hot air up my ass, but since it's my only prayer, I'm gonna explore it."

"You're making absolutely no sense," Brittany said in a frustrated tone, thinking the fever might have made him delirious.

"A guy by the name of Rupert Holt came to see me."

Brittany's jaw dropped, while her heart plunged to her toes. *"What?"*

"Said he was a real close friend of yours who could help me get out of here." Tommy pushed himself up on his elbows, the hope in his eyes disappearing. "From the look on your face, the guy was obviously feeding me a line of bull."

"He was here?" Brittany choked the words out, unable to accept that Rupert had actually come here and talked to Tommy. Was there no end to the man's hideous influence on her life?

"Sis, what's going on?"

She stiffened. "Nothing's going on. He's not to be trusted, so forget he was here."

"That's easy for you to say. He looked like he had money and clout. And he said he really cared about you, and that if you cooperated, he'd make things great for both of us."

Brittany's bones turned as brittle as ice. "He's not a

nice man, Tommy. You can't believe anything he tells you.''

''Shit, I could've sworn—''

''Forget it! It's not going to happen.''

''If I have to depend on you, you're damn right it's not going to happen.''

''Please, Tommy…''

''Go away,'' he mumbled in a defeated tone, falling back against the pillow and closing his eyes. ''I don't wanna talk to you anymore.''

Brittany opened her mouth to argue, then thought better of it. Instead she whispered, ''You'll just have to trust me. I promise I'll get you out.''

And she would, she vowed. And soon, too. Otherwise she feared Tommy might crack mentally. There had to be a way.

''I was just about to call you.''

''Oh, really,'' Collier muttered, unable to look at his dad, deep-seated anger laced with pain usurping everything else.

''Yeah. I have some great news.''

When Collier had arrived at the mansion, he'd headed straight for the study after Maxine told him Mason was there. For a second he'd been tempted to call Jackson down and let him in on this set-to with their dad. But then he'd thought better of that. He suspected it would be an ugly scene, and it would be better not to involve Jackson, not at this point, anyway.

Rupert Holt's less than admirable conduct hadn't surprised him. He'd concluded long ago that underneath the man's polish and glib manner was a slimy lowlife who couldn't be trusted, despite his money and influence.

But Mason, the man he'd looked up to all his life,

wanted to emulate, wanted to *please* more than anything, flagrantly breaking the law was unthinkable and unconscionable.

"My news isn't so great," Collier said at last, staring at Mason, who stood by the fireplace, a glass of wine in hand.

"It's not the appointment, is it?" Mason asked in an appalled tone.

"No," Collier bit out.

Mason raised his eyebrows as if to ask what burr he had under his saddle. Instead he said, "Help yourself to a glass of wine. You look like you could use one."

Silently Collier crossed to the small fancy bar area, where he poured himself something much stiffer than wine. After taking a drink and feeling it land in his stomach with the burn of a lighted stick of dynamite, he set down the glass. In order to have his say, he needed a clear head. He knew Mason wasn't going to take this confrontation lightly.

"Since you apparently aren't going to ask what the good news is, I'll tell you anyway." Mason lifted his glass and grinned widely. "Your brother's getting married. Not only that, he's returning to work."

For some reason Collier pretended to be surprised by the news. He sensed it was important to his dad to be the first to know about his eldest son's good fortune. For a moment he buried his ax to grind and asked, "Since when?"

"Since a little while ago."

"Way to go, Haley," Collier said, raising his own glass.

"I second that. After I got home, I saw her car and went upstairs." Mason paused with a chuckle. "They wouldn't let me in, which makes me think they were having a good time." His gave a knowing smile. "A very good time."

"Making love, huh?"

Mason's eyes twinkled. "Another miracle, wouldn't you say?"

"That it is, and I couldn't be happier. I never thought he should've let Haley get away in the first place."

"You just missed them. They left a few minutes ago."

When Collier failed to respond, Mason continued. "If I have my way, we'll have a blowout of an engagement party." He leaned his head to one side and narrowed his eyes. "You wouldn't be interested in making it a dual engagement party, by chance?"

"You know the answer to that."

"You—"

Collier held up his hand. "Don't start, Dad. It's not going to happen."

"I just hope you know what you're doing," Mason said, his mouth thin. "I suppose you're still seeing that little—"

"Don't," Collier interrupted again, harshly. "Don't say it."

Mason's features darkened. "How you can do this to your brother is something I can't figure out. After what her brother did to yours, you ought to be ashamed."

"Don't talk about shame to me," Collier lashed back, his fury reigniting.

His words seemed to pull Mason up short. "Suppose you tell me what that means?"

"Oh, I think you know," Collier said bitterly.

"The hell I do."

"Does paying off Darwin Brewster ring a bell?"

Mason's face turned white. "Who told you that?"

"Please, Dad, don't insult me."

Mason merely stared at his son, the veins bulging in his neck.

"Yeah, your fair-haired lackey got tired of waiting for his just deserts, as he so delicately put it, and came to see me."

"Why didn't he come to me?"

"Guess he wanted to jerk my chain right along with yours."

"And you believed the cockamamy crap he fed you?" Mason's bitterness rivaled Collier's.

"He sounded pretty convincing to me." Collier felt as though his vocal cords were strained to the max. "Especially when he started throwing your promises in my face, along with accusing you of blatantly breaking the law. You, of all people, who always preached the sacredness of the laws of our land."

"I can't help it if Brewster misinterpreted what I said. Hell, son, as an officer of the court, do you think I'd do anything to undermine that or my integrity?"

"So Brewster made all that up?"

"Did he have anything in writing?"

"No."

Mason shrugged. "Then it's his word against mine."

While he didn't totally believe his dad, God help him, Collier didn't have the stomach to call him a liar. Besides, Brewster was a first-class sleazeball. Who was to say he hadn't read more into his and Mason's conversation than was there?

"But you were opposed to Rogers walking," Collier pressed, still far from satisfied with Mason's explanation.

"Damn right, I was. I didn't want that little upstart to get by with putting Jackson in a wheelchair."

"Maybe that wouldn't have happened. Thanks to

Brewster, we'll never know. He obviously didn't give due process a chance to work.''

The veins in Mason's neck thickened even more. ''You know how some of these bleeding heart liberal judges and juries are. They would probably have bought his sob story.'' He paused and took a shuddering breath. ''If Rogers had walked out of that jail a free man, I think I would've killed him myself.''

Collier's mind reeled. How could he reason with someone whose hatred had taken over, rendering him totally unreasonable? This was a side of Mason he'd never seen before.

''If you had been here,'' Mason added, ''you would've felt the same.''

''And whose fault was that?'' Collier countered. ''My not being here, that is?''

''Mine. You were better served by staying on the job.''

''No. That's another wrong call. But I blame myself for not listening to my own instincts and coming home.''

''It's too late now. And I don't want to discuss it anymore.''

''Well, I do, dammit! I know Rogers claimed he was duped, that his drink was doctored at a party, which could've been shot down easily enough without using illegal means.''

''Not when it was the truth.''

Collier froze. ''What?''

''That's right. When Darwin and I talked over dinner, he admitted he could get Tommy Rogers off, that he'd tracked down his girlfriend, who said she'd actually witnessed a guy named Chad Creekmore put something in his drink.''

''And what did you say?''

Mason didn't so much as flinch. "I didn't respond one way or the other."

Sure you didn't. "So why did Rogers end up doing time?"

"Apparently Brewster went back to the girl and offered her money not to testify. She took it, and Tommy got what was coming to him."

Collier merely stared at Mason, his head spinning. So Brittany had been telling him the truth, only he hadn't believed her. Suddenly he felt as if he had fallen in a tub of shit and desperately needed to take a shower and wash the stench off.

"And you had no hand in that?" Collier demanded harshly.

"I told you, I can't help it if Brewster misinterpreted me." Mason's tone was cold and brooked no argument.

"You know Brewster's not going to take this lying down. He's going to cry foul like a stuck pig."

"Not if you let sleeping dogs lie," Mason said fiercely.

Collier's tone and look were just as fierce. "You're asking me to turn my head?"

"Look, I know you don't agree with the way the situation was handled," Mason said, his voice tempering and his features taking on a haggard look. "But if you care about our family, the firm and your future, you'll forget we ever had this conversation."

Collier merely stared at him, then turned on his heel and headed toward the door.

"Where are you going?"

Collier didn't bother to answer. He just kept on walking.

Thirty-Five

Collier stood at the window in his office, feeling like a weight was tied to his chest. How could Mason have pulled such a stunt without his knowing it? Easy. He hadn't been around. Now, in his heart, he knew Mason had lied. But he had no way to prove it, thank God. His dad had covered his tracks well.

He gritted his teeth. How was he ever going to tell Brittany the truth? That thought turned his blood to ice. But how could he not tell her? He was the first to admit he could be a jerk at times, but to withhold that information would make him a real ass. He simply couldn't do it and live with himself—or continue to sleep with her.

At first the beep coming from the phone didn't register. Then, muttering a curse, Collier swung around, strode to his desk and answered it.

"Mr. Smith," Pamela said, "a Mr. Richard Robb is here from the bar committee. Shall I send him in?"

Collier cringed. Of all days for him to have a key interview. He'd better be glad, he reminded himself, since he was expecting to learn at any minute that he'd been dropped, thanks to Rupert's efforts. Maybe that was what this visit was about. He held his breath, then released it, realizing that Senator Riley would be the one to deliver that news. This guy was here to question him.

Pulling himself together, Collier said, "Of course. Send him in."

"Don't forget you're due in court in a couple of hours."

"I won't, and thanks."

Seconds later he welcomed a bespectacled middle-aged attorney with a wiry build. Once the handshake and the pleasantries were out of the way, Robb took a comfortable chair. Collier sat across from him, feeling as though he was about to go before a firing squad. If he blew this…

"You know why I'm here," Robb said without preamble.

"Fire away."

Robb smiled, though his posture was all business, especially when he crossed his leg over his knee, then opened his plush leather notebook. "Actually I'm following up on the documents you filled out." He pulled them out of his briefcase and slotted them into the notebook.

"Which means I'm still in the hunt, and I'm grateful. However, I pretty much covered all bases in those forms you have in front of you."

"Everything?" Robb's gray eyes were hard and piercing.

"Except every time I took a crap." The moment he said that, he wanted to kick himself. But hell, what else could they possibly want? Dirt. The fact that he didn't have any mud in his background obviously made him more of a target.

"So nothing of significance has happened since these papers were filed?"

Had the committee learned about his affair with Brittany? Had he been mistaken about Rupert? Had he squawked to the senator? Or was this just a formality?

Another routine fishing expedition? Collier didn't know. What he did know was that his relationship with Brittany was neither illegal or immoral, and therefore none of their business.

His breath constricted. *Only they would make it their business.*

But how could he air his feelings about Brittany to this man? He couldn't.

"You obviously have something on your mind. Let's hear it."

Collier flushed. "I'm not sure you even care."

"Trust me, we care," Robb said emphatically.

Baring his love life seemed so Harry High School, he wanted to throw up. Maybe if he just touched on the outer edges, he could get through it.

"I'm involved with a woman."

Robb's lips twitched. "I would hope so."

Collier didn't respond to his dark humor. "Her brother's the one who's responsible for putting my brother in a wheelchair."

Robb's eyebrows rose. "Is she public knowledge?"

"My family knows."

"And do they approve?"

"Not really, but if the press were to get hold of that information they'd—"

"Rip you to pieces," Robb said bluntly.

"There's that possibility."

"With that in mind, are you going to continue to see her?"

Collier didn't hesitate. "Yes."

"Then we'll just have to wait and see what fireworks erupt, if any." Robb paused. "Are you still trying that harassment case?"

"Yes. But things seem to have settled down in the

press. Of course, we're still dueling it out in the court-room. I won't deny that. In order to defend my client, however, I'm convinced my conduct is right on target.''

"We're not trying to tell you how to do your job. The committee's just questioning your choice.''

"I believe in my client's innocence. In any case, I took the case before I knew I was being considered for the bench, which I stated.''

"Well, as you say, the furor seems to have settled, and so far the feminists haven't tarred and feathered you.''

"That might happen yet," Collier pointed out calmly, though there was nothing calm about him. "Especially if I get my client off.''

"Think that will happen?''

"Sure do. I told you, I firmly believe he's innocent.''

From the frown on Robb's face, that declaration didn't please him, but Collier couldn't afford not to prepare him for any possible fallout. The attorney, however, didn't dwell on the subject, choosing to move on.

"Anything else?''

"Not to my knowledge.''

"Still think you're up to the job, Smith?''

"Absolutely, although I know holding people's fates in my hands will not be easy. And does that bother me? Give me sleepless nights? You bet it does. If admitting that undermines my—''

"Quite the contrary, actually," Robb interrupted. "If you didn't feel that way, then you would already have been nixed. While a judge's job is often thankless, it should never become heartless.''

Collier figured that was as close to a compliment as he was going to get from the Judicial Committee. Robb shut his notebook and stood, then extended his hand. Collier followed suit and shook it, suddenly feeling vulnerable again, just as he'd felt growing up, hoping he'd pleased his stepdad but never sure. The attorney's face gave nothing away.

"Good luck in court," Robb said, an impersonal smile briefly touching his lips.

"Thanks."

Robb nodded. "We'll be in touch."

Once he was alone, Collier released a shaky breath, then peered at his watch. He wanted to talk to Brittany. More than that, he wanted to see her. Before he could do anything along those lines, though, he had something else to do. His hand was on the receiver when he heard another tap on the door.

"Yeah?"

Kyle strode in. "Got a minute?"

"Actually, I was about to buzz you."

"Does it have to do with your visitor?" Kyle asked, sitting down. "Pam just told me."

"Yeah, I got grilled, but I think I held my own." Collier rubbed the back of his neck. "But who knows. Politics is a cutthroat business."

"I still think you're the man for the job."

"You're prejudiced."

Kyle smiled. "You'd better hope so."

Collier remained sober. "Look, I'm due in court shortly, so I'm going to make this as quick as possible."

As if he sensed Collier was upset, Kyle didn't respond. He merely sat calmly and waited for his boss to elaborate.

"I've got a real mess to clean up," Collier said gravely.

"Does it involve the Banks woman?"

"Yes." Collier told him the gist of his conversations with Darwin, then Mason.

"Well, I'll be damned," Kyle said in a low voice. "I

didn't think anything could ever shock me again, but I was wrong.''

"I don't have to tell you the fallout from this, if it gets out.''

"So are you saying you're keeping your mouth shut?''

"For now. Or at least until you get me the information I need. Don't leave a stone unturned when it comes to Tommy Rogers.'' Collier hesitated, feeling as if he had a death sentence hanging over him. "And find that girlfriend of his,'' Collier added tersely.

"Then what?'' Kyle's gaze was piercing.

"I'll cross that bridge when I come to it.'' Collier's tone was bleak.

"Are you sure you know what you're doing?''

"Nailing my own coffin closed, more than likely,'' Collier muttered.

"So you haven't said anything to the woman?''

Collier's eyes glinted. "Her name is Brittany.''

Kyle flushed, then shuffled his feet. "Uh, right.''

"Look, I know you don't approve, and I understand why.'' Collier heaved a deep sigh. "So let's just leave it at that and move on.''

"Whatever you say.''

"I say start with the court transcript, go over it with a fine-tooth comb.''

"If Brewster wasn't just blowing hot air and using the accident to get what he wanted out of Mason, and the girl's on the up and up, then Rogers will probably walk.''

Collier compressed his lips. "I'm aware of that.''

"What about Jackson? Is he aware of what's going on?''

"No.''

"I don't have to point out the obvious, then.''

"No, you don't.''

"Thank God your old man won't be hung out to dry," Kyle said. "That sly fox was smart enough to cover—"

Collier cut him off with a savage gesture. "You just take care of the legwork, then we'll go from there."

For a moment Collier thought Kyle might press his point, but he didn't. Instead he took a deep breath, then said, "Sure thing, boss."

Once Kyle reached the door, Collier stopped him. "This demands kid gloves, Kyle." His voice turned hard. "Don't let me down."

Her body felt on fire. Yet it felt wonderful, which didn't make sense. Was she dreaming? Of course she was, Brittany assured herself. In reality, nothing could feel this good.

It was her own groan that made Brittany realize she wasn't dreaming after all. She was in Collier's bed, and his head was between her legs. He was making love to her with his tongue.

"Oh," she whimpered, giving in to the magic raking her body, especially after he eased a finger along the crevice between her buttocks. "Oh!" she cried again, bucking her hips until release finally came.

Then he gathered her lethargic body next to his and whispered, "Go back to sleep, my darling."

But she couldn't. Though she was drained in both body and soul, her mind wouldn't quiet. It kept going over the events that had led up to another marathon evening of lovemaking.

Out of the blue, he had called and asked her to dinner, taking her to another out-of-the-way restaurant. While she enjoyed his company, along with the wine and food, she knew that sooner or later she was going to have to take her pride off the shelf, where she'd stored it, and give him up. Apparently he wasn't going to take the drastic step of taking their relationship public, not unless he was forced to.

While she didn't have nearly as much at stake as he did, she deserved better than a back-alley affair. Her solid work ethic, her drive, her pride and her good name were all the bragging rights she had. And continuing to let him use her was beginning to destroy her.

Still, when they had gone inside his condo, she hadn't objected, especially not after they stripped naked and got into the shower. Once her body was wet and slippery, he'd backed her against the tile, hoisted her to his waist and pierced her with his erection.

Following several thrusts and grunts, they were spent. A short time later he had carried her back into the bedroom, dripping wet. When he would have put her down on the bed, she stopped him.

"What?" he asked in a strained voice, his eyes questioning.

"A treat," she answered breathlessly. "For you." Then, getting out of his arms, she stood in front of him. Beginning with his lower lip, she drew it into her mouth and sucked. He moaned a deep belly moan, clutching her shoulders as though to stop his knees from buckling.

Finally she let go of his lip, opting to investigate another moan zone. Using her tongue, she licked an imaginary line down the middle of his body, from his chin to his penis, licking the water off his body as she went.

"Oh, yes, yes."

Following those thickly muttered words, he tangled his fingers in her hair the second after she landed on her knees in front of his distended flesh and took it into her mouth.

"Oh, Brittany," he cried, trying to bring her to her feet.

Purposely ignoring him, she continued to suck the moist, velvet tip, tasting him on her tongue, massaging his balls at the same time.

"I can't wait!"

She still didn't stop.

Now, as she lay motionless against his sleeping body, she felt her face flush with color at her boldness. She had done to him something she'd never done to another man, never even considered. But with Collier, it seemed so right. Perfect, in fact. Besides, she had to take advantage of him and his body when she could, reveling in the feel and smell of him, ever conscious that this might be the last time she saw him.

Hot sex came with no guarantees.

Yet she knew it was much more for her. She loved him. She might as well admit it, though it sickened her to do so, knowing he would end up stomping her heart into tiny pieces.

It was only after she felt him jolt that she realized she must have dug her nails into his skin.

"How long have you been awake?" he asked in an indulgent tone.

"Not long," she lied.

"We...we have to talk."

"I know," she whispered.

"Look—"

Swallowing her rising panic that he was truly going to end it, she interrupted, blurting out, "Tommy's in the hospital." She hadn't meant to say that; the words had just come out.

"So that's why you were so quiet at dinner."

She fingered his hair. "What's your excuse?"

He didn't respond. Instead he just looked at her, a tormented expression on his face. She turned away from the pain mirrored there.

"I don't know how much longer I can keep leaving you."

Her soul rejoiced. That was as close to a commitment as he'd ever come. Dare she hope? No, she wouldn't do that to herself. She would simply savor their time together.

At this moment his lips were surrounding a breast and a finger was slipping inside her warmth.

She sighed and gave in to the exquisite sensations once again filling her body.

Thirty-Six

Rupert knew things should be easy, so why the hell weren't they?

All he had to do was attend one of his wife's highbrow parties and drop a word or two here and there about Collier's affair with Brittany and the damage would be done. Gossip would spread like wildfire, and Smith's ass would be grass.

First out of the gate to blast Collier would be Senator Riley and the committee; they wanted no hint of scandal to touch their candidates, wouldn't tolerate it. Next would be Bill Frazier, Lana's overprotective father, who wouldn't stand for his little girl being bested by a waitress from the wrong side of the tracks.

So why hadn't he made his move?

Brittany. She was who held him back, who had a lock on his tongue. She would know who had ratted on Collier, maybe not right away, but she'd figure it out. If not, Smith would tell her. Then he would be dead in the water as far as she was concerned. He couldn't bear that.

At least he had her hoodlum brother on his side. Pulling strings and getting into the pen to see Rogers had been a stroke of genius. Before Smith, helping her brother and getting that freaking education had been all Brittany cared about. But once Smith entered the picture, things had changed. *She* had changed.

Rupert knew he was to blame for her change in attitude toward him. He never should have gotten drunk and assaulted her. Before that, he'd had her eating out of his hand. Why, the minute he would walk into the agency, her face would light up and she would be so friendly.

But dammit, friendship hadn't been what he'd had in mind. He wanted to make love to her. That fateful night, following dinner, when she'd cringed at his touch, he'd lost it. No woman had ever treated him in such a manner. Still, he'd been so sure that he could make that sin up to her and she would forgive him, especially if he was patient and used her brother's plight to his advantage.

His ploy would have worked, too, if Smith hadn't messed things up.

Rupert felt his temper rise as he bounded out of his chair and prowled the office. How had the two of them met? Hell, it didn't matter. All that mattered was that Smith was fucking her and he wasn't.

Maybe her stupid brother could convince her that she should let him help them. At least that would bring them back in contact away from the travel agency. Brittany would be forced to see him then.

The only person who could thwart those plans was Collier Smith.

Apparently she was smitten by the arrogant attorney. Damn him. Damn them both.

Rupert knew that this train of thought was forcing his blood pressure sky-high. His head was pounding so hard he feared it might explode. Following several deep breaths, he crossed back to his desk, opened the drawer and removed a bottle of pills. Pitching his head back, he tossed one down the back of his throat, hoping it would eventually knock out his headache.

If her brother didn't bring Brittany to heel, he just

might have to resort to slandering Smith. Right now his gut still assured him Travis Wainwright was going to get the nod from the president. While old Mason had the clout and the money, his stepson didn't have the experience, which was a huge strike against him.

However, the decision as to who sat on the bench wouldn't affect his feelings for Brittany. He just wanted Smith out of the way. And whatever that took, he would do. Patience, however, was not his strong suit. This mess had gone on long enough; he wanted it resolved.

As trusting and naive as his wife was, he could have a long-lasting affair with Brittany and Angel would never know. Of course, he would have to be careful; he couldn't flaunt his extracurricular activities for fear of some of her friends finding out. They might not be as gullible as Angel.

For now, he didn't have to worry about that. The woman he was screwing while waiting for Brittany lived in Houston, where he spent a lot of his time. He would keep her until Brittany came to her senses.

What if she didn't?

Feeling a desperate need for a drink, Rupert jerked open the bottom drawer of his desk and took out a full bottle of whiskey. After twisting off the cap, he pitched his head back and took a healthy gulp. Once the alcohol hit his stomach, he reveled in the punch it gave him before guzzling again.

He had just replaced the cap when he heard a knock on his door. Quickly he dispensed with the bottle, wiped his lips, crammed a piece of gum into his mouth, then made an effort to pull himself back together. No way could his secretary or anyone else in the office know he nipped faithfully on the job. Then he remembered that his secretary was on vacation, and he hadn't bothered to get a sub. Still, he had to be careful. Too much was at stake.

"It's open," he finally said.

Darwin Brewster strolled through the door. Hoping he was adequately covering his amazement, Rupert got up and came out from behind his desk. He didn't know the young man very well. They had been at the same parties and had visited socially, but that was the extent of it. Yet he'd heard unflattering rumors about him. Had it been necessary, Brewster was the one in the firm he would have tapped to spy on Collier.

"I hope I'm not intruding," Darwin said, stopping midway into the room.

"Not at all," Rupert responded, then extended his hand. "Here, have a seat." He gestured toward the plush chairs and love seat adjacent to his desk.

"Thanks."

"How 'bout some coffee?"

"No thanks. Just a little of your time, that's all."

"You got it," Rupert said, barely able to contain his curiosity and excitement. Yes, excitement, he told himself. One of Smith's cronies wouldn't be here unless something was up.

"I understand you're backing Travis Wainwright for federal judge." Darwin gave an almost apologetic shrug. "I think you've made a wise choice."

Rupert's excitement waned. Surely Brewster hadn't come to discuss Travis and his merits as a candidate. No, there was more to this visit than that.

"Thanks for your vote of confidence," Rupert said, filling the short silence. "I think Travis'll make a fine judge."

"Look, may I be blunt?"

"By all means," Rupert said, taken aback by Brewster's sudden in-your-face attitude. He shouldn't have been surprised, though. After all, Williams, Smith and Rutledge didn't hire losers or attorneys without balls.

"If I'm out of line, I apologize in advance, and we'll forget this conversation ever took place."

Rupert's excitement rejuvenated itself, along with his curiosity. "Why don't you just say what's on your mind, then we'll go from there?"

"If you're really interested in kicking Collier off the list, then I have the ammunition."

Rupert kept his voice bland, refusing to tip his hand and show any emotion. "Oh, really? I'd say that's a tall order, young man."

"I realize you have no reason to believe me."

"Wait a minute. I didn't say that. After all, you work for his firm. That alone makes you privy to certain information."

It was obvious his words brought Brewster the confidence and relief he needed to go on, because he straightened a bit, and his eyes took on a steely glint. Yet when he spoke, his voice was slightly unsteady. "But I have to know there's something in this for me."

Ah, so that was the kicker. This young upstart wasn't going to give unless he got something in return. "If your information's worth it, I'm sure we can come to a mutual agreement," Rupert said in a calm, easy tone.

"You'll have to do better than that, Mr. Holt. You see, I'm involved up to my eyeballs already, to the extent I could lose my license to practice law."

Rupert's eyes widened, but he kept his cool. "And you're willing to share your information with me and only me?"

"If the price is right," Brewster stressed.

Rupert needed another drink badly, but he refrained

from getting up and going for the bottle. At least his pounding head had subsided without the benefit of another drink.

"Mr. Holt?"

Rupert focused his attention back on the attorney. "Fire away, young man. You have a captive audience."

Tommy was better. She had just called the prison, and they had told her he'd been released from the infirmary. Thank goodness their disagreement over Rupert hadn't set him back.

Brittany flinched visibly. Every time she thought about the verbal slanging match that had taken place between them, she felt sick. How could she have lost her temper that way? On the other hand, how could Tommy have been taken in by Rupert?

Easy. Rupert had offered to help him, and he certainly had the means to do it. Too, her brother hadn't known Rupert was the one who had assaulted her. Maybe if she'd told him the truth from the start, this wouldn't have happened. He wouldn't have fallen for Rupert's promises. Now Tommy just wanted out, and he didn't care by what means.

Sudden bitterness welled up inside her as she pulled up in her driveway. Instead of getting out, she rested her head on the steering wheel, weary to the bone.

When had things become so complicated?

The only bright spot in her life right now was Collier. And in the end, he would break her heart, too. But until he did, she intended to make the most of their time together. So lost in thought was she that she didn't hear the other car. Only when she reached for the door handle and looked up did she see him.

Frozen in place, she watched helplessly as Rupert

walked toward her. Her first thought was to start her car and back out. She couldn't. He had her blocked in. She scrambled out of the seat just as he reached her. "I told you never to come here again," she said, her voice shaking with fury.

"Well, I'm here," Rupert said flatly. "And unless you intend to carry on our conversation outside, then you'll let me in." His features were harsh. "I'm not leaving until I have my say."

"Damn you, Rupert, leave me and Tommy alone."

"Ah, so you've talked to your brother."

"How could you stoop so low?"

"Hey, I've always told you I was willing to help, if only you'll return the favor."

"Don't you get it? I loathe you."

He smiled, though it failed to reach his eyes. "You won't always feel that way, sweetheart."

"Don't you dare 'sweetheart' me," she lashed back, her chest heaving. Watching his eyes settle on that part of her anatomy further infuriated her. "You have five minutes, and not a second longer."

"Or what?" he challenged, his smile turning indulgent.

"I'll call the cops," she flared back.

He laughed out loud. "I don't think so."

Clamping down on her fury, Brittany swung around and headed for the trailer. After he had followed her inside, just over the threshold, she whipped around. "This is as far as you go. Now, what do you want?"

"Okay, here it is. I have the evidence to prove Collier Smith and his family are responsible for your brother rotting in the pen."

Brittany steeled herself not to show any reaction whatsoever to those words. She wasn't about to give him the satisfaction of knowing how they hurt her, how her knees almost buckled under the pain. "I don't believe you," she declared, that sick feeling in her stomach having returned with a vengeance.

"I think you do. Right after I met you and learned about Tommy, you told me how you thought he hadn't gotten a fair shot, that the cards had been stacked against him by Jackson Williams' family."

Brittany bit her lower lip to keep it steady.

"The truth hurts, doesn't it?"

"Get to the point," she said dully, clinging to the doorknob.

"In good time, sweetheart. All in good time."

"Dammit, Rupert!"

He laughed again, then said, "Actually, I don't want to wait, either. It's past time you knew exactly how lover boy betrayed you."

Brittany felt her jaw drop. "Lover boy?"

"Yeah," Rupert said smugly. "I know Collier's been between your sheets. I saw him sneaking out of your trailer the other morning."

"You've been spying on me?" she screeched, her mind spinning. If Rupert used this information against Collier, it would ruin him.

"Only because I care."

Rupert paused with a chuckle, while Brittany, little by little, was dying on the inside.

"I'm listening."

"So I finally have your undivided attention," Rupert said. "To get on with the juicy details, Mason, Collier's stepfather, offered Darwin Brewster a free cruise and a junior partnership in the firm to suppress the evidence that would've gotten your brother off, or at least bought him a lighter sentence."

"What evidence?" Somehow Brittany managed to force those words through her numb lips.

"Your brother was telling the truth, after all. His girlfriend admitted she saw Chad Creekmore, whoever the hell he is, doctor Tommy's drink and was prepared to testify on his behalf. Shortly thereafter, Mason went to Brewster and the girlfriend disappeared." Rupert paused with an offhand shrug. "And the rest is history, as they say."

Brittany stood stiffly, barely breathing.

Each damning word against Collier was tantamount to being stabbed in the heart with a sharp instrument. More than anything, she wanted to run out of the trailer, jump in her car, find Collier and confront him. But first she had to put an end to Rupert's torment of her. "You've had your say. Now get out!"

Rupert's face contorted, and he gave her a disbelieving stare. "Hey, you're taking your anger out on the wrong person. I'm your champion here. Because of me, your brother will likely get his walking papers. So you owe me big time." He took a step toward her.

She stepped back. "Don't!"

"I want you, Brittany." His eyes were hard. "Now that Collier's out of your life, I'm willing to step in and take his place. You'll never want for anything again. I know I'm married, but that can change. If I thought you'd marry me…"

"Stop it!" she cried, covering her ears. "Don't say another word. I never want to see you again. Do you hear me? Never! You've invaded my life long enough. You've spied on me. You've *assaulted* me. You've—" Brittany couldn't say any more; fury choked off her words.

Rupert grabbed her arm. She jerked away and glared

at him. "I mean it. Any man who would hit a woman is the scum of the earth."

"I've already apologized for that, damn you! But if you're too stupid to know a good thing when you see it, then I won't hesitate to bury you right along with Tommy."

He was looming over her now, his fury so acute that spittle had gathered in the corners of his mouth. "I'll keep my mouth shut about what I told you, and your precious brother will continue to rot in that cell until he serves his full sentence. Maybe even longer, if I have my way."

Brittany didn't back down, though every nerve in her body was strained to the breaking point. She knew she was about to take a gamble that could cost her dearly. "You go right ahead and do what you have to do."

"You're bluffing. You don't have what it takes to fight me and win."

"Try me," she seethed. "I can still file charges on you! And I can go to your wife and tell her about your extracurricular activities, especially your penchant for beating up on women." Brittany paused for emphasis. "Wonder what she'd think about that?"

"Good try, bitch, only I didn't just fall off a turnip truck. Tommy's your main weakness. No way would you choose getting back at me over getting him released."

Brittany purposely held her tongue for a moment and listened as his heavy breathing gave the silence stiff competition.

"But you can't be totally sure of that," she whispered at last, giving him a lethal smile. "Can you, Rupert?"

Thirty-Seven

Brittany kept on walking, despite the crippling fear that threatened to hinder her determination. When she'd pulled up in the parking lot of Williams, Smith and Rutledge and killed the engine a few minutes ago, she hadn't been able to move, not for what seemed like the longest time.

Had she taken total leave of her senses? That question had plagued her ever since she'd made her decision. Once Rupert had left her trailer, she'd taken off her clothes, crawled into bed and curled into the fetal position.

After Tommy had been sent to prison, she had been totally alone and vulnerable. The stake this new knowledge about Collier had driven through her heart had re-created that same feeling.

But wallowing in self-pity hadn't been the answer then, and it wasn't now. Come morning, she had to right a terrible wrong. In order to live with herself, she had to confront Collier, no matter how much such a confrontation would cost her. The fatal wound shouldn't have come as a surprise. She had warned herself he would hurt her.

Only not like this! her heart cried. Not such a harsh betrayal. Emotionally she was a wreck. Part of her still loved Collier, while the other part hated him. But until she'd faced him down, she couldn't move ahead with her life.

Now, as she made her way inside the building, her heart jumped from her chest to her throat. What if he wasn't in? She had called the courthouse and learned he wasn't in court. That much she knew. Still, he could be anywhere, doing anything. His Lexus wasn't in the lot, but since he was one of the partners, she figured he had undercover parking.

What if he was out of town? If that were the case, he would have called her, since he had no clue she was on to him and his family.

A bitter feeling rushed through her. Considering their circumstances, she was a fool to assume that or anything else. It didn't matter, anyway. Even if she had to camp out in his office, she would. She didn't have to go to class today, and she'd called Sissy and told her she might not be in to work. Sensing she was upset, Sissy had tried to question her. But Brittany had rebuffed her, though as gently as possible, telling her that she would talk to her later.

When she finally located Collier's suite, the desk out front was unoccupied and the door to his office was closed. Was he in? Should she wait for his secretary?

No. This wasn't a social call. She had wanted to catch him off guard; that was the point.

"May I help you?"

Brittany swung around, her eyes wide and her heart still jammed in her throat. She swallowed and stared at an older woman, who was attractive despite the frown that marred her features. "I'm looking for Collier."

The older woman's frown deepened. Brittany suspected it was because she had called him by his given name. Since the woman had never seen her before, it was only natural that she would be both suspicious and curious.

"Is he expecting you?" Though her lips were tight, her tone was cordial.

"Is he in?" Brittany demanded, answering the woman's question with one of her own, though her face felt scalded with color. She'd never been this pushy or rude in her life, and neither sat well with her. Too bad. She didn't intend to be thwarted.

Nothing would stop her from seeing Collier.

The woman's frown deepened even more, and when she spoke again, some of her cordiality had disappeared. "If you'll please have a seat, I'll—"

Brittany did something else she'd never done. She turned and opened the door, all the while tuning out the woman's horrified sputtering. Once she was inside, she closed the door and leaned against it.

Empty.

Her confidence eroded. All her blustering courage had gone for naught. Collier wasn't here after all. Damn! Scrambling to come up with another plan, she took several deep breaths and waited, expecting his secretary to come barging in behind her.

But it wasn't the secretary who barged in. A door across the room suddenly opened. In walked Collier, along with a puff of chilly wind.

He pulled up short and stared, slack-jawed.

For a moment speech failed Brittany, as well, her guard having slipped with the initial letdown of his absence. Now he was in front of her, in the flesh, looking so disheveled, *so fractured,* that her first inclination was to close the distance between them, throw her arms around him and comfort him.

Then her sanity and her self-respect reasserted themselves. She had come to exact her pound of flesh, vowing to condemn him for what he'd done. Yet...

"Brittany," he finally said on a hoarse note. "What—"

"Am I doing here?" She made herself move forward, plastering a plastic smile on her lips.

"Well, yes, but it doesn't matter. I'm damn glad to see you."

"You mean you're not ashamed? Afraid for your family to see me?"

As if he'd just picked up on the bitterness in her tone and the forced smile, he seemed to hesitate, though he didn't say anything right off. Instead he put down his briefcase and stepped toward her.

"I take it this isn't a social call." He gave her a lopsided smile, but it lacked its usual warmth.

She felt her control slip. She had resolved to be strong and decisive, to say what she had to say, then walk out. But doing that was turning out to be harder than she'd ever thought.

The hardships of her past, Tommy's accident—even Rupert's assault—hadn't brought her to her knees the way Collier could. She could have taken it if he'd just used her sexually, which was what she'd expected all along. But what he'd done defied all decency.

"Let me get you a cup of coffee," he said into the building silence.

"No."

He pulled up short again at her sharp tone, then muttered a curse before saying, "Well, I'm going to have one."

She merely stood still and watched as he filled a mug while the tension around them mounted.

Once he'd taken a sip, he stared at her over the rim of his cup, his eyes bleak. "How did you find out?"

She didn't pretend to misunderstand. "Does it matter?"

"Holt told you, didn't he?"

"Yes."

"That son of a bitch!" Collier spat, sitting his cup down and rubbing the back of his neck.

"Is that all you have to say?"

"It's not what it seems like," Collier said.

She lifted her eyes upward, mostly to avoid the pleading in his.

"I can explain everything."

She lowered her head. "Oh, I'm sure you can."

"Sarcasm doesn't become you."

"Why, Collier?" Her voice cracked. "Why?"

She'd had no intention of asking that, knowing he'd just deny any involvement in the illegal handling of her brother's case, pass the buck on to his father, perhaps even his brother.

"I don't know why," he muttered harshly, looking beaten down.

She blinked, then regrouped, refusing to feel sorry for him just because she didn't understand his response.

He took her silence as an opportunity to go on. "I know Darwin Brewster deliberately botched the case."

Know. Not *knew*. That took her aback.

"That's right," he said, as though reading her mind. "I just found out myself. Brewster came to my office, demanding to know when my father was going to deliver on the rest of their deal."

"I didn't come here to listen to your excuses."

Collier sucked in his breath, then blew it out before

continuing through tight, white lips. "Well, you're going to, dammit. I have a right to defend myself."

"Like hell you do."

He ignored her and went on. "When I asked Brewster what he was talking about, he informed me that Mason, *not me,* had promised him a cruise and a partnership in the firm to suppress evidence that would get your brother off."

His words rang so sincere that for several heartbeats he'd almost made a believer out of her. Then she recovered quickly and lashed out, "Stop it! You don't have to lie anymore. Of course you knew. How could you not?"

"I'm not lying! This was all done behind my back. Jackson's, too. Hell, I wasn't even in the country when it happened. That bastard Holt is the one who told you all this, isn't he? He's been spying on you and saw me leave your trailer."

There was a frantic edge to his tone, an edge she forced herself to ignore or she would be duped again by his seeming sincerity.

"I know what Rupert's been up to, but that's not the issue here."

"You're right. It's the truth."

While she groped for a suitable comeback, he went on. "Mason says he didn't promise Brewster anything, that Brewster put his own spin on their conversation. Now, whether I entirely believe that or not is another matter, though I can't prove otherwise, since nothing was in writing." He paused and drew a harsh breath. "Now you know everything I know."

"Sure I do."

"I've never lied to you, Brittany."

She gave an almost hysterical laugh. "Our whole sordid affair has been nothing but a lie."

He flinched visibly, his face draining of color. "There's nothing sordid about what's between us, and you know that."

"God, Collier, how can you say that when you've kept me hidden like some backstreet—" Her voice cracked in two, and she turned away.

"Don't," he said in a thick voice. "Don't say that."

That was when she felt his breath on her neck and knew he'd closed the distance between them. Her breathing constricted, and she swallowed hard before moving out of harm's way. If he touched her... Ashamed of those thoughts, she shut them down and swung around, her eyes daring him to make another move.

"Why not?" she asked painfully. "That's the truth."

"When I took you out to dinner the other night, I hoped many other nights would follow, only—"

"You got caught," she interrupted in a low, dull tone.

"Brittany, please, let's stop the personal insults." He stepped toward her once again, then pulled up short, as if he'd reached the imaginary line she'd drawn between them.

"You're right, Collier, this isn't about us." She paused, tempted to add, *There is no us and never will be.* But she refrained, determined not to prolong this agony with any more useless words. "It's about Tommy and the injustice that was done to him."

"Which is something I intend to fix," he responded roughly.

She let loose another hysterical laugh.

Color shot back into his face, but when he spoke, his voice was controlled. "Even as we speak, I've got my best investigator looking for the girl. And I can guarantee you that when this all shakes out, Brewster will lose his license to practice law."

That news was unexpected and even managed to shake her resolve. But only for a second. Regardless of what measures he took now, nothing he could do would make up for his past duplicity. "What about your dad?"

"Not a damn thing will happen to him," Collier responded in a listless tone. "Is that honest enough for you?"

"I should've gone to the D.A. first, you know," she said, still not convinced he was sincere.

"Why didn't you?"

"I wanted you to know that I knew what you were all about. What *we* were all about."

An incredulous look deepened the lines on his face. "You think I used you as a pawn in order to keep this covered up? That I knew who you were all along?"

"Under the circumstances, why wouldn't I?" she flared, her chin jutting.

A groan parted his lips. "God, how can you even think that?"

She closed her eyes against the agony in his, feeling her resolve weaken even more.

"I love you, Brittany."

His carefully spoken words fell into the silence with a resounding boom. As she winced against the mental impact, her eyes popped back open.

"I always will," he added in an unsteady voice. "And furthermore, I want to marry you."

"Please, Collier," she whimpered. "Don't."

"Don't what? Tell you the truth? It can work. *We* can work."

There was a wrenching twist to his voice that cut her to the quick. She desperately wanted to believe him, but long years of mistrust and bitterness resurfaced, and she

cried, "You're just saying words that don't mean anything. What about your family?"

"What about them?"

"They would never approve of me." She paused and
searched for enough air to continue. "And what about
the precious judgeship? Marrying me could jeopardize
that."

"Loving you means more than either one," he countered, a fierce note in his tone.

"Oh, Collier, I don't believe a word of that, and neither do you."

His mouth worked. "Dammit, I'll prove it to you."

"Even if you married me, I could never live in your
world, in the shadow of your family."

He went white again, as if she'd slapped him. "It
doesn't have to be that way."

"Yes, it does."

"Someway, somehow, we could make it work."

"Tommy's my only concern now. He needs me."

"He'll never need you *or* love you as much as I do,"
Collier said in an agonized voice.

She wished she could believe that, but she couldn't.

"It's too late for us, Collier. The damage is too severe."

"Don't say that," he begged.

She fought back the tears. "And know this—if Tommy
isn't released or doesn't get a new trial, I'm going to
hold you personally responsible."

With that, she turned and left.

Thirty-Eight

It was over.

And just as she'd predicted, her heart was in a million pieces. Despite that, the world didn't stop. The sun still rose and set. He would pick up his life where he'd left it before he met her, and she would do the same. No! her soul screamed.

Without Collier, nothing would ever be the same.

She missed him so much. If only she could believe he'd been in the dark about Tommy, that he hadn't known from the get-go about the underhanded deal, then maybe...

Brittany snuffed out that thought. Even if he hadn't known, how could she ever be part of a family that had such flagrant disregard for what was right? They used power and money to run roughshod over anything and anyone who got in their way. She could never accept that. A shudder shook her. Collier wasn't like that, she told herself. He didn't use his wealth and power in that manner. But since her heart was her only gauge, she couldn't be sure.

All she knew was that she loved him, loved him with every fiber of her being. And he'd said he loved her and wanted to marry her. Every time she thought of his tormented confession, her heart stopped beating for a few seconds.

If she'd said yes, would he really have married her? It was hard for her to believe he would defy his family, forsake his friends, jeopardize his job, all for her. No way. If push had come to shove, he wouldn't have gone through with it. She had convinced herself of that, which was how she'd survived these last few days without him. Still, a part of her ached to hear from him.

Ring, phone, please, she'd begged silently.

Ring, doorbell, please, she'd prayed silently.

Now Brittany forced herself to get up and water the plant on the waiting area coffee table. Now was not the time to rehash her feelings. She'd just arrived at the agency, though she hadn't officially opened the door for business. But dear Lord, how she missed him, missed his smell, his touch, his being inside her for hours at a time.

That crushing feeling in her chest suddenly stilled her hands. She didn't think she could stand it, the pain was so intense. Then she panicked, knowing she had no choice. If she didn't get hold of herself, she wouldn't make it. Besides, she had work to do, which she hoped would be her salvation.

Now that the dirty dealings had been brought to light, she had to take action. She couldn't depend on Collier to right that wrong, though when he'd sworn he would, she'd almost believed him. If nothing else, as soon as his father found out what was going on, he'd put a stop to the investigation.

She felt driven to do something on her own. But what? The district attorney's office would be the logical place to start. As she'd told Collier, she should have gone there to begin with. And she certainly should have gone there after their conversation. But at the time her raw hunger for him had kept her from thinking rationally.

However, if Collier didn't get back to her soon, she

would make that move. She couldn't sacrifice her brother or betray him out of her own selfish needs.

She hadn't seen Tommy yet to tell him that soon he would get a new trial or even just simply walk out. She was waiting until she knew for certain. She couldn't bear to get his hopes up, only to see them crushed. Until Renee was found again and agreed to testify on Tommy's behalf, then Mason Williams and Darwin Brewster would get by with duping her brother.

Brittany's temper suddenly kicked in. If Tommy wasn't released, then she would make them pay. So what if it took a lifetime? It would be worth it.

"My, my, you look like you could take on a lion and win."

Brittany swung around, her hand on her chest. "Jeez, Sissy, you scared the you-know-what out of me."

"Sorry. I figured you heard the back door open."

"Well, I didn't."

"I know. You were too deep in thought. Not good ones, either, from the look of you."

"You're right." Brittany paused, toying with her lower lip. "There's a lot going on, things I probably should talk to you about."

"You know I'm here for you, always have been."

"I know," Brittany responded dejectedly. "It's just that I think I should be able to handle my own problems. I hate to burden others with my whining."

"There comes a time in everyone's life, my dear, when they have to depend on others. Perhaps that time has finally come for you. Anyway, whining's not so bad. Lord knows, when Tommy went away, you crawled into a shell and didn't come out for ages." Sissy paused and angled her head. "What say we go to the break room and get some coffee? We have a while before we have to open.''

Brittany didn't hesitate; Sissy's offer was suddenly a godsend. Once they were settled with cups of coffee in front of them at the small table, Sissy said, ''Fire away.''

''I don't know where to start,'' Brittany said, uneasy now that it actually came to unburdening her soul.

''How about with who assaulted you?''

''I'm not sure you want to know.''

Sissy raised her eyebrows, looking shocked. ''Why not? Whoever he is, the bastard ought to be tarred and feathered.''

''It was Rupert Holt.''

''What?''

''I swear it's the truth.''

Sissy opened her mouth again, but nothing came out. Finally she snapped it shut.

Brittany went on to explain the details, how she and Rupert had struck up a friendship, then how he'd mentioned helping Tommy.

''Which was the only reason I ever went to dinner with him,'' she stressed. ''Otherwise, I never would have stepped out the door with him.''

''Oh, honey, I know that,'' Sissy said, shaking her head as though still trying to come to grips with what Brittany had told her. ''The thought just blows my mind, that's all. Rupert, a drunk and abuser. Never in a million years would I have guessed that.''

Brittany lifted her chin a notch. ''He'll never bother me again, though. I threatened to expose him.''

''Well, I'm going to nail his ass where it counts,'' Sissy said with fire. ''*I'm* going to expose him. I intend to tell his wife.''

Brittany's eyes widened.

"That's right. Angel's one of my dearest friends. I can't sit by and let him go ballistic on her one of these days when she crosses him."

"Whatever you think is best. I know he's a good customer, so if—"

"Are you nuts? He'll never be welcome here again. Now that we've settled that, what else is bothering you?"

"Oh, Sissy," Brittany said, "I feel so bad about dumping on you."

"Spit it out."

Brittany drew a breath, then slowly let it out. "It's a long story."

"We can open the doors a few minutes late. It won't be the end of the world."

Brittany hit the high spots of meeting Collier, their affair and how all that was connected with Tommy.

When she finished, Sissy gasped. "My God, girl, how have you survived?"

"It hasn't been easy."

"It's unbelievable that the guy who rescued you turned out to be the stepbrother of the guy your brother ran over."

"I know," Brittany said, biting her lower lip. "I still can't believe it."

"Do you really think he knew about the suppressed evidence?" Sissy asked.

"He swears he didn't."

"I don't know him personally, of course, but I know *of* him. And he's considered one of the best attorneys in this state. The fact that he's being considered for a judgeship bears that out."

"Even if he's innocent, Sissy, it wouldn't work out. His family... God, can you imagine him bringing me home to Daddy?"

Sissy smiled. "Stranger things have happened."

"Right now, my concern is getting Tommy released. I can't sit around and wait." Brittany tapped nervous fingers on the table. "I wish I could find that girl myself. I tried early on, but to no avail. Any suggestions?"

"Wait on Collier," Sissy replied. "I think he'll do right by you."

"Maybe, maybe not," Brittany said, frowning. "But I can't take that kind of chance."

"Were the girl and her mother close to anyone in the neighborhood?"

Brittany hesitated, thinking back. "Their next-door neighbors. I do remember that. And I've thought about going back, but—"

"That's what I'd do. If those neighbors are still there, maybe they've heard something from Renee." Sissy shrugged. "I know it's a long shot."

"But definitely worth a try," Brittany responded thoughtfully. "Especially when that's all I have."

"Want me to come with you?"

"No, but would you mind holding down *your* fort till I get back?"

Sissy half smiled, then stood. "I think I can handle that. In fact, forget about coming back. Take the day off." Her features clouded. "I hope all this works out for you. I wish you and Collier—" She broke off, then went on, "You deserve some happiness, my dear. Life with that man would open up a whole new world for you."

"That's not going to happen. Too much water under the proverbial bridge."

"You still love him, don't you?"

"Always." Brittany's voice trembled.

Sissy grabbed her and hugged her. "Good luck."

* * *

Brittany ignored her racing heart as she stepped onto the porch, careful not to put her boot on a rotten board. That was hard, since the trailer was in a worse state of disrepair than hers.

She knocked on the door several times before she received a response. A woman with scraggly hair and rotten front teeth poked her head out. Brittany couldn't remember if this was the woman she'd spoken to three years ago or not.

"Yes?" The woman's voice had a bourbon-rough edge to it.

"I'm sorry to disturb you," Brittany said in a halting voice, suddenly sensing the futility of this visit. This woman didn't even know the time of day, much less where her long-lost neighbors were. Still, she was here; she might as well see it through.

"Whatcha want?"

"Uh, I'm looking for Renee Youngblood. She used to live next door."

The lady's eyes were suspicious. "What for?"

"I just need to talk to her. It's really important."

"They don't live around here no more."

"I know, but do you know where they are? I thought you might have heard from them or know where they're living now," Brittany finished lamely, giving in to the sinking feeling inside her. So much for her stupid idea; it would die right here.

"You got anything in that fancy purse?"

Brittany gave a start. "Excuse me?"

"Your purse, lady. You got any money in it?"

"A little, but—" Brittany aborted the rest of her sentence. It had finally dawned on her what the woman was getting at.

Hope was reborn.

"I'm awfully thirsty," the woman was saying.

"First tell me what you know," Brittany responded firmly, clutching the strap of her purse, which the lady was eyeing sharply.

"Renee and her mamma have moved back."

"Here?"

"Nope. They live in a trailer park over in Mayberry. I seen 'em last week at Wal-Mart, then they come home with me to visit."

Brittany had trouble containing her excitement. For a second she wanted to grab the old hag and hug her. Instead she fumbled in her purse and drew out a twenty-dollar bill, then handed it to her.

The woman grabbed it, clasped it against her chest, then asked, "Anything else?"

"No, that's all," Brittany murmured. "Thanks. Thanks very much."

Wordlessly the woman slammed the door in her face.

Where was Kyle?

Collier sat behind his desk and stared down at the stack of folders in front of him, then at his computer, but the screen didn't even register. His mind was elsewhere. He'd been expecting to hear from his investigator all morning, either by phone or in person. Nothing so far.

He had heard from Mason, though, shortly after he'd arrived at the office. His dad had been waiting for him. Collier didn't have to be told why he was there. Since they'd had it out, Collier had purposely kept his distance. He'd been so angry with Mason that he hadn't trusted himself to go anywhere near him. And while that anger was still raw and festering, avoiding Mason indefinitely wasn't the answer.

"Are you due in court?" his dad had asked.

Collier had picked up on the uncertain note in his tone, but at that moment he was in no mood to cut his dad any slack.

"Not today. The judge is out sick again."

"Amberson seems to be sick a lot," Mason responded.

"Too much," Collier returned in a clipped tone. "But you didn't come here to discuss my work."

Mason's lips tightened, and he said tersely, "No, I didn't."

Collier held his tongue, waiting for Mason to make the next move.

"I hope you're enjoying yourself."

"Meaning?"

Mason's eyes were piercing. "You're making this hard on me and your brother."

"Me?" Collier clamped down on his rising temper, though his insides were quivering.

"Yes, you. You couldn't let sleeping dogs lie, like I asked."

"No, Dad, I can't. And you know that."

Mason released a bitter sigh. "So what have you decided to do?"

"It'll depend on what Kyle finds."

"He's looking for the girl, right?"

"Right," Collier finally replied.

"Have you spoken to your brother?"

"Not yet." Collier's eyes drilled Mason. "Have you?"

"No," Mason said hoarsely. "I haven't."

"He's going to be pissed, Dad. Just like me."

Mason stiffened. "You might be wrong. He just might pat Brewster on the back for not letting that piece of scum walk."

Collier laughed without humor. "You know better than

that. Even at his lowest period, Jackson never would have condoned Brewster breaking the law.''

''What about Brewster?''

Collier didn't pretend to misunderstand. ''As soon as possible, I'm going to fire his ass, then go after his license. Any objections?''

Mason shrugged, then slid his eyes away. ''Go ahead. I never liked the son of a bitch anyway.''

''He's going to squeal and do a lot of finger-pointing.''

''Let him go right ahead. Like I've already told you, it's his problem if he misinterpreted something I said.'' Mason paused and rubbed his chin. ''But you've made it clear where you stand. *She* obviously means more to you than your family.''

''No, Dad. Stop right where you are. This has nothing to do with choosing sides. It has to do with what's right, regardless of who's involved.''

''But that piece of shit's going to walk.''

''Not necessarily. If he does, though, you'll have to accept it.''

Before Mason could reply, Kyle opened the door. ''Oops, sorry, I should've knocked. I'll come back later.''

''No, you won't.''

''Come on in, boy,'' Mason said, waving his hand. ''I was just leaving.'' At the door, he swung back around with narrowed eyes. ''I hope you know what you're doing, son.''

Collier didn't say a word.

Once Mason was gone, Kyle cocked an eyebrow. ''He's not happy, I take it.''

''He'll get over it,'' Collier said abruptly. ''Now, what have you got?''

Kyle hitched his slacks and sat down. ''The girl. I found Renee Youngblood.''

Thirty-Nine

The trailer in front of her didn't look half-bad, Brittany thought with relief. She was sitting in her parked car against the curb, perusing her surroundings. Two cars were parked in the driveway, a sure sign someone was home. She'd found the mobile home park easily enough, since the town, an hour's drive from Chaney, had a population of only five hundred.

Grabbing her purse, she got out just as a vehicle pulled up behind her. She froze. *Collier*. It couldn't be, but it was. He got out, as well, and walked over to her car. For a long moment neither one of them said a word. Brittany's senses were clamoring from shock, as well as from the heat in his eyes, which he didn't bother to disguise.

"I see you've been busy," he said, his voice low and tense.

Brittany swallowed, wanting to shift her gaze, only she couldn't. He held her captive. "You're the last person I expected to see here."

"I told you I was going to do what I could to right a wrong." He paused. "But you didn't believe me."

She licked her lips. "No, I didn't."

Silence fell between them.

"I miss you." Collier's eyes were dark and searching. "God, how I miss you."

"Don't." Her voice broke.

She missed him, too. Terribly. With him standing before her in the flesh, she inhaled his scent, making her crazy with longing. It was all she could do not to launch herself into his arms and pretend everything was all right between them. But everything wasn't all right, and it never would be. Fate had seen to that.

"How did you find her?" he asked.

"Dumb luck."

His smile didn't quite reach maturity. "So what's next?"

"I'm going to see if she'll talk to me."

His hungry eyes delved into hers one last time before he said, "Lead the way. I'm right behind you."

With her stomach tied in knots, Brittany turned. That was when the front door opened and a young woman walked out. When she saw them, she pulled up short. Keeping her excitement to a minimum, Brittany, with Collier beside her, met her at the edge of the driveway.

She could have been attractive, Brittany thought, had her hair not looked like a pile of yellow straw with black roots, and if she hadn't been so sloppily dressed in baggy jeans and a big sweatshirt that hung too freely on her thin frame.

"Renee?"

The girl's eyes turned instantly suspicious. "Depends on who wants to know."

Brittany faced Collier for a second. "He's Collier Smith, and I'm Brittany Banks, Tommy Rogers' sister." Once she had identified herself, Brittany waited with suspended breath.

"What do you want?" The girl's gaze was pinned on Brittany.

Brittany sensed that Renee knew what she wanted.

Something had flared in her eyes for just a second before it disappeared.

"I want to ask you about what happened that night at the party you attended with Tommy."

"You're the second person who's come here today about that very thing."

Without looking at Collier, Brittany asked, "Who was the first person?"

Renee shrugged. "A man. Said he was an investigator for some law firm."

"I sent him," Collier said. "He works for me."

Brittany's heart was pounding. So Collier had delivered on his promise after all. But she couldn't think about that—or him—right now, even though that was impossible with him standing so close to her. "What did you tell the investigator?"

"The truth," Renee said. "But not until he promised I wouldn't get in no trouble."

"Would you mind telling me the same thing?" Brittany asked.

"I told him I saw Chad Creekmore put something in Tommy's drink. When that other attorney came to see me three years ago, I told him the same thing."

"Darwin Brewster?" Brittany's words were barely audible.

"Yeah, I think that was his name. Anyway, I told him what I'd seen, and that I'd say so in court if it'd help Tommy. But I also told him he'd have to keep Chad away from me. He scared me shitless." Renee clamped her hand over her mouth. "Uh, sorry."

"No problem," Brittany said a trifle impatiently. "Go ahead."

"Later that Brewster guy came back and told me he'd give me some money *not* to tell the truth."

Brittany felt rather than saw Collier stiffen.

"My mamma was real sick at the time, and my daddy had just taken off, so I took it," Renee added with a defiant lift of her chin. "Tommy would've done the same thing, I bet."

Brittany winced at those words but didn't dwell on what that said about her brother. "What about now, Renee?" she pressed. "Would you be willing to come forward and tell the truth?"

"Yeah. Me and Tommy used to be real close."

"He's in prison now, you know," Brittany said in an uneven voice.

"He don't deserve to be."

"With your help, that just might change," Brittany said eagerly.

"That lowlife Chad should take his place."

"Right now, my only concern is Tommy."

"What do you want me to do?"

"My office will be in touch with you," Collier interjected. "Soon."

Renee shrugged. "No problem. I'm not going nowhere."

Brittany let out her pent-up breath, then reached out and hugged her, tears of joy filling her eyes. "Thank you. Thank you. Somehow I'll make this up to you."

"Forget it," Renee declared, her eyes glinting. "I owe Tommy."

Brittany didn't try to stem the flow of tears that ran down her cheeks. "Bless you. And thank you again."

Brittany felt Collier's eyes on her, but she didn't look at him, nor did she say anything. She wished she hadn't given in when he'd urged her to get into his car. Her vulnerability made that a crazy move, though she felt she owed him that much, which was also crazy. Just because he'd found the girl, too, that didn't mean their relationship was on the mend. Tommy still might not be freed.

Trust.

That was what it came down to, and she didn't trust him. With that admission, another chunk came out of her heart.

"It's going to be all right," Collier said in a low tone. "You just have to trust me."

She shifted startled eyes to him. Had he read her thoughts? "I wish I could, but...I can't."

"God, Brittany," he groaned. "Don't say that."

She moistened her lips.

"Don't *do* that," he said, heat in his eyes. "As it is, I can barely keep my hands off you."

"Has anything changed, Collier?" she asked brutally, effectively destroying the mouth-drying sensuality hovering between them.

He didn't pretend to misunderstand her question. "You mean do we have my family's blessing?"

"Yes, that's exactly what I mean."

"No, but I don't care."

"You will, Collier. The day will come when you *will* care, and then you'll blame me."

"Never," he said fiercely.

"Please, I can't fight this battle over again."

"Then don't. Just marry me."

God, she was tempted to throw caution and sound judgment to the wind, fling herself into his arms and say yes. But she couldn't. It was devastating being without him. But if she married him, then lost him, she wouldn't survive.

She simply wasn't prepared to take the risk.

"I'll even withdraw my name from the short list for

the judgeship," he said into the silence, desperation sharpening his voice. "Whatever it takes."

Her eyes widened in horror. "Are you crazy? That's the chance of a lifetime. I would never ask you to give that up."

"I may not get it, anyway," he said harshly.

"Oh, Collier, there's just so much wrong between us." Her voice shook uncontrollably.

"There's so much right, too. For starters, we love each other and we want each other. We *need* each other."

Before she realized his intentions, he grabbed her hand and placed it on his crotch. His erection was hard and throbbing. "See how much I need you?"

"That's not fair," she whimpered, withdrawing her hand.

"And you're wet, too, I'll bet." His words were barely above a whisper.

Air rushed out of her lungs. Of course she was wet. He only had to come near her and her insides turned to mush.

"Brittany?" His voice cracked.

Feeling her resolve weakening, she cried, "What about Tommy? Have you forgotten him?"

"He'll walk. I'll see to that."

Would he? Until it happened, she wouldn't believe it.

"Isn't that what you want?"

"Yes."

"Then you'll have it."

"Would he ever be welcome at our dinner table? At your father's?"

He opened his mouth, then closed it so hard, his jaws turned rigid. Seconds later, he spat an expletive into the loud silence.

"There *you* have it. I won't desert my brother." Her

eyes flashed. "Ever." Suddenly feeling like a trapped animal seeking release, Brittany clawed at the door handle.

Collier clamped down her arm. "No, please."

The panic she heard in his voice matched her own. She jerked free, her stomach quivering. "It's over, Collier. Get on with your life and let me get on with mine." She paused, tasting her salty tears. *"Please."*

Forty

"**D**id you look for a job today?"

Tommy opened one eye and peered up at Brittany from a prone position on the sofa, a pillow clutched to his stomach.

"Nah, didn't feel like it."

She hadn't needed to ask that question. The second she'd walked through the door after an extra-hard evening at the diner, the answer had been quite clear. Since he'd been released from prison six days ago, he'd been on that sofa. Day seven had been no different.

Swallowing her disgust, she had left him, taken her bath and put on her robe before dragging her weary body back into the living room.

Now, as she continued to stare at him, she tried to stifle her frustration and disappointment, but her patience had run out. "How much longer are you going to lie there?"

"What?" Tommy asked, being deliberately obtuse.

"You heard me."

"I told you I don't feel good."

"Then let me take you to the doctor."

"I don't need a doctor."

"That's right. What you need is a job."

He bounded to an upright position and glared at her. "Get off my ass, will you?"

Brittany's eyes sparked. "Don't talk to me like that."

"Sorry," he muttered, shifting his gaze. "It's just that I don't know what I want to do."

Brittany sat in the chair across from him. "When you first got out, you were praising the Lord all over the place, excited about looking for a job, making something out of your life. What happened?"

"Who's going to hire an ex-con?" Tommy demanded in a petulant tone.

"How do you know till you've tried?"

He shrugged. "I just know."

"So you're just going to lie on this couch and rot? Is that it?"

His eyes narrowed. "Without money and without friends, life pretty much sucks."

"What about Renee? She's your friend. Look what she did for you."

"Yeah, but she's seeing someone else now."

"So make some new friends."

"Hey, sis, get off my back, okay?"

Brittany rose suddenly. "No, I won't get off your back, as you put it. In fact, I'm through mollycoddling you. It's time you took charge of your own life. And if you choose not to do so, then that's your problem, not mine."

"Are you kicking me out?" He looked as if she'd kicked him in the stomach.

She steeled herself not to soften. "Only if you don't get a job. We need a dishwasher down at the diner."

"You've got to be kidding!"

"No, I'm not," she spat. "If I can wait on tables to keep food in the house, then you can sure as hell wash dishes."

"That really sucks."

"You're right, it does. But that's the way it is. Take it or leave it."

With that she walked to her room and slammed the door so hard, she felt the trailer shake. Moments later, she was in bed, her heart too broken to cry.

Tommy's attitude had crushed her spirit, while losing Collier had crushed her heart. She had known it would be bad when the final tie was severed, but not this bad. Tommy's homecoming, thanks to Renee and Collier, had been a shot of hope. Now that hope had been dashed and she was left with nothing but an empty shell for a life.

She didn't know if she'd gotten through to her brother or not. But she'd meant what she said. If he didn't change, then she would kick him out, though that would kill her. If it would get his attention, however, help make a responsible human out of him, then she'd do it.

If she could give Collier up, she could do anything.

How was he? she wondered for the umpteenth time. She hadn't seen anything in the paper about the federal appointment, but she knew he had won the sexual harassment suit, which was good.

On top of that, Rupert had gotten at least part of what he deserved. Sissy had made good on her promise to tell his wife about his extracurricular activities. As a result, Angel had filed for divorce and booted Rupert out of the company. Surely that good news had reached Collier's ears.

She truly prayed he was faring well. Because she loved him, she wanted the best for him. If he wanted that appointment to the bench, she prayed he would get it.

He'd gone on with his life, just as she had.

"Only mine sucks," she muttered into the silence, echoing Tommy's phrase.

If she had it to do all over again, would she make the same decision? That uninvited question made her heart falter. Still, she couldn't let it go. Was she having second thoughts about taking the easy road, opting for her boring but secure life over an exciting but dicey one?

Yes, God help her. She didn't want to live her life without him. That admission took her breath away. Was it too late? Had she killed his love? She pulled her knees up to her stomach and closed her eyes, her breathing on hold.

What if she tested the waters and, out of the blue, just showed up at *his* door?

Forty-One

Senator Newton Riley's face was all smiles.

Collier's heart hammered as he met the senator in the middle of his office, hand outstretched. "Is this an official visit, sir?"

Riley shook Collier's hand vigorously while slapping him on the shoulder with his free hand. "You're damn right it is. You're the chosen one, my boy. The president said you were a slam dunk."

"Yes!" Collier exclaimed, both thrilled and shocked. He knew that shock would deepen when it really hit him that he was soon to don a robe.

"Where's your dad?"

"Probably on the golf course."

"I wondered why I always liked Mason." Riley's lips twitched. "Now I know. And the fact that he's so generous with his money, of course."

Collier answered his smile. "Of course."

"So how does it feel to be a federal judge?"

Suddenly Collier felt uncomfortable. "I haven't been confirmed yet."

The senator gestured impatiently. "Hell, boy, that's just a formality. The powers that be, including myself, know everything there is to know about you."

"No surprises, huh?"

"Not unless something's changed in the last few weeks."

Just my life. It's fallen apart. "Nothing that I know of."

"By the way, congratulations on winning that harassment suit."

"Thanks, sir. But personally, I'm glad that case is behind me."

"I can understand that, especially with so much at stake," Riley replied. "Where the public's concerned, sexual harassment ranks right up there with abortion and child molestation. Those things can get them stirred up quicker than anything."

Collier let out a sigh. "I was just doing my job."

"That's why you're going to occupy a judge's chamber. That case ended up actually helping you. I sat in on your closing argument, and it was pure genius. Believe me, that kind of news gets around to the right people."

Collier felt both proud and humbled at the compliment. "You're pushing all the right buttons today, Senator."

"Good. That's what I'm here for."

"Dad will want to have a blowout to celebrate. I hope you'll come."

Senator Riley slapped him on the shoulder again. "Wouldn't miss it for the world. You be sure and give that old codger my regards."

"Be glad to."

"And tell him next time he hits the course to give me a call."

"I'll do that, too." Collier sobered. "So when will this all be official?"

"Details of the confirmation will follow. Meanwhile, celebrate. You've earned it."

That conversation had taken place the previous week,

and since then he'd barely had a moment to himself, which was a gift. He'd been able to keep his personal demons at bay, at least during the day.

First of all, he'd put the wheels in motion to get Tommy a new trial, but that hadn't been necessary. After the D.A. looked at the new evidence, including Renee's sworn testimony, Tommy had been released for time served.

Once that was out of the way, Collier had made good on his vow and fired Darwin Brewster. Although tempers had flared, Brewster had quickly come to the realization that he had run headfirst into a wall of steel. To try to implicate Mason would be futile.

"You're a real bastard, Smith," had been Brewster's parting shot to him. "One of these days, I hope you get what's coming to you."

Although it was apparent Mason had not been happy with Tommy's release, he'd kept his thoughts to himself, especially since events had quickly turned in his favor— the appointment and Jackson's wedding.

As predicted, Mason had thrown a blowout party, basking in both his sons' good fortunes. Jackson's return to the firm had become official, and so had his plans to marry Haley. The appointment and the engagement had been announced and celebrated at the same time.

A great time seemed to have been had by all, including Lana, who was sporting a new, much younger man on her arm. Collier had been glad to see that. He wanted her to be happy.

The media had been at the party, as well, having a field day with the appointment, later filling the paper with article after article about how the hometown boy had made good.

The sad part was that he would have given it all up if he could have had Brittany.

Now, as a groan escaped him, Collier let his head fall back against the leather headrest. He couldn't believe it had been just two weeks since he'd seen her. To him, it seemed a lifetime. There was now a hole in his chest where his heart had been.

Although the judgeship was something he'd wanted for himself as much as Mason, the victory was not nearly as sweet without Brittany.

Yet he kept up a good facade, hiding his broken heart, something that he'd never experienced before. He was dying without her. Nights were the worst. When he closed his eyes, he saw only Brittany, how she looked, how she smelled, how she *tasted.*

Another groan tore through his lips. For a couple of days after they had split, he'd stayed at home and gone on a drunken binge, trying to mend his heart with liquor. That had backfired. He'd merely added a broken head to his broken heart.

Soon he would be sworn in as a federal judge.

Suddenly Collier felt the urge to chuck it all—the bench, the firm, the town—and haul ass. But that wasn't the answer. Brittany's ghost would follow him. Would his heart ever heal? he wondered. Or would he have to endure this ache for the rest of his life?

He couldn't take it.

"I thought you'd be gone by now. After all, it's dark outside."

Collier lifted his head and watched as his brother rolled his chair into the room. "It's been so long since you've worked, big brother, you've forgotten how it is to burn the midnight oil."

It felt damn good to be able to speak freely to Jackson.

Gone were the moodiness and volatility. Now, with the promise of a new life on the horizon, he was the Jackson of old. Collier couldn't have been happier or prouder.

Or more envious, God help him.

"Chalk that one up to you." Jackson grinned. "But just so you'll know, I won't ever be burning the midnight oil again. I have better things to do."

Collier's lips twitched. "I just bet you do."

"Wouldn't hurt you to get laid, you know." Jackson's gaze was direct. "Maybe it'd improve your disposition."

"That isn't going to happen," Collier said curtly. "Ever."

Jackson frowned, though his tone was mild when he spoke. "That's a long time, little brother."

Wordlessly Collier got up and made his way around the desk, then perched on the edge, folding his arms across his chest.

"You look like hell," Jackson said.

"I feel worse."

Jackson sighed, then angled his head, his forehead creased. "Look, you didn't end it with Brittany because of me, did you? Or Dad?"

Collier smirked. "I didn't end it. She did."

Jackson looked surprised. "Does she love you?"

"Said she did."

"Then I don't get it. Why would she do a thing like that?"

"For several reasons," Collier responded in a weary voice.

"I'm listening."

"Would you sit down at the table and share a meal with Tommy Rogers?"

Jackson was clearly taken aback. He stiffened, and his features darkened. "Not in this lifetime."

"There you have it," Collier said bitterly.

"And Dad—well, he'd croak."

"She knows that, too."

"Why the hell couldn't you have fallen in love with Lana?"

Collier threw Jackson a fierce look.

"You're right." Jackson smiled. "Forget I said it."

A smile flirted with Collier's lips, only to quickly fade as he stared off into space, his chest feeling as though it was going to cave in.

"Look, I was out of line when I said what I did earlier, if it makes any difference."

Collier faced him again but didn't say anything.

"While I wouldn't want that hoodlum at my table, I'd tolerate him if that's what it'd take to wipe that desperate look off your face." Jackson paused. "Now Dad, he's a different matter. I can't speak for him."

"It doesn't matter what he thinks. As for you, thanks for saying that. It means a lot."

"Haley would have my hide if I didn't relent."

"There are other reasons why she…we aren't together. She doesn't think she would ever fit into my world."

"That's crazy."

"Not when you think about it and know where she's coming from. She lives in a trailer, goes to school and works two jobs, one of which is waiting on tables in a diner."

"Damn," Jackson muttered.

"Even though losing her is killing me, I have to admire her. She had a chance to have every material thing she's ever wanted, and she turned it down."

"Are you going to let her get by with that?"

Collier gave Jackson a blank stare. "I don't follow you."

"If she loves you, then there has to be a way to work through those stupid problems."

"I'd give up the judgeship for her, Jackson," Collier said in a bleak tone.

"Man, that's heavy-duty stuff."

"I mean it. That's how much I love her."

"Then if I were you, I'd camp on her doorstep until she came to her senses."

"You would?"

"In a New York minute."

Collier massaged his neck. "I don't know."

"You think about it. I'm betting you'll know then. Meanwhile, I'm outta here."

"Me, too," Collier said absently, his mind stuck on what Jackson had said.

A short time later, at his condo, he was still mulling over that conversation while pacing the floor, feeling like those fire ants were loose in his gut again. Should he really camp on her doorstep? What did he have to lose?

He bit down on his lower lip until he tasted the blood. That was when he heard the doorbell chime. He cursed; the last thing he wanted was company.

Yet he strode to the door and muttered, "Yeah?"

"Collier, it's…me. Brittany."

When he opened the door and stood larger than life in front of her, Brittany lost all ability to speak. Instead she just stared at him, hoping he could see the pain and remorse in her eyes.

"I'm so sorry," she finally whispered. "And I love you so much."

"I love you more," he rasped, grabbing her and holding her so tightly against his chest that she had difficulty breathing. Then, between groans, he nipped at her lips, her throat, his mouth leaving a trail of hot moisture wherever it landed.

She felt his erection press into her stomach. Boldly, she reached between them, into his sweatpants, and surrounded him with her hand.

"I can't wait," Collier rasped, jerking her slacks and panties down simultaneously. Once her legs were locked around his waist, he guided his shaft inside her.

Two hard thrusts and moans later, they clung to each other, giving in to the orgasms wracking their bodies.

"Taking you like this seems to have become a habit," he whispered, his breath warm and labored against her ear.

With him still inside her, she smiled at him, placed her palms on either side of his face and gave him a hard kiss, opting for some wild, out-of-control tonsil hockey. "A habit I hope you won't break."

"God, Brittany," he said in a crazed tone. "I love you."

That was when she felt him come back to life inside her. However, this time he managed to make it to the bed before his juices once again mixed with hers.

Finally, too spent to do anything but cuddle, they lay there for the longest time. Then, feeling him brush a damp strand of hair off her forehead, she raised her eyes to meet his.

"Does this mean you'll marry me?" he asked.

"If you still want me," she said in a halting voice.

His eyes burned into hers. "Only for the rest of my life."

"Oh, Collier, I was such a fool," she cried. "You're the best thing that ever happened to me, and I almost let you go."

"Shh, don't beat up on yourself, my darling. You're

here now, and that's what counts. And this time I'm not going to let you go.''

''Thank God,'' she whispered, kissing his chin, then snuggling back against him.

''What about Tommy?''

Lifting her head, she told him what had transpired between her and her brother. ''It was after that confrontation that I realized how big a price I'd paid for him, and he didn't even appreciate it.''

''He will, after we get him some counseling.''

Her eyes widened. ''You'd do that?''

''Would you like me to?''

''Oh, yes, though I'm not sure he'll do it.''

''Then we'll go to Plan B.''

''Which is?''

''I'm not sure yet, but we'll think of something.''

She smiled inwardly, then said, ''I don't deserve you, Collier Smith.''

''Oh, yes, you do—and much more.''

''What about your family?'' She couldn't mask the catch in her voice.

''Dad'll either come around or he won't. That's his choice. And Jackson—hell, he and Haley are all for us getting together.''

''Maybe we could have a double wedding.''

His features darkened. ''To hell with that. I don't want to wait. I intend to marry you now.''

''That's fine with me. The thought of a big blowout wedding isn't something that appeals to me anyway.'' Brittany fell silent for a moment, then said, ''What about the appointment?''

She felt him stiffen, and her heart faltered. She would be crushed if he chose the appointment over her.

''If my being a judge is going to make you unhappy

or uncomfortable, I can stay with the firm and continue to practice law.''

"That's crazy. I don't intend to stop going to school. Obtaining my degree is my dream, and I won't give it up. How could I expect you to give up yours?''

"Brittany, Brittany,'' he crooned, leaning down and licking one nipple, then the other, before raising his head and saying, "I'll love you always.''

"Me, too,'' she whispered breathlessly, smiling through her tears. "Always.''